D1291863

FULL FATHOM FIVE

WRECKS OF THE SPANISH ARMADA

COLIN MARTIN

With Appendices by Sydney Wignall

THE VIKING PRESS NEW YORK

Published in 1975 by The Viking Press, Inc.
625 Madison Avenue, New York, N.Y. 10022

LIBRARY OF CONGRESS CATALOGING IN PUBLICATION DATA
Martin, Colin.
Full fathom five.
Bibliography: p.
1. Armada, 1588. 2. Shipwrecks—Ireland.
3. Shipwrecks—Scotland. 4. Underwater archaeology.
I. Title.
DA360.M27 1975 942.05'5 75-1420
ISBN 0-670-33193-7

Printed in U.S.A.

CONTENTS

ILLUSTRATIONS

COLOUR PLATES

following pages 128 *and* 160

MONOCHROME PLATES

between pages 192 *and* 193

ILLUSTRATIONS

MAPS AND PLANS

PREFACE

This book gives an account of the identification and excavation of three ships which sailed in the Spanish Armada of 1588. The first was the *Santa Maria de la Rosa*, a large vessel, temporarily converted into a warship, which was wrecked in Blasket Sound off the south-west coast of Ireland. The second, *El Gran Grifón*, was a Baltic supply hulk which foundered in the narrow inlet of Stroms Hellier off Fair Isle, and the third was *La Trinidad Valencera*, a Venetian merchantman requisitioned for the invasion, the fourth largest ship in the fleet, which sank in the bay of Kinnagoe on the Inishowen Peninsula in North Donegal.

NOTE

All dates have been adjusted to conform with the New (Gregorian) Calendar which the Spaniards, but not the English, were using in 1588. Contemporary English dates, which were based on the Old (Julian) Calendar, would appear to fall ten days earlier than their Spanish equivalents unless so adjusted.

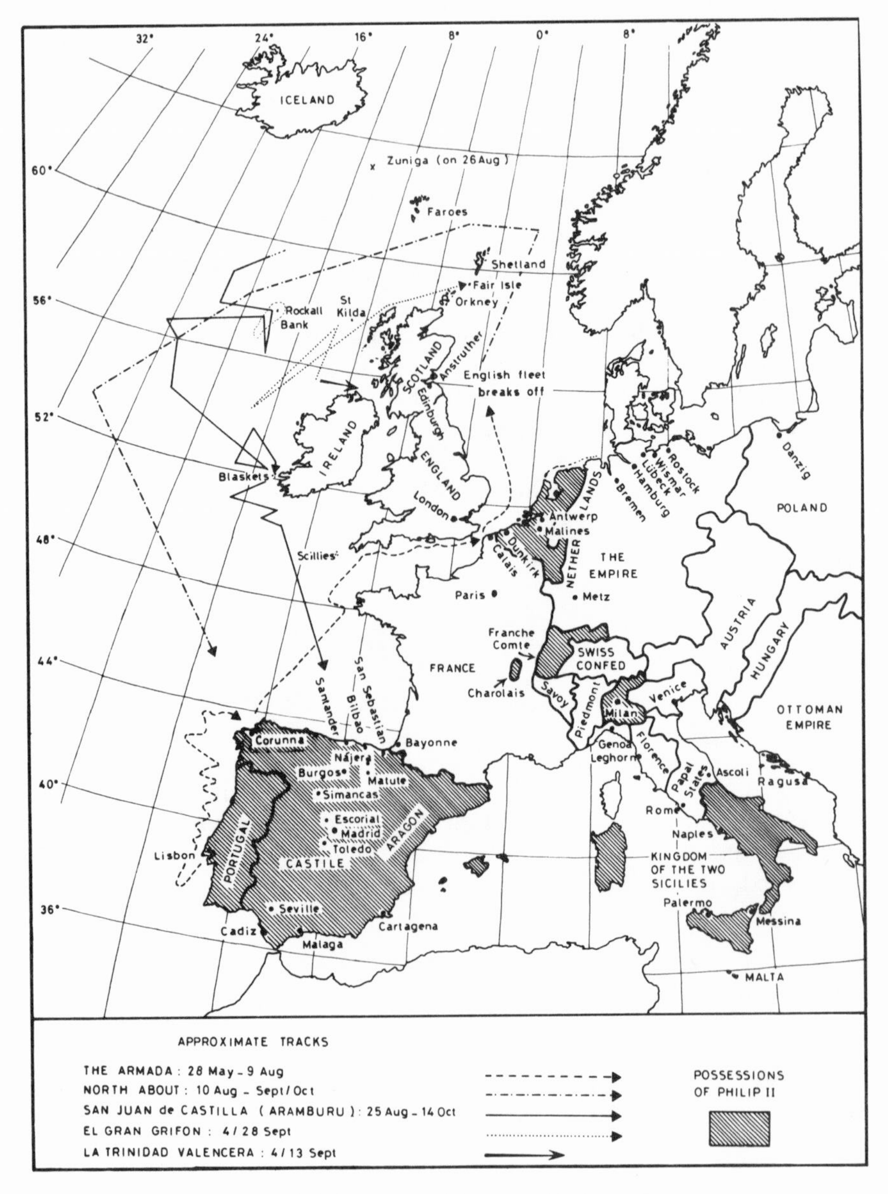

Fig. 1. The route of the Spanish Armada

Introduction

THE ENTERPRISE OF ENGLAND

ON 28th May 1588 an enormous fleet warped slowly out of Lisbon harbour, booming out gun salutes and exchanging trumpet fanfares with the grim fortresses of Belem and St. Julian which guarded the entrance to the Tagus estuary. *La Armada Felicissima* — the 'Most Fortunate' fleet of Imperial Spain — had at last, and after almost insuperable difficulties, embarked upon its crusade.

> 'Famous floating army of many standards
> Defenders all of the red-crossed crusade
> Masts of the Faith, from which there streams
> A fine white pennon at each yard's end'

wrote Lopez de la Vega, Spain's great poet and playwright, who sailed as a soldier with the fleet. What de la Vega's pen could put into words must have echoed in the thoughts of his 30 000 or so comrades aboard the 130 ships which sailed for England. Few of them can have doubted that the magnificent and powerful Armada of His Most Catholic Majesty Philip II, King of All the Spains and Indies, was invincible; it sailed, they believed, not only in the just cause of Spain but also as the chosen and divinely protected instrument of God's will. The holy standard of crusade rippled at the high masthead of the galleon *San Martín,* the 1 000-ton flagship of Philip's Captain General of the Ocean Sea, Don Alonson Perez de Guzman, 'El Bueno', seventh duke of the noble and powerful house of Medina Sidonia. Over a pure white background the banner was blazoned with the arms of Spain between a Virgin and a Crucifixion, and crossed with the blood-red diagonals of holy war. Beneath these symbols was embroidered the battle-cry: 'Arise, O Lord, and vindicate Thy Cause!' This sacred emblem had been consecrated a month earlier at the High Altar of Lisbon's great cathedral, after which it had been borne by the Duke himself between the ranks of fighting men who filled the nave and thronged the wide plaza outside.

Now, as the fleet sailed, a pious fervour ran through these same men as they went about their duties aboard the ships. To every one, of whatever rank, God as Spain's omnipotent ally was close, terrible, and all-seeing. Priests and members of holy orders, numbering 180, ready both to comfort the faithful and convert the heretics, were listed as part of the Armada's fighting strength along with the soldiers, the munitions, and the guns. Officers and gentleman-adventurers wore red crosses on their tunics to remind themselves and those who served under them that they were knights in pursuit of a holy quest. Fleet orders rigorously forbade blasphemy, foul language, and hard liquor, and the presence of women on the ships was expressly banned. Daily routines were, on the special instructions of the King, framed with as much emphasis on religious piety as on the practical running of the vessels. As well as calling the watches, the ships' boys, each day-break, chanted their 'Good Morrow' at the foot of the mainmast, and each evening they sang the 'Ave Maria'. At least once a week the 'Salve' and 'Litany' were chanted by every ship's company, and the daily watchwords were chosen as a constant reminder of the expedition's sacred mission: Monday was 'Jesus', followed by 'Holy Ghost', 'Most Holy Trinity', 'Santiago' (Spain's warrior saint), 'The Angels', 'All Saints', and 'Our Lady'.

The Armada was probably the mightiest assemblage of armed force the world had ever seen. An Englishman who, some weeks later, saw the whole fleet under sail was to describe it as 'the greatest and strongest combination that was ever gathered in all Christendom'. There were nine galleons of Portugal, including Medina Sidonia's *San Martín*; big, tough, weatherly Atlantic-built ships which, although rather old, had been designed specifically for war. To this squadron had been added a tenth ship, a new galleon belonging to the Grand Duke of Tuscany which had been commandeered the year before at Lisbon. Along with the Portuguese squadron sailed another powerful but rather less well armed group of front-line warships, the squadron of Castile—ten recently built galleons of the King's Indian Guard, based at

Seville, whose normal duties were to escort treasure fleets across the Atlantic. Also present were four sleek galleys from the Lisbon squadron. Originally there were to have been forty such vessels in the Armada, but at almost the last moment they had been withdrawn. Galleys, for large-scale naval operations in the Atlantic at least, were becoming obsolete by the late 16th century; the four which sailed were probably included more with nostalgic pride for what had once been the main striking arm of the Spanish navy than with the serious expectation of their achieving much in action. In the event, bad weather forced the galleys to fall out of the fleet before the fighting started.

Four large galleasses provided by the Kingdom of Naples made up a very heavily armed group. These were experimental battleships, intended to combine galleon firepower and seaworthiness with galley manoeuvrability, and they consisted in essence of the heavily armed bow and stern sections of a galleon with the rowing banks of a galley slotted between, and a full three-masted galleon rig over all. In action, however, they did not prove to be a success.

Most of the other fighting ships in the fleet had originally been merchantmen but, to the unpractised eye at least, they were scarcely recognisable as such now. Their deep and beamy hulls had been built up with new fighting castles fore and aft, and the larger of them boasted an armament quite as heavy as that carried by the galleons. There were forty-four of these converted auxiliaries — four atttached to the galleons of Castile and the rest arranged in squadrons of ten apiece representing Spain's maritime provinces of Guipuzcoa, Biscay, Andalusia and Levant.

The Armada, as a self-sufficient invasion force, necessarily included a fleet of stores vessels, as well as small boats for reconnaissance, dispatch work, and inter-fleet communication. Twenty-three stores ships, or hulks, had been chartered from Spain's Hanseatic allies in the Baltic; these were tub-like cargo carriers, capacious and seaworthy but not very weatherly or manoeuvrable. A general-purpose communications squadron, made up of a variety of light craft, some of which were driven by oars as well as sails, completed the fleet.[1]

Between them the 130 ships carried 2 431 guns of all sizes, of which 1 497 were bronze and the rest iron. The better pieces in all categories were bronze, and the larger guns almost exclusively

[1] See Appendix 3.

so. In size the guns ranged from heavy ship-smashing *cañones*, *pedreros* and *culebrinas* which made up the offensive batteries of a relatively small group of front-line warships down to light defensive and anti-personnel pieces carried aboard every vessel. The ships' holds were filled with the ammunition, weapons, gun carriages, field equipment, accoutrements, water, provisions, firewood, wine, cooking utensils, medical supplies and pack animals needed for the voyage and for the invasion campaign which was to follow.

The Armada's most vital cargo, however, was men. Distributed among the ships, in companies and half-companies, were 19 295 soldiers and their officers. The main body of this force was organised into five brigades or *tercios* of heavy infantry — pikemen, arquebusiers and musketeers—each some 3 000 strong and commanded by a brigadier (*Maestre de Campo*). The other soldiers were light skirmish troops and field pioneers, about 5 000 in number, and the whole military force was commanded by the ruthlessly efficient Don Francisco de Bobadilla. Attached to Bobadilla's regular officer corps were 214 *entretenidos* (aspirants to military posts receiving reduced pay) and 123 *aventureros* (young adventurers from noble families).

Spain drew both her ships and her seamen from two main sources — the Mediterranean, particularly Italy, and the Atlantic coasts of Spain and Portugal. It is clear that Atlantic seamen were considered the best, and with reason, for the seaboards of Biscay and Portugal are stern training grounds for any mariner. Some had gained their experience as deep-sea fishermen, while others had sailed on the transatlantic or Baltic shipping routes. But although some of the Mediterranean seamen may have lacked the instinctive adaptability and courage of the Atlantic-bred mariners, they were by no means fair weather sailors — it should be remembered that Columbus was a Genoese, and John Cabot a Venetian. The standard of seamanship shown by the Armada throughout the campaign and its aftermath was exceptionally high, in spite of claims to the contrary by contemporary Englishmen and most of the historians who have followed them.

From the first the Duke of Medina Sidonia had stressed the need for close co-operation between the seafaring and military elements of the expedition. Soldiers' equipment was to be stowed well out of the way in their quarters below decks, and the most comfortable accommodation — that in the fore and after castles — was to be reserved for the seamen so that they would be conveniently placed for working the ship and changing watches. Doubtless the soldiers were expected to lend a hand in ship's routines when required, and they certainly provided the bulk of the gun crews in action. Without such co-operation the fleet, with only 8 050 seamen in all, would have been drastically undermanned.

The instructions which had been issued by the King to Medina Sidonia for the Armada campaign were detailed and strict. The fleet was to sail through the English Channel and rendezvous with a Spanish army under the Duke of Parma off Dunkirk and Nieuport, whence a springboard invasion was to be launched into the Thames estuary. Parma's army would cross in a fleet of small boats, protected by the Armada, and after a beach-head had been secured (probably at Margate) the Armada would land its own troops as reinforcements and off-load the munitions and supplies needed for the campaign which would bring about the overthrow of Protestant England. The Armada's primary job was not therefore to fight the English fleet, but to ensure the successful invasion of England itself.

The Spaniards recognised, however, that Queen Elizabeth's aggressive and well-equipped Navy Royal was not likely to allow such an event to pass unopposed. Philip had long realised that the naval might of the two rival nations would ultimately clash, and as early as 1574 he had been studying detailed reports about English naval strength and tactics. 'The Queen's ships,' runs one such report, 'are powerful vessels with little top hamper and very light (i.e. manoeuvrable), which is a great advantage for close quarters, and with much artillery, the heavy pieces being close to the water . . . if the fleets come to hostilities it would be well to give orders that, when our ships approach them, the ordnance flush with the water should be destroyed broadside on, and so damage their hulls and confuse them with smoke . . .'

But Spain was a military power in the old-fashioned sense, with a huge standing army and a warrior aristocracy to lead it. The use of gun-power and manoeuvrability alone was foreign not only to traditional Spanish codes of naval warfare but also to the design and capabilities of the ships and guns with which she was furnished. In the past the Spaniards had relied on galleys to provide their main striking arm at sea, but against heavily gunned sailing ships, it was becoming realised, these were ineffective and vulnerable. However much Philip might strive to employ modern tactics against his enemies — and he certainly had a strong theoretical grasp of such tactics — he could not escape the limitations of the weapons at his disposal. Because the Spaniards tended to regard boarding and physical capture as the ultimate naval tactic they had concentrated on short-range heavy artillery (cannon-types and perriers) with which they hoped to cripple an enemy into immobility before coming alongside to grapple and deliver the *coup de grâce* with pike, musket and sword. Their sailing ships, most of which had been constructed for trade rather than war, were capacious and well suited to accommodate battery guns and large companies of soldiers, but ill-designed for speed or manoeuvre. The English, on the other hand, who possessed faster and more manoeuvrable ships but whose military steel, in terms both of sword blade and *esprit,* was less well tempered than that of the Spaniards, tended to utilise their superior mobility to keep out of reach of the heavy Spanish ship-smashers and away from the danger of disablement and boarding. They therefore concentrated on the lighter shotted but longer range class of guns (culverin types) with which they could hit the enemy while standing clear of the range of his main weapons.

That all this was abundantly clear to Philip is evident from the instructions he gave, in his precise manner, to Medina Sidonia just before the Armada sailed. 'Above all,' he wrote, 'it must be borne in mind that the enemy's object will be to fight at long distance, in consequence of his advantage in artillery. The aim of our men, on the contrary, must be to bring him to close quarters and grapple with him, and you will have to be very careful to have this carried out.' What the King failed to do, however, was to tell his unfortunate Captain General *how* he was supposed to close with the nimble English ships. Some years ago the late Professor Mattingly discovered the text of a conversation which took place at Lisbon between a papal emissary and a senior but unnamed Spanish officer just before the fleet sailed (Mattingly believed that he might have been Juan Martinez de Recalde, the Armada's second-in-command, who will figure stirringly in later pages of this account). The Spaniard's reply to a direct question as to how he expected the Armada to fare in battle with the English fleet is a monument to realistic fatalism and the Iberian penchant for irony:

'It is well known that we fight in God's cause,' said the officer. 'So, when we meet the English, God will surely arrange matters so that we can grapple and board them, either by sending some strange freak of weather or, more likely, just by depriving the English of their wits. If we can come to close quarters, Spanish valour and Spanish steel (and the greater masses of soldiers we shall have on board) will make our victory certain. But unless God helps us by a miracle the English, who have faster and handier ships than ours, and many more long-range guns, and who know their advantage just as well as we do, will never close with us at all, but stand aloof and knock us to pieces with their culverins, without our being able to do them any serious hurt. So we are sailing against England in the confident hope of a miracle.'

The hoped-for miracle failed to materialise. After a disastrous start, in which rotting provisions and bad weather had forced the fleet to spend a month revictualling and refitting at Corunna, the Armada eventually sighted the south-west coast of England on 30th July — two full months after it had left Lisbon. The main part of the English fleet, which had been lying at Plymouth under the command of Lord Admiral Howard and his vice-admiral, Sir Francis Drake, managed by skilful seamanship to gain the commanding weather-gauge of the Spaniards and remained in this position as both fleets sailed up the Channel, snapping at the heels of the great Armada as it advanced in a stately crescent-shaped defensive formation intent upon the rendezvous with Parma. During the first four days of fighting there was a good deal of confused artillery skirmishing, mostly at long range, in which both fleets needlessly expended a great deal of irreplaceable ammunition, and though the Spaniards did sustain two major losses these were through accident and bad management rather than English action. The first casualty was the *San Salvador,* a big vessel belonging to the Guipuzcoan squadron, which blew up after her magazine caught fire. The English later captured her burnt-out hulk. The second loss was the Andalusian flagship

Nuestra Señora del Rosario, which, after colliding with another Spaniard, fell astern of the Armada and was eventually captured by Drake.

On 6th August the Armada, its formation and discipline still unbroken, dropped anchor off Calais to await news from the Duke of Parma. Thus far Medina Sidonia, in spite of his inexperience in naval operations, had carried out his instructions to the letter. But Parma was not ready, and in any case was unwilling to bring his troops out in unprotected barges through the shallows of the Flemish Banks where the nimble and formidably armed flyboats of Justin of Nassau's blockading Dutch fleet (the Sea Beggars) could operate but the deep-draught ships of the Armada could not. All along this had been the glaring weakness of the plan; a weakness which, in the fervour of his crusading passion, the King had steadfastly overlooked or ignored. Because of it Medina Sidonia and his Armada had been forced, with terrifying inevitability, towards a situation in which there was room neither for action nor escape.

To leeward lay the treacherous sandbanks and shallows and waiting Sea Beggars; to windward, a long culverin-shot away, the anchored English fleet. The action which the English chose to take was more obvious than it was brilliant. Wind, tide, and the Armada's dilemma provided perfect conditions for one of the oldest stratagems in naval warfare—fireships. Eight blazing vessels packed with combustibles were sent scudding towards the helpless and crowded Spanish fleet, and panic immediately gripped the majority of the anchored vessels. Without waiting for orders they severed their anchor cables (most of them, in this fierce tideway, had two or even three anchors down) and jostled helter-skelter for the sanctuary of the open sea. No actual damage was caused by the fireships, though the galleass flagship *San Lorenzo* ran aground in the confusion, and was later boarded by the English. But at a stroke the Armada had been changed from a strong, coherent fighting force into a crowded gaggle of individual ships, some panic-stricken and all in imminent danger of grounding in the shallows to leeward. Medina Sidonia had no alternative but to abandon the anchorage completely and try to save his scattered fleet.

A sudden change of wind providentially saved the Armada from the sandbanks, but not from the English fleet. Off Gravelines Lord Admiral Howard, now reinforced with fresh ships, fiercely attacked at close range. Medina Sidonia gathered together his strongest ships and formed a protective rearguard. The English attempted repeatedly to break this rearguard and cut out its individual members but the battered galleons held firm in each other's support, and still the English would not come near enough to allow the Spaniards to grapple, though at times they came very close to it. In one pass an English ship actually came close enough to the galleon *San Mateo* to allow a single foolhardy Englishman to swing across to the Spaniard's deck. No one followed him, and he was instantly cut down.

Pedro Coco Calderon, an officer on board one of the hulks, vividly describes a fragment of the battle which he witnessed.

> The enemy inflicted great damage on the galleons *San Mateo* and *San Felipe,* the latter having five of her starboard guns dismounted . . . in view of this, and that his upper deck was destroyed, both his pumps broken, his rigging in shreds and his ship almost a wreck, Don Francisco de Toledo[1] in the *San Felipe* ordered the grappling hooks to be got out, and shouted to the enemy to come to close quarters. They replied, summoning him to surrender in fair fight; and one Englishman, standing in the maintop with his sword and buckler, called out, 'Good soldiers that ye are, surrender to the fair terms we offer ye!' But the only answer he got was a gunshot which brought him down in sight of everyone, and the *Maestre de Campo* then ordered the muskets and arquebuses to be brought into action. The enemy thereupon retired, whilst our men shouted out to them that they were cowards, and with opprobrious words reproached them for their want of spirit, calling them Lutheran hens and daring them to return to the fight.

During the following night the *San Mateo* and *San Felipe* drifted on to the Flemish Banks and were lost.

Again and again we hear, in this final battle, of grievous injury inflicted at close range upon the Spanish ships. Martin de Bertendona's huge Levantine flagship *La Regazona* came lurching past one of the hulks, her main guns dismounted and blood gushing from her lee scuppers. Musketeers were still doggedly firing from her decks and tops. The Biscayan *Maria Juan* sank as the direct result of English gunfire, the only ship, in all the battles, to do

[1] *Maestre de Campo* of the *tercio* of Flanders.

so. The *San Marcos,* one of the great Portuguese galleons which had been in the thick of the fighting alongside Medina Sidonia, actually had to be tied round with three great cables to hold her splitting hull together. Many other ships received damage which later on, in the Atlantic and on the wild coasts of Scotland and Ireland, was to be their undoing. At the same time we hear almost nothing of retaliatory damage inflicted on the English ships; an impression later confirmed by shipwrights' reports when, after the fighting, the Queen's ships went into dock for repair and refitting. Very little shot damage is mentioned at all, and none whatever of a major nature. Yet these same ships had been engaged, at point-blank range and for considerable periods of time, with some of the strongest and best armed ships of the Spanish Armada. For some reason the Spanish battery guns, which should have been at their most devastating at this very close range, proved in the event to have been all but impotent.

After Gravelines the Duke of Medina Sidonia was left with a fleet which had been heavily mauled, which was short, though not destitute, of ammunition, and whose supplies of food and especially water were becoming critically low. He had a straight choice: whether, without hope of reinforcement or replenishment, in the face of the prevailing winds and against an enemy who had already proved his superiority over the Armada in battle and was operating close to his home bases, to attempt the rendezvous with Parma again or force a landing somewhere on the south coast; or whether to nurse his crippled fleet around the British Isles and back to Spain as best he could, and so keep its losses to a minimum. He chose the latter course; in the circumstances it was hardly even a choice. The Armada was no longer in a condition to fight, the carefully laid invasion plan was in shambles, and nothing whatever could be gained by wasting more ships, guns, and men in a hopeless gesture. If they could be brought safely back to their home ports they might at least fight some other day.

So the Armada, still more or less in formation (though one erring captain had to be hanged and paraded round the ships to re-establish shaken discipline), moved into the North Sea. The English fleet shadowed the Spaniards until they were level with the Firth of Forth, and then broke off. Howard, Drake and the others would have followed them 'to the furthest they durst have gone' — had provisions and ammunition only lasted. But both the store-rooms and shot-lockers of the English ships were bare, and so, reluctantly, they abandoned the pursuit, uncertain of what the Armada might yet do but certain, at least, that its predicament was far worse than theirs. The terrible 'north-about' journey, which was to cost the Spaniards one-third of their ships and two-thirds of their men, had begun.

I · *Santa Maria de la Rosa*

'A MOST EXTRAORDINARY AND TERRIFYING THING . . .'

THE Blasket Islands lie off the Dingle Peninsula in County Kerry: great craggy flakes of rock which rise from the open Atlantic beyond Ireland's south-west tip to form Europe's most westerly archipelago. The largest of the group, *Inish Mór* or the Great Blasket, is a narrow four-mile ridge with precipitous cliffs and a humped spine which rises almost to 1 000 feet. Between it and the mainland runs an open sound, some four square miles in extent, which is nipped by headlands at its narrow neck to create a rushing, turbulent tide-race. Blasket Sound is notorious, even on this wild coast, for its ever changing eddies and rips, for sinister pinnacles of rock which rear close to its surface, and for sea conditions which can, without warning, change from calm to cataclysmic.

From the jetty at Dunquin, on the mainland side of the Sound, traditional tarred canvas *curraghs* still ply between the shore and Great Blasket Island, though the village nestled on the island's north face is ruined and deserted now. This unique and famous little community, which has produced some of the finest folk literature in Europe and is said to have spoken the purest Gaelic in all Erin, was forced by economic necessity to evacuate in 1954. But Gaelic lovers and others from all parts of the world still come to visit the Great Blasket, and cross the wild Sound in fragile-looking, although wonderfully seaworthy *curraghs,* rowed by gentle hardy men who once lived on the island and who still run their sheep on its sweet grassy sward.

Hidden in an overgrown glade close to Dunquin, amid a tangle of thorned bramble and drooping fuchsia, stands a low mound topped by a rough grey monolith which local people still call

Uaig Mhic Rí na Spaínne — the Grave of the Son of the King of Spain. It is today the only visible reminder of a series of great and terrible events which took place in Blasket Sound nearly four centuries ago, when several storm-battered ships of the Armada sought refuge there, and left the broken wreckage of at least one of their number scattered beneath these bleak and inhospitable waters.

At dawn on 15th September 1588, in blustery weather, the Blasket Islands were sighted from the west by the 24-gun Spanish warship *San Juan Bautista,* of 750 tons, as she attempted to beat her way south with a westerly wind on her beam. The *San Juan* was Castile's vice-flagship; sleek-hulled, low-decked, and (for her time) fast, manoeuvrable, and well-armed. Her commander was Marcos de Aramburu, Supervisor and Paymaster of the squadron, and it is to his log, now preserved among the archives of Simancas Castle in Northern Spain, that we turn for details of the *San Juan*'s adventures in the Atlantic and off the Irish coast.

Aramburu had been attempting to follow the orders of the Duke of Medina Sidonia, given more than a month before, when the defeated fleet was passing the latitude of the Firth of Forth intent on making a 'north-about' passage back to Spain by circumnavigating the British Isles. 'The course that is first to be held,' ran the navigating instructions, 'is to the north-north-east, until you be found under 61 degrees and a half; and then to take great heed lest you fall upon the Island of Ireland, for fear of the harm that may happen to you upon that coast'.

On 27th August, Aramburu's *San Juan* had become detached from the main body of the fleet, somewhere to the north-east of Rockall. How he fixed his position at that time can be deduced from his log. The latitude of 59 degrees would have been taken, simply enough, by measuring the sun's angle at mid-day with cross-staff or astrolabe. The method by which he calculated his longitude, which is much more difficult to determine, displays considerable navigational skill as well as an intimate knowledge of North Atlantic waters. He dropped a sounding lead, he tells us, 'and found ourselves in 120 fathoms deep with a gravel bottom'. In this latitude, and in this approximate position, the only area of such shallow depth which has a coarse gravel bottom (a sample of which Aramburu and his pilots would have been able to run through their fingers when the tallowed lead was hauled on deck) is the Rosemary Bank, which lies about 10 degrees west of the present-day Greenwich meridian or, on such charts as would have been available to Aramburu, some '60 leagues west of Ireland', as he recorded in his journal. In fact, the stark headlands of Mayo and Kerry thrust beyond the 10 degree line, but most charts of the time ignore these jutting outcrops of land and suggest that the line lies well clear of the Irish coast. This gross inaccuracy was certainly a factor which contributed to the Armada wreckings.

Three days later Aramburu sounded on a rock bottom at 125 fathoms and judged that he was over the Rockall Bank, 'in 58 degrees, 95 leagues from the Irish coast'. The weather was far from good; heavy squalls were making it difficult to trim the ship to any course, and winds were coming all too often from the south and west quarters. By now the *San Juan Bautista* was in company with another ship, *La Trinidad* (872 tons, 24 guns), one of the four converted merchantmen which had sailed with the ten royal galleons of Aramburu's squadron. Gradually, in zigzag legs, making what use they could of every remotely favourable wind, the ships tacked southwards. On 4th September they were in 56½ degrees, by reckoning 120 leagues from the Irish coast. By the 8th they had reached 55 degrees, and on the 9th 54. On the 10th they made good progress south, and at dawn on the 11th islands were sighted. The pilots were uncertain whether they were the Ox and Cow, off the Slieve Miskish peninsula, or the Skelligs, slightly further to the north. In any event, they were clearly to be avoided. Taking advantage of a breeze which had sprung up from the south-south-west the two ships headed north-west to gain sea room. Aramburu now takes up the story in his own words:

> At 4 o'clock in the evening the wind began to freshen and the sea to get up. On the 12th September we held the same course out to sea. At 5 p.m. it began to blow from the south with such force that at night there was a most violent storm with a very wild sea, and great darkness on account of the heavy clouds. The ship *Trinidad* was sailing close to us, under foresail and

mainsail, but after midnight we lost sight of her, though we showed her our lantern.

On the 13th, at daybreak, the wind went rapidly round to the north-west, and the sea began to go down. Our course was south-east. On the 14th we continued the same course with the same wind, and at noon we saw to our leeward a big vessel with a tender almost in view (i.e. nearly hull-up on the horizon). We gradually worked down on her, and at nightfall were a league off, but could not follow her, as it was dark. We kept our lantern burning all night, that she might see us.

On the 15th, running south with the wind west, two hours before daybreak we saw a vessel to windward of us, showing us light and going north, and another to leeward which had no lantern burning.

We suspected they were the same as those of the previous evening, and that like us they were trying to beat clear of the land, of which we were in dread, though for the short time before it was light we kept to our southerly course. At dawn we found by the prow two big islands, and on the larboard side, to the east, the mainland; and as we could not weather it, we turned to the north-north-west. The two other vessels were also beating to seaward, and these we now recognised as the flagship of Juan Martinez de Recalde, and a tender. We turned towards the flagship with the wind on our beam, for we were totally ignorant of this coast, and despaired of any remedy. The admiral cleared one of the islands and then headed towards a part of the mainland, which he saw before him, steering an easterly course. We followed to windward, believing him to have some knowledge of this landfall. He kept bearing down on the mainland, and then ran into the haven of Vicey through an entrance of low rocks about as wide as a ship is long, and anchored. We came in behind the flagship, and after us the tender. This day we saw another ship to leeward close to the land. We must hope that God will have come to her aid, for she was in great danger.

From Aramburu's vivid account of these events, and in the light of our discoveries in Blasket Sound during 1968, we can reconstruct exactly what happened. At dawn on 15th September the three vessels found themselves off the Blaskets, probably just to the north-west of the northern island, Inishtooskert, from which position that island, and the Great Blasket some 5 miles off, would loom large and menacing. Beyond, to the east, the hilly

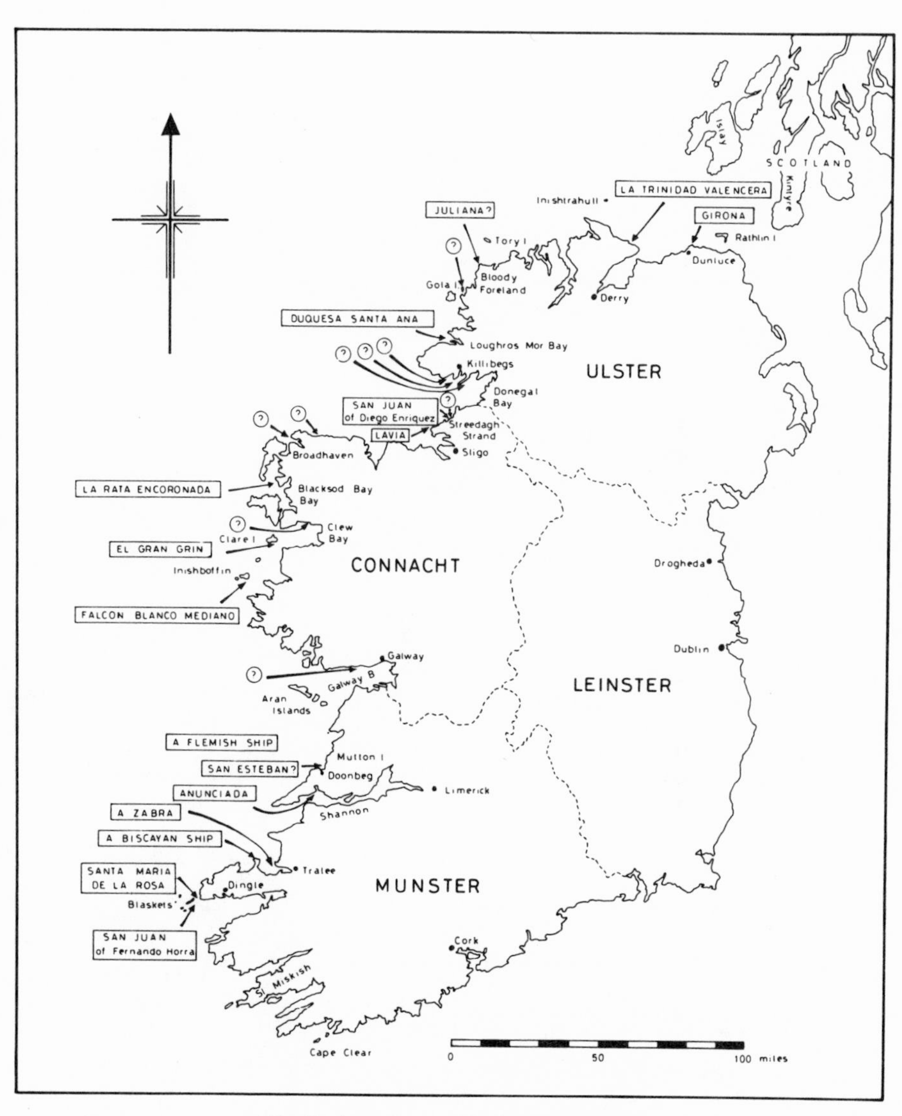

Fig. 2. Armada wreck sites off Ireland

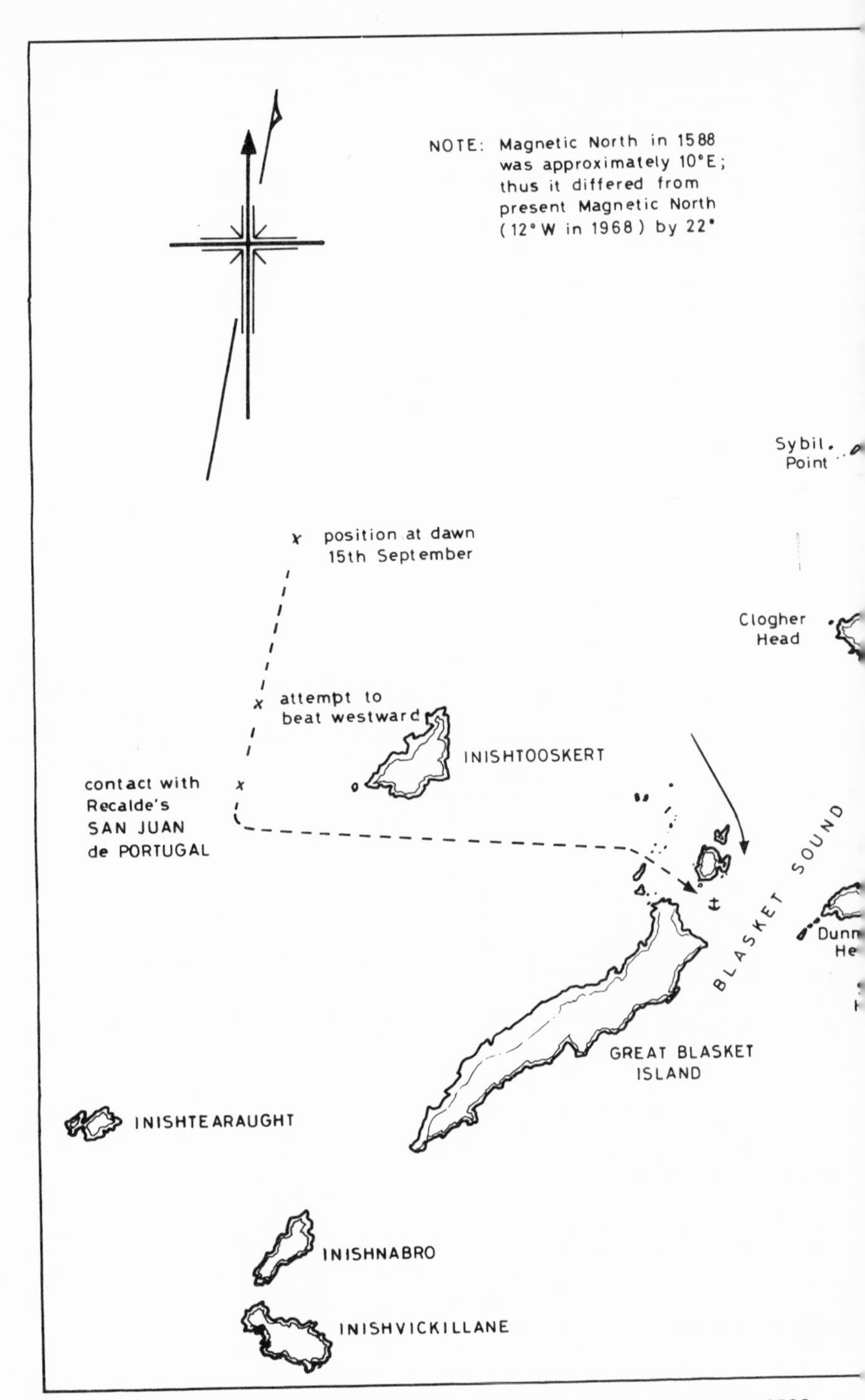

Fig. 3. Dingle and the Blaskets showing the Spanish landfall, September 1588

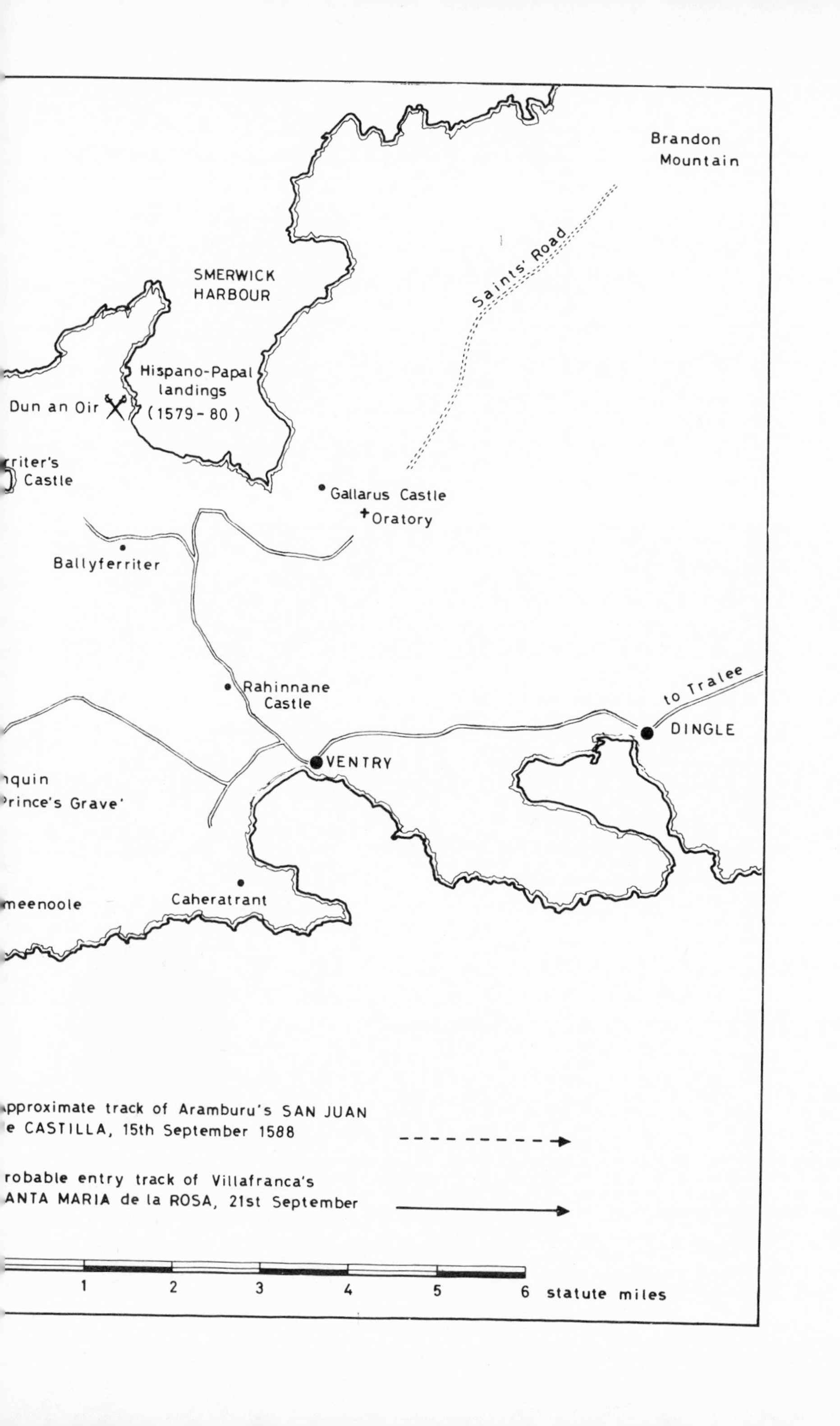
Brandon
Mountain
Saints' Road
SMERWICK
HARBOUR
Hispano-Papal
landings
(1579 - 80)
Dun an Oir
rriter's
Castle
Gallarus Castle
Oratory
Ballyferriter
Rahinnane
Castle
to Tralee
DINGLE
VENTRY
nquin
Prince's Grave'
meenoole
Caheratrant
pproximate track of Aramburu's SAN JUAN
e CASTILLA, 15th September 1588
robable entry track of Villafranca's
ANTA MARIA de la ROSA, 21st September
1
2
3
4
5
6
statute miles

mainland from Sibil Point to Dunmore Head would plainly be visible, white breakers forming a dancing line along the base of its unbroken cliffs.

Seeking to escape this reef-strewn, terrifying coast, Aramburu tried to beat seawards, as did the other two ships. These Aramburu had now recognised. The smaller was a 40-ton dispatch boat, one of the Armada's swift *pataches.* The other was the great *San Juan de Portugal,* vice-flagship of the squadron of Portugal and of the whole Armada; 1 050 tons, carrying 50 guns and commanded by the vice-admiral himself, Don Juan Martinez de Recalde, Knight of Santiago, grim hero of the Channel fights and unquestionably the most experienced seaman officer in the fleet. Recalde was a nobly born Basque from Bilbao, related by kinship to the famous Iñigo Lopez de Recalde who, under the name of Ignatius de Loyola, had founded the Jesuit Order. Like Ignatius, Juan Martinez de Recalde had received in his youth a full training in the military arts but he had then turned, unlike most young *aventureros* of his class, to the sea. He had risen to command escort fleets of the Indian Guard, and he had undertaken a number of successful expeditions in European waters. At the great naval battle off the Azores in 1582 he had fought as the Marquis of Santa Cruz's second-in-command. For a time he had been Controller of the Royal Dockyards, and had supervised shipbuilding programmes throughout Spain. Ninety years ago the Spanish naval historian Fernandez Duro described Recalde as 'one of the greatest mariners of his time', an opinion shared by a more recent English historian, Michael Lewis, who wrote of him: 'His ships, his weapons, his men, his superiors might fail him: but he never failed them: a lionhearted, competent, trustworthy old man, unquestionably the most valuable officer they had.' Off this bleak and almost uncharted corner of Ireland, far away from the flags and the fighting, Recalde was to display his magnificent qualities of courage and seamanship as never before.

The *San Juan de Portugal* had fallen away from the main body of the Armada with seventeen or so companions about the beginning of September; much the same time at which Aramburu himself had become detached. Most of this group were in desperate need of water, and it included many of the ships which were to be wrecked on Irish coasts during the following weeks.

Recalde's group was itself split up by the storm of 12th September and thus it was, 3 days later, that Aramburu came upon the flagship and her tender trying, like him, to beat their way clear of the Blaskets to leeward.

It proved impossible, in the teeth of that strong westerly wind, to make any headway out to sea. At this point Aramburu seems to have given up all hope, 'despairing of any remedy' for their predicament. Not so Recalde. Handling his lumbering galleon, which was suffering badly from heavy damage she had sustained during the battles, with consummate skill, he suddenly reversed his heading and cleared the breaking reefs south of Inishtooskert to run eastwards with the wind towards the white wall of foaming water which stretched between the northern point of Great Blasket Island and the neighbouring islet of Beginish. Aramburu and the *patache* followed in blind faith close on his stern. There was not much else they could do. Either the admiral had taken leave of his senses and was leading them all to certain destruction on the reefs and cliffs to leeward, or he knew something about this landfall which they did not.

Between Great Blasket and Beginish, in the lee of the larger island's rising bulk, there is a broad stretch of sheltered water, protected from the crashing Atlantic rollers by a low fringe of islets and reefs. It is marked on the Admiralty Charts as a storm anchorage today, and Recalde clearly knew of its existence in 1588. The entrance to this haven from the landward side of the Sound is wide and easy. But, in a westerly wind, a sailing ship cannot approach from this direction. The only other entrance, from seaward, is blocked by the protecting reefs, except for a channel so narrow and difficult to negotiate that even small modern craft find the passage tricky and only attempt it in the calmest weather. In a heavy westerly sea the reefs, in breaking the force of the rollers and thus creating the haven beyond, become themselves a terrifying maelstrom of rocketing spume and mountainous waters.

It was through this passage, and under such conditions, that Recalde took his 1 000-ton, damaged flagship; at speed, too, for otherwise the ship would have had insufficient steerage to allow her inefficient whipstaff-operated rudder to bite. The *San Juan*'s mighty lead-sheathed keel, 20 ft or more below the surface, must have scraped the bottom. As one follows today the course Recalde took, between the northern tip of Carrigfadda and the reefs of Ballyclogher and Wig Rock, one is amazed by the seamanship, courage, and sheer audacity of his act.

Off the clean white beach which curves at the foot of Great Blasket Island's northern face, the *San Juan de Portugal* dropped anchor and held firm on sandy ground. Further to the north, off Beginish, Aramburu's *San Juan Bautista* loosed her ground tackle and rode safe. The *patache* moored somewhere clear of the big galleons. As Recalde had clearly intended, and had achieved by his outstanding seamanship, the three ships were now safely sheltered from all quarters except the north-east. And from that direction would come the fair wind that would take them to Spain.

How had Recalde known of this sheltered anchorage, and of the terrifying passage from seaward by which it had to be won? Most certainly such information was not to be found on the scanty and wildly inaccurate charts which seamen of those days possessed. But, by an extraordinary co-incidence, the old admiral had himself been in close and bitter contact with this very stretch of coast some years before.

In the summer of 1579 Sir James Fitzmaurice, who 6 years earlier had gone into exile after failing to bring about a national rising against the English in Ireland, landed at Dingle with a Papal-sponsored band of Spanish and Italian mercenaries. The Earl of Desmond rallied to his support, and by that winter most of the province of Munster was in revolt. Vigorous counter-measures were taken by the English land forces under the acting Lord Deputy, Sir William Pelham, with a squadron of the Queen's ships giving support by sea. That winter Fitzmaurice was killed, one of Desmond's kinsmen was captured and hanged, and the foreign mercenaries were scattered throughout Munster with marauding bands of Irish irregulars.

Meantime a new mercenary force, some 800 strong, had been gathering on the north Spanish coast at Santander. On 28th August 1580 these soldiers embarked with their Italian colonel Sebastian di San Guiseppe in a flotilla of six Spanish ships commanded by Juan Martinez de Recalde. Ireland was sighted after 15 days at sea, and in spite of a storm which scattered the small fleet most of the soldiers and their stores were landed at the wide natural harbour of Smerwick, on the same peninsula off which the Blaskets lie. Recalde remained to supervise the establishment of the bridgehead and the unloading of some light field artillery, and at the beginning of October he returned to Spain.

Smerwick Harbour is only some 6 sea miles from Blasket Sound, and in the fortnight he was there Recalde must have come to know this whole coastline well. While seeking out the lost members of his scattered fleet he must have ranged over much of its length, and it would be strange indeed if a seaman of his calibre did not observe that the lee of Great Blasket Island might provide emergency shelter for a ship caught on that coast in a westerly gale, or if his professional curiosity did not prompt him to reconnoitre the passage through the reefs by which such shelter would have to be gained. First-hand knowledge of this kind was, after all, the only way in which a seaman could familiarise himself with a strange shore in days when adequate charts were unknown. One never knew when in the future such information might prove useful, or even vital. Filed away in the vast bank of Recalde's sea experience, this particular fragment of knowledge was still there in all its detail when, eight years later, the moment of crisis arose.

From the deck of the *San Juan de Portugal,* as she rode gently at anchor off Great Blasket Island in 1588, Recalde would clearly see, beyond Sybil Head, the three sloping peaks which guard the entrance to Smerwick Harbour. He will surely have reflected, with that grim irony for which he was notorious, that this was not a place of happy associations. The Kerry landings had been a tragic fiasco; the mercenaries had been inexperienced and abysmally led, and were, as a Vatican official later complained, 'so little inflamed with military ardour that they were accustomed to use their swords as spits, and their helmets as pots when cooking their meat'. Instead of thrusting inland to gain the strategic heights and seize the passes San Guiseppe stayed encamped within his bridgehead fortification at Dun an Oir (the Fort of Gold), a small promontory jutting into Smerwick Harbour on which the remains of the mercenaries' earthworks can still be seen. The position was vulnerable to attack by land and sea, and the English were not slow to exploit both possibilities. On 5th November 1580 Dun an Oir was blockaded by a fleet commanded by Sir William Winter, and subjected to a heavy bombardment. Two days later a military force arrived under the new

Lord Deputy, Grey of Wilton, and proceeded to invest the fort from the land side. Siege trenches were dug and 10 guns landed by the fleet were manhandled into position. What then followed is described in a report later sent to Philip II by the Spanish ambassador in London:

> After firing a few shots the English dismantled one of the cannons in the fort, and the besieged at once hoisted a white flag to parley. Notwithstanding that they made not the slightest resistance and did not fire a shot, the Lord Deputy delayed parleying with them, for fear that it might be a stratagem to keep him in check until reinforcements arrived and attacked him in the rear, since it was impossible for any soldier to believe that there could be so few brave men in the fort, which they had been strengthening for two months, as to surrender without striking a blow. On being told that they (the defenders) came by orders of the Pope, Grey said that he could not treat them as soldiers but simply as thieves.
>
> In spite of this, they surrendered on condition of their lives being spared. Twelve of the leaders came out, and were told to order their men to lay down their arms. When this was done, the Lord Deputy sent a company of his men to take possession of the fort, and they slaughtered 507 men who were in it and some pregnant women. Besides which they tortured and hanged seventeen Irish and English men, amongst whom was an Irishman named Plunkett, a priest, and an English servant to Dr. Saunders [the Papal Legate who had been attached to the expedition].
>
> In the fort were found 200 corslets and arquebuses and other weapons sufficient to arm 4 000 men, besides great store of victuals and munitions enough to last for months, in addition to money.

A number of the Italian officers were spared for ransom, including San Guiseppe, and whether he was a traitor as well as an incompetent coward is a matter over which historians have speculated. One of the English soldiers who was present at the savage butchery of Dun an Oir was Walter Raleigh, who was then serving as a young captain with the Lord Deputy's forces. Of Lord Grey himself, the phrase 'Grey's faith' became an expression long used in Ireland to denote the vilest perfidy.

The knowledge that a similar fate was the likely prospect of any of his men who set foot on the forbidding shore opposite can have brought little comfort to Juan Martinez de Recalde as, from the Blasket anchorage, he considered his next move. But food and especially water were desperately needed. He sent eight seamen to the mainland in one of the *San Juan*'s boats, with orders to make contact with the local inhabitants. With luck, he hoped, there might be no English troops in the vicinity. In case there were, the reconnaissance party was given a formal letter to the Governor of Munster stating that the three Spanish ships had been driven by stress of weather upon the Irish coast and wished only to take on fresh supplies, after which they would depart in peace. The eight men pulled away into the tossing waters of Blasket Sound and eventually vanished from sight among the dark mainland cliffs, two miles to leeward. They never returned. 'We suspected,' wrote Aramburu two days later, 'that they had been lost at sea, or taken prisoner.'

In fact, the men suffered the latter fate, which was certainly the least enviable of the two. The English were as certain of how they would deal with landings from the Spanish ships which were daily being reported from all parts of the Irish coast as they were uncertain of whether these were survivors of the dispersed Armada or a fresh invasion force from Spain. In either event the sparse, badly equipped, and disorganised forces by which the Queen's Lord Deputy held down the wild outlying mountains and coasts of Ireland could not afford battle-hardened Spanish troops to land and rally the dissatisfied Celtic clans. 'We look rather to be overrun by the Spaniards than otherwise,' wrote the Lord Deputy anxiously a few days later, from Dublin Castle. At the same time, he issued instructions to his officers in the western provinces of the country 'to apprehend and execute all Spanish found, of what quality soever. Torture may be used in prosecuting this enquiry.'

Thus the eight captured men from the *San Juan de Portugal* were brought to the little walled town of Dingle and there incarcerated. Recalde's letter of friendship was brusquely forwarded by Dominick Rice, the Sovereign (Crown Officer) of Dingle, to the Vice-President of Munster, Thomas Norrys. The Vice-President's reaction was predictable enough; he immediately dispatched 200 foot-soldiers and fifty cavalry with orders to watch over the Spanish ships and repel any attempts to land. Meanwhile the captured men were interrogated before Rice. One of them was a Scotsman who with six others had been captured by the Duke of Medina Sidonia's flagship *San Martín* from a fishing boat off the Scottish coast, and had been transferred as a pilot to the *San Juan.* He had probably been included in the reconnaissance party with the hope that the savage gibberish which — to Spanish ears — he spoke might be intelligible to Gaelic speaking inhabitants here on the Irish coast. The unfortunate Scotsman informed Rice that the ships 'were destitute of victual, and in great extremity for want of knowledge'. Whether he was then released — he had after all been taken by the Spaniards against his will — is not known, but there is nothing to suggest that he was spared. Other innocents who had forcibly been pressed into the Armada found the fact no defence from the hangman's noose in Ireland. Still less is it likely that his seven companions were treated with any compassion at all. The depositions of four of them, taken down during formal interrogation and perhaps under torture, survive today in the Public Record Office. They are moving documents. In one Emanuel Fremoso, a Portuguese seaman, gives harrowing details of conditions aboard the stricken *San Juan*:

> He says that out of the ship there died 4 or 5 every day of hunger and thirst, and yet this ship was one of the best furnished for victuals. . . . He says that there are 80 soldiers and 20 of the mariners sick and (some of them) do lie down and die daily, and the rest, he says, are very weak, and the Captain (Recalde) very sad and weak. . . . There is left in this flagship but 25 pipes of wine, and very little bread, and no water but what they brought out of Spain, which stinketh marvellously, and the flesh meat they cannot eat, the drought is so great. . . . He says the Admiral's purpose is with the first wind to pass away for Spain. . . . He says also that it is a common bruit among the soldiers that if they may get home again, they will not meddle with the English any more.

Another Portuguese, Emanuel Francisco, tells of the crippling battle damage in spite of which the *San Juan* reached the Irish coast. The flagship, he says 'was many times shot through, and a shot in the mast, and the deck of the prow spoiled. . . . He says the flagship's mast is so weak, by reason of the shot in it, as they dare not abide any storm, nor to bear such sails as otherwise they might do. . . . And further, the best that be in the Admiral's ship are scarce able to stand, and that if they tarry where they are any time, they will perish . . .'

The shot in the *San Juan*'s mast was a relic of the earliest bout in the Channel engagements almost two months before. As the Armada had advanced in a defensive crescent formation intent on the rendezvous with Parma, the English fleet, lying in a commanding windward position, at first held back, wary of making a decisive move. Though many hot-headed Spaniards—particularly the young *adventureros*—must have been longing to stand and fight, Philip's master-plan strictly forbade it. No one had been more conscious of this plan than the Duke of Medina Sidonia, whose detailed orders from the king sailed with him aboard the flagship *San Martín*. He was not to plunge (as the normal tenets of Spanish honour demanded) into an all-out close quarter mêlée; instead, he was to maintain a rigidly disciplined defensive formation and fight only when it was necessary to do so in order to keep this formation intact and moving. The whole plan hinged on a successful rendezvous with Parma. Only if that rendezvous should fail for some reason, ran Philip's secret instructions to the Duke, was the Armada to attempt any other course — the seizure, perhaps, of a port on the south coast or a straight battle of attrition with the English navy. But Philip did not expect failure. Had he not provided for every conceivable eventuality, and issued comprehensive instructions to all who were to participate? Was this not the largest and most powerful fleet that had ever sailed? Was it not, moreover, God's will that they should succeed?

The Armada battle began with an incident which was almost medieval in its flavour. There emerged from the English ranks a tiny pinnace, the *Disdain* (surely the most aptly named vessel in the annals of naval warfare), which bore down on the Spanish rear until she was almost amongst the towering galleons to fire, into their midst, a single token shot — Lord Admiral Howard's 'defiance', or formal challenge. Although Medina Sidonia was too conscientious of his orders to be thus provoked into halting the Armada's progress and joining battle, old Martinez de Recalde, in the vice-admiral's position at the rear of the formation, presented his broadside to the enemy, supported by his Biscayan vice-flagship *Gran Grin.* Recalde had already expressed to the King his personal conviction that the English fleet would have to be defeated at sea before the invasion could take place. Perhaps he therefore intended, against orders but from the highest motives of patriotism and honour, to precipitate the close quarter mêlée in which all his instincts and experience told him that the heavy short-range Spanish guns and massed companies of soldiers would prove decisive.

Recalde clearly hoped that by exposing himself and his ship — both valuable prizes — as bait, the English might be tempted to close. They did close, but only to short culverin range, 300 yards or so. As an anonymous naval strategist (it might even have been Recalde himself) had feared just before the Armada sailed, the English intended to stand aloof and knock them to pieces with their long-range culverins. For 2 hours Recalde held grimly on while Drake's *Revenge,* Hawkins' *Victory,* Martin Frobisher's huge *Triumph,* and others poured their fire into him. His foremast was twice hit, his rigging and tackle badly cut about, and some fifteen men were killed. In terms of contemporary sea warfare, such damage and casualties were relatively slight, but the chastening thing for the Spaniards was that they had been inflicted on the *San Juan*, one of the Armada's most powerful vessels, without her being able to reply effectively at all. It was a grim omen for the battles which later would have to be fought.

Under questioning in Dingle John de Licorino, one of Recalde's fellow Biscayans, confirmed the reports of the other prisoners but added little himself. The fourth seaman to be interrogated, a Fleming called Pier O'Carr, says of his staunch, proud admiral: '. . . after such time as the fight was at Calais (he) came not out of his bed until this day week, in the morning that they ran upon the shore [O'Carr was being examined on the 21st September, a week after his capture] . . . he says this Admiral is of Biscay and of 57 years of age, and a man of service . . .'

Ever since the fleet had left Corunna on 22nd July Recalde (who was in fact 62) had been suffering from severe attacks of sciatica which had, after the gruelling week of action in the Channel, driven him pain-racked and exhausted to his quarters. In the hour of dire necessity, however, he had struggled to his feet and once more taken up the commander's position on the *San Juan*'s poop, determined to put up a sustained fight to the last. During the terrible fortnight in Blasket Sound Recalde displayed endurance and leadership even above that he had shown in the battles, pressing his failing men on not by threat but by example, struggling with almost superhuman courage to carry out what he believed to be his duty, and far more. On the day following the ships' entry into the Blasket anchorage he was busy supervising with seamanlike efficiency the important business of ensuring that both vessels had serviceable ground tackle to cope with any future emergency. Aramburu stood in need of cables, for he had only the one he was anchored by, so Recalde gave him two of his, and a small broken anchor. In return Aramburu sent over a 30-cwt. bower anchor, which Recalde had lacked.

On the next day, 17th September, Recalde dispatched his longboat with a landing party of fifty arquebusiers to make another attempt at getting supplies from the shore. 'They found only large rugged rocks,' recorded Aramburu in his log, 'against which the sea pounded, and ashore 100 arquebusiers were marching, bearing a white standard with a red cross. It was concluded that they were English. . . .' The President of Munster's men had arrived, and were guarding the Dunquin cliffs.

The detachment of English soldiers was commanded by James Trant, one of the Sovereign of Dingle's officers. Trant was an Anglo-Norman who could trace his ancestry back through the five centuries which had passed since his forebears came to Kerry at the time of the Norman conquest. As hereditary feudal landlords the Anglo-Normans were often even more fiercely attached to the cause of an independent Ireland than the native Irish themselves. But in these troubled and confused times a man could often do no more than base his loyalties on local circumstances, and to James Trant, prosperous merchant in the port of Dingle, allegiance to the English crown suited him and his townspeople best. His father had raised the alarm when the Papal mercenaries landed at Smerwick, and James himself had on more than one occasion acted as a negotiator between the rebel forces and the English. Now, as a trusted holder of the Queen's Commission, he had been charged with watching over the Spanish ships anchored off Great Blasket Island.

Trant at once judged that they would give little trouble. 'We do not fear their landing here,' he wrote a few days later, 'for they are in a most difficult road (anchorage), and themselves in a miserable state. We have 200 men watching upon the shore every day. We stand in no fear of them, for they are so much afraid of themselves.'

After Recalde's arquebusiers returned to the *San Juan de Portugal,* the Spaniards made no further attempts to land on the mainland. Instead, they directed their energies towards taking on water from the tiny spring which still wells on the cliff-top above the beach on Great Blasket Island. Recalde was able to use his longboat to get the casks and men ashore, and Aramburu recorded that the flagship was able to 'take on a little water, but with much work'. It must indeed have been a gruelling task. Each barrel would have to be landed through the surf, rolled up the beach and parbuckled up the cliff to the spring, and then, with even more labour, brought down to the boat again. Aramburu's *San Juan Bautista,* which had no boat, was not able to take on any water at all. Trant, on the mainland cliffs, viewed these operations from afar, and reported that 'they go ashore every day on the island to refresh themselves and take on water'. The watchers on the cliffs could also see, half a dozen or more times each day, the dismal little ceremony which was performed every time a fresh corpse was tipped over one of the ships' weather-blackened sides.

At dawn on the 21st September, just a week after the Spanish ships had come into the Blasket anchorage, the worst gale of that whole wild autumn came howling out of the north-west. Edward White, clerk of the Council of Connacht, described it later as 'a most extreme wind and cruel storm, the like whereof hath not been seen or heard a long time'. Like many sudden Atlantic gales, the result of cyclonic conditions in mid-ocean, it came without warning, out of a cloudless sky. Marcos de Aramburu, eye witness and participant in the events which followed, wrote:

> On the 21st, in the morning, the west wind came with some terrible fury, but cloudless and with little rain. The flagship of Juan Martinez (Recalde) drifted down on our ship, cast anchor and another cable, and having smashed our lantern and our mizzenmast tackle and rigging, the flagship secured herself. At mid-day the ship *Santa Maria de la Rosa,* commanded by Martin de Villafranca, came in by another entrance nearer land on the north-west side. She fired a shot on entering,

as if seeking help, and another further on. All her sails were in pieces except the foresail. She cast her single anchor, for she was not carrying more, and with the tide coming in from the south-east side and beating against her stern she stayed there until two o'clock. Then the tide waned, and as it turned the ship began dragging on our two cables, and we dragged with her, and in an instant we could see that she was going down, trying to hoist the foresail. Then she sank with all on board, not a person being saved, a most extraordinary and terrifying thing. We were dragging on her still, to our own perdition.

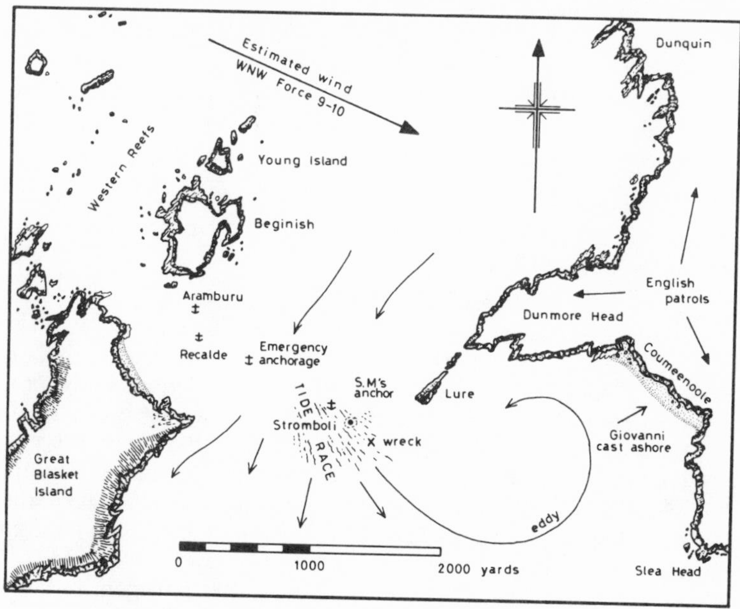

Fig. 4. Sequence of events, 21st September 1588

But Our Lord had willed us, in case of such necessity, to put a new stock to an anchor which had only half a stock, which Juan Martinez had given us, with a cable. We dropped this anchor, and the ship turned her prow; and we hauled in the other anchor, finding only the stock with half the shank, for the rest was broken, and the cable chafed by the rocks over which we were lying. There also entered with this ship (i.e. with the *Santa Maria*) the ship of Miguel de Aranivar.

The same afternoon, at four o'clock, the ship *San Juan* of Fernando Horra came in with her mainmast gone, and on entering her foresail was blown to shreds. She let her anchor go and brought to. Owing to the gale it was impossible to communicate with her, or give assistance.

On the morning of the 22nd the ship lowered her longboat and made known her distressed condition. Seeing it to be hopeless, Juan Martinez decided that I should take on board the whole company of Gonzalo Melendez while that of Diego Bazan should be distributed among the *pataches.* I urged him to leave, putting before him my own distressed condition, pointing out how without a boat I could not replenish water, while bread and other stores were constantly being used up, and suggesting that the abandoned ship should be fired and that we should all depart. But he wished, as will be seen, to remove the guns from that (Horra's) ship, and to make a supreme effort to do so, though it was an impossible task. Nonetheless, he gave me open permission to run for Spain.

These dramatic events had been seen from the shore by the ever watchful James Trant who, on 22nd September, reported in writing to his superiors that :

> . . . the ships ride at anchor between the Ferriter's Main Island (the Great Blasket) and the shore. There are three great ships, the biggest of them is of 900 tons, and is Admiral of the whole fleet of Spain. The other two are great ships also. One of them has her main mast broken. They have two small barques. There came from the sea unto them yesterday a mighty great ship of 1 000 tons, wherein was Il Principa Dastula (the Prince of Ascoli), base son of the King of Spain. The name of this ship was *Santa Maria de la Rosa,* and as soon as ever they cast anchor they drive upon a rock, and there, was cast away into the middle of the sea, with 500 tall men and the Prince, and no man saved but one, that brought us this news, who came naked upon a board.

The *Santa Maria de la Rosa* was a large merchant vessel, one of the temporary warships which made up the bulk of the Armada's fighting strength, displacing 945 tons and carrying 26 guns. She had sailed from Lisbon as vice-flagship to Miguel de Oquendo's Guipuzcoan squadron; originally, she was to have been his flagship, but she lost this status when a bigger and more heavily gunned ship, the *Santa Ana* (1 200 tons, 47 guns) became available.

The final muster-roll before sailing shows that the *Santa Maria* had a complement of 64 mariners and 233 soldiers, and it also lists the names of gentleman adventurers (*aventureros*) and military captains who sailed with the ship. These included Don Diego Pacheo, son of the Marquis of Villena, with nineteen retainers (*criados*), and four other *aventureros* of less noble birth — they had no retainers at all — Jusepe Justin, Juan de Alba, Juan Cler, and Pedro Dere. The latter two were almost certainly renegade Englishmen, John Clarke and Peter Dare. The military captains, who sailed with their companies of soldiers, were Lupercio Latras and Lope Ochoa de la Vega (not to be confused with the famous Lope de la Vega Carpio, who also took part in the Armada), both of the Sicilian Regiment, and Christobel Rivero of Don Francisco de Toledo's Regiment. We also know from other sources that the ship's captain was Martin de Villafranca, a Basque from the port of San Sebastian, and that the senior military officer on board was Francisco Ruiz Matute, of the Sicilian Regiment.

In the storm which scattered the Armada off Corunna the *Santa Maria* had been one of those most severely damaged, losing her mainmast with all its tackle. She had limped into Corunna, a shattered confusion of fallen spars, broken decks, and injured men, with most of her provisions spoiled. The job of repairing the *Santa Maria* was one of the many problems which faced the Duke of Medina Sidonia at Corunna, and it cannot have been easy to find a new mast and spars for a ship so large. Somehow he succeeded; 'the Duke is working with great energy, as usual', wrote Recalde to the King. 'We have finished (10th July) putting the new mast into the *Santa Maria de la Rosa* of Oquendo's squadron, after a great deal of trouble, as we were over 6 hours in getting it upright', the Duke himself was able to report the following day. He added with a touch of understandable pride, for stepping a large mainmast is a complex and heavy task, that 'when I saw it finished, I thought we had not done badly'.

While the *Santa Maria* was non-operational because of these repairs the squadron's vice-flag evidently passed to her sister-ship *San Salvador* (958 tons, 25 guns), though when a muster was held before the Armada left Corunna the *Santa Maria* is once again listed as the *almiranta,* or vice-flagship. There is some confusion as to the relative status of these two ships, however, for the *San Salvador* (which later blew up and was captured in the

Channel) continues to be referred to, by some Spanish sources, as Oquendo's *almiranta.* The squadron cannot, surely, have had two vice-flagships. In any event, when the *Santa Maria*'s loss off Ireland is finally recorded in Spain, she is clearly described as Guipuzcoa's *almiranta.*

Though we are nowhere specifically told of this ship's part in the battles, Guipuzcoa's station was towards the Armada's rear, and a vice-flagship's post was at the rear of her squadron. In such a position the *Santa Maria* must have been exposed to the main English attacks from windward and seaward, and that she was indeed heavily engaged during the fighting is implicit in her only survivor's statement that 'this ship was shot through four times, and one of the shots was between the wind and the water, whereof they thought she would have sunk, and most of her tackle was spoiled with shot'. She may well have taken part in some of the more offensive actions, too. In the fighting off the Isle of Wight, when the Duke of Medina Sidonia's *San Martín* had been cut off by several English ships, including Sir Martin Frobisher's *Triumph,* the Guipuzcoan squadron counter-attacked in line. 'The plan (i.e. the English attack) would have succeeded,' writes a Spanish witness, 'if Oquendo had not kept up so close a luff, and sailed towards the flagship with other ships following him, thus covering her (the *San Martín*), and receiving the chief brunt of the attack, which was very heavy.' It would be strange if the *Santa Maria,* as Oquendo's vice-flagship, was not one of these 'other ships' which fought in their squadron commander's close support. In all, reports the survivor, the ship suffered 200 casualties 'by fight and sickness'.

According to the survivor's testimony the *Santa Maria de la Rosa* stayed with the main body of the fleet on its north-about course until early in September. Then a storm dispersed them. 'Where he left the Duke he knoweth not . . . he saw no land and therefore can name no place but they feared by tempest, the Duke kept his course to sea; we drew towards the land to find Cape Clear, so did divers other ships, which he thinks to amount to the number of forty ships . . .'

Again, in his third interrogation, the survivor states that 'the whole navy were dispersed by tempest, some eight in one company, and four in another; and thus dispersedly passed on the seas . . . he said that after this first tempest which was about

25 days now past, growing of a south-west wind, they had sundry tempests before they were lost (i.e. sunk) with various winds sometimes one way, and sometimes another . . .'

Only one other vessel reported having seen the *Santa Maria* as she struggled through the north Atlantic. She was the *San Salvador* (not the Guipuzcoan *San Salvador* already mentioned, but the vice-flagship of the clumsy supply-hulks, 650 tons and 24 guns, commanded by the Armada's chief stores officer, Pedro Coco Calderon). 'From the 24th (of August),' wrote Calderon, 'we sailed without knowing whither, through constant storms, fogs and squalls. As this hulk could not beat to windward it was necessary to keep out to sea, and we were unable to discover the main body of the Armada until the 4th of September, when we joined it . . . on this day, as we were sailing to leeward of the body of the Armada, we saw the ship Villafranca of Oquendo and another Levantine ship fall away towards the Faroes and Iceland. These ships were far to leeward of us.' The ship 'Villafranca of Oquendo' can only have been the *Santa Maria de la Rosa,* for Martin de Villafranca was that ship's captain, and Miguel de Oquendo her squadron commander.

Who was the *Santa Maria*'s only survivor, and how did he alone, of several hundred men, come to escape drowning when she was wrecked? He had saved himself, James Trant tells us, 'upon a board'. On the day after the wrecking the survivor was interrogated at Dingle, and the transcript of his first statement (now in the Public Record Office) is headed: 'John Antony de Manona. An Italian. Son to Francisco de Manona pilot of the ship called *Santa Maria de la Rose*, of 1 000 tons, castaway in the Sound of Bleskey.' A second statement, taken four days later, adds further detail: 'He saith his father and himself with others came to Lisbon in a ship of Genoa about a year since, when they were embarked by the King of Spain, that ship was of about 400 tons. He saith his father, after this, was appointed pilot in the ship called *Our Ladie of the Rosarie,* of the burden of 1 000 tons being the King's'.

The first problem, in seeking to identify the survivor, is to deduce his proper name. The names in the Armada interrogation depositions, which were orally transcribed, are often inaccurate; indeed, when a selection of them were published in London some weeks later it is admitted in the preface that 'there may be some errors in the writing of the Spanish names in English, because the same are written by way of interpretation'. In his first statement the survivor is named as John Antony de Manona; in his second as John Antonio of Genoa; and in the third as Giovanni de Manona. The one sure fact seems to be that he came originally from Genoa and, for someone who hailed from that city, Giovanni is a much more likely name than John Antony. Very probably he was really called Giovanni de Genoa — a common enough form of name — and the 'Manona' (later further corrupted into Monona and even Menesis) is simply a transcriber's error for 'Genoa'.

If we assume that the name 'Manona' is a red-herring, we can go some distance towards guessing who he might have been. His father, he tells us, was called Francisco, and he was the ship's pilot. Giovanni also tells us that the first ship in which he and his father were embarked 'was of about 400 tons'. Now in a list of the Armada's pilots, drawn up at Lisbon before the fleet sailed by the Duke of Medina Sidonia, there is a certain Francisco de Martiato, who appears originally to have sailed aboard the *Nuestra Señora del Pilar de Zaragoza*, the 300-ton flagship of the communications squadron of swift *zabras* and *pataches*. He could be our man and, if so, he might have been transferred to the *Santa Maria de la Rosa* during the fleet reorganisation at Corunna, as Giovanni suggests.

Whatever his correct name, young Giovanni has much to tell us. He was, of course, the only surviving witness from the wrecked ship. 'This ship broke against the rocks in the Sound of the Bleskies a league and a half from land upon the Tuesday last at noon, and all in this ship perished saving this examinate, who saved himself upon two or three planks; the gentlemen thinking to save themselves by the boat, it was so fast tied as they could not get her loose, thereby they were drowned. . . . He saith as soon as the ship broke against the rock, one of the Captains slew this examinate's father, saying he did it by treason . . .'

On being pressed for details of 'ordnance, wines, and other matters of moment', Giovanni states that 'on the ship here castaway . . . were 50 great brass pieces, all cannons for the field, 25 pieces of brass and cast iron belonging to the ship, there is also in her 50 tuns of sack. In silver there are in her 15 000 ducats, in gold as much more, much rich apparel and plate and cups of gold.' In a later statement the survivor adds that 'this ship that is drowned hath in her three chests full of money'.

Much of Giovanni's testimony is taken up with details of officers and noblemen who sailed with the Armada, and in particular of those who perished in the wrecking of the *Santa Maria de la Rosa.* This, of course, does not reflect his own interest in or knowledge of such matters, but rather the importance attached to them by his interrogators. The English were after ransom money and salvage, and if circumstances denied these to them they sought at least to extract propaganda value by stressing the immensity of the loss, both in terms of material and men. It is with this in mind that we must regard what Giovanni has to say.

The presence on board the *Santa Maria* of two important individuals who are named by Giovanni can easily be confirmed. One is the ship's captain, Martin de Villafranca, who is first mentioned in connection with the vessel in Medina Sidonia's report of 24th June 1588, when the *Santa Maria* lay at Corunna without a mainmast. That he was still captain at the time of her wrecking is attested by Aramburu's log. The other officer mentioned by Giovanni is a Francisco Ruiz Matute, commander of the Sicilian infantry aboard the ship. His presence on the *Santa Maria* was dramatically confirmed by our expedition in 1969, when we found pieces of his named campaign tableware on the wreck site.

It is natural that Giovanni should have known both of these men well, for he would have been in frequent contact with them during the voyage. If the Duke of Medina Sidonia's standing orders to the fleet were carried out properly on board the *Santa Maria,* Villafranca and Matute would have been present when, three times each week, these orders were read out to the assembled ship's company. Captain Matute, moreover, if he was a conscientious officer, would have been on hand for each day's rations issue at which ' . . . the ship's notary must be present at and take proper account of all distribution of rations, his book to be signed every day and countersigned by the Captain of Infantry. . . .'

Most of the other names listed by Giovanni as being on board the *Santa Maria* when she sank seem to have been those of *aventureros,* or noblemen, even perhaps survivors brought off other foundering vessels. It is unlikely that these men would have had much to do with the day-to-day running of the ship such as would bring them into contact with the ordinary members of her crew. So strong were the barriers of caste that men of this quality would scarcely have deigned to mix with a humble Genoese seaman, who can thus hardly be blamed for getting at least some of them wrong. Many famous names must have been bandied around in lower-deck gossip, in whatever context, and no doubt poor Giovanni will have been pleased enough to blurt out any name which seemed to give his grim tormentors satisfaction.

At any event, grand-sounding names rolled off his tongue: the Prince of Ascoli, base son of the King of Spain; Miguel de Oquendo, Captain-General of the Guipuzcoan squadron; Captains Suarez, Gorrienero, Lupino de la Vega, Montinese and Francisco; John Rice, 'an Irish Captain', and Francis Roche, another Irishman; Don Pedro, Don Diego, Don Francisco, and many other 'gentleman-adventurers, but not of the reckoning of the former'. It is an impressive list. Unfortunately, apart from de la Vega and Don Diego, it is a difficult one to reconcile with the official fleet lists and muster-rolls of Lisbon and Corunna, a difficulty encountered by no less an authority than Philip II himself when he was presented with a copy of Giovanni's statement some months later. Against the list of names he wrote, in his spidery scrawl: 'He is wrong about most of these, perhaps he is so about the rest.' If Philip of Spain, who organised the whole affair, can make neither head nor tail of Giovanni, who then are we to try?

We should, however, comment on two of the names he has given. Miguel de Oquendo most certainly was not on board the ship. This proud old officer who men called 'The Glory of the Fleet', who had been the terror of the Turks in the Mediterranean, who had smashed his way to the rescue of his admiral at the Battle of Terceira, and who was said to handle his ship 'with the dash of a light cavalryman', struggled back to Spain with his squadron flagship *Santa Ana*. Oquendo himself landed at San Sebastian, where he died within a few days. The *Santa Ana*, shortly after anchoring, blew up and sank with 100 men on board.

It is less easy to dismiss Giovanni's clear and very detailed statements concerning the Prince of Ascoli, the noblest of all the Armada's colourful band of *aventureros*. These were men of gentle birth who held no specific appointments in the fleet and whose function can only be seen in the context of a strongly feudal order. All had been trained from boyhood in the art and etiquette of chivalry, and were duty bound both to lead and to protect those socially inferior to them. Though not necessarily rich they were, to a man, aristocratic. Such men were expected to lead their countrymen in the forefront of battle like knights of old, both through privilege and implied feudal contract, and no one thought it strange that in order to do so they should hold freelance roving commands over the organised elements of the army and navy. Promotions to the high command were invariably made from this group, usually but not always on merit. One of these men was Don Alonso de Leiva, a dashing 24-year-old favourite of the Spanish court, who became one of the few real leaders thrown up by the whole unhappy campaign and who had secretly been destined by the King to take supreme command should Medina Sidonia fall. Don Alonso was drowned with 1 300 others when the galeass *Girona* was dashed against the rocks of Antrim, and all Spain is said to have mourned him.

In practice, of course, many *aventureros* were little more than figureheads; brave enough in their example, no doubt, but unsuited to the direct command of fighting units. The Prince of Ascoli had been one such. Antonio Luis de Leiva[1] was an Italian princeling, said to be a base-born son of King Philip himself, who had sailed as a member of Medina Sidonia's staff aboard the flagship *San Martín*. According to several witnesses, including Giovanni, he had left the flagship at Calais on a staff mission to the Duke of Parma and had been on shore when the English fireship attack took place. A seemingly veracious letter was sent by him to his father from Dunkirk on 12th August (by which date the Armada was off the coast of Scotland), explaining why he had been left behind and declaring his fervent wish '. . . to serve your Majesty and do my duty in a manner worthy of my birth . . . when my person shall be of service it shall be exposed to the death on your Majesty's behalf'. However he does not appear to have made this supreme sacrifice in 1588, either in Blasket Sound or anywhere else. Strong evidence shows that he lived long afterwards, and spent much of his subsequent life in Flanders and Italy.

[1] Distantly related to, but not to be confused with, Don Alonso de Leiva.

Giovanni's statement is in quite specific disagreement over the matter. The Prince was, he says, on board the *Santa Maria de la Rosa,* and he perished in Blasket Sound. He explains, moreover, how Ascoli came to be on board the *Santa Maria.* 'He saith the Prince of Ascule the King's base son came in the company of the Duke's ship called the *S. Martine,* of 1 000 tons, but at Calais when Sir Francis Drake came near them, this Prince went to the shore, and before his return the Duke was driven to cut his anchors, and to depart, whereby the Prince could not recover that ship but came into the said ship called *Our Ladie of the Rosarie,* and with him there came in also one Don Pedro, Don Diego, Don Francisco, and seven other gentlemen of account that accompanied the Prince.'

In his third examination Giovanni was pressed for a detailed description of the Prince: '. . . (he was) a slender made man of a reasonable stature of twenty-eight years of age, his hair of an acorn colour stroked upwards; of a high forehead; whitely faced with some little red on the cheeks. He was drowned in apparel of white satin for his doublet and breeches, after the Spanish fashion cut, with russet silk stockings. When this Prince came into their ship at Calais, he was appareled in black raised velvet laid on with broad gold lace.

'He saith that this Prince's men for the most part were in the ship that this examinate was, from their coming out of Spain; and when they were at Calais the Prince passed in a little *phelocke* (small boat) with six others to give order to them, and some said that he went on shore at that time.'

But if the Prince of Ascoli really had been on board the *Santa Maria de la Rosa* on 21st September 1588 he could not have lived for many years after that date, as he appears in fact to have done. Neither is the strong tradition that he was buried at Dunquin of any help to us, for this tradition itself clearly derives from Giovanni's testimony (no doubt someone from the wrecked ship is buried there, but who he really was is another matter). It is to that testimony, therefore, and the circumstances under which it was obtained, that we must turn if a possible explanation of the mystery is to be found.

The most telling factor seems to be that Giovanni was examined no less than three times. No other Armada captive was so closely interrogated. His first examination gives some details of the ship and its contents, and lists the names of those supposedly aboard, including the Prince of Ascoli. Only brief mention of the Prince is made, describing him as a 'base sonne of the King of Spaine'. But when this statement was later perused by the authorities, one fact must have stood out above all the others. The King of Spain's own son — albeit an illegitimate one — drowned like a dog! What a catch for the propagandists! What material for the broadsheets lauding the Armada's defeat which were already coming off the London presses! The boy must be questioned again, and more details of this high born prince and the manner of his death secured. Here, surely, we see the reason behind the second and third interrogations.

Much of Giovanni's second statement is given over to a careful enquiry as to how the Prince came to be on board the *Santa Maria,* and fresh details of the wrecking are sought. Almost all of his third and final statement, recorded a full week after his capture, is taken up by a personal description of the Prince. The impression that the whole line of questioning was directed by someone whose main intention was to verify the story of the Prince's death is very strong indeed.

What may have happened, I believe, is this. Giovanni was a young Italian seaman, of no great rank, who after the most harrowing series of misadventures imaginable suddenly found himself, quite alone in a hostile foreign land, facing the terrors of a formal 16th century interrogation. He would, of necessity, be questioned through an interpreter, and his answers, once given, would have to be retranslated before they could be written down. The possibility — indeed the likelihood — of error is very great. We even have a proven example. When Giovanni spoke of Miquel de Oquendo in his first interrogation he was probably telling who his squadron commander was, without meaning to imply that he had actually been on board the *Santa Maria.* It is inconceivable that Giovanni really thought that a man of Oquendo's standing was on the ship when he was not. But in the second interrogation it is stated, much more emphatically, that 'Michael d'Oquendo was General of this ship'. Suppose that when Giovanni was being re-examined it dawned on him that his captors would be pleased if Oquendo had been drowned in Blasket Sound. Nothing could then be more natural for him, if they had taken him up wrongly in the first place, than to agree that Oquendo *had* been on the ship. And so it was written down.

What clearly happened in the case of Oquendo might surely also have happened in the case of the Prince. Possibly some of his thirty-nine *criados* (retainers) really did sail with the *Santa Maria,* as Giovanni states ('this Prince's men for the most part were in the ship that this examinate was'), thus occasioning a first mention of the Prince's name. For the boy then to agree under questioning that the Prince himself had been on board might quickly follow, regardless of the truth. But once the lie had been told, it would have to be substantiated whatever further questions were asked, and such questions — lots of them — clearly were asked about the Prince of Ascoli. How did he come to be on the ship? Who came with him? Was he not originally on board the *San Martín* (the Armada fleet-lists, including the names of *aventureros* and the ships on which they had sailed, had already been widely publicised throughout Europe)? What did he look like? What kind of clothes did he wear? To each question he was asked, Giovanni would have to find an answer. Had he been asked similar questions about Oquendo no doubt he would have described him in the same vivid but imaginary detail. It would be unreasonable to expect him to have done otherwise. Giovanni was unconcerned about what future historians might make of his statement. He was a lonely frightened boy trying desperately to please his captors, and so delay the dark fate which inevitably awaited him when they wanted to hear no more.

It seems likely that the whole misunderstanding sprang from faulty interpretation during the interrogations, and we have reason to suspect its cause. The interpreter responsible was a certain David Gwynn, a Welsh soldier of fortune about whom we know a good deal. Gwynn had been, of all things, a galley-slave on board one of the Armada galleys, the *Diana,* which had been wrecked at Bayonne (like the other three galleys, which were totally unsuited to Atlantic conditions, the *Diana* never reached the Channel). He claimed, with more bravado than truth, to have led the revolt of slaves which had caused the wreck; at any event, he had found his freedom in France whence he had made his way through England to Ireland where he arrived just in time for the Armada wreckings on that coast. His services as an interpreter for the interrogation of prisoners were siezed on by the authorities, and Gwynn had a part in most of the examinations of Armada prisoners taken in Ireland. But fate soon caught up with him. In October 1588 he was arraigned on charges of 'manifest falsehood and perjury touching the embezzling of certain gold and coin received by him of the Spaniards', as well as on more serious charges of treasonable talk. Though probably not a traitor Gwynn was certainly a scoundrel, whose life was a tissue of lies and underhand dealings. Such a man can have had little more personal concern for the truth than had poor Giovanni. Neither do we know what fluency he had in the language (Spanish or Italian?) in which the questioning was conducted. It may not have been great.

The sinking of the *Santa Maria de la Rosa* was not the termination of activity and incident in Blasket Sound. Recalde and Aramburu were still there, as well as the rather mysterious 'ship of Miguel de Aranivar', and the *San Juan* of Fernando Horra which arrived in a distressed condition two hours after the sinking with a broken mainmast.

There is no mention in the Armada fleet lists of a captain named Miguel de Aranivar, though of course changes in command might easily take place through casualties or for other reasons. As to the identity of the ship herself there is nothing to go on other than Giovanni's brief statement concerning what is obviously the same vessel that 'there came in their company a Portingall ship of about 400 tons who coming into the same sound cast anchor near where they found the Admiral at anchor . . .' If this ship did indeed belong to the squadron of Portugal, and if Giovanni's estimate of her size is approximately correct, there are only two likely candidates. These are the Portuguese galleons *San Cristobal* and *San Bernardo*, both of 352 tons and of 20 and 21 guns respectively (the next in size in the squadron was the *Santiago* of 520 tons). Both these ships returned safely to Spain and one of them, the *San Bernardo,* seems to have been in company with Recalde's *San Juan* when she eventually reached Corunna. It may well be that she was Miguel de Aranivar's ship.

There is no doubt at all about the identity of the other ship, the *San Juan* of Fernando Horra. Though her captain's name is variously mistranscribed in the Armada lists as Fernando Ome, Fernando Oume, and even Fernan Dome, the ship involved is always the same; she is the second *San Juan Bautista* of the Castile squadron (Aramburu's was the other) though she was not, like Aramburu's ship, a true galleon but an armed merchantman of 650 tons and 24 guns. In common with the other three merchant ships attached to that squadron (one of which was the same *Trinidad* in whose company Aramburu had been for some time off the Irish coast) she was a fast, Atlantic-built vessel normally used on the West India passage, and she is mentioned by the Duke of Medina Sidonia as being one of the two speediest vessels in the fleet. One of the military captains aboard her was Don Diego de Bazan, whose father, the Marquis of Santa Cruz, was to have commanded the Armada until his untimely death in February 1588 precipitated the Duke of Medina Sidonia into reluctant leadership.

What happened to this ship in Blasket Sound is rather more of a mystery. We know that Bazan's company of soldiers, and another unit under Gonzalo Melendez, were taken off the *San Juan,* and that Recalde intended to salvage her guns and then scuttle her. But at this point we lose our key witness, Aramburu, who sailed for Spain. Later, however, the Venetian ambassador at Madrid reported to his government that a ship had 'gone to the bottom' in an uninhabited Irish port, though her crew and some of her guns were saved by Juan Martinez de Recalde. This is confirmed in the correspondence of Sir George Carew, one of the Queen's Commissioners in Munster who, in listing the Armada losses, includes

'. . . one ship of 500 tuns sunk in the Sound of Blaskie . . . the men were saved by Don Joan de Ricaldo (sic)'.

Both these references can only be to the *San Juan* of Fernando Horra, and they clearly indicate that she was scuttled, though it seems that Recalde was at least partially successful in what Aramburu had considered to be the 'impossible task' of bringing off her guns. At a moment like this, when he and his comrades were half dead from sickness and privation, and all seemed hopeless, to transfer heavy guns from a sinking to a damaged ship in foul sea conditions in order to bring them back to Spain to fight another day says a great deal for Recalde's indomitable will and unbreakable spirit, and that of his men too.

Marcos de Aramburu survived the Armada and went on to serve with distinction in the Indian Guard until the beginning of the 17th century. In 1591 he was to play a leading part in the immortal fight against Sir Richard Grenville in the lone English galleon *Revenge* (Drake's flagship in the Armada battles) off the Azores. Aramburu left the Blasket anchorage on 24th September by the hazardous passage through which he had come, between the western reefs, and after a nightmare voyage the *San Juan Bautista* reached Santander on 14th October.

A few days later grim old Recalde, quite literally dying on his feet, brought the broken *San Juan de Portugal* to a safe anchorage in Corunna roads. One hundred and seventy of his ship's company had perished during the campaign and its aftermath, and all the survivors were sick and emaciated, having been reduced in the end to a daily ration of only a quarter pound of biscuit per man. Recalde himself, his duty both to Spain and to his beloved Biscayan seamen discharged to the last ounce, went quietly ashore to die. He refused to see family or friends, though he managed to write a brief note of condolence to his King. This letter is now in the Simancas archives. The shaky signature at its foot, penned by a proud but heartbroken man very close to death, somehow epitomises the whole tragedy of the Armada. Within four days of landing this magnificent man was dead. In his way he had been as great as any who had served in the campaign on either side.

Because of Recalde's stubbornly heroic efforts in Blasket Sound to recover guns from Horra's sinking *San Juan* the old admiral had been forced to wait several more days after Aramburu's departure for another favourable wind. On 25th September, according to an English report, the ships had 'weighed their anchors and essayed to go, but the wind turned them back again'. About this time a Breton salt-boat which came to Galway town informed Sir Richard Bingham, the Governor of Connacht, that four Spanish ships were still sheltering in Blasket Sound; they were, we may presume, Recalde's *San Juan,* the unidentified 'ship of Miguel de Aranivar', and the two *pataches.* Not until about 28th September were they finally able to clear the Irish coast.

When the battered ships and their spectre-like crews finally quit this unhappy place they left the remains of the *Santa Maria de la Rosa,* Guipuzcoa's once-proud *almiranta,* lying somewhere on the sea bed beneath the four square miles of Blasket Sound's bleak and unpredictable waters. But if anyone ever knew exactly where, it was soon forgotten. Only the tradition remained: the tradition that a great Spanish ship had been lost there at the time of the Armada, and that a son of the King of Spain lay buried beneath a green mound at Dunquin. In 1837 Blasket fishermen brought up in their trammel nets a small bronze gun emblazoned with a coat-of-arms, which is now lost, and in more recent times local men spoke of encrusted muskets which had been dredged from the sea floor.

But no one could remember the spot from which they had come.

THE SEARCH

THE idea of looking for Armada wrecks is not a new one. Even as news of the wreckings came in, Lord Deputy Fitzwilliam ordered his Commissioners to 'make enquiry by all good means . . . to take all hulls of ships, stores, treasure, etc., into your hands . . . much treasure (is) cast away, now subject to the spoil of the country people . . . also great store of ordnance, munitions, armours, and other goods of several kinds, which ought to be preserved for the use of her Majesty . . .' One of these Commissioners was Sir George Carew who, in the summer following the Armada, wrote to the Lord Deputy from Dunmore Castle in County Clare, hard by the ledge on which a large Spanish ship had struck, informing him that

'. . . already we have weighed three pieces of artillery of brass. Yesterday we fastened our hawsers to a cannon of battery or basalyke, as we suppose by the length, for they lie at 4 fathom and a half of water; which was so huge that it break our cables. Our diver was nearly drowned, but Irish *aqua vitae* hath such virtue as I hope of his recovery. If the diver of Dublin with his instruments were here, I would not doubt to bring good store of artillery from hence; for if I be not deceived out of our boats we did plainly see four pieces more . . . Command some victuallers of Galway to bring us beer and bread; and an oyster dredge or two, in hope to scrape somewhat out of the seas.'

Sir George next hastened to Ulster to salvage the wrecked galleass *Girona* only to find that the local chieftain, Sorley Boy McDonnell, and some of his Scottish kinsmen, had been there before him and had recovered several large guns as well as 'great store of gold and silver'. Naturally, when the wrecks lay in shallow water, or had been driven high and dry, local people salvaged them clean. *La Rata Encoronada*, the great Genoese carrack of Don Alonso de Leiva, was rifled by the picturesquely named brigand 'Devil's Hook' Burke as she lay grounded and burning in Blacksod Bay, County Mayo. So enthusiastic were the people of Dunbeg and Troma in County Clare in their efforts to salvage to the bones the two ships wrecked there that Nicholas Kahane, a local official, was only able 'by much ado' and a bribe of 40 tescons to persuade a local youth to break off plundering and carry news of the wreckings to the Mayor of Limerick. In later years, too, successful salvage was carried out on Armada wrecks. Work on the wreck in Tobermory Bay, on the Island of Mull, was in full swing by the mid 17th century. The remains of this ship — probably the *San Juan de Sicilia* (800 tons, 26 guns) of the Levant squadron — lie ten fathoms down on a bottom of deep mud. The first divers, who worked from a bell, were for the most part Swedes, some of whom had already recovered guns from almost twice this depth from the *Wasa,* a Swedish royal ship lost in Stockholm Harbour on her maiden voyage in 1628. Several guns have been recovered from the Tobermory ship, and one of these can be seen today at Inveraray Castle, Argyll. During the 18th century a visitor to Tobermory could watch divers 'sinking three-score foot under water, and returning with the spoils of the ocean, whether it was plate or money'. In more recent times similar operations have continued. From 1906 to 1908 a number of 'strange and pleasing relics . . . were brought to the upper air by gentleman-adventurers styled "The Pieces of Eight Company" '. Further efforts to salvage the wreck and its supposed treasure have continued, with varying success, to this day.

Two bronze guns were recovered in 1728 from the wreck of *El Gran Grifón,* flagship of the hulks, on Fair Isle. Some years later off Gola Island in West Donegal, an enterprising group of young men raised from an unidentified Armada wreck a number of bronze guns crested with the Spanish arms, which they broke up over a peat fire and took away by the cartload, selling the metal as scrap at 4½d a pound. They also recovered several boat-shaped lead ingots, and a quantity of coin.

Up to the 1960s, however, those who sought Armada wrecks were invariably motivated by the hope of valuable salvage recoveries, particularly of treasure, with a measure of adventurous curio-hunting thrown in. Little thought was given to the archaeological potential contained by such wrecks even though, from the late 19th century onwards, great advances had been made in the historical study and interpretation of the Armada fight. Much documentary material which had lain unstudied in the archives for centuries was transcribed and published, particularly by Captain Fernandez Duro in Spain and by Sir John Laughton in England. For the first time the uncritical and wildly misleading legends which had grown up around the Armada were subjected to a scholarly appraisal and rejected in favour of a more balanced interpretation of what had really happened. This has further been carried forward by the important studies of Professors Michael Lewis and Garrett Mattingly during the past 30 years.

In spite of this, however, there had remained much concerning the Armada about which the available sources said little or nothing. Of the political and strategic background to the campaign, of the general outline of the fighting and of the terrible voyage back to Spain, there is documentary evidence in almost overwhelming abundance. But this is not the whole story. Concerning the living stuff of the Armada — the ships, the guns, the accoutrements and the weaponry — there was almost nothing. Shipwrights of that age made no detailed plans of their work, relying rather on tradition and rule-of-thumb, so that when the ships they had built perished or were broken up details of form and construction were lost. What were the Armada ships really like? Were they as strong and formidable as had often been supposed? And what of the guns? Much has been written on naval artillery at this vital period of its development, but most of what has been written is theoretical, and above all else gunnery is a practical business. What sort of guns did the Armada ships carry? What kind of tackles and carriages did the Spaniards use? Had effective gun-drills been evolved for use at sea? Most puzzling of all, why did the heavy Spanish guns fail when set against the lighter English pieces at close range, when they ought to have been at their most devastating? It has long been known that answers to these questions are not to be found among the archives. Might they, perhaps, be found among the debris of the wrecked ships themselves?

The exciting and at the time revolutionary idea of seeking an Armada wreck for the purpose of studying the Armada campaign through archaeological method was conceived by Sydney Wignall in 1961. He began by consulting the published State Papers of Spain, England and Ireland, and then he began to delve into the manuscript archives of the Public Record Office in London and

Simancas Castle in Spain. Soon he had built up a dossier on all the known Armada wrecks, and had supplemented the historical evidence with a careful study of modern maps and charts. He visited many of the sites himself, and probed deeply into local traditions and folklore. It would surely, he reasoned, be possible to locate one of the wrecks with a carefully planned diving expedition. But which one to choose?

One by one he considered the wrecks, and one by one he rejected them as unsuitable for the operation he had in mind. Almost all of those whose position seemed easy to pin-point had come to grief on shallow beaches or against the mainland cliffs. From an archaeological point of view they would at best be meaningless jumbles of scattered artefacts, with little hope of any of the ship surviving, and in any case most of them had probably been salvaged long ago. What Wignall wanted was a ship — or at least part of a ship — with her contents and guns lying in some kind of coherent relationship. Only then, he reasoned, would a relevant study of the ship *as a complete fighting unit* be possible. A few coins, or a surf-abraded gun, would not be enough.

But in order to survive in the kind of condition Wignall hoped for, the ship would have to have gone down suddenly, in fairly deep water, over a relatively flat sand or shingle bottom. There, she would stand a good chance of breaking up in a progressive sequence. Her upper works would collapse first, and her guns would probably fall to either side. As her decks and sides fell in, her contents would cascade into the hold among the packed stone ballast. With luck the very bottom of the ship — the keel and lower ribs — might even remain intact, pinned beneath a mound of ballast and artefacts and drifted sand.

As Wignall sifted through the evidence, looking for such a wreck, two particular documents drew his attention. One was Marcos de Aramburu's account of the happenings in Blasket Sound on 21st September 1588: 'In an instant we could see that she was going down, trying to hoist the foresail. Then she sank with all on board, not a person being saved, a most extraordinary and terrifying thing.' The other was James Trant's description of the same event: '. . . and as soon as ever they cast anchor they drive upon a rock, and there, was cast away *into the middle of the sea . . .*'

Of all the Armada wrecks this — the sudden foundering of the *Santa Maria de la Rosa* — had been the most dramatic, and it had taken place in deep open water; a league and a half from land, the survivor tells us. Somewhere beneath the four square miles of Blasket Sound the ship's remains presumably still lay. If any Armada wreck offered archaeological potential, that was surely the one.

In spite of the enormous difficulties inherent in locating such a wreck in open exposed water Wignall felt he had no option but to choose the *Santa Maria* as his target. The time had come to move out of the archives and into the cold grey waters of Blasket Sound. Wignall already had a staunch ally in Desmond Branigan, a marine consultant and historian, whose Dublin-based organisation, Marine Research, had helped to piece together the evidence contained in the National Library of Ireland. Branigan was, in addition, an experienced diver. During Easter 1963, at Wignall's request, he took a party of Irish divers to Blasket Sound to make a preliminary reconnaissance and assess the diving problems at first hand. The weather was perfect, and they were able to make several exploratory dives in the anchorage off Great Blasket Island. Even so, Branigan stressed, in the report he wrote afterwards, the 'most hazardous' nature of Blasket Sound, particularly in the tide-race at its narrow neck. This preliminary search was the first known attempt to locate the wreck of the *Santa Maria de la Rosa.*

Wignall himself came over to Blasket Sound in June of that year with his friend and associate Joseph Casey, and a party of divers from the St. Helens Underwater Group, to which they both belonged. Bad weather dogged their visit, and diving operations had to be abandoned after only a few days. Wignall had been following the theory of William Spotswood Green, an authority on the Armada wrecks, who believed that the *Santa Maria* struck Stromboli Rock, a reef which rises close to the surface at the eye of the tide-race. 'For those who have the time and means at their disposal,' Spotswood Green had written prophetically in 1909, 'this part of the Blasket Sound would be an interesting field for discovery.' Wignall himself dived on Stromboli and ranged with the tide on a free-swimming search through its pinnacles southwards to the shingle bottom beyond the 100-foot mark. Ironically enough, he must have passed very close to the wreck on this dive, for this is the area in which it was eventually found. But he saw nothing, and as he swam over the flat desert of stones and sand in the green-blue twilight of deep water 'without a cannon in sight' he concluded that Spotswood Green had been wrong. He now recalls this sweeping judgement with wry humour, and confesses 'how very little we really knew of Blasket Sound in those early days'.

That dive, though, taught Wignall one lesson which he never forgot. He surfaced from it just as the tide was beginning to ebb strongly from the broad basin of the Sound into its constricted neck. A south-westerly wind had sprung up against this tide, and what had been a choppy but otherwise docile sea when he went down had become a confusion of mountainous waves, crashing and breaking in every direction. The nearest land was more than a mile away, and a three-knot current was bearing him away from it. He caught occasional glimpses of the diving boat, several hundred yards to leeward, when he and it happened to be on a wave crest at the same time, but his shouts went unheard. As the waves built up, the boat's crew had lost sight of Wignall's small marker buoy, and they were now searching frantically for the surfaced diver. Happily, they found him, but his experience remained firmly embedded in Wignall's mind. Never once, in all that was to follow, did he lose the deep respect for Blasket Sound that he gained on that day.

In 1964 a party of divers from a London branch of the British Sub-Aqua Club visited the area to search for the *Santa Maria.* The company which was to have hired them a mobile aqualung compressor let them down, and they arrived with only the supply of air contained in their cylinders. Without means of replenishment their search time on the sea bed was drastically reduced, and they had no better luck than the 1963 expeditions.

Meantime Wignall had been looking into the legal question of protecting the wreck from plunder if it was found. Maritime law in the United Kingdom and the Irish Republic at that time recognised no special category for shipwrecks of historical importance and, if found, they were often subjected to indiscriminate looting and souvenir-hunting which diminished or even destroyed their archaeological value. There would be little point or justification in locating the *Santa Maria* if the discovery resulted in a free-for-all for selfish private speculators and curio-hunters.

Wignall first approached the Irish authorities and was advised to get in touch with the Spanish Government which, as successor to Philip II, still seemed to be the legal owner of the wreck. An agreement with Spain was duly ratified in 1967, in which Wignall deposited a bond of £1 000 in respect of his good faith, and agreed to pay over to Spain 20% (the old Royal Fifth) of the value of whatever recoveries were made. In return he was granted a sole licence to excavate the wreck, extending over a period of 10 years. Thus armed with the ability to protect the *Santa Maria*'s historical integrity should her wreck be found, Wignall began to organise a full-scale expedition.

Then, in 1967, an unexpected bombshell burst. The St. Helens group, now operating independently of Wignall and without his approval, claimed to have located the *Santa Maria* in Blasket Sound. It was a strange story. The St. Helens divers had been using towed diver searches, in which a weighted line is towed behind the diving boat with a diver or divers hanging on to its end. The boat steers a prearranged course, and the divers scan the sea bed as they pass close over it. On one September morning two divers dropped into the water off Young Island, in the northern part of the Sound, to be towed on a southerly course towards the Blasket Island anchorage. Two miles away, on the shore at Dunquin, Wignall's friend Joe Casey watched the boat as it manoeuvred into position. Then a sea mist fell with blinding suddenness, blotting out Casey's view of what was happening. From the boat itself the fog completely blanketed the landmarks afforded by coast and islands on which those on board relied to judge their position.

Some ten minutes after they had entered the water the divers surfaced, almost incoherent with excitement and distress. In rapidly worsening conditions they were hauled on board. They had just, they said, passed over a mound of rubble and stones, amongst which they had seen three guns, one of which stuck at an angle from the sea bed. They had not been able to tie their line to the find, they explained, because the current was so fierce that their masks were almost ripped from their faces, and so they had made an emergency ascent to halt the boat. Fearful of losing the position, the St. Helens men peered into the mist, seeking in vain for a navigational landmark. The sea was becoming rougher. They had no clear idea of where in the Sound they were.

One thought he could hear surf beating against the flat rocks of Beginish; another believed that they were somewhere off Great Blasket Island. There was no marker buoy in the boat, and in view of the heavy sea and the uncertainty of their position no one was willing to give up his lifejacket with which to improvise one. Eventually they set an easterly compass course which brought them to the mainland cliffs, and then they hugged the shore until they reached the jetty at Dunquin.

Over the next few days the St. Helens men went over every clue, trying to work out exactly where they had been when the sighting was made. It proved impossible. They made further towed searches, attempting to re-create the conditions of the first dive. At length, without result, they abandoned their searches and returned home.

From the nature of their evidence, however, the sighting appeared to have been genuine enough. Wignall felt that he should now attempt to locate the site himself at the earliest possible moment, so that a proper archaeological survey could be conducted without fear of interference. With dedicated urgency he began planning a full-scale expedition which would work non-stop from April to September 1968 with the aim of finding the wreck and of surveying and excavating whatever remained. Though he could ill afford it, he put up the required capital himself, amounting to more than £5 000 for the first phase of the operation. Joe Casey, an engineer by profession, supplied and checked over compressors and diving equipment, and found a heavy lorry with which to transport the gear to Ireland. Numerous organisations and individuals added their help in various ways.

The gathering together of the right equipment was not in itself enough to find the *Santa Maria.* The keystone of the whole operation was whether an area the size of Blasket Sound could effectively and systematically be searched, and whether the right men could be found to do it. Even if the alleged St. Helens sighting proved genuine, the area involved was a huge one. But if—as was always possible — they had somehow been mistaken in what they saw, then the problem was truly gigantic. In that event the whole of Blasket Sound might have to be covered, and covered *systematically,* for only by a process of elimination is it possible to search a large area with any hope of success.

Suppose a man loses a valuable ring somewhere in a large field. He might wander at random all over that field looking for the ring, and the statistical chances of his finding so small an object in so large an area would be minimal, however long he was prepared to continue his unsystematic search. If, however, he has the sense to start at one end of the field and search carefully up and down, furrow by narrow furrow, he would almost be bound to find it in the end, for he would eventually have visually covered every square inch of the field. But momentary carelessness could spoil his whole search. If, just once, he allowed his concentration to wander from the immediate furrow to his front, he would invalidate the entire operation, for he could not then *know* that the area already covered was clear.

The bottom of Blasket Sound was, in effect, a field some 4 square miles in extent, somewhere within which the perhaps not very obvious traces of an Armada shipwreck rested. But here there were no closely defined furrows to follow, and a single diver swimming over it would have his vision restricted to a few feet in any direction. Strong and complex currents would affect him, and there would be no reliable fixes from which to navigate his course or plot his position. The inevitably crooked furrow of his progress, at most 10 yards wide, could not therefore be plotted with any accuracy after he surfaced, nor could he hope to use previous searches in such a way as to guarantee that no areas had been missed — and quite a small area might contain what he was looking for.

But was there, in practice, an alternative? Was there any method by which Blasket Sound could actually be covered by divers, area by progressive area, in such a way as to *guarantee* that nothing would be missed on any single search? A systematic diver search on this scale, or in these conditions, had never been attempted — let alone accomplished. This being so, Wignall's Blasket Sound project might never have got beyond the planning stage had he not, at just the right moment, met just the right man.

In 1965 the Royal Navy's Middle East Clearance Diving team in Malta, a specialist unit trained for underwater search, demolition, and offensive diving operations, was commanded by Lt. Commander John Grattan, R.N. Clearance divers are hard and efficient men, who have to qualify in what is probably the navy's toughest course, and like most members of dangerous specialised

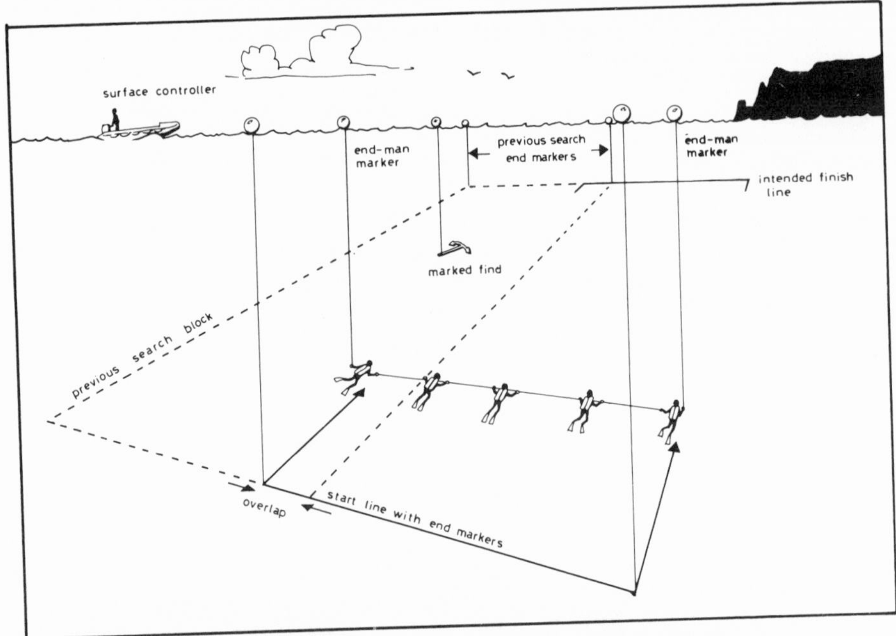

Fig. 5. Swim-line technique (simplified diagram). In practice between eight and fifteen divers were on the line

units they are courageous without being foolhardy, disciplined without being over-respectful of authority, and above all full of dedicated professional enthusiasm for their work. Clearance diving officers win the respect of such men on physical leadership and example rather than on rank. John Grattan was such a man. Fit and wiry, in his early thirties, he was later to be awarded the O.B.E. for his work in Malta and in 1968 he took command of H.M.S. *Reclaim,* the Royal Navy's deep diving research ship.

In 1965 Wignall's business interests took him to Malta, and the two men met. They soon began to find that they had common interests. Wignall's Armada research was by this time far advanced, and already he was beginning to think seriously of mounting an expedition to look for the *Santa Maria.* Grattan listened carefully as Wignall explained the background to the wrecking, and described the experiences he had already encountered in Blasket Sound. Only the enormous problem of searching the Sound, Wignall concluded, was holding him back. Was there any way of covering an area this size?

Underwater search techniques happened to be Grattan's particular speciality, and he had been instrumental in the development of a method for the visual location of small objects lost in wide areas which, if properly applied, was virtually infallible. The technique is called the 'swim-line' system and, in theory at least, it is very simple. It involves a team of divers — usually six or more — spaced at intervals along a thin nylon line, who swim in line abreast over the search area holding on to the line and keeping it comfortably taut. It followed that, provided the spacing allows their ranges of vision to overlap (a factor which naturally varies with the clarity of the water), any visible object on the sea bed over which the line passes will be spotted by one or other of the divers. The swath covered by the swim-line is sufficiently wide to allow scope for overlapping with previous search blocks, and in this way the effective coverage of an unlimited area can be guaranteed, building it up block by block of eliminated ground. A six-man swim-line with divers spaced 20 yards apart, for instance, will cover a 100-yard swath; on a 1 000-yard swim, therefore, 100 000 square yards of ground would be cleared. Ten divers on a similar swim would cover 180 000 square yards. These are respectable areas by any standard, and they are large enough to be plotted on a chart. Most important of all, by means of lightweight markers towed on the surface by each diver, a surface controller who is able to navigate by surface visual methods can see the position and progress of the swim-line at all times. He can, moreover, pass signalled instructions to the divers *via* the markers and so make navigational corrections during the course of a search. The technique permits a skilled controller to direct a given swim so as to overlap previous search patterns, and to plot the patterns, block by block, and so build up the areas of elimination until the sought-for object is found.

Grattan had used this simple and very adaptable technique many times with clearance divers in the Mediterranean, and had achieved outstanding successes there. But could the system be used to cover a much greater area than hitherto attempted, in the fierce tidal conditions of Blasket Sound, using a team made up largely of part-time amateur divers? Grattan believed that with determination, organisation, and training it could be done, though neither he nor Wignall were under any illusions about the difficulties of carrying out such an operation. There are dangers inherent in the swim-line system that set very high demands on individual discipline and initiative; so much so, indeed, that it is not generally accepted by Royal Navy units as a workable operational search system. An enormous responsibility rests with the surface controller. In him the divers must be able to place their absolute trust. It is he who must ensure that they do not risk decompression sickness — the 'bends' — by diving too deep and too long, and he must pick them up safely when they surface, often exhausted, in rough open water. At the same time he must be able to navigate and control the progress of the search, and take accurate surface fixes so that its precise coverage can be plotted on a chart. Overriding everything else, he must anticipate and deal with any possible emergency affecting the safety of his divers.

With a good controller, who must of course be a highly experienced diver himself, the system is virtually foolproof *providing* the divers carry out his instructions implicitly and clearly understand their own responsibilities. But while most divers of average experience and intelligence can readily understand the system when it is explained to them in safety and comfort on shore (simplicity is its great strength), considerable extra qualities of courage, tenacity, team-work and common sense are needed to put it into practice.

Sydney Wignall's appeal for divers went out in the February 1968 issue of *Triton,* the official journal of the British Sub-Aqua Club. Some extracts from his article will indicate the sort of volunteer he was looking for:

> Those readers who know me well will be aware that my main interests are marine archaeology, closely followed by the filming of underwater documentaries for television. This is not a treasure hunting expedition. If there is any treasure, and we find it, then that will be an added bonus. Any share-out will be on an equitable basis. However, I do reserve the right to reward any member of the expedition, by means of an added share, for outstanding efforts.
>
> The expedition is financed solely by the organisers (Wignall and Casey), so participants are offered the unique opportunity to work (note the word 'work') on a wreck of great historical

importance at a minimum cost to themselves. Accommodation will be provided free, but participants will be responsible for their own feeding arrangements. The only other cost is that of return transport to Dingle, County Kerry.

It sounds too easy and soft, doesn't it? Well it isn't, and here comes the crunch. Blasket Sound is not a place for the inexperienced. Participants must be in sound health, and have no history of heart or respiratory complaints. Discipline for obvious reasons will be tough. Everyone will have a job to do and will be told to do it, or pack up and go. The expedition officers will have the authority to dismiss at a moment's notice any member who is either not pulling his weight, or who by his actions is deemed an unproductive or disruptive person.

I (Wignall) as sole licensee will have overall control of the project, but during April and May I am standing down as leader of the expedition in favour of a professional diver of international repute (Grattan).

There are not, nor will there ever be, any committees involved in this expedition, and it will be run almost entirely on naval lines and discipline. In the light of having experience in organising both underwater and Himalayan expeditions before, I would not under any circumstances take part in an expedition that is run by a committee.

Certificates and paper qualifications alone mean little to me. They comment only on a man's physical prowess. They tell me nothing of his character or temperament. Temperament is most important. A sense of humour is absolutely essential; also an aptitude for tackling unpleasant tasks voluntarily or by direction, without bitching. A certificate does not tell me whether its owner is a bore, crank, dead-beat, bum, free-loader or hypochondriac, any one of which can cause dissension and destroy an expedition. For these reasons, there is no room for friends or passengers. Every volunteer must be a diver. If you want a 'jolly time' by the seaside at our expense, do not apply. If you like hard work, don't mind being soaked to the skin and frozen, cut, and bloodied, fed up to the teeth with the word 'Armada', and tired but still determined to soldier on with a smile, then you are probably just the chap we are looking for. And you will probably have one hell of a ball.

Are you interested?

In all, no fewer than 116 young men applied to take part in the expedition that first season. Of these a total of forty-three were eventually accepted. They came from many walks of life, from a Bermondsey lorry-driver who *thought* the whole project was insane to a graduate in psychology who *knew* it to be so. But insanity, after all, often implies nothing more than an inability or unwillingness to conform blindly to the common herd : to set out on a hazardous adventure such as this one, in which the rational certainty of success is less important than the challenge, could be considered, in this materialistic age, to be insanity of a sort. If so, Sydney Wignall possessed this kind of madness in abundance, and transmitted it infectiously to his expedition. The expedition owes much to its dedicated and selfless volunteers, just as those of them who stood up to the hardships and met the challenge gained immeasurably from the experience themselves.

It is easy to overlook the immense task of organising an expedition on this sort of scale, though to subject the reader to a day-by-day account of the administrative processes by which it came into being would be almost as tedious as the job itself. For more than a year Sydney Wignall, helped by Joe Casey, had worked full-time on this thankless slog, seldom away from typewriter and telephone, organising equipment, replying to applications and selecting volunteers, and attending to the countless tasks and problems which, though often seemingly petty and unimportant individually, together produce that complex and indefinable combination of humanity, spirit, and equipment that is a successful expedition. All this labour bore fruit when, on Saturday 13th April 1968, eleven men met together in Paddy Bawn's famous pub in Dingle for the first time. Over glasses of rich black porter we began to get to know each other.

Wignall, myself, a cockney ex-Royal Marine called Michael 'Smudge' Smith and a young man I will call 'X' were the only civilians present on that first day. The remaining seven, led by John Grattan, were Servicemen, though it should be explained that Service departments were in no way connected with the expedition. All Service personnel who took part did so on their annual leave and came under the same blanket invitation as the other volunteers. None the less, since five of them were qualified clearance divers, their participation assured the expedition of a highly professional hard-core in its critical early stages. Grattan had recruited them for this very purpose. They comprised two other clearance diving officers, Lt. Commander Karl Lees and Lt. Brian Barrett, and two very experienced petty officers, Ken Snowball and 'Mick' Roberts. Lt. Nick La Hive, a ship's diving officer, and Brian Maidment of the R.A.F. completed the initial team. Maidment had already worked with Wignall on an R.A.F. marine archaeological expedition to the Aeolian Islands in 1962.

Though Dingle is almost 10 miles from the jetty at Dunquin from which the expedition boats would operate, our accommodation was in the town since we felt that to live in civilised surrounding where maintenance and other facilities were on hand would more than offset the disadvantages of travelling twice daily to Blasket Sound. Wignall had rented two houses, one of which became a headquarters in which most of the permanent members were to live, while the other served as accommodation for visiting divers and was run with Royal Marine efficiency and discipline by Smith. Our landlady was Mrs. O'Connor of nearby O'Connor's garage, who won our hearts by keeping us supplied with home-baked Irish soda-bread.

With domestic arrangements complete, the expedition members gathered at headquarters for a detailed briefing. Grattan was to take charge of the search operation, and while this continued Wignall insisted on being treated as a working diver or boat-handler. Charts were spread on the table along with Wignall's photo-copies of the historical documents concerning the *Santa Maria de la Rosa,* and Grattan delivered his appreciation of the situation before outlining the search plan he intended to put into effect. Because everything pointed to the St. Helens sighting having taken place somewhere in the vicinity of Young and Beginish islands, in the north-west part of the Sound, he considered that a swath some 500 yards wide running alongside those islands to be the first 'high probability' area to be covered.

Grattan's plan was to use what he called a 'running jackstay' swim-line system. A weighted line would be run out between fixed surface points at high speed, in such a way that it would drop quickly to the sea bed while still taut and so provide an anchored datum which the end man on a swim-line could follow. The whole line could thus move up one side of the datum, covering a swath of about 100 yards, and then move down on the other side to cover a similar search block. A second jackstay would then be laid further across to provide the next datum, allowing a sufficient overlap to ensure certain coverage. The first jackstay would be reeled in after the first search had been completed and leap-frogged over the second jackstay to provide the third, and so on. By using the jackstays the operation would be relatively simple from the point of view of the divers, who would only have to keep the swim-line straight and taut, and would not have to bother about navigation.

Some time later, on the local golf course, the team was put through a dry run of swim-line procedures. Its members were strung out, blindfolded, each grasping the plaited nylon swim-line with both hands. Grattan explained the simple code of signals that was to be used underwater, in combinations of 'pulls' (steady, rhythmic tugs) and 'bells' (shorter, sharper jerks) which could be passed between the divers themselves through the swim-line or to individual divers from the surface *via* their towed 'blobs'. There were signals for 'go', 'stop', 'move right', 'move left', 'hurry up', 'slow down', 'come up', and finally—most important of all—the five bell signal for 'I have made a discovery and am marking it'. With a little practice the blindfolded team learned to move in formation, responding at once to corrective signals passed to the line by the controller.

In the meantime Joe Casey had arrived with the heavy lorry which he had driven over from Liverpool with the expedition's diving gear and compressors. A hard afternoon's work completed the assembly and charging of the ten twin-cylinder aqualung sets, and the rigging and preparation of the two 16-foot inflatable 'Gemini' craft and their outboard engines. That evening the team members relaxed in Paddy Bawn's, talking divers' shop and looking forward, with some trepidation, to their first encounter with Blasket Sound.

Dunquin Jetty, which was to be our shore base, is reached by a steep path inaccessible to wheeled traffic, which twists down from the cliff top 200 feet above. Our gear and boats had to be manhandled down the path, and although the boats could then stay there, hauled clear of the water when not in use, the heavy aqualung cylinders had to be carried up after every dive for recharging at Dingle. It was a chore we never really enjoyed, especially after a hard dive, but it kept us fit!

The first Gemini was rigged up as John Grattan's command boat, with a lightweight free-running reel in the bow which would be used for laying both the jackstays and the swim-lines. A 1 000-yard weighted jackstay was reeled on, and then Grattan, accompanied by Wignall and Lees, pull-started the 20-horse-power motor and roared off in the direction of Beginish Island to lay the first datum. An hour later they were back, having successfully put out the line parallel with the east side of the island. The first swim-line jackstay search would be attempted the following day; meanwhile, all the expedition divers kitted up and were dropped in pairs in 60 feet of water to test and check their gear.

Because of the tremendous tidal flow in Blasket Sound diving operations had to coincide with the short periods of slack water between tides. This meant that each day's work was entirely governed by the tide-tables, and if for any reason we missed a tide (there are usually two workable periods of slack water each day, about 6 hours 20 minutes apart) the dive would have to be abandoned. The team quickly fell into a disciplined routine of work, in which unpunctuality was the unforgivable sin. Though this was second nature to the service divers, some of the amateurs, used as they were to treating diving as a recreational activity, had to make a considerable effort to fall into line. Most of them, to their credit, did so without fuss.

The diving routine, which was to remain in essence unchanged for two full seasons, began on the first day of the search. Each evening the time by which the team had to be ready to move out on the following morning was posted in both houses. This time was calculated backwards from the first workable period of slack water in Blasket Sound, allowing the time taken to drive to Dunquin, kit up, get the boats in the water, and travel to the search area. Sometimes this would mean a 6 a.m. start. By move-out time everyone had to be ready with his own personal kit, and the vehicles loaded with charged cylinders for the dive. Charging was done by team members on a roster basis with an electrically driven compressor which the expedition had set up in a shed next to O'Connor's Garage.

On Wednesday 17th April, the first day of the search, the weather was blustery, with a westerly wind gusting to Force 7. The waters of Blasket Sound were dotted with white cresting breakers. Grattan thought hard before deciding to go ahead that day. The team was untried, some of its members were inexperienced, and he had no idea of our capabilities. On the other hand, each volunteer had known what to expect, and if

Blasket Sound was going to be searched at all there would be no room for the faint hearted. By working the team on a day like this — quite literally by throwing it in at the deep end — Grattan reckoned that he would at least find out what its members were made of.

The two Geminis, piloted by Grattan and Wignall with nine divers aboard, battled their way across the Sound, aquaplaning smoothly across the downward slopes of the big Atlantic rollers and crashing, bow foremost to avoid capsizing, into the steep breaking crests. When we arrived off the northern headland of Beginish Grattan found that the buoys he had laid the previous day to mark the beginning and end of the jackstay line had disappeared, and a diver was sent down to see whether the line was still there. He surfaced within minutes to report that the line was broken and tangled everywhere, torn from its anchored position by the currents.

That he did not immediately order the boats home so that a new plan could be formulated and explained in comfort emphasises Grattan's peculiar genius for directing this kind of operation. If jackstays could not be laid in Blasket Sound because of the current then we would have to learn to do without them, and Grattan considered that now was the time to start. He called the second boat over, and tossing crazily together in that fearsome sea he re-briefed us, shouting to make himself heard above the spray. The end men on the swim-line would have to navigate by compass, without the laid jackstay to guide them. He would drop the line exactly where he wanted the search to begin, and mark the point by dropping an anchored buoy there. The line would have to be laid at maximum possible speed in order to keep it running straight and to cut surface drift to a minimum. The divers would have to get down to the sea bed fast, or the search line would be dragged by the current away from the planned start position.

While Grattan had been issuing these instructions we divers had been sitting along the gunwales of the two boats, in full gear except for our facemasks. Briefing complete, it was the work of seconds to clench the demand-valve mouthpieces in our teeth, suck in a couple of reassuring gushes of air, and adjust the masks to our faces. Grattan stood, legs bent and slightly apart, against the engine, one hand on the tiller and throttle and the other leading the looped end of the swim-line from the forward mounted reel. Mick Roberts, who was well versed in this kind of thing, was to be first man in. He looped the end of the swim-line on his wrist, and in his other hand held the expanded polystyrene stick-blob coiled with line which would unwind as he descended. Grattan manoeuvred into position, checking his exact location from shore transits. Go! Roberts toppled backwards into the water, taking the end of the swim-line with him. Grattan immediately gave the Gemini full power and the swim-line reel began to spin, the nylon rope running freely between his forefinger and thumb. Number two ready . . . go! The second diver rolled over the side of the now speeding boat, 20 yards from the end man, and swam to his position on the line. Numbers three and four followed at similar intervals. Now there was only one man apart from Grattan in the lead boat — the last man, number nine. Numbers five, six, seven, and eight were in the second boat, piloted by Wignall, which was tucked in close on Grattan's stern quarter. Grattan continued full ahead, the flat bottom of his Gemini banging and skidding over the wave tops, still paying out the line. As the second Gemini drew abreast of number five position Grattan cut his arm down in a signal, and number five rolled off the second boat, followed by six, seven, and eight. Now only number nine, the second end-man, was left. Grattan slammed the throttle shut and as his boat wallowed to a standstill he sliced through the swim-line with his heavy diving knife, separating it from the reel, and handed the cut end to the last man who immediately dropped overboard. Now the nine divers, each with his separate coiled blob, were evenly spread out along the line in the water. Grattan sped round to the front of the line, checking that all was in order. Then, waving his outstretched arms downwards, he signalled the divers to descend.

I later recorded my own impressions of that first swim-line search, which was to be the first of more than 100: 'We were all somewhat confused by the change of plan, trying to sort out our gear and remember what Grattan had told us, and not a little frightened by the size of the waves and by the seas which were pounding on the stark rocks of Beginish 100 yards away. It was a relief to get underwater. Visibility was about 20 feet, so it was impossible to see the man on either side of one, although the thin white swim-line bowing out in either direction gave one a sense of confidence. We hit the bottom 60 feet down. The sea floor was very broken with rock gulleys, shingle, pinnacles, and a lot of kelp. Within a few seconds two sharp tugs came down the line — two bells, the move-out signal. I started swimming slowly, about 10 feet from the bottom, which Grattan had told us was the optimum height for spotting things. I concentrated on keeping my head and eyes moving, making sure that no part of the ground over which I was passing evaded my gaze, looking for the slightest clue. Naturally each of us expected at any moment to come upon a heap of bronze guns or something equally exciting, but we were disappointed. After I had been swimming for what seemed like a long time but was in fact less than 5 minutes a moving shape loomed out of the murk to my front. Momentarily I started, before recognising it as another diver. It was someone from the opposite end of the line, swimming in the opposite direction. Our straight line had turned into a circle!

'Total confusion followed, which was only resolved when someone had the sense to pass the "come-up" signal through the line, and we all surfaced. Grattan brought his Gemini over to pick the end man up and take the line aboard; then, by winding it back on the reel, he pulled the complete team towards him. It was still very rough, but the swim-line was now our lifeline, and so long as we held on to it we were safe. Within a very few minutes we were all back in the boats and Grattan was briefing us for a second attempt. This turned out to be no more successful than the first, and after a third attempt had failed we headed back for Dunquin, miserable at what we felt to be our total inability to carry out a swim-line search.'

To our surprise Grattan had no recriminations. In fact he was pleased. For a first effort in this sort of weather, he said, the drills had gone well and above all safely, and with more practice we should have few problems. Direction keeping was always difficult underwater, but we would soon get the hang of it. What was more important was that we were beginning to think and work as a team.

The following day the weather was settled and the team much more confident. Everything went well, and in the morning the search task which had failed the previous day was successfully completed. Grattan carefully plotted the first block of 'covered' ground on his chart. In the afternoon a second block, butting up to the first, was added. Nothing had been found.

At this point the team had an unusual visitor. Bert Snowdon was an ex-major in the Royal Engineers, and he was a dowser; that is, he claimed to be able to locate water or other buried objects using special rods which he held out in front of him. Dowsers are often regarded with scepticism, but there is little doubt that under some circumstances the technique works. Snowdon did not claim that he *could* locate a sunken shipwreck, but only asked for the chance to try. It was certainly an interesting experiment. We took him out into Blasket Sound, and he reported getting reactions in the same area off Young and Beginish Islands that we were searching. It was a curious coincidence, for Snowdon had had no idea of where we had been concentrating, but spot-dives revealed nothing. My view now is that while there is clearly much more to dowsing than scientific explanation can provide, it has not been found to function effectively on underwater sites. It tends, in my experience, to build up hopes rather than facts.

New members were joining the team, and some of the originals were leaving. Newcomers included four more clearance divers who had been with Grattan in the Mediterranean team: his second-in-command, Lt. Mike Stewart, Neil Primrose, 'Wiggy' Bennett, and 'Tug' Wilson. Two members of the Naval Air Command Sub-Aqua Club also joined. A quiet-spoken civilian commercial diver, Chris Oldfield, also arrived about this time. Oldfield stayed with the team until the project ended in 1969, while Wilson later returned to skipper the expedition's 50-foot boat *Jimbell* during the final stages of the excavation.

By now the weak links (and the strong ones too) were making themselves felt. The first to drop out was a young man who never lost an opportunity to impress on all he met what a fine and bold diver he was; the deeper and murkier the water, he said, the more he liked it. Unfortunately this attitude found its best expression in the pub, and crumbled when faced with the harsh realities of Blasket Sound. He washed out of the first three dives, and refused the fourth, so was relegated to a shore job. When he fell down on this he was told to leave. Another man, who claimed to have a phenomenal amount of diving experience, actually broke down and cried when told to go over the side. Yet another arrived with a carefully cultivated hard-man image and an exotic French girl friend whom he had evidently intended to impress by emerging from the depths, lantern-jawed and no doubt smelling of the latest male deodorants, laden with glittering treasures. Blasket Sound soon cut him down to size, and he returned to his comfortable civilisation where men can pretend to be men without the embarrassing necessity of having to prove it.

I doubt whether anyone who took part in the expedition was not from time to time afraid — I for one was frequently terrified, and on occasion the impulse to give up was very strong. Wignall, Grattan, and several of the others have frankly admitted the same to me.

It was not just those who failed as divers who created problems. One extremely experienced and competent man had a manner so brusque, and a tendency to try to take over the direction of all operations in which he was involved, that he was in danger of disrupting the entire team and consequently had to go.

The inevitable weeding out process left a team which was strong, capable, confident and above all close-knit. A fortnight after the start of the expedition we were regularly carrying out successful swim-line searches twice daily, and the plotted blocks on John Grattan's chart now covered the whole 'high probability' area off Young and Beginish Islands. We had found no trace of the wreck, but we had made a discovery which explained, we thought, the sighting claimed by the St. Helens divers in 1967. Just off the south-east tip of Young Island we had come upon several pieces of iron piping, one of which stuck at an angle from the sea bed, which might well have appeared to divers under hazardous and distressing conditions to have been cannons. If this was true, we were literally back to square one, for it meant that the hypothesis which had prompted us to search this area was based on a false premise. It was beginning to look as though we might have to search the whole of Blasket Sound if we wanted to find the *Santa Maria de la Rosa.*

The dives off Young and Beginish had not been without incident. On one occasion Wignall had almost been capsized by a breaking wave while he was alone in an inflatable during one of the dives. Wignall was also taking part in many of the dives himself, and he had christened a series of swims we had done at mid-tide in the centre of the Sound the 'Shanghai Express'. By carrying out these searches while the tide was at its fastest, perhaps three knots or more, the line was carried at what appeared on the bottom to be the speed of an express train with very little swimming effort needed from the divers. These swims covered great areas of ground, and were extremely exhilarating to take part in. On one day, in two such swims, we completed a total area coverage of half a million square yards.

About this time schools of migratory basking sharks passed through the Sound on their way to summer feeding grounds off Norway. These huge creatures, up to 30 feet in length, are totally inoffensive, feeding on nothing except the colossal quantities of plankton which they filter out of the water simply by swimming with their vast mouths open. Underwater they are an awesome sight, and if encountered unexpectedly a very disturbing one. Normally they swim very close to the surface, with their great triangular dorsal fins sticking out of the water. Sometimes we followed them in the boats, and dived with them. Then on 9th May we found the first anchor.

Once the area east of Young and Beginish Islands had been cleared, and our suspicions that the St. Helens sighting had been a false alarm confirmed, the searches had moved southwards into the sheltered water off Great Blasket Island where the Spanish ships had probably first anchored. Right in the middle of the anchorage, on a sandy bottom some 60 feet deep, the swim-line snagged on a large and heavily concreted iron anchor, which was immediately marked with a buoy. Wignall and I later went down to inspect and measure the find. It was 13 feet long, about the right size for the bower anchor of a large sailing vessel, and it was obviously very old. Moreover the ship it had once held had broken free of it, for one fluke was missing and the ring had burst.

Could this have been one of Recalde's anchors? We re-read Aramburu's account, and much seemed to fit. On the stormy morning of 21st September 1588 the *San Juan de Portugal* had indeed broken free of her moorings, presumably leaving an anchor behind. 'The flagship of Juan Martinez,' wrote Aramburu, 'drifted down on our ship, cast anchor and another cable, and having smashed our lantern and our mizzenmast tackle and rigging, the flagship secured herself.'

Were there perhaps other anchors in the vicinity? Aramburu himself had definitely lost one, and probably two. And what of the other ships? In the days of sail ground tackle was frequently lost, since it was often impossible to make headway in the direction necessary to work an anchor free. For this reason large vessels invariably carried six or more main anchors. Finally, what of the *Santa Maria*'s own anchor, her single remaining one, the one she had cast close to Aramburu shortly before she was wrecked? Might it and the wreck also lie somewhere in the vicinity?

The discovery of the anchor — our first positive find in a month of unremitting work — was a great boost to the team's morale. Everyone was keen to get on with the search. But on the following morning the weather had deteriorated, and although we went out into the Sound sea conditions were far too rough to put divers down in safety. By the next day, however, the weather had moderated somewhat and it seemed safe enough to work. Our two boats battered their way across the Sound in a short, choppy sea towards the Blasket Island anchorage.

Off Beginish a violent squall hit us. Without warning a series of four huge waves piled out of nowhere, and in the trough of one of them Grattan glimpsed a pinnacle of rock standing 4 feet proud which he knew normally lay 10 feet below the surface — an observation which confirmed that these waves were some 28 feet from trough to crest. At the same time a viciously gusting wind sprang up against the still running tide. It was an appallingly frightening situation. The boats could do nothing except attempt to keep their bows into the oncoming sea, for to swing broadside to it would have brought certain disaster. The fourth wave was the biggest of them all. In horrifying slow-motion it began to crest, a line of spume spinning from its curling, collapsing peak. It broke just as it hit Wignall's boat, in which I and five other divers were sitting, fully kitted up. With an exploding crash of spray the inflatable was tossed on its side, catapulting its occupants into the water.

All I can recall of the incident is that the whole world suddenly appeared to turn wet, green, and opaque (I was not wearing my facemask, so could see nothing clearly). I was heavily weighted for diving, and must have sunk 10 or 15 feet before gathering my wits. Had I knocked my head on my equipment as

I had been catapulted from the boat I might easily have gone straight to the bottom and drowned. As it was, I started finning up towards the surface. As I rose I became aware of a loud roaring sound, very close to me, and I suddenly became convinced that I was swimming straight into one of the boat's propellors. Then I grasped my breathing tubes, and found to my intense relief that the roaring was nothing more sinister than a rush of air escaping from the mouthpiece.

I surfaced close to the boat, which amazingly was still right way up, lurching crazily up and down in the 30-foot sea. Beside it the other divers who had gone overboard were surfacing, all apparently unhurt. By good fortune one had managed to stay in the boat and soon everyone was pulled safely inboard.

The situation was still perilous. Some 50 yards away Grattan's boat was heading into the waves, attempting to edge closer to give assistance. Wignall managed to get our engine started, and gradually the two boats worked their way into slightly less rough water in the lee of Beginish. By now the whole of the Sound had been affected by the squall, and conditions were far too bad to attempt the crossing back to Dunquin. Only Recalde's well-chosen anchorage off Great Blasket Island was relatively sheltered, and this we made for, beaching the boats on the strand and settling down to wait for the storm to pass.

Wignall and I sat together on the cliff above the beach, recovering from the shock of our recent experience. Only luck, aided by the discipline and seamanship which Grattan's training had instilled into the team, had saved us from disaster. Sitting there on the island, looking across the wild, frightening, and yet hauntingly beautiful sound which had almost claimed our lives, we felt strangely close to the events of four centuries before. It was not difficult to imagine Recalde's long-boat pulled up on the beach below us, where our own boats now lay, or to see his soldiers struggling to replenish water casks at the spring where we ourselves had just refreshed ourselves. Out in the middle of the anchorage, where the red buoy we had tied to the big anchor was just visible bobbing among the waves, we could almost visualise the black silhouette of the mighty *San Juan de Portugal* herself. The wreck of the *Santa Maria de la Rosa* must surely lie somewhere close. We felt certain that we were near to discovery, and that the clue was to be found in the anchors the ships had left behind. We did not know how true this was, or how much lay ahead before the mystery would finally be solved.

Next morning when we dived we found another anchor, 200 yards north of the first. This anchor lay on a shingle bottom, surrounded by kelp. It was broken, only the bottom part of the shank and its two flukes remaining. Once again Aramburu's words came ringing out of the past: 'We hauled in the other anchor, finding only the stock with half the shank, for the rest was broken, and the cable chafed by the rocks over which we were lying . . .'

Aramburu, it seemed, had recovered part of an anchor — the top part of an anchor which had broken half way down its shank. It looked as though we had found his missing lower half.

There could no longer be any doubt that these two anchors bore mute witness to the first events which occurred on the day of the *Santa Maria*'s sinking. Recalde had broken free of his moorings and had drifted down on Aramburu. The force of collision had snapped the fluke end off Aramburu's own anchor and the two ships had drifted together into the middle of the Sound. But to where did they drift? We reckoned that the components of wind and tide, which Aramburu describes in such detail, would have carried them towards the south-east. Gradually, therefore, our searches moved out in this direction, towards the Sound's narrow neck and the fierce tide-race which rips through it.

Right in the eye of the tide-race, and partly responsible for the constriction which causes it, stands an underwater reef which, at its highest point, comes very close to the surface. This is Stromboli, so named from a steam gunboat, H.M.S. *Stromboli,* which struck it, though she did not sink, more than a century ago. We began to probe the foothills of the reef; a series of jagged flakes of rock rising sharply from the flat shingle sea floor into a landscape of soaring pinnacles and deep gullies. The whole reef teemed with life: armour-plated crawfish and lobsters creaked like big primeval insects among the rocks, sleek salmon glided purposefully past on their way back to spawn in the rivers of their birth, and busy colourful reef fish darted everywhere. We could only intrude on this beautiful but alien place at dead slack water, for at all other times a tidal current raced over it with unbelievable ferocity.

To the north-west of the reef we found the third anchor, and on the northern ledge of the reef itself the fourth and fifth.

The third anchor, we guessed, probably marked the position at which Recalde and Aramburu re-anchored; the position in which they were to be joined by the *Santa Maria de la Rosa,* the unidentified 'ship of Miguel de Aranivar', and later by the *San Juan* of Fernando Horra. Any one of these ships, apart from the *Santa Maria,* could have left an anchor at this spot. The fourth anchor, which was still hooked foul 6 feet up on a rock overhang at the edge of the reef, was very large indeed, measuring 17 feet from crown to ring. It had almost certainly been a big ship's sheet (or main) anchor, the largest carried aboard, a type described by Sir Henry Mainwaring (writing about 1625) as 'that which the seamen call their last hope, and is never used but in great extremity; this is the true *Anchora Spei,* for this is their last refuge'.

Was this then the *Santa Maria de la Rosa's* sheet anchor, her last and largest, the single anchor which Aramburu tells us she cast 'for she was not carrying more'?

Not far from the big anchor we found another rather smaller one. Could this be the one Recalde had given Aramburu 'with a cable' during the exchange of ground tackle just after the ships had first entered the Sound, to which Aramburu had prudently fitted a new stock 'in case of such necessity', and with which he had saved himself from the same fate as the *Santa Maria*'s? Aramburu had been very close to the *Santa Maria* when she foundered, dragging with her 'to our own perdition' before the *San Juan Bautista*'s anchor at last held firm and turned the vessel's head into wind. Had Aramburu perhaps been forced to abandon this anchor when eventually the tide turned and enabled him to limp back into the shelter of Great Blasket Island? According to his log, he was to lose all his anchors save one in the course of this eventful day.

Shortly afterwards, slightly to the south-east of the big anchor, we located the main pinnacle of the reef. It was not quite where the chart had led us to suppose it would be, but some distance west of the main reef complex: a sinister stalagmite-like finger of rock which stretched its menacing point to within 7 feet of the surface at low water. We had previously thought it unlikely that the *Santa Maria* could have struck Stromboli, as Spotswood

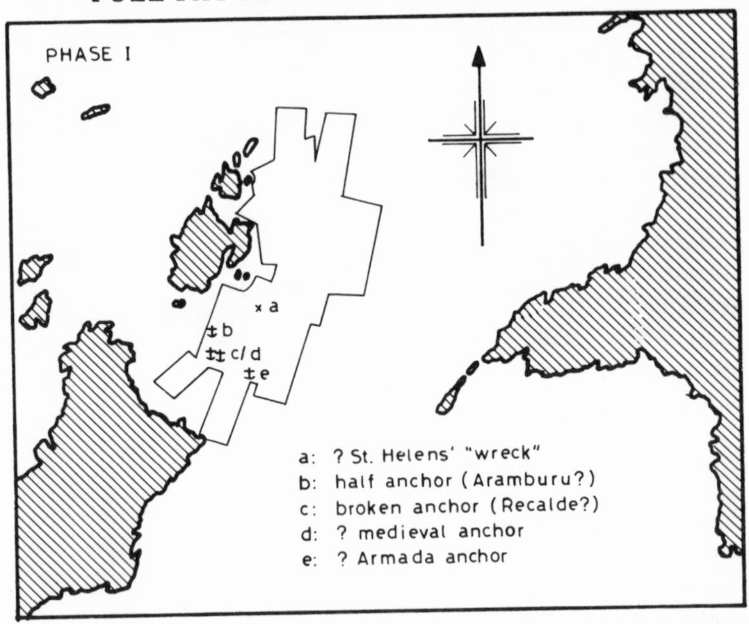

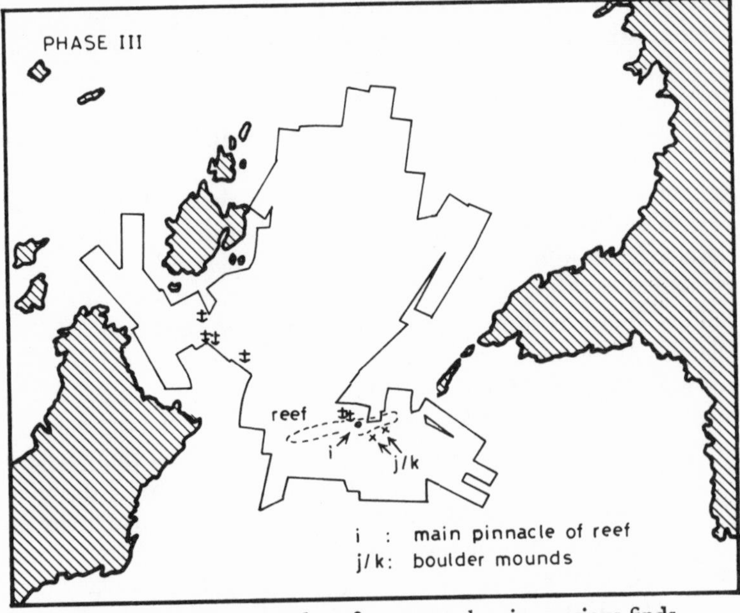

Fig. 6. Swim-line searches; four maps showing various finds

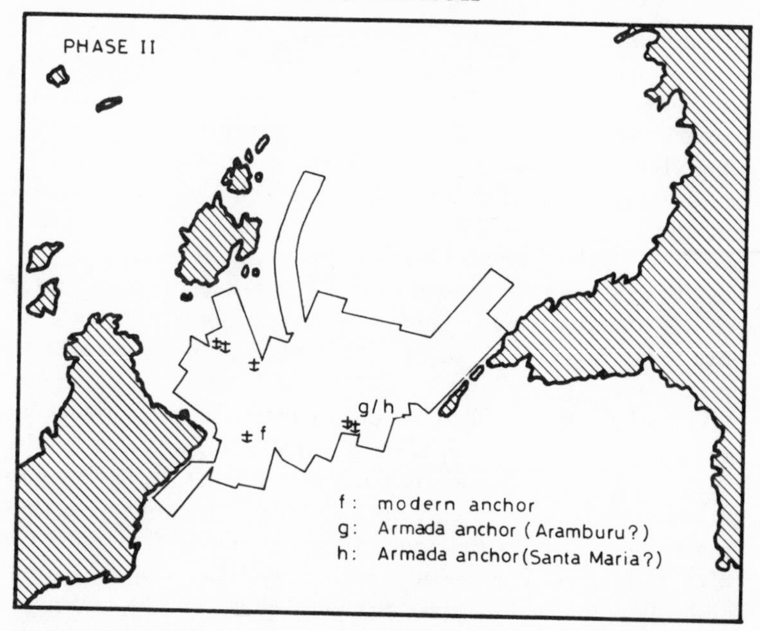
PHASE II
g/h
f
f: modern anchor
g: Armada anchor (Aramburu?)
h: Armada anchor (Santa Maria?)

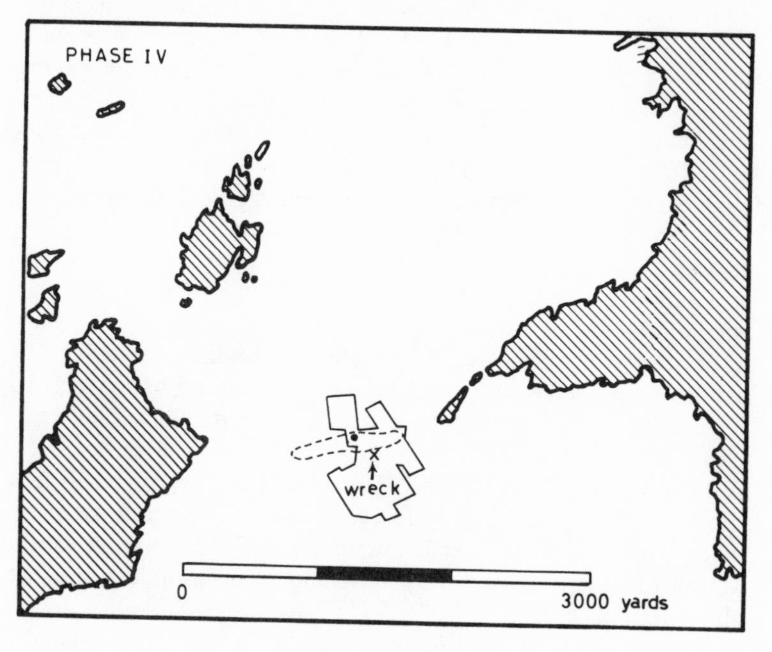
PHASE IV
wreck
0
3000 yards

Green had suggested more than 60 years ago, since at high water — at which time the wrecking took place — the reef should have had more than 25 feet of water over it. The discovery of this new pinnacle, which had eluded the hydrographers' sounding-leads when Blasket Sound was charted in the middle of the 19th century, put the matter in quite a new light. It now appeared that the pinnacle would have had no more than 17 feet of water over it when the *Santa Maria* dragged to this area, and the ship would have probably drawn up to 20 feet — perhaps more, for she was already in a half-sinking condition. She would not even have to be caught in a trough for Stromboli to smash her bottom open.

The inference was plain: if our deductions were correct and the ship had hit Stromboli, her wreck should lie somewhere to the south of the pinnacle. John Grattan decided that the best way to search this area was to carry out a series of swim-line searches from deep water to the south, running northwards until we reached the reef. This meant working in deep water; 300 yards south of the reef the sea bed dropped below the 120-foot mark, which was the effective limit to our operations. Beyond this depth the problems of decompression sickness — the 'bends' — become unacceptably great, and we dared not risk the necessity of having to decompress divers (the only cure for bends) in stages below the boat in the unpredictable conditions of Blasket Sound. Because of this Grattan had wisely insisted that we should at no time exceed the 'no-stop' limit at any depth: that is, the limit of time beyond which decompression stages are needed before surfacing. The time allowed decreases sharply with depth; at 60 feet it is safe to spend a full hour before surfacing, while at 120 feet the limit is only 14 minutes.

For these deep water searches we were dropped some 400 yards south of the reef, with a slight flood tide helping us towards it. The swim-line would descend to 100 feet (at which depth we had a no-stop limit of 25 minutes), and set course towards the reef swimming at first 'blind', for the bottom perhaps 150 feet down would be lost to view. The sea floor would usually show up when it was about 30 feet below us, around the 130-foot mark. We would then carry on until we hit the base of the reef, at about 100 feet.

It was flat, featureless ground, bathed blue in the eerie twilight of deep water. A week of patient searching in these quiet, cold depths revealed nothing. Then, on the morning of Tuesday 11th June — the 60th day of the expedition — Joe McCormack spotted a big pile of stones close to the base of the reef. He thought they might be ballast stones, but some were very big and appeared to be natural; moreover they were scattered over quite a wide area and there was absolutely no sign of anything which could be associated with a wreck. At the same time Jack Sumner, some 200 yards away on the other end of the line, had come upon the main pinnacle of Stromboli reef.

We did an overlapping search of this area that afternoon, moving slightly further towards the west. This time Sumner, flanked by Chris Oldfield and Joe McCormack, crossed over a long low mound of medium sized boulders. They were not the ones McCormack had spotted that morning. However, none of the three divers could see anything out of the ordinary, and the search moved on.

Might either of these mounds, particularly the second one, have been a wrecked ship's ballast stones? But if they were, where were the guns and other artefacts which would surely also be lying in the vicinity? We all felt at the time that the find was negative — probably nothing more than a natural phenomenon. The positions of the mounds were noted on the chart, just in case — and we moved on.

That evening the team went through a heart-searching debriefing. Full coverage of Blasket Sound had at last been achieved — and apart from the anchors we had found nothing. Was the *Santa Maria* there at all? Had we missed the wreck? Had she drifted into impossibly deep water before she sank? Or was she totally buried in deep sand? Serious doubts were beginning to form when a chance remark by one of the divers made it clear that, in the early days of the search, two of the less experienced members of the team had not always covered their sectors properly through 'flying' too high over the sea bed, which meant that details of the terrain over which they passed might have been obscured or lost. This was indeed a bitter revelation. We were acutely conscious that the wreck might occupy a very small area, and that the signs of it might not be at all obvious. Even the elaborate theories we had built up around the anchors and Stromboli Reef began to crumble, and the possibility of the so-called

St. Helens wreck really existing somewhere off Beginish again nagged us. This meant — on the analogy of the searcher for the ring in the field — that every square yard of the areas we had previously regarded as clear was once more suspect. The implication was daunting. If we wanted to be sure, we would have to search the whole lot again.

That is just what we did do, and we did it in three hectic, gruelling weeks. Not only did the team search the full extent of Blasket Sound a second time, but coverage to the north and west of the Sound and anchorage was substantially extended. That our coverage was total was proved beyond doubt by the relocation of all the anchors we had previously noted, by finding once more the iron pipes of the 'St. Helens' wreck, and even by the recovery of small items of diving equipment members of the team had lost during the previous searches. But we found nothing else, not the merest hint of a shipwreck. And when we had finished the researching of the Sound, the time had come for John Grattan to leave.

We had searched the whole of Blasket Sound, just as John Grattan had said we could, and that we had achieved this colossal feat was a tribute to his skilled guidance and dynamic leadership. But, apparently, it had all been for nothing. On the eve of Grattan's departure the whole team was plunged in deep gloom. It is difficult to describe the strain that all of us, but particularly Wignall and Grattan, had been going through. The purely physical strain of continuous diving in difficult open water conditions, coupled with acute mental strain, had sapped our morale to a very low ebb. That at the end of it all we had found nothing brought about a sense of deflation and anti-climax which was almost unbearable. At the same time we knew we had searched Blasket Sound as thoroughly as humanly possible, and in that we could draw a certain grim satisfaction.

We resolved, nevertheless, to continue searching to the south of Stromboli reef. Having gone through so much, we felt irrationally disinclined just to pack up and go. Moreover, though Grattan was leaving, the permanent team had been transformed by its experiences from a mixed group of amateurs to a highly professional team. We could carry on just as long as Wignall's money and our own determination lasted. Wignall's determination and optimism itself remained unquenchable.

Sydney Wignall now took charge of the swim-line laying, and in the course of the next three days we searched fruitlessly over the deep sandy bottom close to Dunmore Head. We saw nothing but tide-rippled dunes and fat starfish, small return for continued diving beyond the 100-foot mark. Then Wignall himself had to leave on several weeks of urgent business in the U.K. and Malta. It looked as though the expedition must collapse in failure.

The night before Wignall left the whole team gathered in Paddy Bawn's, and we got very drunk. Insobriety, however, loosened our tongues and our minds. To a man, it transpired, we all wanted to go on. But was there any point in staying in Blasket Sound? If not, was there anywhere else we might find an Armada wreck? (Finding an Armada wreck — any wreck — had become an obsession.) Wignall had researched the known ones, and with the aid of his charts he went through them all with us. Twenty or more Armada ships had been lost on the Irish coast. Some had been well witnessed and well recorded, like the *Santa Maria de la Rosa*; others were no more than shadowy traditions which had passed down to the descendants of the men who saw the disasters take place, or who had come upon piles of wreckage and bodies washed up on some remote beach. There was *La Trinidad Valencera* (1 100 tons and 42 guns), a great-ship of the Levant squadron which was wrecked in Kinnagoe Bay, Donegal, with one of the Armada's military commanders, Don Alonso de Luzon, aboard. The discovery of her wreck in 1971 by the City of Derry Sub-Aqua Club will be described on later pages. On 20th September another large ship, possibly the *San Estéban* (736 tons and 26 guns) of the Guipuzcoan squadron, was lost near Dunmore Castle in County Clare with heavy loss of life. The traditional spot is remembered locally, and mounds nearby which are said to mark the victims' graves are still pointed out. Not far away, on the same day, a large ship went aground in the shallows off Mutton Island. All the survivors from these two ships were executed at a place still called *Pairc na Croha* (The Field of the Hangings) by the Sheriff of Clare, Bothius Clancy, whose name was formally cursed in memory thereof every 7th year in a little Spanish church until well into the 19th century.

On the day that the *Santa Maria* was wrecked in Blasket

Sound, the 21st September, the foundering *Anunciada* (703 tons, 24 guns) of Levant was scuttled in the mouth of the Shannon by her crew who then escaped to other ships which were sheltering there. On that day too (or, just possibly, the day after), *El Gran Grin* (1 160 tons, 28 guns), the battle-scarred vice-flagship of Recalde's Biscayans, struck rocks off Clare Island, County Mayo, and sank. Her survivors were put to the sword. Finally, on that dismal, stormy Tuesday, there was wrecked one of the Armada's proudest ships, *La Rata Santa Maria Encoronada* (820 tons, 35 guns), in which the noble cream of Spain's young *aventureros* had sailed with the dashing Don Alonso de Leiva at their head. This big Genoese carrack, which had been hotly engaged in every battle during the fighting, ran helplessly aground while seeking to anchor in Blacksod Bay, County Mayo. Don Alonso brought his men ashore in good order with their arms and equipment, and then fired the stranded ship. It is said that the burnt stumps of her frame timbers could still be seen protruding from the sand at low water as recently as the beginning of this century. Shortly after the wrecking Don Alonso and his men were able to embark on another vessel, the hulk *Duquesa Santa Ana* (900 tons, 23 guns), but this ship, in making her way north, was herself wrecked in Loughros Mor Bay, Donegal. Don Alonso, although injured, again successfully brought his people ashore and, on hearing that one of the Armada's four galleasses was lying at Killibegs harbour, marched across 19 miles of mountain and bog to join it. The galleass was the *Girona,* and she had entered the port to make repairs to her hull and damaged rudder. Don Alonso took charge and at length the galleass, now carrying the combined complements of three ships, set sail in an attempt to reach Scotland. Off the coast of Antrim her jury-rudder broke. Caught helplessly on a lee shore, she was driven against a reef close by the Giant's Causeway, where her scattered remains were found by Robert Sténuit in 1967. There were only nine survivors. Don Alonso and some 1 300 others, galley slave and dashing hidalgo alike, were drowned.

About 25th September three large vessels, none of them identified with certainty, were wrecked on Streedagh Strand, near Sligo. Eleven hundred bodies were counted as they lay washed up on this sweeping, 5-mile beach; even today bleached human bones are exposed from time to time in the shifting dunes. Sir

William Fitzwilliam, the Queen's Lord Deputy in Ireland, saw wreckage lying along this strand '. . . more than would have built four of the greatest ships I ever saw . . . and such masts, for bigness and length, as in my knowledge I never saw any two that would make the like'. From one of the Streedagh wrecks — possibly that of the *Lavia* (728 tons, 25 guns), vice-flagship of Levant — there escaped a certain Captain Francisco de Cuellar, who was to write a vivid and harrowing account of his adventures in Ireland and Scotland when, more than a year later, he succeeded in reaching Antwerp.

These, the most important of the Irish wrecks and consequently the best documented, account for only half the known tally. One of the hulks, the *Falcon Blanco Mediano* (300 tons, 16 guns), was lost somewhere in Connemara, perhaps on a reef near Inish Boffin. Most of her survivors were hanged or beheaded in Galway. Another ship, evidently a large one, was wrecked on Gola Island in Western Tirconnel. A big vessel, perhaps a Biscayan, sank in Tralee Bay. Three ships were lost in Donegal Bay, in and around the entrance to Killibegs, where the *Girona* had sought refuge. Other wrecks occurred in Galway Bay, Clew Bay, Broadhaven, and on the wild coasts of Tirawley and North Donegal. Yet other ships, large and small, may have foundered unwitnessed in the open sea, or have been smashed on reefs or shores so remote and desolate that no one ever knew of them.

On balance, Wignall reckoned that the Streedagh wrecks offered the best prospects for discovery. Grattan, before leaving, had strongly advocated that the team should move there. It would not be difficult to carry out a ribbon on swim-line searches running along the full length of the 5-mile strand, covering the depth range to the 30-foot contour within which the three ships must have grounded. Plans were laid for the now highly trained permanent members of the team to move to Streedagh for an all-out, last ditch effort to find an Armada wreck.

But somehow none of us who were left felt quite ready to make the move. We were uneasy about leaving Blasket Sound; it was niggling the back of our minds that something we had not yet seen, or recognised, lay around or near Stromboli. We decided to search the reef once again, and if we found nothing we would then move to Streedagh.

On this basis Wignall departed, leaving me in charge. There followed an exchange of letters between us. In them, there is not so much as a mention of Streedagh Strand. The first was written by Wignall immediately he arrived home:

Dear Colin,

Having left the Sound, and sitting here re-examining the evidence, I find I can adopt a more detached attitude to the problem. With the hours we have been working, plus the strain, I feel that we were too eager to jump at wild theories without tempering them with calm consideration.

I have re-read the documents and have concluded that, in the main, Aramburu is of little direct help to us. All we can really deduce from his log is that both his ship and the *Santa Maria* dragged anchor, and that the *Santa Maria* sank.

The only man who really knew what happened was the sole survivor, Giovanni. Look again at what he says. 'This ship was shot through four times, and one of the shots was between the wind and the water, whereof they thought she would have sunk.' This was the condition she was in when she entered the Sound, under her solitary foresail.

Clearly, at that time, she had not hit a rock. Go back to Giovanni's statement. 'This ship broke against the rocks in the Sound of the Bleskies a league and a half from land upon the Tuesday last at noon.' Now go back to Aramburu '. . . the ship began dragging on our two cables, and we dragged with her, and in an instant we could see that she was going down, trying to hoist the foresail. . . . We were dragging on her still, to our own perdition.'

If we had only found the two 'anchorage' anchors, including the one with the broken shank, and taking into consideration the areas we have searched, I can only conclude that the *Santa Maria* and Aramburu's ship dragged south-east from the Blasket anchorage, and that therefore the *Santa Maria* probably hit Stromboli Rock.

We can now see the full significance of Aramburu's words 'we were dragging on her still, *to our own perdition*'. Dragging on to what? Towards, surely, Stromboli, which in that wild storm would be breaking into a great chaos of white water. The big anchor clinches it for me. Its shape and dimensions are right for a ship the size of the *Santa Maria,* and of her period. Its position is exactly right for this theory to be true. It lies just on the north-western edge of Stromboli's main pinnacle.

The fact that the disaster was sudden and quick is verified by

Giovanni's statement that the officers, attempting to save themselves by the ship's boat, found it 'so fast tied as they could not get her loose, thereby they were drowned'.

I am now quite certain in my own mind that Spotswood Green was right and I was wrong. Stromboli may look too far east on the chart, but we now know that its true pinnacle lies 150 yards west of the charted position, in direct line with the big anchor and with the anchors we located in the anchorage.

Giovanni's testimony is the only one on which we can place any credence. The ship struck a rock and sank quickly. She must be somewhere on the south or south-east side of the Stromboli complex. Keep plugging away at that area. I have a feeling she is down there.

Best of luck,

Syd.

But before I received this letter I had myself sent the following one to Wignall:

Dear Syd,

I think we are getting warm. I am sure that the key lies in following the sequence of events which took place on 21st September 1588. The anchors prove that this sequence developed in a south-easterly line running from the anchorage towards Stromboli. This south-easterly movement also reflects the mean influences on a sailing ship of a westerly wind and an ebbing tide, conditions we know from Aramburu's log to have been present in Blasket Sound at the time of the *Santa Maria*'s sinking. Stromboli must therefore be the rock she hit, and the big anchor on the north of the reef must be hers. Having now actually seen Stromboli's pinnacle twice myself under water, I am convinced that such a rock would punch the bottom out of a ship so savagely that she would indeed sink 'in an instant'. Where else in the Sound could such a catastrophe occur?

We have now almost covered the Stromboli reef complex itself — this afternoon's swim, if all goes well, should complete it. We have been carrying out very short swim-lines dead on slack water. The timing is critical — it must be right literally to the minute — and the tides are not always obeying the published tables as they should. The other day we had to abort a perfectly good swim because the line simply could not cope with a rising flood over the pinnacles, and in fact we were swept backwards off the reef into the tide-race. Visibility is extremely good among the pinnacles at the moment — why, I don't know, for the weather itself has been lousy. But for the first time we are managing to see clearly into the deep gulleys.

When we finish the reef I plan to re-do the swims up to the reef from deep water, as close to mid-day as possible. I think this is important, for we did many of these deep swims early or late in the day when light conditions down there were bad. We could have missed something. I only hope the wreck is not in very deep water, or completely buried in sand.

This area must be considered a very high probability one. And it contains those mounds of stones we found earlier. What about them? Could they be ballast stones, with most of the guns buried at either side? The boys feel particularly confident about these mounds, and I must say I do too. We will find them and look at them very carefully. Morale is at present quite high, and discipline holds. The equipment is still working, and is being properly maintained and repaired. In other words, the expedition is still plodding systematically on.

Yours ever,
Colin.

On Thursday 4th July we relocated the mounds of stones.

At one end of the swim-line 'Smudge' Smith came upon a jumbled pile of huge boulders, just at the base of the reef. As instructed, he made his marker float fast on them, and signalled the line to come up. Meanwhile, on the other end of the line, Flight Lieutenant (now Squadron Leader) Mike Edmonds, an R.A.F. friend of Wignall who had been with him on the 1962 Aeolian expedition and who was now spending his leave with us in Blasket Sound, had spotted another pile of stones, long, low, and regular in appearance. At one edge he noticed a larva-like concretion, apparently stuck to the boulders. Quickly, for the line was coming up on Smith's signal and in any case we were close to the 'no-stop' time limit for the depth (which was 110 feet), he hacked into this concretion with his knife. Part of the outer shell of the object fell away, in a cloud of black oxide, revealing the glint of a spherical metal object beneath. He had no time to examine it further, or to mark it, so reluctantly he kicked his fins and followed the line to the surface.

Next day we carefully examined Smith's pile, and found nothing to suggest that it was not of completely natural origin. It seemed, in fact, to be the result of an underwater avalanche which had broken away from the cliff face above. Then we tried to locate Edmonds' unmarked stones, and failed to find them (the swim-line, as still occasionally happened, lost direction and fouled itself). We returned home that evening angry and disappointed with ourselves. On the following morning, however, we found and marked the second mound without difficulty. It was the mound Jack Sumner had seen a month before.

By the end of that day we had found, amongst the stones, great piles of iron roundshot (including one with the mark of Edmonds' knife-cut on it), lead musket bullets, a small piece of glazed pottery, a cluster of six boat-shaped lead ingots and one rectangular one. We had seen, protruding from the shingle at the edge of the mound, the blackened ends of oak beams and planks. We had swum all round the mound, noting that it rose about 3 feet from the sea bed and ran 100 feet in a north-south direction and was 40 feet across at its widest part. It was clearly the stone ballast of an ancient shipwreck. The deepest point of the wreck was 115 feet below the surface at high water.

When we surfaced the Sound was unnaturally calm, almost oppressively so, its waters shimmering like molten lead under a grey sky. The whole situation breathed with an air of total unreality. Only the heavy musket bullets rolling in our palms, their mould flashes as crisp as when they were cast, told us that we had really reached our goal, that we had found the Armada ship in Blasket Sound. For what else could it be? From where we sat becalmed, immediately above the wreck, we could trace the line of orange buoys we had tied to the anchors running straight towards the Blasket Island anchorage 1 mile away, revealing the terrible events of four centuries ago so clearly that we could almost feel the shock of them taking place. In the shelter of the island's rising bulk, Recalde's great *San Juan de Portugal,* caught in the sudden dawn squall of 21st September 1588, breaks free of her moorings and drifts uncontrollably down on Aramburu's *San Juan Bautista,* anchored nearby, smashing her stern lantern and mizzen tackle. The impact of collision causes Aramburu's own anchor to snap across the shank, and the two ships are sent scudding helplessly before the wind towards the mainland cliffs. Halfway across the Sound they manage to get their reserve anchors down (Recalde's foresight in preparing emergency ground tackle a week earlier probably saved both ships in this crisis) and hold precariously on at the edge of the tide-race, unable to work back into the shelter of Great Blasket Island, and in imminent danger of being wrecked on the breaking reefs and cliffs only a few hundred yards to leeward.

At this critical point, unexpectedly, two more Armada ships limp into the Sound from the open sea, coming in by the wide northern entrance. One of them, which Aramburu recognises as the Guipuzcoan vice-flagship *Santa Maria de la Rosa,* is in a highly distressed condition : her sails are in tatters, her hull is shot through, and she is making water fast. Worst of all, she has only one anchor remaining. In a desperate plea for help her commander, Martin de Villafranca, fires two distress signals, but the anchored ships, themselves in dire peril, can do nothing to help. The *Santa Maria* works her way close to Aramburu's *San Juan,* and drops anchor. The massive plaited hemp cable snakes out of the hawse-hole and pulls taut, turning the ship's head into a wind which is blowing so strongly that her stern is forced into and against the fast flood tide which is coming up from the south-east. At this point, with the wind directly against the tide, conditions in the Sound are appalling, and the tide-race over the reef only a few yards away boils in a terrifying inferno of crashing white water. But at first the *Santa Maria*'s anchor holds firm. As the tide slackens conditions become a little better, but only temporarily. The flood tide which has filled the broad basin of Blasket Sound must now drain back through the narrow constricted neck in which the ships are lying. Both wind and tide begin to pull together on the *Santa Maria*'s anchor where before they had countered one another. The extra strain is too much for the holding power of the anchor. Slowly at first, but with increasing violence and momentum, the anchor bounces and jerks as the fluke alternately digs into and then rips out of the shingle sea bed. Inexorably, to the unspeakable horror of those on board, the *Santa Maria* drags into the tide-race, which once again is beginning to boil as the tide gathers speed. As she drags, her cable fouls Aramburu's cable, and the *San Juan Bautista* is herself momentarily placed in deadly danger, from which however she is able to extricate herself by casting another anchor.

Suddenly the *Santa Maria* strikes the hidden fang of Stromboli : with a terrible splintering crash, heralding what to those on board was quite literally the end of the world, the great rock thrusts deeply into the ship's bowels, smashing through planking, ribs, and decks as though they were matchwood. She shudders momentarily on the impaling rock and then the ebbing tide carries her off it, mortally stricken. Panic breaks out in the foundering vessel, although at least someone has the presence of mind to attempt to raise the foresail in a desperate bid to bring the ship's head round towards the shore. If the vessel could be run into the lee of Dunmore head before she sank, it might be possible for some survivors to reach the shore. They stood little chance if they remained where they were. Could this sensible action — indeed the only possible action — have been instigated by the ship's pilot Francisco, young Giovanni's father? Did he also order the anchor cable to be cut, as he would have to do if the vessel was to be got under way? Was this incident perhaps linked with the otherwise inexplicable slaying of the ship's pilot by 'one of the (military) captains'. Did a fierce argument break out on board the doomed ship, in which the seamen wisely insisted on raising the foresail, cutting the anchor cable, and heading for the shore, while the panic stricken landsmen (who would have outranked them in nobility) wanted instinctively and irrationally to remain anchored, perhaps to be saved by the other ships?

While the seamen fight to save the ship and the soldiers struggle to save themselves the breaking hull lurches and settles in the tossing waters amid a confusion of springing timbers, falling spars, and wind-snatched rigging. As the seas close over the upper decks hundreds of scurrying, helpless figures are engulfed. Soon nothing can be seen of the ship except a white froth of bubbles aerating a strangely flattened, seething surface, among which countless bodies, timbers, and casks bob pathetically. Only one man, clinging desperately to a couple of planks, reaches the shore alive. The rest are swept out of the Sound, along with the floating debris of the wreck, by the 3-knot flush of the ebbing tide. Within a few minutes nothing remains on the storm-driven surface to show that Guipuzcoa's 945-ton vice-flagship and the 300-odd people aboard her had ever existed.

CAPTAIN MATUTE'S PLATES

Now that we had found the wreck there was a great deal to do. We telegraphed the news to Wignall in Malta, following up with a detailed written report. For the next two or three days we carried out a number of exploratory dives on the site, familiarising ourselves with it and seeking signs of the guns which we felt sure must lie somewhere near. But all that we could find were a few sherds of glazed earthenware pottery; there seemed to be little else visible among the great pile of stones. This pile was undoubtedly the ship's ballast, and we calculated that there was more than 200 tons of it — a striking indication of how tall and top heavy the ship that carried it must once have been.

From a diving point of view the wreck could not have been in a more inconvenient spot. It lay right in the eye of the tide-race, so we could only work there for a brief 20 minutes on either side of slack water. It was also a very difficult place in which to moor a boat, and because of its open tidal nature there was an acute danger of divers being swept away and lost if they failed for some reason to surface up the mooring line. To reduce these risks a strict code of safety regulations was laid down and enforced. Moreover, the site was very deep; at low water the wreck lay at 110 feet and at high water the depth increased a further 10 feet. These depths gave us 'no-stop' limits on the site of 17 and 14 minutes respectively; thus diving twice daily on high and low water slack allowed each man to carry out only half an hour of effective underwater work.

The team was now considerably reduced in size. Only the hard core which had evolved from the early days of the search remained, including Oldfield, Smith, Sumner, and myself. We had recently been joined by a new member, Karl Bialowas, who had elected to stay with us permanently. Mike Edmonds, whose knife-cut had led to the discovery of the wreck, completed our present number.

Our first task was to make a plan of the visible remains. We began by laying a 15-foot grid of weighted lines across the ballast mound, but the tidal currents were too strong and the lines quickly became tangled and carried away. We then set up four permanent markers around the site, from which any position on the wreck could be fixed by taking tape measurements from two or more of the markers and plotting the intersections. The markers consisted of welded tubular metal posts and stands which we pinned securely to the sea floor by building cairns of rocks around them. This system allowed us to plot the general features of the site quite rapidly, and map the shape and extent of the ballast mound. Spot heights were fixed relative to one another by means of an inverted plastic hose filled with air — the air level at each end providing an accurate datum from which to measure height differences.

In order to map the more complex areas, and to permit the quick and accurate recording of finds once excavation started, we built two movable 15-foot square grids with adjustable legs. The grid frames, which were dismantled for ease of transport to the sea bed, were constructed in 14 hours of non-stop work by the team's two engineers, Jack Sumner and Chris Oldfield. The grids were immediately christened 'Beasts', and in their livery of black and white scale markings they looked smart and efficient. We decided to set up the first 'Beast' very early the following morning, as we wanted to avoid awkward questions about their purpose. News of our discovery had not yet broken, nor did we want it to. The team set out sleepily before daybreak, at 4.30 a.m., and we were moored over the wreck in flat calm conditions as a mountain sunrise was bathing the Sound and islands in soft, pastel light. Three of us swam down with the dismantled grid sections. It was very dark and cold at the bottom, and the wreck felt eerie and hostile. Sumner and Oldfield followed close behind to assemble their creation. In almost total blackness they put the grid together, without fumbling, in a matter of minutes, and then trued it level and square. After their labours with welder and hacksaw the previous evening they had had a very heavy night out — which did not, however, affect their skill as divers and engineers at 6 o'clock the following morning. They were a good pair of men to have around.

The other 'Beast' was set up the following morning, at a

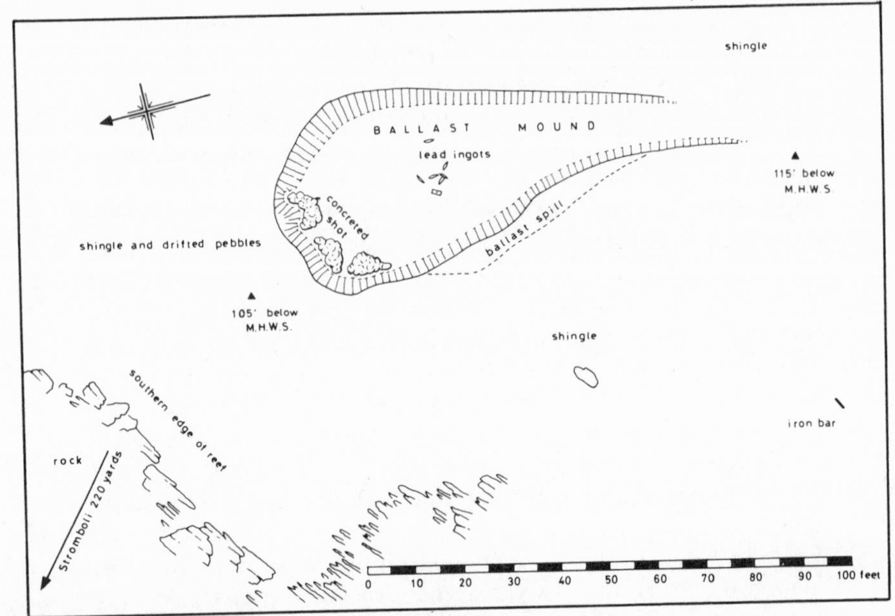

Fig. 7. Wreck of the *Santa Maria de la Rosa* when first discovered

similar hour. Once the grids were down and the markers fixed we proceeded with the survey. The preliminary measurements, which allowed us to draw a general plan of the wreck and the surrounding area, occupied myself, Bialowas, and Edmonds for the next fortnight. At the end of it we were able to plot on a drawing board an overall picture of what the site looked like, a picture which the limited visibility of the sea bed had never allowed us to see in real life. What, if anything, could this picture — this 'pre-disturbance' site plan — tell us about the wreck?

The long mound of ballast stones, tadpole-shaped with a broad head and narrowing tail, presumably indicated the lie of the bottom part of the ship. Which end then was the bow, and which the stern? In its distinctive shape we seemed to have a clue: a clue which, when we looked up our researches into Armada period ships, gave us the answer. In the Bodelian Library, Oxford, there is an original eye-witness account of what an Armada wreck looked like to a salvor working on it underwater from a diving bell about the year 1670. The wreck was the well-known Tobermory

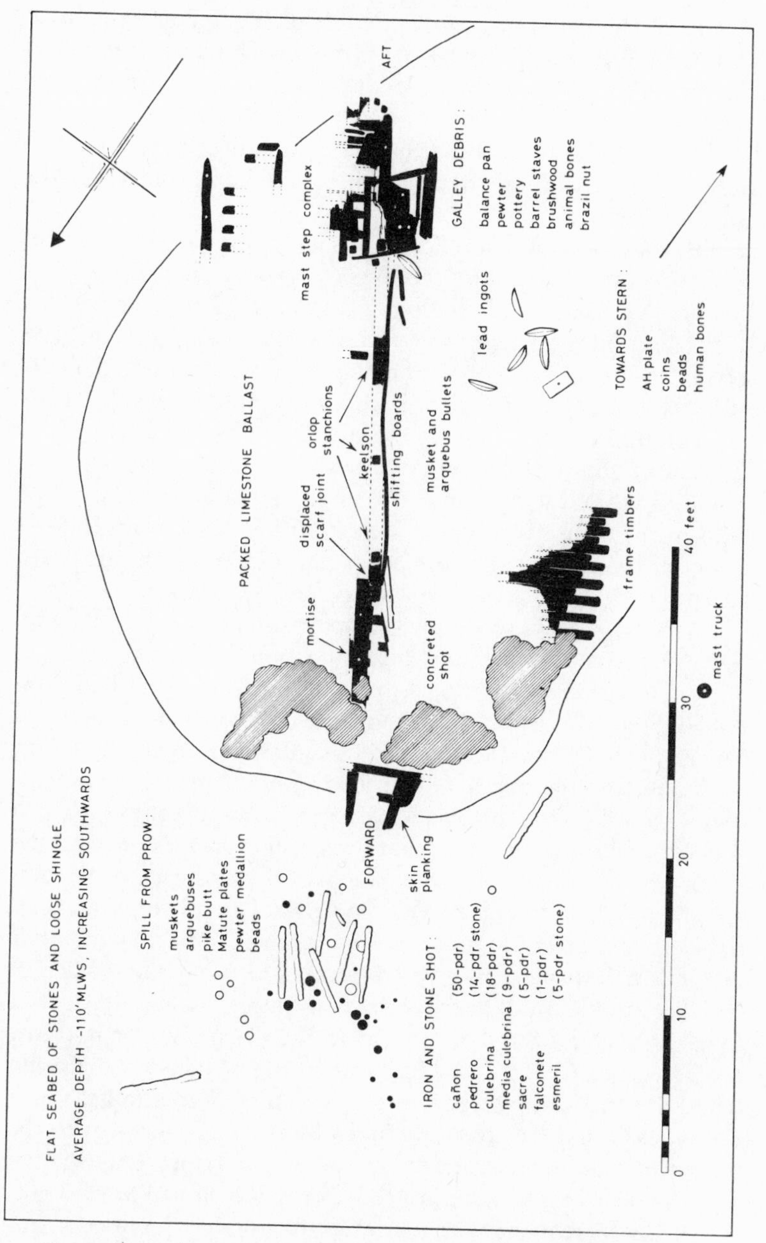

Fig. 8. *Santa Maria de la Rosa:* plan of wreck site after excavation

ship (probably the *San Juan de Sicilia,* of the Levant squadron), and the salvor, Archibald Miller of Greenock, has this to say of the remains as he saw them less than a century after the ship had sunk:

'There is no deck upon her except in ye hinder part . . . in the fore part of the ship lies many great ballast stones and some shot amongst them . . .'

Miller's description implies that the greatest mass of ballast occurred in the fore part of the Tobermory ship. Consideration of the factors involved in ballasting a ship of this kind suggests why this should be so. The towering castlework of the stern, with its associated armament and fortification, would have exerted a considerable stern-down component in the trim of the vessel. Ballast concentrated forward, tapering gradually aft from midships with the run of the hull, would have corrected this imbalance, and would leave on a wreck site a greater spread of ballast in the bow than in the stern, as Miller observed on the Tobermory ship. It is logical to suppose, therefore, that the broad head at the north end of our ballast mound represents the bow of the ship.

By the time we had completed the preliminary survey Wignall returned from Malta. I took him on a tour of the site, pointing out the features we had noted and the survey grids we had positioned. Soon afterwards we raised some of the roundshot and two of the lead ingots for detailed examination. Eric Reynolds, Wignall's accountant and close friend who had joined the expedition for a week, then discovered that gently tapping the misshapen and corroded surface of the shot with a light hammer caused the outer casing to flake off, revealing an apparently perfectly preserved iron ball complete with its original moulding lines and, in some instances, foundry marks. Almost immediately after extraction, however, fresh rust began to form on the surface of the shot, and so we immersed the balls in fresh water and got in touch with Peter Start, a lecturer in the Chemistry Department at University College, Dublin, whom Wignall had met during his Malta trip and who had most generously offered to help with the analysis and treatment of finds. Start came down to see the balls and take away samples, and after laboratory examination he was able to explain the protective crust which had formed outside them. By reacting with sea water the iron had produced complex sulphides and oxides which had acted as a strong adhesive cement, to which sand, pebbles, and shells bonded themselves to form a solid concrete several inches thick. Within this concretion the original object remained preserved, at least in so far as its shape was concerned; but in chemical composition it had undergone a radical transformation. The reduction process had taken away most of the pure metal to leave only ferrous impurities, mostly graphite, which retained within the concretion mould the exact shape of the original object. What the iron objects did not retain was their original weight; the loss of pure metal had reduced this in some instances by as much as two-thirds, so that what appeared superficially to be a solid lump of iron weighed little more than a similarly sized pumice stone.

Such objects, on being exposed to the atmosphere, became highly unstable. Oxidisation set in so fiercely that in some instances balls became hot and began disintegrating before our eyes. Even apparently well preserved samples did not remain unaffected for long. Keeping them in water held the decay in check, but it was not until Wignall and Casey between them constructed a vacuum chamber in which the iron could be impregnated with stabilising chemicals that the problem was finally solved.

Mr. Start was able to make another observation regarding the iron shot. When the concretion was first broken off we found that the surfaces of the balls were covered in an extremely thick, smelly grease. On analysis this proved to be chemically broken down animal fat, perhaps pig lard, with which the Spaniards had evidently coated the balls to prevent rusting.

The shot also provided us with evidence which helped to confirm that our wreck was an Armada ship. Although we knew from the Lisbon Muster that the *Santa Maria* had carried 26 main guns, there was no indication in documentary sources of their type and size. However, we did possess some details of the guns mounted by her sister ship *San Salvador,* which had an almost identical tonnage and numerical armament: 958 tons and 25 guns. The *San Salvador* blew up during the fighting and was captured by the English, and later her captors made a careful inventory of her guns. These records survive, and though they do not tell us her complete armament—she probably lost some in the explosion and others were stolen by gun-hungry English captains before the official inventory could be made—they do give actual examples of the kind of guns carried by a ship of this class.

From the roundshot we had now recovered from Blasket Sound we could also list the various calibres of guns carried by our ship, and if they proved similar to those known to have been on board the *San Salvador* the case that the Blasket wreck was indeed her sister Guipuzcoan *Santa Maria de la Rosa* would be stronger than ever. The results are expressed in the table below:

Gun Types

Blasket Sound wreck (based on average shot sizes plus ¼ inch allowance for windage)	*San Salvador* (numbers from English inventories)
Whole cannon (7½ inch bore; 50-pounder shot)	2
Perrier (6½ inch bore; 14-pounder stone shot)	4
Culverin (5½ inch bore; 18-pounder shot)	1
Demi Culverin (4½ inch bore; 9-pounder shot)	1
Minion or sacre (3½ inch bore; 5-pounder shot)	4
Falconet (2-inch bore; 1¼-pounder shot	1
Esmeril (4½ inch bore; 5-pounder stone shot)	1

The types of guns carried by the two ships thus appear to have been identical in all respects. Our roundshot, it seems, would have neatly fitted into the *San Salvador*'s guns. Moreover, this particular combination of artillery is exactly what all the evidence would lead us to suppose would have been carried by a front-line Armada ship. It is an aggressive rather than a defensive armament, with a strong main battery of short-range cannon-types and perriers, intended to deliver ship-smashing broadsides at point-blank range. Such a combination is unlikely to be found aboard a vessel of any other nationality or period.

We next turned our attention to the lead ingots we had found. They weighed about 100 pounds apiece, and were stamped on their flat upper faces with Roman numerals. Similar ingots had been recovered earlier that same summer by Robert Sténuit from the site of the *Girona,* the Armada galleass which had been wrecked off Antrim. They are also mentioned in an account of recoveries made from an Armada wreck off Donegal during the 18th century, where they are described as 'pieces of lead a yard long, triangular, the sides being pointed towards the ends, getting thick in the middle'. Lead ingots were also listed in the English inventories of stores aboard the captured Armada ships *San Salvador* and *Nuestra Señora del Rosario*; in the latter instance they are described as 'sows' of lead weighing a hundredweight apiece.

Lead was an important war commodity which the Duke of Medina Sidonia had substantially increased among the ships shortly before the fleet sailed. In discussing the issue of lead to the various units, he speaks of the three forms in which the metal was accountable: 'made up into arquebus and musket bullets' (i.e. previously cast and shipped as shot); 'quintals of lead for making into bullets' (i.e. ingots); and finally 'in respect of the Armada' — that is, for the operational maintenance of the ships themselves (patching, scuppering, and the like) — 'lead in blocks (*planchas*)'. We know from the Armada inventories that the *Santa Maria* had been loaded with about 2 000 pounds of lead at Lisbon before she sailed.

In the boat-shaped ingots, a type which could easily be handled by two men or slung in pairs across a pack animal, the individual quintals (100 pounds) 'for bullets' may surely be recognised. The Roman numerals stamped on them probably indicate adjustments to this standard tally-weight. These ingots were part of a field army's stores, and would be hacked up for issue to individual soldiers to cast into shot with their bullet moulds. The large rectangular ingot, which weighed nearly 300 pounds, would have been far too heavy for infantry to carry in the field, and so it is probably one of the *'planchas'* from the ship's stores.

The lead bullets, which we were picking up all over the site, were of two sizes, $\frac{1}{2}$ inch and $\frac{3}{4}$ inch in diameter and weighing $\frac{1}{2}$ ounce and 2 ounces respectively, the smaller being suitable for the arquebus and the larger for the musket, the two standard infantry firearms in service with the Spanish Army at the end of the 16th century. Lead shot was also used for close quarter work by the ship's main guns and swivel pieces, bagged in cases of several hundred bullets to form deadly close-range 'scatter' ammunition.

Pottery was also to be found scattered around the ballast mound in some quantity. We collected several dozen broken sherds, mostly quite small, the majority of them a rather poorly fired red earthenware with a gaudy green or brown internal glaze. This must have been the everyday crockery in use aboard the ship, and it brought to mind a huge order for pottery which had been placed with the potters of Seville and Lisbon by the Marquis of Santa Cruz for the fleet in 1586, when planning for the Armada was just getting under way. The order specified 100 000 pieces of 'glazed earthenware (*barro vidriados*) . . . including plates, bowls, pots, and pitchers . . .' It looked very much as if the mass-produced, rather cheap scraps of pottery we were finding were part of this official 'Armada issue'. Almost identical Seville pottery can be recognised in the rough kitchenware depicted in some of Velazquez's earliest paintings.

Thus from a pile of old cannon balls, a great heap of stones, some lead ingots and bullets, and a few scraps of pottery, we had been able to deduce a great deal of information. Ignoring all the strong circumstantial evidence which pointed to our wreck being that of the *Santa Maria de la Rosa*, we knew that we had found the remains of a large stone-ballasted ship, armed according to Armada front-line specifications, carrying soldiers equipped with arquebus and musket, having in her hold lead ingots of a type associated with other Armada ships, and containing domestic pottery probably made in Seville or Lisbon.

But where were the guns? Once the wreck survey was complete we turned our full attention to the mystery. John Grattan returned for a week, carefully examined the wreck, and formed the opinion that they probably lay buried in the loose shingle on either side of the ballast mound when they had fallen as the ship's sides collapsed outwards. If so, there was a lot of digging to be done. It was too late in the season to organise heavy excavation gear — that was planned for the following year — so we began to dig outwards from the western edge of the ballast at a point about midships, using hand tools. Working in shifts for several weeks, we completed a trench some 3 feet deep and 30 feet long. The result was negative: we found nothing in it at all.

Clearly there was now little we could do until the following season. Before we left, however, Wignall arranged a Press Conference to announce the discovery of the wreck. This conference was held at the Shelbourne Hotel, Dublin, under the generous sponsorship of Guinness Limited, and was attended by representatives from all the main Irish national and provincial papers and many British dailies, as well as by other interested parties. The conference was chaired by Mr. Aiden O'Hanlon of the Irish State Tourist Board (Bord Failte). Wignall first outlined the history of his researches into the *Santa Maria,* emphasising the important historical value of the wreck, and Grattan went on to describe the search techniques which had made the discovery possible. Finally Wignall's solicitor, Mr. John P. King of Dublin, who had assisted Wignall from the very early days of his interest in the Irish Armada wrecks, summarised the legal position. Our aim in presenting the story to the Press was to emphasise the serious intentions of our project, and to play down any sensational treasure hunting angle. If we were treasure hunters we were extremely unsuccessful ones, for we had not yet unearthed a single coin!

Before the close of the season we produced and published, through a prodigious feat of writing and organisation (mostly on Wignall's part), an illustrated 128-page report on our work to date. This was circulated to our many supporters, and to various potential sponsors. We also submitted it, through the British Sub-Aqua Club, as the expedition's entry for the Duke of Edinburgh's gold medal award for underwater achievement. To our great joy the expedition won this award, though it was not until late in the following year (1969) that our success was announced. Wignall received the medal — on behalf of the whole team, as he was at pains to insist — from H.R.H. Prince Philip at Buckingham Palace on 9th November 1971.

In 1968 we had found and surveyed a wreck which we believed to be the *Santa Maria de la Rosa*; in 1969 we planned to find out what lay beneath the ballast mound and among the drifted shingle surrounding it. Most particularly we wanted to find the ship's guns. The iron roundshot we had already raised told us that there had been whole-cannons on board, monster 50-pounders of bronze weighing perhaps 3 tons, as well as an assortment of other guns: stubby stone-throwing perriers; slender long-range culverins, demi-culverins, and sacres; light falconets and swivel pieces. So far we had not seen one of them. If we could discover at least a few we would be able to examine, at first hand, the actual armament carried by an Armada ship, something which no historian had yet been able to do. At the same time we wanted to recover a cross-section of the thousands of different objects which a ship of this kind would have carried. We expected to find rich things, certainly; perhaps coins from the three great iron-bound chests carried in the ship's strong-room, personal jewellery worn by the officers and *aventureros,* or the sumptuous plate off which they ate their meagre sea rations. But commonplace objects interested us too; objects which, in themselves, might seem mundane, fragile and inanimate, but which if properly studied would help to bring to life the people who once used them and tell of the conditions under which they lived and worked. Finally we wanted to uncover and survey parts of the ship's hull which we knew lay pinned beneath the pile of ballast, in order to learn something of the *Santa Maria* herself.

Once again the administrative and financial burdens of organising the expedition fell on Sydney Wignall, who planned to carry out a full 6-month season on the wreck, starting in April. We decided to rely mainly on the small permanent team which had grown up during the previous season, for we now had proved that we could work well together. Part-time voluntary help would still be used, but on a much smaller scale than before — strictly limited to those who had worked with us satisfactorily in 1968, or who had special qualifications or skills. The great depth at which the wreck lay and the time limit which this imposed meant that every diver-minute would have to count.

We gathered at Dingle for the 1969 season on 2nd April. There were seven of us in all; Wignall, myself, Chris Oldfield, Tony Long, Jack Sumner, 'Smudge' Smith, and Karl Bialowas. Shortly after the start of the season we were joined by two Navy friends, Mick Roberts and Karl Lees, and a few days later John Grattan arrived with his Chief Petty Officer from Malta days, Alf Slingsby. We spent several days preparing the equipment and putting it in working order, and on 7th April we launched the Geminis at Dunquin and set out to relocate the wreck.

The first task of the season was to carry out a metal detector survey of the entire area surrounding the wreck in an attempt to locate the guns, which we still felt convinced must be lying buried around the edges of the ballast mound. During the winter we had approached Dr. Edward Hall, Director of the Oxford Laboratory for Archaeology, about the metal detection apparatus which the laboratory had developed for underwater archaeological work and had already used with considerable success on ancient shipwreck sites in the Mediterranean. Dr. Hall kindly agreed to co-operate in a survey of the *Santa Maria* site, and arranged for Jeremy Green, a member of his staff who had been particularly closely involved in the development of the underwater detector and was an experienced diver himself, to come over to Blasket Sound with the necessary equipment and organise a survey. The aim was not to prospect at random for isolated contacts (or 'targets') but to build up a systematic pattern of information about the positions and nature of buried metal deposits surrounding the wreck to give us an idea of how the ship had broken up, and how best, in consequence, to set about excavating the remains.

In order to mark out the area in which the metal detector was to work we had made up a number of concrete anchor blocks with wooden pegs sunk into them (for obvious reasons we could use no metal), and these we set up as terminal points around the ballast mound. Light jackstay lines were then stretched between them. An area 200 feet long by 100 feet wide was laid out in this way, involving thirty-six individually positioned anchor blocks and eighteen jackstay lines. The speed and accuracy with which this quite complex operation was carried out confirmed the wisdom of our policy in using an experienced and close-knit team; it was indeed a joy to watch the ease with which a plan mapped out on the drawing-board was put into precise effect on a twilight sea floor 20 fathoms down at the tail of a fierce tide-race.

Jeremy Green arrived shortly after the first lines had been successfully laid out. I took him down on the wreck with his detector, a neatly compact unit which could easily be operated by one man, and together we worked out a practical system for using it to cover the ground systematically. A two-man team was needed, consisting of operator and assistant. The operator would move slowly up the side of a line, sweeping the circular coil of the instrument in a 5-foot arc over the sea floor. Any contact would immediately register on a dial, and further investigation with the detector would indicate whether the buried object was large or small, and whether it was close to the surface or deeply buried. The assistant would follow with a bag of markers to indicate the extent of individual targets as they were spotted by the detector. These contacts were then plotted on a grided survey board.

Like the rest of us Green was limited by the depth to two 15-

minute diving sessions each day, and a calculation based on his average rate of progress with the detector showed that it would be impossible for him to cover the planned survey area in the fortnight that he and the equipment were available. He therefore suggested that other members of the expedition should be trained to use the instrument. Four teams, each consisting of an operator and assistant, were selected, and after a day's theoretical training on land followed by practice in an area of shallow water in which an assortment of tin cans, iron bars, and coins had been buried, the teams could guarantee to spot and mark every target in the seeded area.

As soon as all was ready to proceed into the survey proper Blasket Sound rebelled with a Force 9 gale and diving became out of the question. Wignall suggested that the metal detector might be usefully employed on land to give the teams further practice, and we all felt that a survey at Dun an Oir — the old fort on Smerwick Harbour where Juan Martinez de Recalde had landed the ill-fated Papal force in 1580 — might yield interesting results. The earthwork defences of the fort can still be traced across the neck of the promontory which the mercenaries had fortified, and among our research files we had a copy of a plan of the fort made in 1580 by one of San Guiseppe's officers. The original of this plan is now in the Vatican archives. It clearly shows the earthwork bastions strengthened with a timber palisade and a moat defending the cluster of tents, store huts, and gun positions inside the fort. Above it all, on a tall flagstaff, flies the crossed-keys of the Papal banner.

In this same area, now overgrown with thorns, we located numerous targets with the metal detector, and after these had been carefully plotted on a measured survey of the fort we dug up a small area of shallow contacts to see what they were. We avoided digging deeply for fear of causing damage to the site, which had probably been used as a fortified refuge since prehistoric times. Even so, many relics of the 1580 siege came to light. There were several pieces of iron roundshot, a couple of lead bullets, some iron nails, a few potsherds (very similar to the pottery we had found on the *Santa Maria*), a soldier's belt buckle, and the remains of a copper powder ladle for a 3-pounder gun, with part of its wooden haft still in position. The iron shot indicated what kind of artillery the mercenaries had with them; these were the very guns, it will be remembered, which had been off-loaded from Recalde's ships as they lay at anchor off the fort. The guns were evidently quite small, 2, 3, and 4-pounders (a 4-pounder *minion* would have weighed, with its carriage, about three-quarters of a ton), just the kind of guns one would expect of light field artillery which was to be deployed in wild and mountainous country such as this. However, as we know, San Guiseppe never got his guns further than the bridgehead fort.

At the very tip of the promontory, where the 1580 map clearly shows a gun emplacement facing out to sea, the detector located a number of fractured pieces of bronze. On closer examination these proved to be shattered fragments of a gun which had evidently exploded on firing. We identified pieces of the breech, including the touch-hole, and deduced from the curve of the bore that the gun had been a 3-pounder or thereabouts. This was a very exciting find, for the mishap which destroyed it must have happened during the siege and there is documentary evidence to suggest that an accident of this nature had indeed taken place in the fort. It is to be found in the Spanish Ambassador's report of the episode in which he says that 'after firing a few shots the English dismantled (i.e. put out of action) one of the cannons in the fort'. But was it the skill of the English gunners which had destroyed the gun? Our find suggests otherwise. If the fragments we found are from the same gun then it disintegrated while being fired and not as a result of enemy action, for the pieces clearly point to an internal explosive fracture. A badly made gun, and not the efforts of the English, may therefore have been the real cause of the accident. Almost unwittingly we had stumbled on the Achilles Heel of Spain's military might in the 16th century — the inferior technical knowledge and craftsmanship of her gunfounders.

The day we spent at Dun an Oir with the metal detector thus added useful data to our study of Spanish military technology at the time of the Armada, and also cleared away any lingering doubts as to the efficacy of the Oxford Laboratory equipment. The following day the weather moderated sufficiently to allow us to take the detector down on the wreck. In the course of the next ten days the survey proceeded well, but to our increasing concern no large contacts were made which could be identified as guns. Jeremy Green calculated that a 3-ton bronze gun should give a signal even if it was buried 8 feet down, and yet neither the ballast mound nor the shingle around it gave the slightest hint of any large object hidden beneath. The results, when the survey was complete, were extremely disappointing. Even the small targets which the detector had picked up were sparse and scattered, considering the tens of thousands of metal objects which must once have been on the ship. We were beginning to suspect that much of the wreck probably lay elsewhere.

We were confident, however, that at least some interesting things remained on the site, particularly in a small area just north of the ballast mound where a concentration of metal detector targets had been marked. We decided to start digging there: first by hand, and then with the air-lift suction gear which was due to arrive shortly with the expedition's 50-foot salvage boat, *Jimbell.* Wignall had bought *Jimbell* at the close of the 1968 season, and now she was fitting out at Dublin under the supervision of Desmond Branigan, our Irish colleague who in 1963 had first dived in Blasket Sound and who ever since had kept in close touch with the expedition. As well as excavating this area, we planned to start shifting some of the ballast in order to examine the well preserved ship timbers which we knew lay beneath it.

At the same time the apparent lack of guns had given rise to a serious doubt which began to nag at our minds. The guns might of course have been carried away with the upper works of the ship when she had broken apart, to be taken into deep water by the ebbing tide, and it was possible that further searching might locate them if they were not too far away. But there was another possibility which could not be dismissed. In spite of the strong circumstantial evidence provided by the anchors, and the way in which everything we had found seemed to fit the eye-witness accounts of the disaster given by Marcos de Aramburu and young Giovanni, it was possible that this wreck was not the *Santa Maria* at all. It was an Armada ship; we were sure of that, but there was another Armada ship which might well lie in or around Blasket Sound—the *San Juan* of Fernando Horra, from which Recalde had rescued the survivors before bringing off some of her guns, and then scuttling her. Was what we had found merely her stripped hulk? We did not think so, but the doubt remained.

Then, on 2nd May, we found Captain Matute's plates.

The first one was found by 'Smudge' Smith and Alf Slingsby as they were digging in shingle close to the ballast mound. Laboriously they had been shovelling away stones and sand to uncover an area about 2 yards square to a depth of 2 feet. At the bottom of the hole was a great mass of concreted magma which contained, amongst the inevitable iron roundshot, several slender objects about 5 feet in length. We carefully surveyed and photographed these objects as they lay *in situ,* and then Smith and Slingsby began carefully to extricate one of them with hammer and chisel. By the end of the dive they had freed it, and beneath it they found a small pewter plate, 8 inches in diameter, heavily encrusted but apparently in good condition. The finds were slung in a net and sent soaring to the surface under an air balloon, to be borne triumphantly back to Dingle for cleaning and examination.

On a bench in the back garden of our house I began, with toffee hammer and soft metal chisel, to remove the concretion from the long object with painstaking care. Whatever lay beneath seemed to be made of wood, which, amazingly, was still hard and solid. Gradually the well preserved stock of a matchlock arquebus began to emerge, complete except for its curved butt, with the remains of its firing mechanism and trigger still in their recessed slots, and with its brass ferruled cane ramrod still intact. The concretion which had protected the stock had been formed by the rusting of the damascene steel barrel, which had almost completely disintegrated although enough remained to show that it had a 0.5 inch bore. As I cleaned away the decayed iron from the breech, a lead ball rolled out.

By this time I was surrounded by most of the members of the team, and in our excitement at the arquebus we had forgotten Wignall, who had been inside the house picking the concretion away from the pewter plate. At this moment he appeared at the back door, looked with interest at the arquebus, and then quietly asked us all to come inside. On the kitchen table the plate lay bottom upwards, its beaten grey metal surface shining dully, all the encrustations now removed. Beneath its rim we could see very clearly six incised letters — M A T U T E. Beside the plate Wignall had placed one of the photostated 16th century documents from the Public Record Office. It was the transcript of Giovanni's second interrogation . . . 'He saith the Captain of this ship was Villafranca of San Sebastian, and Matuta was Captain of the Infanterie. . . .'

The pewter plate had been the property of a man called Matute, perhaps part of a set of tableware for use on campaign. And, according to Giovanni, a Captain Matuta was the senior military officer aboard the *Santa Maria* when she sank. Matute on the plate, and Matuta in the documents, are clearly one and the same. The difference in the last letter is not significant; Giovanni's testimony was, after all, transcribed orally. There was no longer any question as to the identity of our wreck; a man dead for four centuries now confirmed it for us. The Matute plate demonstrated, with as convincing a proof as we could ever hope to find, that our wreck was the *Santa Maria de la Rosa.*

We looked again at the muster rolls drawn up by the Duke of Medina Sidonia at Lisbon just before the Armada sailed, in which all the military officers in the five *tercios* (regiments) are listed, and there we found him, with his company of ninety-five soldiers, in Don Diego de Pimentel's crack Sicilian *tercio* : Francisco Ruiz Matute. From this it appears that his name was Ruiz, an ancient Castilian family from the Burgos region of North Spain. Fifty miles east of Burgos, nestled in a valley among the Sierras de San Lorenzo, lies the tiny village of Matute; here he was probably born. Two other Ruizes, both from the same region, in fact sailed with the Armada; Captain Pedro Ruiz de Torquemada and Don Gaspar Ruiz de Peralta. Both were young *aventureros.* Francisco Ruiz Matute, however, was probably older and more experienced than his two *aventurero* kinsmen, for he held a senior appointment in a tough and battle-hardened regiment. Spain's large regular army had been fighting in various theatres almost without cessation for several generations. The stolid, disciplined, and well-armed infantrymen of the *tercios* were the only fully professional soldiers in Europe, and they boasted with justification that in the century now growing old they had never lost a pitched battle. It was they who had introduced infantry firearms to the world's battlefields, handling their light matchlock arquebuses and heavier muskets with deadly efficient company drills which had banished forever the archers and armoured cavalrymen of medieval days. They had campaigned through Flanders and through Italy, in France and in Germany, and like the ancient Roman legions with whose tactical organisation and grim professionalism they had much in common, they were accustomed to win their battles not through individual flashes of undisciplined courage but through a solid team effort of grinding toil, devotion to duty, endurance, discipline, and skill-at-arms. Spanish troops, the Duke of Parma had written in 1587 to Philip II concerning the forthcoming Armada, would be the 'sinew of the whole business'; he was right; and had the *tercios* actually landed in England the course of history might have been very different.

If the soldiers of the *tercios* were hard, dedicated men, so also were their officers. Captain Matute would have been responsible for the discipline and well-being of the 233 soldiers aboard the *Santa Maria*. He would have had to ensure, as Medina Sidonia emphasised in his General Instructions to the Fleet, that his men did not quarrel with the seamen or 'go down and take or choose their rations by force' — inter-service rivalry was always strong on the ships. He would have had to supervise ration issues and account, with the ship's notary, for all stores on board. He would have to check with the magazine keeper that each soldier was kept supplied with the proper amounts of lead, powder, and match as laid down in standing orders, and he would also — again in Medina Sidonia's own words — have been required to check that 'the soldiers' arms are kept clean, ready for service; and in any case, he must cause them to be cleaned twice a week. He must also exercise his men in the use of their arms, so that they may be expert when needed'.

How did Captain Matute and his men fare in the dark, rotting, vermin-infested bowels of the *Santa Maria de la Rosa* on that terrible north-about voyage? Hardship and privation, even of this magnitude, were no strangers to the 16th century professional soldier. Did they stubbornly maintain the discipline and spirit which their regimental traditions demanded, and for which countless hard campaigns had schooled them? We like to think that they did, and surely that bullet which rolled from the breech of one of their arquebuses four centuries later proves that their weapons were indeed kept 'ready for service' right up to the end.

On our next dive the remains of several other arquebuses came to light, together with another Matute-inscribed plate almost identical with the first. We then found the barrel of a larger weapon, of 0.75 inch calibre. This was clearly a musket, the heavier of the two types of infantry firearms used at this period by the Spanish army. The arquebus was a long, graceful weapon, quite light, which fired a ½-ounce ball; the musket was more powerful but clumsy, 'a terrible arm and heavy to the one who carried it', as a contemporary Spaniard wrote — so much so that it was always used in conjunction with a forked rest which the musketeer stuck in the ground in front of him. It fired a 2-ounce ball. Both weapons were of course muzzle-loaders, and were detonated by a simple matchlock device which brought a burning slow-match of braided hemp impregnated with saltpetre into contact with a pan containing a small priming charge. Such guns were tricky and temperamental to use, and a complicated drill was necessary to load and discharge them. None the less, in skilled and disciplined hands, they could be fired at a rate of up to once a minute.

We chiselled out the concretion surrounding the arquebuses and brought chunks of the matrix ashore each day to be broken apart, a chore which necessitated great care for there was no knowing what delicate artefacts might be hidden inside. The evil-smelling concretion was full of objects: iron and stone shot, fragments of metal, wood, rope and leather; pieces of canvas-wrapped grape shot. We found the end of a wooden pole shod with iron which may have been a pike butt, and two cut glass costume beads. A most interesting find was a pewter religious medallion bearing on one side the head of a protecting saint and on the other the Virgin Mary surrounded by a halo of light. Though crude in design, and obviously mass-produced, the medallion was a particularly touching and evocative find, for it must once have belonged to one of the *Santa Maria*'s ordinary seamen or soldiers. The knotted end of the string on which it had hung round his neck was still tied through its loop. He must have worn it, whoever he was, at the great Cathedral of Lisbon when all the men who were to take part in the Armada had been paraded in kneeling lines as the holy fathers, led by the Archbishop, confessed and communicated them, and granted absolution to their souls should they fall unshriven in battle. Did this unknown soldier clasp the medallion in nervous piety during the mind-splitting cannonades of the Channel battles? Did it comfort him through the terrible days of the voyage around the British Isles, and during those horrific final moments of despair in Blasket Sound? This battered memento somehow symbolised for us the thousands of ordinary men of the Armada — most of them decent, simple folk with modest hopes and aspirations, about whom the history books say nothing.

At the other end of the wreck, close to the ballast 'tail', Chris Oldfield had been examining another of the metal detector targets. As he cleared away ballast stones he came upon a badly crushed pewter plate, 14 inches in diameter. Beneath it he uncovered some human bones — the legs, pelvis, and ribs of a body which must have been trapped by the spilling ballast after the ship had gone down (human remains on ancient wrecks are rare; usually the bodies float away, or are reduced to nothing by the scavenging attentions of crabs, lobsters, and other marine organisms). Among the pelvis, where the man's purse or pocket would have been, Oldfield found a small concreted disc which he thought might be a coin. That evening, in the house, we cleaned and examined his finds. The plate bore a pewterer's touch, or trademark — which we have not yet been able to identify — and beneath the rim were the monogrammed letters 'A H'. Immediately we looked up the Armada lists, seeking a man with these initials. We found two: Don Antonio Hurtado de Mendoza, the officer in charge of the swift communications squadron of light *pataches* and *zabras,* and Don Antonio de Herrera, a captain in the Sicilian *tercio* (Captain Matute's regiment). Unfortunately neither of these men seems ever to have been associated with the *Santa Maria,* and in any case both survived the Armada, so the identity of our 'A H' remains a mystery.

When we came to examine Oldfield's concreted disc we found that it contained not one coin but two, a gold and a silver one stuck together.

These two coins in the dead Spaniard's pocket had come from opposite sides of the Atlantic, from the Old and from the New Worlds, and the legend they both bore was, appropriately, the same:

PHILIPPUS II DEI GRATIA:
REX HISPANIARUM ET INDIARUM—
Philip II by the Grace of God; King of All the Spains and the Indies.

The gold coin was a 2-*escudo* piece of Philip II, with the King's own arms surrounded by the Order of the Golden Fleece displayed on the obverse and the cross of Spain with the lions and castles of

Leon and Castile on the reverse. The mint-mark showed that it had been struck at Seville. The silver coin was a 4-*real* piece, also of Philip II; it had been struck at Mexico City.

We next turned our attentions to what remained of the ship herself. The great mound of ballast stones represented the complete bottom of the hold, the part left behind when the upper works had broken apart and drifted away. With luck the hull beneath it — the keel and lower ribs which could tell us much about the size, characteristics, and structural details of the vessel — would still be more or less intact. Because of their top-heavy design and the weighty hamper of masts, tackle, and guns, ships like the *Santa Maria* needed to carry a quarter of their own weight or even more in counterbalancing ballast. This was usually provided simply by filling the bottom of the ship with manageable sized rocks (none bigger than 50 pounds in weight) up to a depth of 2 feet or more. As we began removing some of these stones we noticed how carefully they had been packed, on exactly the same principles used in the building of a dry stone wall. Stability of the ballast was of course vitally important, for if it shifted the results could be disastrous; nevertheless, it was revealing to see just how tightly and securely it had been loaded into the hold. The stones were packed in such a way, however, as to be quite easy to pull out from the top; this was because the lower timbers had to be checked by the crew from time to time in case they were leaking, and this could only be done by systematic trenching through the ballast until the whole floor had been examined strip by strip. As the *Santa Maria* had battled her way through the Atlantic storms with her shot-weakened hull leaking badly, work on the hull timbers below the ballast must have been a constant and hideously unpleasant task for the ship's carpenters and caulkers as they struggled in almost total darkness to find and stop up the leaks, wading up to their knees in the foul bilgewater which slopped in the ballast trenches. Now, in order to examine these same timbers, we were going to use exactly the same trenching method, and by exposing selected strips through the ballast we intended to examine, measure, and subsequently reconstruct on paper an exact plan of the wrecked ship's remains.

Our first trench followed the line of what proved to be the forward section of the ship's keelson, the structural member which runs along the inner hull directly above the keel, clamping down the ribs and forming, with the keel, the backbone of the ship. The keelson was made up of carefully jointed lengths, 10 inches broad by 8 inches deep, with rib slots cut out of the underside. These dimensions were unusually slight for a ship of the *Santa Maria*'s size; a first hint that the Armada ships were not as solid and massively built as had often been supposed. Along the keelson we found the stumps of upright stanchions or pillars which had carried the beams of the orlop, the lower hold deck. Four of these actually remained in place, and we identified the positions of two more by the mortice holes cut in the keelson to receive them. All the wood was sea-blackened oak, still remarkably solid after four centuries of immersion, with the marks of the shipwright's adzes still crisp upon it.

Hard up against the stanchions, running along the line of the keelson, were two 20-foot planks, each 1 foot broad by 2 inches thick, set on edge one atop the other. They were not fastened in any way, being held in place solely by the pressure of ballast against the uprights. Sir Henry Mainwaring, in his 'Seamen's Dictionary' of the early 17th century, describes loose boards like these which, he says, were used as shoring when the ballast was moved from one side of the hold to the other to careen the ship, or during routine trenching to check the floor timbers for leaks. They would also have helped to prevent the ballast from shooting sideways in heavy seas.

Thirty-five feet from the bow of the wreck, on the axis of the keelson, we uncovered a complex structural arrangement which puzzled us at first. A rectangular box of boards and upright posts, now partly collapsed, had been built up lengthwise directly above the keelson. This box was so constructed as to withstand pressure from outside, and not inside, which suggested that its purpose had been to hold an open well within the ballast in order to keep the stones clear of something which lay inside it.

As we dug further down we reached the conclusion that this box had been built around the step of the ship's great mainmast. Of the step itself, or the massive heel of the mast, there was no trace. But there were a number of clues which told us that this was where the mast had been. First we found that the keelson, where it passed through the box, was double its normal thickness. We knew, from ancient shipbuilding treatises and from more recent parallels, that the keelson was always made thicker at this point to bear the heavy weight of the mast. The keelson inside the box, furthermore, was massively torn and splintered, as though by the ripping out of a heavy structure which had once been bolted to it. We next uncovered three strong timbers running athwartships from the starboard side of the well. Their inboard ends were neatly squared off and bevelled, as if they had been intended to butt into and support some component no longer in place.

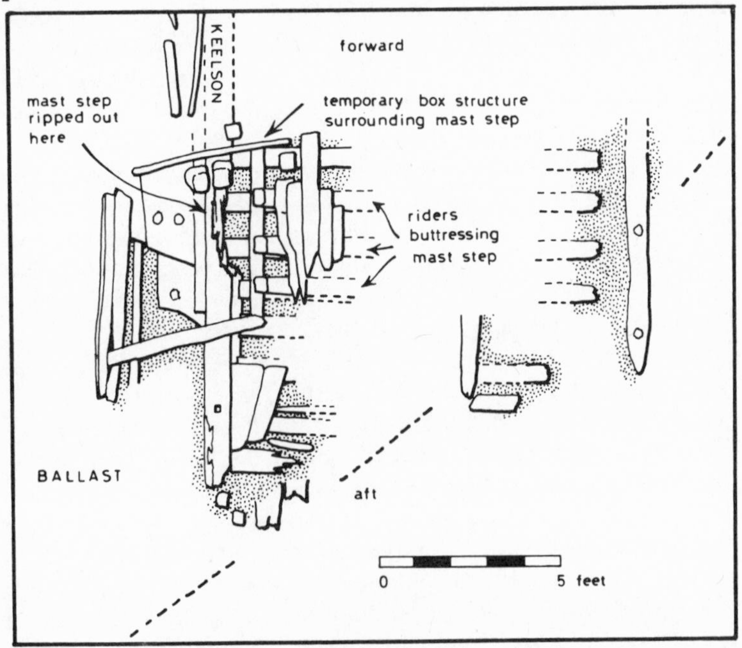

Fig. 9. *Santa Maria de la Rosa:* mast step

It took us more than 6 weeks to excavate and survey this interesting structure but the results, when we had analysed them, told us a great deal about the ship and about the wrecking. We were able to deduce that the mast had been stepped in a recessed wooden block bolted to the keelson, which had been specially reinforced to bear its weight, and was buttressed athwartships by three large riding timbers on each side. On close examination the rectangular box which surrounded the step proved to be a makeshift and evidently temporary structure, its flimsy rough-

and-ready carpentry in marked contrast to the solid strength of the main components. Its function puzzled us until we looked once again at what we knew of the *Santa Maria*'s history before she reached Blasket Sound. Of course! In the storm outside Corunna she had lost her mainmast, and under the personal supervision of the Duke of Medina Sidonia a new one had been fitted on 10th July 1588. 'Yesterday,' he had written to the King the following morning, 'we finished putting the new mast into the *Santa Maria de la Rosa* of Oquendo's squadron, after a great deal of trouble, as we were over 6 hours in getting it upright.' In order to lower the new mast into place the area surrounding the step would have had to be cleared of ballast and revetted with shoring, which is what the box structure was. The realisation brought us very close to that gruelling six-hour operation in which the huge mast, weighing several tons, was set upright in its step, and we could almost visualise the anxious figure of the Duke of Medina Sidonia (who, since he was no seaman, was probably getting in the way) fussing around these very ballast stones and timbers as he attempted to supervise and encourage his men in their heavy task.

The way in which the mast had collapsed and the distortion of the structure around it allowed us to reconstruct with some confidence what had happened when the ship had been wrecked, in just the same way that an accident inquiry can piece together the sequence and causes of a disaster from the wreckage it leaves behind. The collapse of the mainmast was evidently a major factor in the break-up of the ship, and this must have happened very soon after the sinking — probably when the ebb tide began to exert its full pressure on the upright mast, spars, and rigging. The solid block of wood in which the heel of the mast had rested had been ripped away from the keelson, tearing out the great bolts which had held it down in a confusion of jagged splinters. The distortion of the keelson and the buttressing riders at this point shows that the mast collapsed down tide, across the lie of the ship, and its collapse must have helped to break the hull in half. We found abundant signs just aft of the mainmast to suggest that the ship had broken into two parts, and this explained the puzzling way in which the ballast mound sharply changed direction at this point, trailing off down tide some 50 degrees away from the axis of the forward section of the ship.

We could now deduce what had happened when the ship hit Stromboli. The *Santa Maria* probably struck the rock about midships on the starboard side as she swung stern first on her fouled anchor, and the sharp pinnacle must have holed her from keel to waterline. She sank quickly, stern first as she had been when she struck, and landed heavily on the shingle bottom just south of the reef. The impact would further have weakened her structural integrity, particularly amidships, for the mast would have acted like a giant piledriver when she hit the bottom. Then the tide, as it began to ebb strongly, ripped the mast out, continuing the break to port, which had already started on the starboard side, across the weakened keel and keelson. The ship would now be virtually in two halves; the lower forward section weighted down with the bulk of the ship's ballast, and the stern with its tall aftercastle trailing off down tide and taking with it, apparently, the bulk of the upper works and decks of the ship together with their contents and guns. Thus there was left on the site only what we had found — the lower forward section of the ship, and the bulk of the ballast. Even the ballast from the stern section remains; this must have spilled out as the stern lifted up and drifted away, and the cascading ballast rocks entombed one of the disaster's victims and a large pewter plate, for us to find nearly 400 years later. Where the rest of the wreck now lies is anybody's guess; it could be miles away, and it is certainly in very deep water.

We would have to be content, therefore, with the part of the ship we had found. The examination of the structure continued. We uncovered some of the ship's main rib timbers, near the bow end of the ballast mound. Every second timber was 8 inches wide by 1 foot deep, and between each pair of these main frames was a rather smaller timber, fitting into the gap with only an inch or so to spare. The rising curve at the end of the timbers showed that they had broken or rotted away close to the turn of the bilge. The outer planking, which was 3 inches thick, was pinned to the frames with long wooden dowels or 'trenails', studded in groups of twos and threes. We managed to extract one for examination. It had been carefully spokeshaved to a round section (trenails of later date are generally lathe-turned), and the ends were slightly bevelled so that it could be driven home. At each end there was a wedge split to tighten up the trenail once it was in place. Sir

Henry Mainwaring stressed the importance of tight fitting, well seasoned trenails; loose or sappy ones, he warned, will make a ship 'continually leaky, and it will be hard to find'. We did find several trenails with lead patches over them, evidently to seal leaks. Trenails were used in preference to iron fastenings because the latter were prone to salt water corrosion ('iron sickness', Mainwaring calls it), though we found that the plank ends, or butts, where springing stresses were strongest, had been clenched with iron bolts just as Mainwaring prescribes.

In the course of our structural investigations we had made a number of small finds. Most came from around the mast step. One was a brass scale pan with three suspension holes and graduated internal lines. The galley of 16th century ships was usually located in the hold, just forward of the mainmast, and this scale pan was probably one of the officially certified ration measures issued at Lisbon to the fleet before it sailed. A considerable amount of brushwood and charcoal found in the same area indicates the probable location of the galley fire, which was evidently laid directly on top of the ballast stones. This arrangement must have given rise to a severe fire hazard, and we could readily understand the Duke of Medina Sidonia's strict instructions that all galley fires were to be doused before sunset. Fuel for cooking was provided by the brushwood dunnage which was used to pack the water and provision casks tight in the hold, and by breaking up the casks themselves when they were empty. We found among the stones many fragments of barrel staves and hoops, and a great assortment of brushwood including beech, ash, and pine branches.

In this area we also found considerable quantities of bones and pottery. The bones were of sheep, cattle, and chicken, and must have come from the casks of salt meat listed in the Armada inventories. Occasional luxuries, however, supplemented the monotonous and unhealthy official diet, as we discovered by finding — in amazing condition — a whole brazil nut.

1969 was the year of the unfortunate *Grey Dove* affair, which Sydney Wignall describes in the Appendix. This prolonged lawsuit severely curtailed diving and archaeological work on the *Santa Maria,* and it was not until the end of June that we were able to get *Jimbell,* Wignall's 50-foot Motor Fishing Vessel which had been specially converted to our requirements, working in Blasket Sound. *Jimbell* was skippered by 'Tug' Wilson, one of the Clearance Divers who had been with us during the 1968 season and who had since left the Navy. That we were able to obtain the full-time services of so experienced a diver and coxswain was an extreme stroke of good fortune, for Wilson was married and had a family to support, and could not have survived on the same voluntary unpaid basis as the rest of the team. Wignall's expedition funds were by this time precariously low, and he could not afford to pay Wilson a living wage. But we had some good friends in Dingle. All that summer the cast and filming crews of MGM's epic *Ryan's Daughter* had been in the district shooting this Robert Bolt/David Lean production against the magnificent background of the Blaskets. We got to know many of them well, and their Public Relations team was especially kind in helping us in various ways, particularly with photographic work. When the head of the P.R. team, Bayley Silleck, heard about the problem of paying Wilson, he immediately wrote out a cheque on his own account to cover the wages, shrugging off our embarrassed thanks by telling us that he thought what we were trying to do was fascinating, and that he was glad to be able to help. His obvious enthusiasm and belief in what we were doing was even more gratifying to us than the cash.

To provide *Jimbell* with the heavy moorings she would need over the wreck site our good friend and colleague Desmond Branigan, of Marine Research, had at his own expense obtained four massive anchors and heavy chains, and these were laid in position under the skilled direction of Captain O'Shiel of the Irish Lights vessel *Ierne.* With *Jimbell* working we adopted a new daily routine; instead of driving to Dunquin each morning to launch the inflatables from the jetty we sailed direct from *Jimbell*'s berth in Dingle, cooking breakfast and preparing for the dive during the two-hour outward trip. On arrival in Blasket Sound we picked up the buoyed permanent moorings and positioned the boat exactly where we wanted her. This gave us a firm base from which to work and a solid platform for the heavy excavation equipment.

The most important item was the suction pipe or air-lift, which had been built by the expedition's two engineers, Jack

Sumner and Tony Long. This device consisted of a hollow pipe, 6 inches in diameter and nearly 100 feet long, which creates a powerful suction force at the sea-bed via compressed air which is pumped down through a hose from the surface. It is therefore an extremely effective tool for clearing away sand and shingle, although great care has to be taken lest valuable artefacts are sucked up it as well.

We used the air lift to finish clearing the areas of ship structure that we had been examining, and then proceeded systematically to excavate in the shingle around the ballast mound in the hope of increasing our very sparse collection of artefacts. It was not easy to handle the air lift in that fast and unpredictable tide; attempting to control the towering tube was often a hazardous business, especially when it became blocked, for this caused it to become exceedingly buoyant and the whole rig would soar towards the surface only to crash down again in the direction of the hapless operator when the blockage cleared. Fortunately, there were no serious accidents. Sometimes a blockage could not be cleared, and in this event we had to raise the whole air lift to the surface (it was normally kept flat and anchored to the sea-bed when not in use) in order to tow it to Great Blasket Island where we could beach and clear it. This tedious operation would take the best part of a working day.

Now we had *Jimbell* we did not return to Dingle between the two daily dives, but anchored off the Great Blasket to await the next tide. This gave us some 5 hours to recharge the aqualungs with a small portable compressor and cook ourselves a mid-day meal. We enjoyed the fine summer days which we spent anchored in the lee of the island, close to where the Spanish ships had ridden so many years before. We would swim or laze on the long white beach, ramble around the deserted island hunting rabbits for the pot, or simply lie sunbathing on the gently rocking deck until it was time to dive again.

The results of our excavations around the edge of the ballast were very disappointing indeed. We found almost nothing at all; confirming at least our theory that the ship had broken into two parts and that the main part had drifted away was probably the correct one. The only really interesting find we made in two months of intensive effort with the air lift was a mast truck, the iron-bound wooden cap which was placed at the mast head to provide channels for flag halliards to run through. What flag, we wondered, had been run up on this truck? Was it the official crusading banner of the Armada, the red cross on a white background which proclaimed holy war? Could it have been the royal arms of Spain, with the encircling chain of the Order of the Golden Fleece? Or was it perhaps the squadron flag of Guipuzcoa, six silver cannons in pairs on a red background?

Our other preoccupation during these final days of the expedition was the completion of the expedition film. Sydney Wignall, who was an experienced cameraman, had shot 16 mm film sequences of all aspects of our work above and below the water; this he subsequently edited along with film he took in 1970 on the *El Gran Grifón* wreck site at Fair Isle to make a documentary film which was shown on B B C 2s archaeological programme 'Chronicle'.

By the end of August we had reached the conclusion that there was not much more that we could do on the site. We had examined and excavated the wreck as far as we had been able, and we had carefully recorded the results. It was obvious to us that we were not going to find the ship's guns, or indeed much more in the way of artefacts of any kind. Wignall's money was running out, and all of us were reaching exhaustion point, both physically and mentally. It had been a very hard two years. The equipment, too, was beginning to break down under the strain of constant hard use. Without fuss, and with relief as well as disappointment, Wignall decided to wind the expedition up. The team had, he felt, achieved all that could be reasonably expected of it and that was that.

A check on the log books revealed just how much the team had in fact achieved in Blasket Sound. In the course of nearly 100 swim-line searches, during the first three months of the 1968 season, we had covered some 15 million square yards of sea-bed — by far the largest area search ever made. More than 1 000 individual man-dives by a total of 43 divers representing no fewer than 20 sub-aqua clubs went into these searches. The number of dives we carried out on the wreck, for the remainder of that season and for the full 6-month season in 1969, amounted to just under 2 000—some 500 man-hours actually spent on the *Santa Maria de la Rosa.* My own personal tally on the wreck, I calculated, was 72 hours.

At the end, there were only five of us left: five who had been with the team since the very earliest days; Wignall, myself, Oldfield, Sumner and Smith. We decided, before we left Ireland that summer, to go on a brief Armada pilgrimage — a quick journey up the west coast to visit other places with Armada connections, and dive at some of them. The trip was more of a holiday relaxation than a serious expedition. We took a caravan, our diving gear, an inflatable boat, and a portable compressor. Leaving Dingle early one morning we passed by Scattery Island, on the Shannon, where the Levanter *Anunciada* had been fired and abandoned by her crew, and we camped that night near Dunmore Castle, County Clare, close to where Sir George Carew had salvaged guns from a large Armada wreck in 1589. The ruined castle from which Sir George carried out his operations still stands, and the traditional site of the wreck was pointed out to us by the local people. We dived there, but found nothing. That afternoon we searched for traces of the Armada ship off Mutton Island, again without result. Next, passing through Galway town where so many of the luckless Armada survivors had been executed, we visited the Corraun Peninsula, opposite Clare Island in County Mayo. We spent several days in this delightful spot, diving at a number of places which were supposedly associated with the Armada without finding anything of interest. Finally, a brief visit to Blacksod Bay, where Don Alonso de Leiva's great *Rata Encoronada* had been wrecked, and a dive in Broadhaven, brought us to the end of our trip.

We returned to Dingle, packed our belongings, and went our separate ways. Some day, we felt sure, we would find another Armada shipwreck. But, for the time being at any rate, we had had enough.

Now that the physical work in Blasket Sound was complete it remained for us to assess the evidence we had recovered and attempt to place it in its historical context. What had our two years of work on the wreck of the *Santa Maria de la Rosa* taught us, if anything, about the Spanish Armada? We would have to re-examine all the original documentary evidence concerning the Armada, look again at how historians had interpreted it, and see whether our physical findings—unarguable evidence gathered from the actual remains of an Armada ship—added to, or perhaps modified, the understanding of that great historical event. Wignall and I decided to share the research; he would look into the question of the ship's armament, for this had always been his main interest, while I — since I had been the most intimately concerned with uncovering and surveying the *Santa Maria*'s structural remains — would concentrate on a study of the ship herself.

The results of Wignall's research are presented in his chapter on Armada shot. My own task in interpreting the structural evidence was hampered at the beginning by the fact that, although I probably had more practical experience of examining a 16th century great-ship's hull than anyone living, I was also in almost total ignorance of the principles of old-time naval architecture. This subject is, naturally, little studied, and since there were few experts to whom I could turn I set out to become one myself. I spent six months in libraries, archives, museums, and art galleries, soaking up everything I could find on the subject; poring over treatises in English, Spanish, Dutch, French, Italian and Swedish by shipwrights and theorists of the 16th, 17th and 18th centuries; working through contemporary inventories of ships' gear and fittings; examining paintings, prints and sketches of ships by contemporary artists; reading books and papers by modern naval historians and experts. Only when I felt sure that my knowledge of armed wooden sailing ships was as complete as I could make it did I turn my attention once again to the *Santa Maria de la Rosa* and to the plans we had made of her remains at the bottom of Blasket Sound.

What we knew of the ship from documentary sources did not amount to much. She had, according to Spanish calculations, a burthen of 945 tons, and she was vice-flagship of the squadron of Guipuzcoa — the squadron, that is, based on the Atlantic port of San Sebastian. Martin de Villafranca, her captain, himself came from that town. Was she, therefore, one of Spain's new and weatherly Atlantic-built ships, constructed on sleek race-decked lines similar to the latest royal galleons? Or was she, as we know so many of the Armada's ships to have been, a large and beamy merchant carrack of Mediterranean build, a great-ship of the kind which had been plying between the ports of that inland sea and even voyaging as far as the Baltic for a

I. Blasket Sound and Island from the mainland above Dunquin. Recalde and Aramburu sailed into the Sound from the west between Great Blasket and Beginish and anchored south of Beginish (in the centre of the picture). The *Santa Maria de la Rosa* sailed in from the north and later sank just beyond Dunmore Head (at the left).

II(a). One of the massive iron-bound wooden gun-carriage wheels from *La Trinidad Valencera* lying on the sea bed. This discovery has led to the conclusion that the heaviest Armada guns were part of a siege train intended for Parma's march on London. The measuring rod is 1 foot long.

II(b). Two of the bronze guns from *La Trinidad Valencera* in the conservation tank: the larger is a 50-pounder curtow weighing nearly 2½ tons and cast by Remigy de Halut at Malines, while the long culverin-type is by Zuanne Alberghetti of Venice.

century or more? It is misleading to over-simplify the distinction between 'Atlantic' and 'Mediterranean' methods of shipbuilding, for by their nature ships travel widely and developments in ship building and fundamental design tend to spread and intermingle beyond purely geographic boundaries. None the less, long evolutions in different environments produce underlying traditions which are very strong, and broad distinctions can often be drawn. The three-masted sailing ship had evolved in the Mediterranean as a natural development of the 'great' or 'round' merchant ship, the origins of which lie deep in antiquity. Such ships relied on an overall structural integrity based on many small and closely fitting components which, although individually slight, locked together to form a relatively solid self-stressing shell. On the Atlantic seaboard of Europe, however, there had evolved during the course of the 16th century a quite different type of sailing ship, which may loosely be described as the 'galleon' type: a ship specifically designed for oceanic sailing; fast and weatherly, longer and lower in the water than a 'round' ship of the same tonnage, yet still capable of carrying a heavy armament and sufficient provision for long voyages. Shipwrights following the newly developed 'Atlantic' methods apparently favoured an internally stressed hull of fewer but more massive structural components, each of which possessed strength even in isolation.

Technical shipwrights' drawings of this period are extremely rare, particularly in Spain, but I discovered one dating to 1587, the year before the Armada sailed. The draughtsman was Diego Garcia de Palacio, a Spanish nautical expert working in Mexico, so his drawings certainly relate to 'Atlantic' type vessels. The feature I took particular note of was the positioning of the ship's mainmast, which stands exactly over the mid-point of the keel. This feature can be seen on other contemporary ships of known Atlantic-build, including English ones. The mainmast of large Mediterranean merchant ships, on the other hand, was always set much further forward, so as to give the round-bellied hull more directional stability. A Venetian treatise of the mid 15th century actually gives us an exact formula for establishing the mainmast position on a 'round' merchant vessel — 'to fix the mast step . . . divide the keel into five parts and leave three parts (less 1 foot) aft'.

Since we knew the approximate position of the bow end of the

Santa Maria's keel, and the exact position of the mainmast step, it was a simple matter to apply these fundamental 'Atlantic' and 'Mediterranean' criteria to the remains to see which result appeared to be the most sensible. The distance between bow and mast step was $37\frac{1}{2}$ feet; a measurement which gives us, according to the 'Atlantic' formula, an overall keel length of 75 feet. This figure is far too short to accommodate the *Santa Maria*'s listed 945 tons, even allowing for the Spanish tendency to exaggerate tonnages. The result, however, becomes much more plausible if we apply the Mediterranean formula, from which, assuming the $37\frac{1}{2}$ feet between mast step and bow to be two parts *plus* 1 foot forward, the following calculation emerges:

$$1 \text{ part} = \frac{37.5 - 1}{2} = 18.25 \text{ feet}$$

$$\text{Therefore keel length} = 18.25 \times 5 = 91.25 \text{ feet.}$$

If the *Santa Maria* was a broad beamed 'round' ship, as indeed the quantity and spread of her ballast appears to confirm, then a keel length of 91 feet would reasonably accommodate her tonnage. Furthermore, the run of ballast aft of the mast step—that is, the ballast left behind by the stern when it broke away—closely agrees with the theoretical measurement of the stern according to this formula. The inference is clear: the *Santa Maria de la Rosa,* vice-flagship of the Atlantic-based squadron of Guipuzcoa, shows the unmistakable characteristics of a Mediterranean build. The very slightness of her construction, evident in the dimensions of keelson, frames, and outer skin, further point to Mediterranean influence. Perhaps it was for this reason that she failed to cope well with Atlantic conditions, as exemplified by the loss of her mainmast off Corunna. Many Armada ships appear to have been over-masted in relation to their structural strength, for one finds trouble with masts cropping up time and again in Spanish narratives and reports of the campaign and its aftermath. Mediterranean hulls could certainly be strong, but their strength was, as it were, the strength of an egg-shell, which, while intact, can resist great external pressure, but which, if only slightly cracked, easily collapses. A good instance of the inherent weakness of a Mediterranean build, although concerning a ship of much later date, is to be found in the case of H.M.S. *Daedalus,* a 40-gun frigate wrecked on a reef south of Ceylon in 1812. She had been captured from the French, runs her captain's narrative, and had been 'built at Venice, and perhaps never intended by the Enemy to go out of that Narrow Guelph; for when taken into dock at Deptford she was found to possess the Timbers, and Scantlings, of an 18-gun ship . . . the weight of her Upper Works and Guns, when she touched (the reef), crushed her slender frame to pieces.'

A vessel of this kind would indeed be prone to strain if overmasted, and perhaps more than anything else would be desperately vulnerable to gunfire. The *Santa Maria* had been, it will be recalled, 'shot through four times, and one of the shots was between the wind and the water, whereof they thought she would have sunk . . .' In this connection it is also worth noting that the group of ships which suffered the lowest casualty figures in the Armada campaign was the squadron of ten newly built 'Atlantic' galleons of Castile (10% losses), while the heaviest losses (80%) were sustained by the Levant squadron—the only squadron in the Armada whose ships are all known *for sure* to have been of Mediterranean origin.

That the *Santa Maria* should have the build and appearance of a Mediterranean merchantman is interesting, but not inexplicable. Confusion has arisen in the past from the fact that two of the Armada's four auxiliary squadrons were supplied by the wholly Atlantic squadrons of Guipuzcoa and Biscay, and in consequence an Atlantic origin has been assumed for their ships. But this was certainly not the case. It appears that many of the 'great' ships or *naos* of the four auxiliary squadrons (Guipuzcoa, Biscay, Andalucia and Levant) were large Mediterranean merchantmen, especially converted at Lisbon for warlike purposes by the addition of fighting castles and extra armament. Most of these ships were owned by Italian, Venetian, or Ragusan maritime interests, and had been based and therefore presumably built on Italian and Adriatic coasts. The Marquis of Santa Cruz, in his 1586 Armada 'Proposal', states that forty large merchant ships suitable for use in the Enterprise of England were available from the ports of Ragusa (modern Dubrovnik), Venice, Sicily, Naples, and other Mediterranean harbours as far as Cartagena. When the Armada actually sailed in 1588 a great many of its ships indeed came from these very ports. The great maritime city-state of Ragusa, though it owed no direct allegiance to Spain, often supplied ships to Philip II for use in war as well as in peace, and it is known that a number of ships were provided by Ragusa for the Armada, four of them large vessels. And Ragusa was only one source of these big ships. Others which took part in the campaign came from Venice, Sicily, Naples, Leghorn, and Genoa.

When the Armada finally sailed from Lisbon it included sixty-four large fighting ships, exclusive of galleys, galleasses, and hulks. Twenty of these — the ships belonging to the squadrons of Portugal and Castile — were definitely Atlantic-built galleons. Four more — the Indian Guard merchantmen attached to Castile — also appear to have been 'galleon' types. This leaves the forty large ships of the auxiliary squadrons, including the *Santa Maria de la Rosa,* to be accounted for. To what extent, if at all, do these ships represent the forty ships which, in 1586, Santa Cruz tells us were available from Mediterranean ports?

The fact that Santa Cruz's number, and the number of auxiliary ships which actually sailed with the Armada, is exactly the same, is certainly an interesting coincidence. But we must be careful, because Santa Cruz's figures represent a proposal and not an actuality, and we must bear in mind, moreover, that the same proposal shows that a further thirty-five merchant ships were available from the Atlantic coast provinces of Guipuzcoa and Biscay. Did any of these 'Atlantic' ships actually sail with the Armada, or were they entirely replaced with Mediterranean-based vessels?

I believe that the latter hypothesis is the correct one, and Santa Cruz's own figures themselves help to support it. In his 'Proposals' he gives the average burthen of the ships available from Guipuzcoa and Biscay as only 350 tons apiece, while the vessels to be had from the Mediterranean, he notes, average out at 600 tons each. Although there is no evidence of a major shipbuilding programme on the Atlantic coast between 1586 and 1588, the average tonnage of the Guipuzcoan and Biscayan squadrons as they actually sailed in 1588 works out at 650 tons per great-ship — almost double the 1586 figure for the squadrons, and almost exactly the same as the average tonnage of the ships known to have been available from Mediterranean ports in that year. It thus appears almost certain that, between 1586 and 1588, the indigenous ships of the Atlantic squadrons were entirely replaced by large temporary warships of Mediterranean origin.

A convincing reason for this drastic change of policy is not far to seek. Obviously, if all other things had been equal, the weatherly native-built Guipuzcoan and Biscayan ships would have been better suited to operations in the Atlantic than the round, cargo-carrying Levanters. But the Mediterranean *naos* had an advantage over the Atlantic merchant ships which, though it would not have mattered so much in 1586, by 1588 had become all-important. They were much larger, more impressive, and better suited to carrying a heavy battery of armament and soldiers.

In 1586 the proposed auxiliary fleet was to carry a light, mainly defensive armament; one suited to the non-combatant, troop carrying role then envisaged for it. Details of the guns intended for these ships are to be found in Santa Cruz's proposals: they include nothing larger than 9-pounder demi-culverins plus some obsolescent stone-throwing perriers and a mixture of various other light, generally obsolete, pieces. By 1588, however, the larger auxiliary ships in fact positively bristled with heavy, offensive armaments, up to and including 50-pounder whole cannons, as abundant documentary evidence suggests and our recent discoveries confirm. This sweeping change in armament policy is, in every instance for which there is evidence, confined to the auxiliary fleet. That the squadrons of the auxiliary fleet should have been, at exactly the same time as this new armament was introduced, re-equipped with large Mediterranean-built ships cannot be coincidence. The smaller Atlantic ships of Guipuzcoa and Biscay must have been abandoned because their small size made them unsuitable for the proposed new armament. It is a question of cause and effect, and the cause must undoubtedly have been the decision, evidently taken some time during 1587 (in which year the squadron of galleys based at Cadiz had made a pathetic showing against the firepower and manoeuvrability of Sir Francis Drake's ships during his famous 'beard singeing' raid), to abandon the forty-strong galley fleet which was to have sailed against England in direct support of the royal squadrons of Atlantic-built galleons. Galleys, the Spaniards (and particularly Philip himself) had come to realise, were not suited to modern naval warfare under Atlantic conditions; though fast and highly manoeuvrable they were defenceless against broadside artillery, and could carry only a few light prow-mounted guns themselves. A supporting arm upon which so much reliance had once been placed, if abandoned because of proved obsolescence, had somehow to be replaced, and it is in this context that the Armada's reformed auxiliary fleet, with its new and heavy armament, is surely to be seen.

And so, as hastily converted capital ships, these large Mediterranean merchantmen sailed for England. Their poor sailing qualities were a further burden to the unfortunate Duke of Medina Sidonia, who can have obtained little consolation from King Philip's remarks in answer to his complaints about them:

> The reason why the Levant ships and the hulks are longer away than the others [wrote the ever optimistic monarch to his storm-bound Captain-General at Corunna] is that they could not lie to so well, and were obliged to run with the wind . . . I see plainly the truth of what you say, that the Levant ships are less free and staunch in heavy seas than the vessels built here, and that the hulks cannot sail to windward; but it is still the fact that the Levant ships sail constantly to England, and the hulks go hardly anywhere else but up the Channel, and it is quite an exception for them to leave it to go to other seas. It is true that if we could have things exactly as we wished, we would rather have other vessels, but under the present circumstances the expedition must not be abandoned on account of this difficulty.

A great many of the Armada's front-line ships were therefore not real fighting ships at all, but weakly built and clumsy merchantmen, They were big ships, it is true, but very vulnerable ones; scarcely the monsters that a contemporary propagandist described them as being, 'framed of planks and ribs four or five foot in thickness'. On the contrary, many of them were of eggshell-weak Mediterranean build. Little wonder they fared so badly in the fierce gun battles against the powerfully armed, strongly built ships of the English fleet.

Sir John Hawkins, who as the energetic reformer of Queen Elizabeth's Navy Royal can be relied upon to recognise ship-types when he sees them, was able to count, in the confusion of battle, no less than twenty great Venetians and argosies (i.e. Ragusans) of the seas within the Strait' among the Armada. Was the *Santa Maria de la Rosa* one of them? The evidence of her own broken hull certainly suggests she was, and her Mediterranean origin is further hinted at by two pieces of documentary evidence. The first comes from the narrative of Pedro Coco Calderon, of the hulk *San Salvador,* who, out in the North Atlantic, saw far to leeward 'the ship Villafranca of Oquendo (i.e. the *Santa Maria*) and *another Levantine ship*'. And if final confirmation is needed it is surely to be found in the fact that the ship's pilot — an appointment which required him to take full practical responsibility for the running of the vessel — came from Genoa.

II · *El Gran Grifón*

'THIS DAY OF OUR GREAT PERIL...'

TOWARDS the end of 1588 Queen Elizabeth's minister Lord Burghley took a copy of the Armada's Lisbon muster (which had been published as a propaganda broadsheet in almost every European capital before the fleet sailed) and wrote against the appropriate sections, with understandable satisfaction, his own knowledge of the fates which had befallen the various ships and men listed. This document, still bearing Burghley's annotations, is now in the British Museum Library.

Against the name of Juan Gomez de Medina, Captain-General of the squadron of *urcas* (supply-hulks) Burghley wrote: 'This man's ship was drowned 17 Sept; in ye Ile of Faroe neare Scotland . . . this man came to Scotland and passed into Spayn.' Of Gomez de Medina's flagship, *El Gran Grifón* (650 tons, 38 guns) Burghley comments '. . . this was generall of ye urks', noting also that she was 'of Rostock'.

Rostock, on Germany's Baltic coast, was in the 16th century a powerful Hanseatic Lordship, or free-trading city state. The port's heraldic emblem was (and still is) a golden *griffin* and from this, no doubt, *El Gran Grifón* took her name. With the other Hanseatic towns of Lübeck, Wismar, Danzig, Hamburg and Bremen, Rostock played a considerable part in supplying ships and material for the Armada. The reasons for their alliance with Spain are not far to seek. The political fragmentation which the Reformation caused in Northern Europe had placed the largely Catholic enclaves of the Hanseatic League on an isolated and dangerous limb, and the idea of a military counter-reformation led by Spain naturally appealed to them. This consideration, however, did not weigh as heavily as their own economic decline — a decline which could be related, in some measure at least, to the recent and vigorous growth of Dutch and English maritime power.

The Baltic ports, moreover, were vital to Spain's own strategy in Northern Europe. In the 1580s the theatre of operations revolved largely around the Spanish Netherlands, and in view of the hostile neutrality of France and Anglo-Dutch control of the Channel, supply-bases in the Baltic were infinitely preferable to ones on the coasts of Biscay. Hanse merchants transported most of the bulk grain from Germany needed to feed the vast Spanish armies campaigning in Flanders. Sea-supported warfare of this kind also demanded great quantities of raw and manufactured materials most of which were, conveniently, obtainable from the Baltic region. The most important of these was timber, particularly Norwegian pine for masts, but there were other vital commodities too; tar and pitch for caulking and sheathing, cordage and canvas, anchors and military stores, not to mention ever increasing supplies of metal which a growing munitions industry demanded. Manufactured ordnance also found its way to Spanish arsenals aboard Hanseatic ships.

When serious preparations for the Armada were set in hand at Lisbon, therefore, an increase in maritime activity at once became apparent in the Baltic. Records kept at the toll-fortress of Elsinore, where dues were exacted from all traffic into and out of the Baltic, show that no fewer than 377 shipping movements involving vessels from Rostock alone took place in The Sound during 1587. The nature of much of this traffic is also well documented. In June 1586, for instance, twenty-five Baltic hulks, laden with pitch, sails and shrouds, sailed from Hanseatic ports for Spain taking, for security reasons, the longer 'north-about' route around Scotland. Some weeks later nine other German hulks, out from Hamburg and similarly laden, were intercepted and captured by English ships. In retaliation the city of Hamburg wrote to the King of Spain 'offering him (the use of) the port of Hamburg, which is capable of sheltering a large fleet'.

In December 1586 King Philip authorised the requisitioning of all large ships which put into Spanish ports, irrespective of their nationality, to take part in the Armada. Some of the states which owned vessels thus impounded — notably Venice and Florence — protested vigorously, but in vain. There is nothing to suggest that any such complaint was voiced by the Hanse merchants whose ships sailed with the fleet for they were, by choice, already contracted to the Spanish crown, and had evidently intended to take part in the enterprise from the beginning. Less than a month after Philip's requisitioning decree twenty more German hulks docked at Lisbon and discharged cargo.

Baltic hulks were sturdily built ships designed for cargo capacity rather than speed, and although seaworthy they were very clumsy. Their main disadvantage was that they could not sail close to the wind. The Flemish artist Breughel has illustrated this distinctive northern type of vessel in considerable detail, showing its squat deep-bellied hull, its high charged and unstepped stern with two lateen mizzens, and its lack of an elaborate fighting castle at the bow. It is worthy of note that while some of the other merchant ships which sailed with the Armada were fitted at Lisbon with such castles in order to convert them into temporary warships, none of the hulks appear to have been modified in this way. From the first they were not reckoned to be fighting ships.

It is against this background that we must look at the squadron of hulks as they actually sailed with the Armada. In the final muster at Lisbon there were twenty-three of them, with a total tonnage of more than 10 000 tons — a tonnage which made the squadron, incidentally, by far the largest command in the fleet. In some instances their names indicate their origins; the *Barca de Amburg,* for instance, and the *Barca de Anzique* (Danzig). The flagship, we know, came from Rostock, and there can be little doubt that the remaining *urcas* were also Baltic hulks, in generic type if not always geographical origin (several were probably Flemish and one, the *San Andres,* seems to have been Scottish). They were the pick of the Hanseatic vessels which, for almost two years, had carried war supplies in support of the projected Armada. Their function was now to provide the same cargo-support on active service, as well as to act as auxiliary troop-carriers and hospital ships. The Duke of Medina Sidonia himself emphasised their non-combatant role by ordering, in his General Instructions, that 'great care and vigilance is to be exercised to keep the squadron of hulks always in the midst of the fleet . . .' Such armament as they carried, as the discovery of *El Gran Grifón* has now confirmed, was light and essentially defensive in character.

El Gran Grifón was present at the first muster held at Lisbon on 7th January 1588, and when she sailed with the fleet at the end of May she had forty-three mariners and 243 soldiers on board. The soldiers belonged to the *tercio* of Nicolas de Isla, and three of their company officers — Patricio de Antolinez, Pedro Hurtado de Corcuera, and Esteban de Legorreta — sailed with them. Whether or not Gomez de Medina had a large personal staff is not known; none are mentioned, but assistants aboard a stores ship were more likely to have been notaries rather than noblemen, and would not therefore merit inclusion on the official lists. The only *aventurero* to sail with the *Grifón* was Vasco de Lago — and he evidently a minor one, for he boasted only a single retainer.

El Gran Grifón was one of those ships which failed to gain the shelter of Corunna during the storm which dispersed the fleet, and together with many of her sister hulks and some of the larger and clumsier members of the fighting squadrons (including *La Trinidad Valencera*) she made for the next rendezvous position off the Scillies, thinking that the rest of the Armada would do the same. Not until 6th July did these ships straggle back to rejoin the main fleet at Corunna, 'smelling of England' as Juan Martinez de Recalde put it. They had cruised off the Scillies for a fortnight, where they had taken a couple of prizes, and would have taken others had not an accidental fire broken out on board one of the hulks during the action.

When at last the Armada shook itself into battle formation off Land's End, ready for the advance up Channel, Gomez de Medina's unwieldy supply-ships were carefully shepherded into the safety of the great crescent's centre. Only once, amid all the disjointed glimpses of the week-long series of battles which followed, do we hear of a hulk effectively engaged with the enemy. That hulk was *El Gran Grifón,* and it is interesting to speculate on a possible reason for her involvement, against orders, in the fighting. While it may be going too far to suggest that it was actually a dishonour for a Spanish gentleman to serve aboard a non-combatant supply ship, it can have been no great honour either. Captain-General Juan Gomez de Medina was a scion of a noble family, and he had served with distinction before the Armada (as he was again to serve after) as Governor of the great port and arsenal of Cadiz. His personal device as well as the arms of Spain and the crusading banner of the Armada's eighth squadron flew over the squat round hull of *El Gran Grifón.* To Gomez de Medina's Castilian pride this demanded that, whatever his orders might be, he should not shirk action. He had already been hotly involved in the small engagement off the Scillies at the end of June, and in the Channel battles we first hear of him on 2nd August off Portland when, according to a witness aboard one of the big Portuguese galleons, 'Juan Martinez de Recalde came entering in from the south-east, and with him and Juan Gomez de Medina and other ships we came so nigh (to the enemy) that with one piece of cast iron we shot two bullets into the Vice-Admiral of the English, and there was great shot of ordnance....'

When dawn broke the following day off the Isle of Wight *El Gran Grifón* was once again to be seen away from her regular station within the sheltering heart of the Armada, straggling on the tip of the fleet's exposed right wing. But if Gomez de Medina's defiant courage in facing the enemy may have been praiseworthy, his grasp of the situation into which he had precipitated himself was not. The last place for a ship of below average speed and manouevrability is on the weathermost tip of the formation in which she sails; the more so when a nimble and powerful enemy holds the weather gauge. Seeing their chance, several English warships crowded on sail to cut the straggler off. As a battle-situation inexorably developed, the faithful Recalde in his great *San Juan de Portugal* moved to the *Gran Grifón*'s support, and several large Biscayans followed. The English, however, got there first, and though we are nowhere specifically told that Sir Francis Drake was the officer involved, this was the wing of the Armada against which he habitually operated, and there can be little doubt that the *capitana* (flagship) mentioned in Spanish accounts of the action was in fact the *Revenge.* With terrifying ease the Englishman glided abeam the wallowing *Grifón,* gave her a devastating broadside at close range, neatly came about and gave her another, then crossed her stern and raked her at half musket shot. It was a grim illustration of what manoeuvrability and fire-power, skilfully applied, could achieve. The *Grifón* sustained seventy hits to her hull, and seventy killed or wounded on her decks.

El Gran Grifón was now beset on all sides, *Revenge* alone bearing on her more than three times her own weight of gunpowder. But no Englishman offered to board the wounded hulk, for her bloody decks were thronged with more than 200 angry and highly trained soldiers, who can surely have wished nothing better than to come to pike's length with their elusive tormentors. True to form, however, the English held off and plied their culverins, determined to finish off the stubborn Spaniard without recourse to close combat.

This one-sided fight lasted only the few minutes it took for Recalde's column to come into action, when the whole right rear of the Armada became heavily engaged. *El Gran Grifón,* by this time practically disabled, remained in the thick of it until Medina Sidonia sent in the galleasses to bring her out. One of them managed to pass her a cable and she was towed back to the safety of the fleet, where she was able to make emergency repairs.

In spite of her damage, the *Grifón* took an active part in the rearguard action off Gravelines, and managed to keep up with the Armada during the first leg of the 'north-about' voyage, when the prevailing winds were favourable. When the fleet took up a westerly course to round the north of Scotland, however, she began to fall behind. On 20th August the Armada passed between North Ronaldsay and Fair Isle, where Scottish fishermen reported a 'very great fleet of monstrous great ships, being about 100 in number', running westward before the wind. On the same day Don Balthasar de Zuniga, a staff-officer aboard Medina Sidonia's flagship *San Martín,* landed at Scalloway in Shetland in order to take a fast pinnace to Spain with despatches for the King. Somewhere about this time, or perhaps slightly before, *El Gran Grifón* with three other ships lost contact with the main body. Two of the *Grifón*'s companions were hulks, the *Barca de Amburg* (600 tons, 23 guns) and the *Castillo Negro* (750 tons, 27 guns). The third ship was a big Venetian from the Levant squadron, *La Trinidad Valencera* (1 100 tons, 42 guns), about which much more will follow on later pages. It may be noted in passing that Baltic hulks and Mediterranean great-ships alike shared the same poor sailing qualities.

The four ships struggled together towards the south-west for the next 12 days, making almost no progress into an almost ceaseless headwind. Then, on 1st September, the *Barca de Amburg,* her seams open and her pumps choked, signalled that she was foundering. Her company of 250 was transferred to the *Grifón* and the *Valencera* just before she sank. Three nights later, somewhere off the north-west coast of Ireland, the remaining ships lost contact with one another. The *Castillo Negro* vanished in the blackness without trace, never to be heard of again, while *La Trinidad Valencera* was to be wrecked a fortnight later in Kinnagoe Bay, Donegal.

Alone, and in almost continually adverse weather, *El Gran Grifón* beat south-westwards into the Atlantic, until on 7th September a great storm fell upon her causing her seams, already severely strained by battle-damage, to open up; some of them, we are told, gaping as much as a hand's breadth apart. An oncoming sea would certainly sink her, so she had to run wherever the weather took her.

Details of the terrible voyage which followed have come down to us through the diary of one of the survivors. We do not know for certain who he was, but there are some slight grounds for supposing that he may have been Gomez de Medina himself. The diarist records how for 3 days they ran northwards until they reached 'an island of Scotland in about 37½ degrees latitude'. This can only have been St. Kilda, a stark and isolated mass of rocks far beyond the western Hebrides. Then the wind veered unexpectedly into the north-east, allowing the almost helpless vessel to turn once more 'towards our dear Spain'. For three days the favourable wind held, carrying the ship to the latitude of Galway Bay, but then it backed once more into the prevailing south-west quarter. The story is now taken up in the survivor's own words:

> We turned back and sailed for three days more to the latitude we had been in before. But when we got there, we were fit only to die, for the wind was so strong and the sea so wild that the waves mounted to the skies, knocking the ship about so that the men were all exhausted, and yet unable to keep down the water that leaked through our gaping seams.[1] If we had not had the wind astern we could not have kept afloat at all. But by God's mercy during the next 2 days the weather moderated, and we were able to patch up some of the leaks with ox-hides and

[1] On this same day, 400 miles to the south, the *Santa Maria de la Rosa* was wrecked in Blasket Sound. The weather pattern indicates a strong mid-Atlantic cyclone which during the equinox often gives rise to violent storms along Europe's whole western seaboard.

planks. And so we ran until 23rd September, when the wind rose against us, and we decided to turn back again and try to reach Scotland. On the 25th we sighted some islands which the pilots said were Scottish [probably the Outer Hebrides]. And so we sailed till the 26th to the north-east in search of land. On that day we sighted some other islands which we tried to avoid so as not to be lost [these must have been the north Orkneys]. The weather then got so strong that our poor repairs were all undone, and we had to keep both pumps always going to keep the water down. So we decided to sail for the first Scottish land even if we had to run the hulk ashore. Late in the afternoon of the 26th we were troubled to see an island to windward of us [perhaps Westray or Papa Westray], for it was getting dark and we feared to be among islands in the dark. We had hoped we were free of them. During the night we gave ourselves up for lost, for the seas ran mountains high, and the rain fell in torrents. At two in the morning we saw an island right ahead of us [possibly the north part of Sanday] which, as may be supposed, filled us with consternation after all the tribulation we had passed through. But God in His mercy at that moment sent us a sudden gleam of light through the dark night, and so enabled us to avoid the danger. Then the blackness fell as dense as before. Two hours afterwards another island loomed up before us, so close that it seemed impossible to weather it. But God came to our aid as usual, and sent a more vivid gleam than before. It was so bright that I asked whether it was the daylight. This was the Isle of Cream [almost certainly North Ronaldsay], where we had decided to bring up if we could not reach Scotland, though we did not recognise it until later as we had run further than we had thought. At dawn, two hours later, we discovered it, and in fear of the heavy sea we tried to get near the island again, but after trying for four hours we found it impossible. The sea kept giving us such dreadful blows, that truly our one thought was that our lives were ended, and each one of us reconciled himself to God as well as he could, and prepared for the long long journey that seemed inevitable. As to force the hulk any more would only have ended it and our lives the sooner, we determined to cease our efforts. The poor soldiers, too, lost all spirit to work at the pumps. The two companies — 230 men in all, and 40 we had taken from the other ship [the *Barca de Amburg*], had pumped incessantly and worked with buckets, but the water still increased, till there were thirteen spans over the carlings (as they call them) and all efforts failed to reduce it an inch. So we gave way to despair, and each one of us called upon the Virgin Mary to be our intermediary in so bitter a pass; and we looked towards the land with full eyes and hearts, as the reader may imagine. And God send that he may be able to imagine the smallest part of what it was like, for after all there is a great difference between those who suffer and those who look upon suffering from afar off.

At last — when we thought all hope was gone, except through God and His holy Mother, who never fails those who call upon him—at two o'clock in the afternoon we sighted an island ahead of us. This was Fair Isle, where we arrived at sunset, much consoled, though we saw we should still have to suffer. But anything was better than drinking salt water. We anchored in a sheltered spot we found, this day of our great peril, 27th September 1588.

Fair Isle lies half-way between the Orkneys and the Shetlands, a tiny hummock of land set in the midst of one of the most unpredictable stretches of water imaginable, where the tides and currents of the North Sea and of the Atlantic mingle in furious confusion. Those on board the foundering *Grifón,* as they battled through swirling cross-seas from the south-west, can have drawn little comfort from their first view of the rugged Atlantic side of the island; a three-mile stretch of sheer cliffs rising, at the north end, to 600 feet, against which the Atlantic rollers (made all the heavier by the south-westerly gale) pounded with relentless fury. But in a south-westerly good shelter and reasonable anchorage can be gained immediately on rounding the rocky islets off the island's south-eastern tip, and it seems likely that there were those on board who knew these waters well. The *Grifón* was under charter from Rostock, and such an arrangement usually includes a working crew. Many of her forty-three seamen, therefore, were probably Germans. The chances are strong that some of these men had been to the Shetlands before, for a vigorous trade with the Hanseatic ports had been going on from the early part of the 16th century at least, and probably from much earlier. At any event, *El Gran Grifón* unerringly sought out the only sheltered haven to be found, and managed to drop anchor there just before dark.

There is some doubt as to what actually followed since the

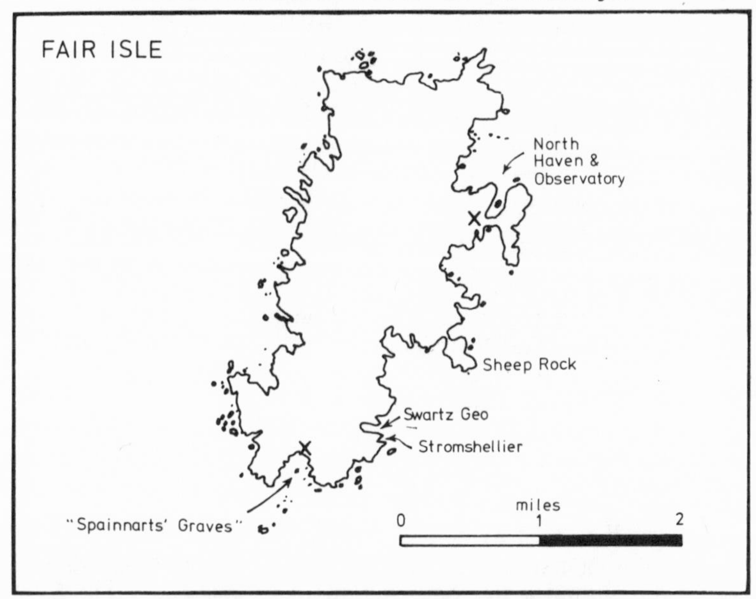

Fig. 10. Fair Isle showing Stroms Hellier

survivor makes no direct mention of the wrecking at all. The ship eventually sank in the narrow inlet of Stroms Hellier, as island tradition relates and our recent discoveries confirm. But how, exactly, did she get there?

There seem to be a number of clues. The survivor tells us, later in his account, that he and his comrades actually landed on 28th September, the day *after* they arrived. This presupposes that they rode out the night of the 27th/28th aboard the ship. Our diarist had, moreover, previously stated that it was their intention, if necessary, 'to run the hulk ashore': this being the best way of getting everyone off alive and perhaps also of salvaging stores and valuables. But since night in late September closes quickly in these latitudes, any attempt to run the ship aground on an unknown and dangerous shore in the growing dusk would have been out of the question. The only course open was to wait for first light, in the hope that the ship could be kept afloat for a few hours longer. With salvation so close, tired hands no doubt found new spirit to work at the pumps. Probably at dawn on the following day — the 28th — the beaching attempt was made.

From the *Grifón*'s anchorage only one place suitable for such an attempt presents itself. At the head of Swartz Geo, a cliff-surrounded inlet some 50 yards wide and 300 yards long, there is a gently sloping pebble beach. To look towards this beach from seaward today confirms that the Spaniards had no other sensible choice; everywhere else within sight are tall overhanging cliffs and breaking razor-edged reefs.

But for some reason their attempt to get in there failed. As we now know, the *Grifón* ended up in Stroms Hellier, a small cave-ended *geo* just beyond the entrance to Swartz Geo. A more unsuitable place in which to run a sinking vessel is difficult to imagine. The cliff above is a terrifying overhang, in places 150 feet high. There are jagged reefs on either side of the *geo,* and a spine-like outcrop runs down its middle, while the sea bed is a contorted fusion of shallow rocks and sheer gullies, some nearly ten fathoms deep.

Stroms Hellier is a name of Norse derivation meaning 'Cave of the Tide-Race', and in this name a clue to the mishap perhaps lies. Though the water inside the inlet itself is calm and sheltered, a fierce current springs up almost without warning mid-way through the tidal cycle and rips across its mouth. It is not difficult to imagine the sinking *Grifón,* her hold full of water, wallowing towards the mouth of Swartz Geo, doubtless towed by her boats and assisted by warps secured ashore. It is equally easy to imagine how she could have become caught in this unexpected current, to be carried past the narrow entrance to Swartz Geo finally to wedge herself tight between the centre rocks of Stroms Hellier and the shore. There, she must quickly have gone to wreck, though she did hold together long enough to allow her people to escape.

Island tradition still recounts how the Spaniards climbed to safety up the masts and over the yards, which were leaning against the cliff, and in the circumstances there are no grounds for doubting that this actually took place. Immediately over the fore part of the wreck as it now lies there is an overhanging ledge 70 feet above the water, against which the foremast must have lodged. After some of the men had scrambled ashore the Spaniards probably rigged a hoist on this ledge, just as we did 382 years later, in order to salvage what they could before the ship broke up and sank. It seems certain that they brought off whatever treasure the ship carried ('they saved their treasure and are come hither unspoiled' wrote a Scotsman when, some months later, the survivors reached Edinburgh), though evidently they were able to recover little else.

Another tradition, more colourful and perhaps more fanciful, relates that when the Islanders saw the Spaniards resplendent in their dully gleaming breastplates and morions advancing cautiously across the hummocky grassland towards the crofts, they thought that the grim strangers were the Angels of the Heavenly Host, and that the Day of Judgement had arrived. The popular legend that the Spaniards introduced the famous knitting patterns to Fair Isle seems to be without substance; apart from more academic arguments (the patterns are almost certainly of Norse derivation) it is difficult to imagine that the hard-bitten warriors of the *tercios* included many knitting enthusiasts in their ranks. But there is an interesting and little known subsidiary tradition, for which I am indebted to Mr. Tom Henderson of Lerwick, that one particular Fair Isle knitting motif — a stylised bird-like shape — supposedly represents the figurehead of the wrecked ship. Could it, perhaps, have been a golden *griffin*?

The Spanish diarist gives a first-hand account of their enforced stay on the island and describes the folk who then inhabited it:

> We found the island peopled by seventeen households in huts, more like hovels than anything else. They are savage people, whose usual food is fish, without bread, except for a few barley-meal bannocks cooked over the embers of a fuel they use, which they make or extract from the earth and call turf. They have some cattle, quite enough for themselves, for they rarely eat meat. They depend mainly upon the milk and butter from their cows, using their sheeps' wool principally for clothing. They are very dirty people, neither Christians nor altogether heretics. It is true they confess that the doctrine that once a year is preached to them by people sent from another island, nine leagues off, is not good, but they say they dare not contradict it, which is a pity. Three hundred men of us landed on the island, but could save none of our provisions. From that day, 28th September, till 14th November, we lost fifty of our men—most of them dying of hunger—amongst others the master and mate of the hulk. We had decided to send a messenger to the governor (i.e. of the Shetland mainland) to beg some boats to carry us to

> Scotland to seek rescue, but the weather was so heavy that we could not send until 27th October, when the weather was fine, and they went. They have not yet returned in consequence of the violence of the sea.

The sudden arrival of 300 desperate men on so small an island was a situation fraught with danger for the inhabitants. Winter was drawing close, and the seventeen crofts would have set aside provisions only for their own survival through the hard months ahead. There would be little to spare for the hungry castaways. Robert Menteith, an Orkney man writing in 1633, would have us believe that considerable trouble resulted:

> . . . the Spaniards at first eating up all they could find, not only cattle, sheep, fishes and fowls, but also horses . . . the Islanders in the night carried off their beasts and victual to places in the isle where the Spaniards might not find them: the officers also strictly commanded the soldiers to take nothing but what they paid for, which they did very largely, so that the people were not great losers by them, having got a great many Spanish *reals* for the victuals they gave them. But now the people fearing a famine among themselves kept up their victuals from the Spaniards; thus all supply from the isle failing them they took up their own bread (which they had preserved) which being dipped in fish oil they did eat, which also being spent it came to pass that many of them died of hunger, and the rest were so weakened, that one or two of the islanders finding a few of them together could easily throw them over the cliffs, by which many of them died.

A comparable tradition survived until quite recent times; it was told to the late Robert Stuart Bruce of Symbister, who made a systematic study of the Shetland wrecks, by a Mr. Walter Traill Dennison of Orkney (Dennison was also reputed to have in his possession 'a rapier which was given to the head of the Traill family by an officer of the Spanish Armada'). This tradition relates that a number of the Spaniards were killed by the Islanders, who caused the heavy flagstone roof of the large turf hut in which they were sheltering to fall in on them. Other versions of this tradition state that the shipwrecked men were 'pitten ower da bauks' (a story clearly derived from Menteith's account), or lured to an open-air feast at the foot of a deep *geo* where they were cut off and drowned by the incoming tide.

These violent tales of murder (which, incidentally, are strenuously denied by the Islanders to this day) do not stand up well to close scrutiny. In particular they are not authenticated by the presumably factual evidence of the Spanish diarist, who makes no mention of atrocities on either side though he speaks movingly of the hunger he and his comrades endured. Fifty of them, he tells us, died — but from hunger, not murder. What is almost certainly their mass-grave was exposed by sea erosion on the south coast of the Isle around the beginning of this century, when bones, buckles, and coins were apparently found. The spot is now known on the Isle as 'the Spainnarts' Graves'.

In any case, it is surely beyond belief that 300 armed men would have allowed a few crofters to take liberties of the kind Menteith suggests. The surprising thing is the *lack* of enmity which appears to have existed between Spaniard and Islander. Indeed, the memory of this friendship remains strong in Island tradition today, echoing an impression given by a report sent to Philip II in 1588 that 'a gentleman of rank (Gomez de Medina) was in the Scottish islands, where the people were very much pleased with him, as he paid well for everything he had of them'.

The true story is probably more compassionate and honourable than Robert Menteith would have us believe. No doubt the Spaniards did feed on fish and sea birds (both abundant on Fair Isle), plus whatever the islanders were willing to spare. As lack of fodder usually meant that non-breeding stock had to be killed off in winter anyway, it may actually have been to the crofters' advantage to sell some of the carcasses for hard cash. Beyond that, Menteith's story seems to be a 'dress-up' job of a kind journalists are ever prone to use, with a touch of gory sensationalism added for good measure. In any case, the clear fact that the Spaniards did not immediately seize all the island's provisions by force reflects the greatest humanity and discipline on their part, and leadership of a high order is implicit in the whole situation. Once again we seem to catch a glimpse of those qualities of courage, endurance and honour which flourished so brightly in 16th century Spain.

We may, perhaps, place more reliance on Menteith's account

of the Spaniards' escape from Fair Isle, sometime about mid-November. 'Notice came to Andrew Umphrey of Burra (in Shetland) who, having a ship of his own, instantly went to the Isle and brought them to Shetland, where for the space of 20 days or a month they met with better entertainment. The Duke (i.e. Gomez de Medina — Menteith, like many later writers, confuses him with the Duke of Medina Sidonia) stayed at Quendale (an estate on Shetland's south coast) till the ship was made ready, where, imagining the people did admire him, he made his interpreter ask Malcolm Sinclair (the Laird of Quendale) if he had ever seen such a man? To which Malcolm replied in broad Scots, unintelligible to the interpreter, "Farcie in that face, I have seen better men hanging in the Burrow-Moor".'

That the Spaniards did stay for a time at Quendale is well confirmed. John Brand, who visited the Shetlands in about 1700, met an old lady who as a girl had spoken to people who in their own youth had actually seen the Spaniards there, and up to the middle of the last century it was said that 'the walls and earthworks which they hastily constructed may yet be traced, along with the foundations of temporary buildings'. Agricultural improvements now seem to have obliterated these remains.

At daybreak on 6th December 1588 one of the town baillies of Anstruther, a seaport on the north coast of the Firth of Forth, woke the local minister, the Reverend James Melvill, to inform him that 'there is arrived within our harbour a ship full of Spaniards'. The Spanish officers, went on the agitated baillie, had come ashore, but had been ordered back to their ship until the magistrates were consulted. 'Up I got with dilligence,' continues Melvill in his diary, 'and assembling the honest men of the town, came to the Tolbooth; and after consultation taken to hear them, and what answer to make, there presents to us a very reverend man of big stature, of grave and stout countenance, grey-haired and very humble like, who, after muckle and very low courtesy, bowing down with his face near the ground, and twitching my shoe with his hand, began his harangue in the Spanish tounge...'

This polite and distinguished stranger was none other than Juan Gomez de Medina, new arrived from Shetland with his men. With considerable tact in the face of Melvill's Calvinistic outbursts, directed against Roman Catholicism in general and the Armada in particular, he sought for himself and his comrades asylum and relief in Scotland so that they could return peaceably to their homelands. In due course authority for the Spaniards to land was granted; Juan Gomez and his officers were spirited off to be entertained by the local laird, while the ordinary soldiers and mariners were 'suffered to come to land, and lie all together, to the number of thirteen score, for the most part young beardless men, sillie, trauchled and hungered, to the which kail, porridge, and fish was given . . .'

Among the officers who came ashore Melvill mentions 'Captain Patricio, Captain de Legoretta, Captain de Lufera, Captain Mauritio, and Seignour Serrano.' Patricio Antolinez and Esteban de Legorreta were, as we have already seen, infantry officers who had joined the ship at Lisbon. De Lufera's name does not appear on the Spanish lists, though perhaps he was a survivor taken off the sinking *Barca de Amburg.* Seignour Serrano was probably one of the Armada's 180 priests. 'Mauritio' was certainly Maurice Desmond, a kinsman of the Sir John Desmond we encountered on an earlier page leading a revolt against the English in Kerry. His brother, Thomas, also seems to have been aboard the *Grifón,* along with another Irishman called Robert Aspolle. Many Irish expatriates, as well as some Catholic Englishmen, sailed with the Armada as *aventureros* or *entretenidos.* Their names had been carefully ticked on Burghley's list, no doubt to indicate that special treatment was reserved for them should they have the misfortune to fall into English hands.

In 1588, however, Scotland was quite independent of her southern neighbour, though her youthful King James VI, Protestant-nurtured son of the Catholic martyr Mary Queen of Scots, was moving towards a union of the crowns which was eventually to become reality when he succeeded to the English throne on Elizabeth's death in 1601. Scotland's position as a neutral power when England's mortal enemies were cast upon her shores was, therefore, a somewhat delicate one. James had no wish to alienate Elizabeth over the matter, but at the same time, since he was still not secure on his own throne and many of his powerful vassals were practising Catholics with declared sympathies towards Spain, he had to tread carefully when dealing with the Armada survivors who were flooding into Scotland. It was a situation which easily might get out of control, and it deeply worried the king and his ministers, as well as the English ambassador in Edinburgh who wrote to Burghley that 'there are 1 000 or more (Spanish soldiers) in this country, which is dangerous among these turbulent spirits (i.e. the Catholic lords); the soldiers may be sent away, the captains stayed for ransom.'

The *Grifón*'s survivors were brought to Edinburgh, where they were well treated. They were, of course, an immediate target for the pro-Spanish Catholic faction's schemes. An English agent, Thomas Fowler, wrote on 15th January 1589 to Francis Walsingham, the shrewd chief of Elizabeth's secret service, informing him that 'Dun John de Medina [*sic*] and divers captains of the Spaniards are going hence with great credit. . . . on Sunday last I dined with Bothwell, where I found four Spanish captains whom he entertains.' Francis Stewart, fifth Earl of Bothwell (nephew of the fourth Earl, James, third husband of Mary Queen of Scots), was hereditary Lord Admiral of Scotland; a wild and unscrupulous bravado who, though posing as a Protestant, was in fact the power behind the plotting Catholic lords. He naturally singled out Gomez de Medina, by far the highest ranking Spanish officer to land in Scotland, for special intrigue. Hopeful of leading a Catholic *coup* in Scotland supported by Spanish arms, Bothwell arranged for one of his fast fly-boats to take Medina and the Irish expatriates back to Spain 'to let the Spanish king know how many well willers he hath in this country, and to procure but 4 000 Spaniards, good shot, and leaders, with a sum of money to be brought hither with speed.' Bothwell clearly intended that the Spanish soldiers already in Scotland should remain there and await these reinforcements. By the end of January Gomez de Medina and his aides were on their way. The situation was potentially critical and very confused; there are even hints that King James himself might have welcomed Spanish support, could he but control it, in prosecuting his own designs on the English crown. In the event, however, Spain proved as disinclined to embark on such a venture in Scotland as she had in Ireland. In March 1590 the Catholic lords were still awaiting the aid promised by the 'King's servant John Medina so soon as wind and weather may serve . . .', but they waited in vain, for it never came.

In any case, the Spanish officers and soldiers whom Medina left behind themselves had no intention of remaining in Scotland, unpaid, in order to further a nebulous political cause which they had no sound motive to support. By late July 1589 Captains Antolinez and Legorreta had 'gathered their companies, which were dispersed through Scotland, to Edinburgh, Leith, Burntisland and Kirkcaldy, 660 ready to be shipped — 400 serviceable men, the rest sick, lame, miserable wretches who will never be fit for service'.[1] There had been considerable difficulties in arranging their passage. First, there was the question of a safe-conduct, lest weather forced them to put into an English port. The Spaniards, hardly surprisingly, refused to sail without one. Then there was the matter of paying for the voyage. The Spaniards had insufficient funds left to cover the ten shillings a head demanded, and the King of Scotland, anxious as he was to be rid of these uninvited guests who were fast becoming an embarrassment to him, none the less balked at paying their fare home. Even Queen Elizabeth was asked to provide the money, though the answer she gave to this request — perhaps fortunately — is not on record. Eventually the harassed and bankrupt Duke of Parma, still slogging away at his thankless and bitter war in the Netherlands, was prevailed upon to put up the cash, and four Scottish merchant ships were chartered.

Even then there were hitches. A Leith merchant called Lamb came forward to claim that his ship had been impounded in a Spanish port, and that his son, its master, had been imprisoned by the Inquisition. He demanded that Spanish hostages be taken against the safe return of his son and property. Finally, just before the Spaniards were due to sail, there was a dockside brawl at Leith in which an English trumpeter was killed. How these difficulties were resolved is not known; resolved they must have been, however, for by 8th August the *Grifón* survivors and their companions had departed.

James Melvill, the Anstruther minister, has a postscript to add. He tells us that when Gomez de Medina got back to Spain he 'showed great kindness to a ship of our town, which he found

[1] These men may be accounted for as follows: 260 from *El Gran Grifón*, 300 'which were in Norway', plus, probably, 100 or so survivors from Ireland. A further hundred who had been ashore when the Tobermory ship blew up did not arrive in Edinburgh until slightly later.

arrested at Cadiz on his home-coming, went to court for her, and spoke on behalf of Scotland to his king, took the honest men to his house, and enquired for the Laird of Anstruther, for the minister, and his host, and sent home many commendations . . .'

Juan Gomez de Medina was not a man to forget his debts of honour.

CAVE OF THE TIDE-RACE

TOWARDS dusk on Friday 8th May 1970 I arrived on the cliff top above Stroms Hellier. Earlier that day I had made the three hour crossing to Fair Isle from Shetland in the *Good Shepherd,* the 50-foot boat which is the island's lifeline with the outside world. The broad tide race of Sumburgh Roost which runs between Sumburgh Head and Fair Isle had been whipped by a strong easterly wind into a chaos of steep and conflicting breakers such as I had rarely encountered before, even in Blasket Sound. But to the crew of the *Good Shepherd,* who make the trip twice weekly for mail and supplies, such conditions are commonplace, breeding in them an instinctive natural seamanship which would be difficult to match anywhere.

The same easterly was driving a heavy sea into Stroms Hellier as I stood looking down into its dark chasm 150 feet below me. I had tried to picture this place many times during the preceding winter as I poured over the historical documents, air photographs, and large-scale maps which had led me to it, but its reality was wilder and more sinister than I had imagined. The north side of the gully was an enormous sloping slab of rock, split by a great fissure called the Kist o' Stoodle. The slab ended in a ragged tumble of rocks which could be reached with difficulty from where I stood by a precarious cliff path. Cutting the inlet into two halves, north and south, ran a shallow spine, breaking the surface at its landward end in a reef which, in these heavy seas, was a confusion of swirling white water and rythmically tossing weed. The southern point of the *geo,* Point Saider, was a flat slab of rock from which the cliff rose 60 feet to a small overhanging ledge, the Cup o' Skairharis. From the big overhang at the geo's apex, on which I stood, I could hear the hollow pounding of the surf as it broke in the twin caves immediately under my feet. This fearsome place was where, according to our researches, *El Gran Grifón*'s remains should lie.

It had been Sydney Wignall's idea to look for this wreck. Not long after our return from Ireland in 1969 he had written to Roy Dennis, warden of Fair Isle's famous bird observatory, to ask whether there was any local tradition of the wreck's whereabouts. Dennis's reply had been quick and enthusiastic. Yes, the precise location was still pointed out by the islanders, and as far as he knew no one had ever dived there in modern times. How soon could we come out to explore?

The seeds of an expedition were thus sown. *El Gran Grifón.* An Armada flagship. Wrecked not in deep water like the *Santa Maria de la Rosa,* but evidently in a gully close inshore. It seemed unlikely that any of her hull could have survived in such a place, but what of the guns? We had lacked Armada guns on the *Santa Maria*; might we perhaps find them here? Wignall and I at once recognised the attractions of mounting a limited expedition to Fair Isle to find out. Both as a search operation and, if we found the wreck, as an excavation, the difficulties and costs would be much smaller than those encountered in Blasket Sound. And there was a great deal, we felt, that might be learned from a study of *El Gran Grifón*'s remains.

What sort of guns, for instance, did she carry? Professor Michael Lewis, in making his assessment of the gun-strength of the Armada, put the *Grifón* into the 'front-line' category; that is, he believed that because of her flagship status she probably mounted a heavy offensive armament which included ship-smashing cannons and perriers, such as the major ships in the fighting squadrons carried. Was he right? If he was, then we might achieve our ambition of finding and studying large Armada guns. We ourselves felt it more likely, however, that the *Grifón,* though a flagship, was *not* armed as a front-line vessel; after all, we did know that the hulks, as a group, were intended to be non-combatant second-line ships. But very little real evidence existed of the nature of these ships' armament at all, and so if the *Grifón* herself proved to be of this category we might also expect to fill an important gap of knowledge.

That winter we laid our plans. Wignall worked on organisation and logistics; I on research. We made contact with the National Trust for Scotland, Fair Isle's owner, and with Tom Henderson, curator of the County Museum in Lerwick. Both endorsed the project, and offered full co-operation. Shetland

County Council, largely through Mr. Henderson's good offices, had already leased a number of historical wreck sites around the islands in order to prevent their indiscriminate plunder, and on our representations we were granted sole permission to carry out archaeological work on *El Gran Grifón*. In the meantime a dossier of research into the ship's background, and the circumstances of her wrecking, was building up. Over the coming summer, we decided, we would test our theories in the field.

Syd Wignall, because of other commitments, could not spend the whole 1970 season on Fair Isle, though he intended to be present during the first week and to come up again towards the end of the season to film the results of the project. We urgently needed two reliable men to make up, with myself, a permanent team. My brother Simon Martin gave up his job with a Public Relations firm to join us. He was not at that stage a diver, but he was a hard worker and he had plenty of enthusiasm, and he had keenly followed the Armada project since its beginnings in 1968. We signed him on; it would be far easier to teach him to dive than it would have been to find a qualified diver with the temperament and aptitudes we wanted. Then we made contact with Chris Oldfield, who since the *Santa Maria* expedition had been salvaging a Second World War wreck in the Hebrides. Oldfield promised to come to Fair Isle as soon as we had established ourselves there, and if the prospects looked good for an interesting season (typically, it was 'interest' rather than 'profit' which motivated him) he would spend the summer with us, and bring along his heavy salvage gear. This was a godsend to the project; partly for the equipment, but more for the man. Oldfield had already proved himself in Blasket Sound to be an ideal expedition member — dedicated, strong, a wizard at mechanical improvisation, and a diver of quite remarkable skill. Most important of all, he, Simon and I were firm friends, and could work in co-operative unison.

We now had that most vital of all expedition attributes — a sound permanent team. But, if things went well, there would be room for part-time voluntary help too. Alan Bax, Director of the Fort Bovisand Underwater Centre at Plymouth, offered to come and help us for a week in June, while a 16-man team from the Naval Air Command Sub-Aqua Club was scheduled to spend a fortnight with us in July, by which time we hoped that excavation work would be well under way.

Money — as ever — was the main problem. Somehow we managed to scrape together a loan of £500, but this was barely enough even to cover running expenses. At this critical moment a private individual very generously donated £250, which tipped the financial balance and allowed the expedition to go forward. Even so, we were still relying heavily on the goodwill and support of our friends. Syd Wignall in particular helped out by providing the diving equipment left over from the previous seasons and by loaning a small air compressor which he had recently bought and an inflatable boat flown over specially from Malta. What would otherwise have been an acute transport problem on the island was solved for us by the generosity of Aimers McLean of Galashiels, who loaned us one of their ubiquitous 'Gnat' hill tractors for the duration of the expedition. Finally, if a serious operation resulted from our initial discoveries, we could rely on Chris Oldfield's compact and highly reliable diving and salvage systems. We planned to start work at the beginning of June and carry through until mid August, by which time we reckoned that our money would have run out. What would happen then was anyone's guess. We were operating on faith and a shoestring.

But before we arrived in force, I planned to visit the island briefly to carry out a reconnaissance of the site, and to make arrangements for our working facilities and accommodation. So it was in early May that I stood looking down on the supposed site of the wreck in Stroms Hellier. But as I leaned into the easterly gale doubts began to assail me. Was the wreck really here? It seemed impossible that the exact spot could have been remembered for almost four centuries. And even if *El Gran Grifón* had sunk in the heaving and crashing waters below, surely all those years of storms such as the one now blowing, and far worse, would have brought down vast quantities of rock from the overhanging cliff to bury any relics beyond recovery?

Here, on the spot, I began to review the evidence we had gathered in the libraries and archives. We knew the traditional story of the wrecking in some detail, and it certainly fitted with what I could now see of Stroms Hellier. One could easily imagine a big vessel wedged tight in here, with her tall masts leaning against the overhanging cliff. Then there were the accounts of recoveries made from the wreck in later years. In 1593 — only 5 years after the wrecking — the notorious Earl Patrick of Orkney signed a contract with William Irvine of Sebay to the effect that he (Irvine) should 'address himself . . . unto the Fair Isle and there, by all means possible, shall win the ordnance that was lost there in the Spanish ship.'

It is very doubtful that this operation was ever put into effect, for no subsequent record of it appears to exist, but more than a century later effective salvage definitely was carried out on the wreck. Detailed information about these operations is to be found in the records of the Admiralty Court of Scotland which are now lodged in Register House, Edinburgh. An entry dated 17th February 1730 records a partnership contract which had been drawn up in 1727 between two noted 'wrackmen' (salvage entrepreneurs), Captain Jacob Row (or Rowe) of London and William Evans, a ship's carpenter from Deptford in Kent. The two men had agreed to fit out a vessel 'with the proper engines for diving upon and recovering a wreck supposed to be lying near the island called the Fair Island in the Orkneys.' On 12th March 1727 Row obtained permission from the Earl of Sutherland, who was Vice-Admiral of the Orkneys and Shetlands, '. . . to raise a Spanish ship, or man of war, called the Grand Admiral of Spain (and one of the Spanish Armada) mounted with 130 brass guns or thereabouts.' Row and Evans were to share equally in the profits of the venture. The diving 'engine' had been invented by Row, who claimed to hold an exclusive patent from the Crown which gave him sole rights to use it 'in all the British seas.'[1] Row's machine was an ingenious but terrifying contraption. Patent drawings of it and the boats and tackles used to work it still exist, and a detailed description of the device is to be found in Desagulier's *A Course in Experimental Philosophy,* published in 1744 (Vol. II p. 215):

> It is a tub or truncated cone made in the shape of a Scotch snuff-mill, in which the diver is shut up by a cover, fortified with hoops, as is also the body of the machine. The arms are put through the holes (in the machine) and made tight, either with or without leather hose upon the hands and arms. The

[1] Though Row held a patent on his engine, patents on almost identical machines had been issued to a number of other rival 'wrackmen'.

III(a). The Remigy de Halut gun from *La Trinidad Valencera* after preliminary washing in the tank. The inscription on the breech records not only the founder's name but also that of Juan Manrique de Lara, Captain-General of Artillery, and the date 1556.

III(b). The escutcheon on the gun showing the full arms of Philip II, with (left) the emblems of Leon, Castile, Aragon, Sicily, Granada, Austria, Burgundy and Brabant, and (right) the leopards and fleurs-de-lys of England. In 1556 Philip was, in name at any rate, King of England, since two years earlier he had married Mary Tudor. Surrounding the shield is the collar of the Order of the Golden Fleece, of which Philip was Grand Master.

IV(a). Dolphins for lifting the Remigy gun.

IV(b). The swivel gun from *La Trinidad Valencera* with encrustations removed: it is revealed exactly as its gun-captain left it in 1588, loaded with a powder-filled breech chamber held in place with an iron wedge and leather packing wad. A $3\frac{1}{4}$-inch stone shot is in the barrel, and there is a twist of hemp in the touch hole to keep the powder dry.

legs are within the machine turned back as when a man kneels. There is a glass to see through, from which the diver can wipe the dew or steam with his nose upon occasion, for his posture is to be let down with his face downwards. The air is shut up with him in his tub, and is about a hogshead in contents . . . a man shut up in it can remain in the water about an hour. Now, though this diving engine be better than a great many, yet it has the same inconveniency of not being fit for great depths. Captain Irwin,[1] who dived for Mr. Rowe, informed me that at the depth of 11 fathom he felt a strong stricture about his arms by the pressure of the water; and that venturing two fathom lower to pick up a lump of earth with Pieces of Eight sticking together, the circulation of his blood was so far stopped, and he suffered so much, that he was forced to keep his bed six weeks. And I have heard of another that died in three days, for having ventured to go down 14 fathom.

The machine was ballasted with a lead keel weighing about a quarter of a ton to counter its buoyancy, and lowered over the tender's side from a swinging jib to which was attached a triple block-and-tackle worked by a team of seamen. The diver was able to pass instructions or emergency signals to the surface by means of a light signal line. As the diver descended the growing weight of water would press on the machine in an attempt to equalise the low pressure air inside it (which, because the machine was totally closed, remained at surface or atmospheric pressure). This force would act directly on the diver's arms through the machine's waterproof sleeves of tightly laced oiled leather. At eleven fathoms the pressure differential would amount to nearly thirty pounds per square inch—close to the physiological limits that the human body could endure. The effect must have been hideously painful and uncomfortable, cutting off the circulation to cause the 'strong stricture' which Desagulier describes. Though the divers undoubtedly reached eleven fathoms (and evidently deeper, though with sometimes fatal results), these must have been short forays only, and most of their work would have been accomplished in much shallower water. Another severe limitation would have been imposed by respiration problems, for only the air trapped in the machine was available to the diver, and since this only amounted to a hogshead (52½ gallons) minus the diver's

[1] William Irvine, Customs Officer at Lerwick in Shetland.

own body volume—about 12 gallons in the case of a 12-stone man—it would require replenishment after a maximum of ten minutes. This was done by hauling the machine to the surface and pumping in fresh air through a bung hole by means of bellows. Only in this way would the working durations of one hour described by Desagulier have been possible.

With such equipment the intrepid Row and Evans proposed to salvage the remains of *El Gran Grifón*. At Leith the two men bought and rigged a sloop called the *Princess Mary* at a cost of £96 and sailed for Fair Isle. Receipts show that they purchased £10 worth of provisions from Robert Sinclair of Quendale (a descendant of the Malcolm Sinclair who had entertained Juan Gomez de Medina) and paid the same man, as proprietor of Fair Isle, £21 for rights to dive on the wreck. A Captain Simon Fraser of Broadland in Orkney contributed £140 : 16/- towards the enterprise, though more funds had to be raised later; in all, £500 was paid out in wages to sailors, hire of boats, and the purchase of provisions and materials.

Row and Evans were convinced that the wreck on Fair Isle was a 'treasure' ship, and had confused her, as did many others, with the Duke of Medina Sidonia's great flagship *San Martín*, which of course got safely back to Spain in 1588. Gomez de Medina's name was obviously the source of the confusion (he was in fact distantly related to Medina Sidonia) and he, as we know, had saved the treasure from the stranded *Grifón* and brought it 'unspoiled' to Edinburgh. Ignorant of this dispiriting fact, and wildly optimistic about the number of guns to be raised from the wreck (even the *San Martín* had only carried 48), the salvors set to their task with gusto, and on 28th July Thomas Gifford of Busta (on the Shetland mainland) wrote to the Earl of Morton informing him that 'the company of divers at Fair Isle have found the wreck of one of the Spanish Armada and have got 2 or 3 brass cannons and talk of a great prospect they have there of no less than 40 or £50 000 stg . . .' The existence of these guns is confirmed in the Earl of Morton's papers, for on 3rd May 1732 John Hay, a Leith shipmaster who had been involved in Row's enterprises, wrote to the Earl from Kirkwall informing him that he had, as instructed, 'engaged a boat to go to Fair Isle for the guns.' On 6th June Hay reported that 'the two brass guns were brought from the Fair Isle and shipped on board James Alexander's ship for Leith . . .' The guns ended up in a Leith box-maker's cellar, where they were eventually seized on behalf of Row's creditors. Their final fate is not known.

In an account of Fair Isle written in 1798 by the minister of Shapinsay in Orkney there is a reference to Captain Row's operations which names the precise location in which they took place. Concerning the natural *geos,* or inlets, he wrote:

> In several parts of this solitary isle, where the rock has been soft, or a stratum of clay has presented its surface, the sea has dug many deep gulfs or gullies to a considerable distance. Of this kind is the one on the S.E. side of the island, called *Stromsceilier,* in which, tradition asserts, one of the ships of the Spanish Armada, in the year 1588, suffered shipwreck. The inhabitants believe she is now converted into a rock, and covered with sea weed. Captain Roe, from England, in 1740 (sic), when fishing the wreck, was fortunate enough to raise two brass guns, of a larger size, and some other articles of a less value; but, having lost a man in the attempt, he desisted. About the year 1770 a ship bolt, long and thick, was thrown ashore in a neighbouring gulf, and is now in the possession of James Stewart, Esq., the proprietor.

At the beginning of August 1728, by which time Captain Row had realised that the *Grifón* wreck was unlikely to yield much of value, he received news which prompted him to abandon this enterprise entirely. He forthwith wrote to his patron Simon Fraser of Broadland stating his intention of 'sailing to the Island of Barra, where an East Indiaman is said to be lost, which I see lately confirmed in the news papers.'[1] He went on: 'I expect to return here by the latter end of this month or the beginning of the next at farthest and in the meantime I have ordered Mr. Robert Ross with a gang of hands to use his utmost endeavours in clearing the ground on the west side of the reef (i.e. the north-west side of the reef in the middle of Stroms Hellier) where I am well assured that the greatest part of the wreck lies.'

But Row never returned to Fair Isle, for the pickings he found off Barra were too good. On 23rd March 1728 the Dutch East India Company ship *Adelaar,* outward bound from Middelburg to Java, had been lost with all hands against the rocky

[1] Several reports of this wreck appeared in the *London Evening Post* and *Caledonian Mercury.*

promontory of Greian Head on Barra's exposed west coast.[1] She had been carrying a valuable mixed cargo, which included a fortune in coined and bar silver, and some gold. The salvage operations proved successful, and by the following spring virtually all the specie had been recovered. But the story has a sad ending; the salvors first fell out with one another over the division of spoils, and then the powerful Dutch East India Company moved in to sue them all for the return of the treasure (the pro-Hanoverian Dutch were able to exert strong pressure on George II's government to support their claim). In the complex litigation which followed Row was ruined, though he later organised expeditions to dive (without much success) on the Tobermory Armada wreck and another unidentified vessel off the Ayrshire coast.

I thought with admiration of these colourful 18th century adventurers as I stood on the cliff-top, trying to visualise Captain Row's salvage boats (he had used traditional Shetland *sixerns* [six oarings] for his work on the *Grifón*) moored in the inlet below, rigged with the jibs and tackles necessary to handle the strange diving engine in which he and his men were plunging 50 feet down to the sea floor. Stroms Hellier! Surely this was the same *Stromsceilier* — the Cave of the Tide-Race — mentioned in the Statistical Account. There in the middle, tangled with kelp, was the large rock which the 18th century inhabitants once believed to be the petrified remains of *El Gran Grifón*'s hull. Though that tradition (which survived into comparatively recent times) is patently untrue, it did seem to confirm that the ship had struck hereabouts. And the present inhabitants — many of them the descendants of 18th century islanders, or for that matter of 16th century ones — were in fairly precise agreement over the spot. It must have been in this very place that Captain Row recovered the two guns, 'and some other articles of a less value'. Anchors, perhaps, or ingots? Then there was the ship bolt, 'with stone adhering,' cast ashore some years later. The description of iron concretion, with which we ourselves were so familiar, was unmistakable. But even if there had been remains there at the beginning of the 18th century, would they still be recoverable now, almost two and a half centuries later?

There was one way to find out. I had brought with me a set

[1] The *Adelaar*'s remains were re-located in 1972 by the author and his colleagues Chris Oldfield, Tony Long and Simon Martin.

of diving gear with a twin cylinder aqualung which would give me a full hour's endurance at medium depth; time enough, I calculated, to search the gullies of Stroms Hellier for any visible clues. If we could find the wreck before we committed ourselves to the expense of an expedition, so much the better. It might even be possible, if we could provide solid evidence of the *Grifón*'s existence, to raise further funds, or perhaps interest a newspaper in sponsoring us. But there was a formidable snag. With an easterly gale blowing, diving in Stroms Hellier was quite out of the question, especially as I would have to dive alone and without surface cover.

The next two days were agonising. The wind showed no sign of abating, and though I was sorely tempted to risk a dive, common sense prevailed. By the Monday, however, the wind had moderated somewhat, and swung into the south-east. Stroms Hellier was still wild, but less wild than before. I was due to leave the following dawn on the *Good Shepherd,* and so this day was my only chance. Rather against my better judgement I decided to make an attempt.

Roy Dennis, the observatory Warden, and his assistant, Ian Robertson, helped to carry the gear down to Point o' Stoodle, and stood by to keep an eye on me. Excitement and expectations ran high. I kitted up and slipped into the water during a lull in the breaking swell. A moment's anxiety as I struggled through the surf, and then I kicked up my fins and descended to the sea floor, 50 feet down. On the bottom it was relatively calm, but the visibility was very poor. I could hardly see a yard ahead. I was in a shingle-filled gully about 15 yards wide, with vertical walls rising on either side. Somewhere in here, on the north side of Stroms Hellier, I expected the wreck to lie. If any wreckage was to be seen — even a small lump of concretion — I ought surely to spot it. Carefully I zig-zagged my way up the gully, expecting at any moment to bump against a cannon, an ingot, or an anchor. There was nothing but flat, clean shingle. All the time the gully was narrowing, and suddenly it became dark. I had swum into the cave at Stroms Hellier's western end. Here, if anywhere, I thought I should find something, but twenty minutes spent digging into the shingle with my bare hands revealed nothing but pebbles and shells. Another twenty minutes searching back along the gully confirmed my fears. There was no visible wreckage in it at all.

I should have listened more carefully to some of the islanders, who had suggested that the wreck perhaps lay on the south-east side of the geo. But by now my air was running low, and I had time only for a quick sortie across the central ridge of rock into the southern gully. There I found more drifted shingle, apparently sterile, though at this point I must in fact have been within yards of a bronze gun. Now I was beginning to pull hard on my air tubes, for the bottles were almost empty, and so reluctantly I headed for the surface.

As usually happens on such occasions, the weather had worsened considerably since I had entered the water. I tried several times to land on the steep slippery rocks of Point o' Stoodle but, weighed down as I was with my heavy gear, the sea tossed me aside like a puppet every time I tried to get a foothold. Frightened, and feeling very foolish (which of course I had been for diving alone and without surface cover), I jettisoned my weight-belt and began the long swim into Swartz Geo, where I landed safely on the shingle beach.

Had the *Grifón,* in spite of the local traditions, gone down somewhere outside Stroms Hellier? Had she perhaps foundered at anchor just offshore? In spite of our doubts, we decided to go ahead with the expedition as planned. The area to be covered was very small. We would carry out a more extensive search and we were confident that, if there was anything to find, we would find it. On Friday 5th June Simon and I arrived by sea with the equipment and on the following morning Syd Wignall flew into the island's rough and tiny airstrip aboard one of Loganair's versatile Islander aircraft. By Saturday afternoon we had the gear unpacked and expedition headquarters set up in one of the old observatory huts at North Haven. Our own accommodation, as it was to be throughout the expedition, was in the newly built and very comfortable Observatory Hostel nearby.

In the evening we charged the aqualung bottles and rigged the 12-foot Gemini and then, under the expert pilotage of Stewart Thompson of Quoy, we took the boat from North Haven to South Harbour, from which we planned to operate. It was essential to get a local man to guide us through the passages between Fair Isle's dangerous reefs and tide-races; one could otherwise spend a lifetime trying to learn the hazards of such a coast, and that lifetime would probably be a short one. Thompson took us through the reefs and islets which afforded a sheltered passage between Stroms Hellier and South Harbour; a very tricky passage to negotiate, but an essential one to know if we chanced to be caught on this side of the island in bad weather. 'When I say "go near" a rock,' shouted Thompson, 'I mean about 10 feet away — when I say "close", we scrape it!' He was not exaggerating.

The next day we were ready to start diving. We loaded the Gnat with our gear and sets and drove the 3 miles from the Hostel to South Harbour. The weather, in contrast to my earlier visit, was perfect; the sea flat calm. Unhurriedly, for there was no worry here about tides, we launched the boat, loaded up, and set off through the reefs for Stroms Hellier. A row of oily grey shags sat motionless along the sloping slab of Point Saider as we arrived, coolly aloof to our presence. I donned my gear and dropped into the water at the mouth of Stroms Hellier.

As already described, I had concluded (quite wrongly, as events were to prove) that *El Gran Grifón* had not gone down in Stroms Hellier at all, but had sunk at anchor somewhere outside. I mention this to show how strong can be the tendency to bend evidence to fit with one's own preconceived theories and ideas. The obvious course would have been thoroughly to search the southern gully, which I had only glanced at before; but no, I thought I knew better, and so we started to search beyond Stroms Hellier.

On that first dive I crossed the mouth of the geo, heading south, and searched the deep gully between the shore and a rocky islet called the Fless. Then I doubled back on my tracks and crossed the entrance to Stroms Hellier again, slightly further out to sea, eventually surfacing north of Swartz Geo. Wignall dived at the mouth of Swartz, and headed seawards into deep water. He surfaced when he reached the 20-fathom mark; like me, he had seen nothing.

On the following day we extended our searches. I dropped into the water a quarter of a mile to the north of Swartz Geo, and followed the base of the steeply sloping cliff southwards until

I reached the geo mouth. Wignall then carried out a text-book search of Swartz Geo itself, boxing across in a series of compass swims. Again we found nothing. That evening I gave Simon, who was already proving to be a competent boatman, his first training dive in North Haven.

Looking back, it seems incredible that the last area we searched was the one we should have covered first. We had done much the same, on a far larger scale, in Blasket Sound. At any event on the third day of diving, Tuesday 9th June, we arrived at Stroms Hellier still determined to search *outside* the geo. Wignall dived close to the Fless, and swam out to sea, surfacing when he reached deep water. We were beginning to suspect that something was wrong, for our searches had been systematic and extensive, and we had found nothing at all. At this point we decided, almost offhandedly, that someone ought to have a closer look in the southern gully of Stroms Hellier itself. It was my turn. I slipped over the gunwale into the calm water and finned gently down, swallowing to clear my ears.

The southern edge of the gully was an overhanging rock face, alive with waving sea anemones and bright yellow sponges, which plummeted to the sea floor 50 feet below. A few feet from the surface I stopped for a moment, for I was having some difficulty in clearing my ears. As I blew to get my eustachian tubes to 'click' and equalise the pressure in my inner ear I noticed, immediately below me, a short length of what at first appeared to be a length of drainpiping sticking out of the shingle at the bottom of the gully. As I descended slowly towards it, my mind began to grasp what I was really seeing. It was the muzzle of a bronze gun, bright and green and quite unmistakable.

Leaving my ears to sort out their own problems, I dived down and grasped it in both hands, feeling the cold metal and reassuring myself that it was real. About 3 feet of the muzzle protruded from the shingle. Its bore, which I gauged with my shaking fingers, was a fraction under 3 inches; just right for a *media sacre,* a peculiarly Spanish type. Robert Sténuit had found such a gun on the wreck of the galleass *Girona,* off Antrim, 3 years before. I looked quickly round to see if there was anything else. Yes! Close to the base of the cliff were three more guns, iron this time, almost buried in the shingle. I had only been in the water five minutes, but I had seen enough. There could be no doubt at all that this was the wreck site. I surfaced and mouthed the news to Wignall and my brother, who had patiently been following my bubbles.

They hauled me into the boat and helped me off with my gear, as I gasped out to them what I had seen. Everything now fitted. Immediately above us we saw the overhanging ledge of Cup o' Skairharis against which the ship's masts must have leaned. The locals had been absolutely right. There, a few feet away, was the ridge of rock in the middle of the geo which they had once said was the ship's hull, turned to stone. This was where Captain Row and his men had successfully dived for guns more than 2 centuries before. And they had left much behind, for I had just seen it lying there with my own eyes.

Wignall, who had just completed a dive and could not go down again for fear of the 'bends', had to wait until the following day to see his first Armada gun. Next morning we were on the site early, and we both dived on the wreck together. Wignall removed his mouthpiece and kissed the muzzle of the bronze gun, and then he shook me by the hand. We grinned inanely at each other in sheer exuberance through our face masks. Here we were, the pair of us, doing the one thing we wanted to do, experiencing a moment of triumph after years of effort and frustration we had gone through. To us that little gully, with the ancient Spanish guns lying tumbled around its walls, was a secret and hallowed place.

Such emotional moments are fleeting ones, and when they pass there is work to be done. I began searching the seaward end of the gully for more evidence of wreckage, while Wignall went to explore the neighbouring gully which ran towards the southern cave. Ten minutes later he was back, gesticulating for me to come with him. I followed him up a deep and narrow cleft, almost bare of shingle, until we reached what he had found — a cluster of lead ingots. Just beyond them lay another iron gun, so badly abraded by the ground swells of 4 centuries that its top half had been completely rubbed away, leaving what was in effect a longitudinal section of the gun, with a 3-inch iron ball still lodged in its exposed breech.

Two of the ingots were boat shaped, and weighed about a hundredweight apiece. Such ingots seem to be the hall-mark of an Armada wreck; we had found six of them on the *Santa Maria,* and Robert Sténuit had recovered a great many from the *Girona*. Another ingot, a heavy rectangular one with a hole in the middle, was very similar to one we had found on the *Santa Maria* and this kind, we believed, was the one described as *planchas*, or blocks, in Spanish inventories of ships' stores.

Further searching over the next two days revealed no more visible wreckage, and so we carefully photographed everything as we had found it and considered our next move. Obviously much more was buried in the shingle, so the first job was to carry out a detailed survey of the site and then arrange for the plant and gear necessary for proper excavation. At this moment, as if on cue, Chris Oldfield arrived, and after a brief dive to look at the site he became wildly enthusiastic about the whole project. Together the four of us worked out a plan of action. We would need an efficient air-lift, as on the *Santa Maria*, to remove the shingle overburden. In this instance, however, we would be able to station the compressor on the cliff top and run an air line direct to Stroms Hellier, so avoiding the necessity of a large supporting boat. All we required was a second hand plant compressor, a 500-foot length of air hose, and a 60-foot-long 6-inch air lift. Oldfield reckoned that he could fix this up in about a week.

A few days later the three others left for the mainland; Wignall to start other projects and researches, Chris Oldfield to collect his heavy salvage gear and assemble components for the air lift rig, and Simon Martin to sound out the Press in Edinburgh and London for possible sponsors. Simon and Oldfield would meet in about a fortnight to return with the equipment and, we hoped, the promise of a sponsorship cheque.

Meantime I remained on Fair Isle to carry out a pre-disturbance survey of the wreck site. By a very fortunate coincidence Alan Bax of the School of Nautical Archaeology at Plymouth arrived at the moment the others left. He and I made an efficient survey team, and in the week he spent on Fair Isle perfect weather conditions enabled us each to put in about 3 hours diving every day. This allowed us to complete an unhurried and detailed survey of the entire wreck area, using tape triangulation and barometric levelling.

As we surveyed Stroms Hellier's contorted geology, amongst which the tumbled wreckage lay, we gave the various features names. The gully which appeared likely to contain the main deposit of buried artefacts became 'Grifon Gully'. Other features we honoured with Spanish names. Thus 'Leon Gully', where we had first discovered the guns, with its flanking rock outcrops of 'Aragon' and 'Castile', reflected the three great kingdoms of Philip II's Spain. 'Cabreras' described a jagged ridge akin to the Sierra Cabreras in north-west Spain, a mountain range in which Simon and I had climbed some years before. A large expanse of featureless boulder-strewn shingle became 'La Mancha' after the wide plain in Murcia across which Cervantes' Don Quixote once rode with his faithful squire.

When Alan Bax left, the sea bed survey was complete, but a corresponding survey of Stroms Hellier's land features was lacking. The large-scale Ordnance Survey map, based on surveys carried out a century ago, was hopelessly inaccurate for our purposes, and in any case of too small a scale to show the detail we required. Fortunate coincidence once again came to our aid. As I was puzzling how best to survey the geo without proper instruments an Ordnance Survey team arrived on the island to carry out a complete revision of the maps. We immediately became friends, and in return for my transporting the team in our Gnat to the more inaccessible parts of the island (a Gnat, incidentally, really will go almost anywhere), the team supervisor, Robert Morison, specially surveyed Stroms Hellier for us to a scale of 50 inches to the mile. When I had scaled this to our own underwater survey, we had an accurate and fully detailed map from which to plan operations.

In the meantime Chris Oldfield had moved his equipment from Coll, the Hebridean island on which he had been working, to Leith, whence it could be shipped to Shetland. He had also purchased a suitable air lift compressor and had designed a 60-foot air lift pipe in detachable 20-foot lengths. Simon Martin met him at Leith after a mammoth and disappointing trail round Fleet Street. One leading Sunday newspaper, after almost agreeing to sponsor the whole project, dropped it when it transpired that we were serious archaeologists and that there was little prospect of underwater battles with rival gangs, or of chests dripping with doubloons.

By the beginning of July most of the heavy gear was in Fair Isle. The trip over in the *Good Shepherd* was a particularly rough one and the air lift compressor, which had been lashed to the deck, was almost lost overboard. Because the *Shepherd* could not carry a vehicle, the Land-Rover had to be left behind, though we were able to arrange for it to be brought across later by a larger vessel which was due to deliver road construction materials to the island. But since we still had the Gnat, and had borrowed an old tractor for the power take-off needed to run Oldfield's big aqualung compressor, we could manage for the meantime without it.

We decided to use the air lift first to clear shingle from around the guns in Leon Gully. From the survey it had seemed that this was not the main deposit, but rather spill from an upper deck, and was therefore a good place to start. After a weekend of preparation during which Oldfield set up his welding plant and worked almost non-stop to rig the air lift, we clamped the whole 60-foot tube together on the cliff top above Stroms Hellier and then — with some tricky and hair-raising moments — we lowered the complete assembly into the water 120 feet below. We next block-and-tackled the air lift compressor into a convenient hollow on the cliff top from which the man operating it would be in hand-signal contact with the boat moored over the wreck site. The air line from the compressor ran down to a lower ledge (the same ledge by which the shipwrecked Spaniards escaped in 1588) where it was coiled up when not in use. From there the hose could be dropped directly into the water, to be collected by a diver who would take it down and attach it to the air lift nozzle. When air was passed into it the loose end of the air lift pipe would rise and disgorge; when the supply was cut off it would fall back on the sea bed, safe from surface disturbances.

It was a simple arrangement and therefore an effective one. Our work routine became equally uncomplicated. Now that we had Oldfield's large sea-going Gemini we could work with safety in most weathers directly from the expedition HQ at North Haven, a three-mile voyage each way. Two of us would come round with the boat bringing, as well as our own equipment, the third man's diving gear. He meantime would have made his way overland to Stroms Hellier to start up the compressor on the cliff top, and drop the air line into the sea when required. The first diver would link the air line to the air lift head, while his mate acted as boat cover and signal link with the compressor operator.

At a given signal air would be delivered to the air lift, and its exhaust end would rear to the surface in a froth of bubbles and gushing water to be lassoed by the boatman and dragged to wherever we wanted it to discharge its spoil. The three duties were completely interchangeable (Simon Martin was by now a fully trained and accomplished diver), and by virtue of the cliff path the man at the compressor could be relieved when the first diver had completed his stint. In the course of a working day each of us would dive (we were working on a 50-foot 'no-stop' limit of 85 minutes) and also take his spell as surface cover and compressor man.

We began to make finds in Leon Gully almost at once. Chris Oldfield uncovered, close to the bronze *media sacre,* the broken muzzle of a rather larger bronze piece. It was evidently the end of a 4½ inch *media-culebrina,* a 9-pounder which overall would have measured 10 feet or more, though we had found only the last 26 inches of it. Surprisingly, and disappointingly, there was no sign of the missing part anywhere near. Had the gun perhaps blown up during the fighting? Guns of this period — particularly Spanish ones — quite frequently did burst on firing. We had found exploded fragments from a bronze gun at Dun an Oir in 1969, and a number of 'muzzles' and 'broken pieces' are listed among English inventories of captured Armada material. But on clearing out compacted shingle from the bore of the Fair Isle muzzle we found, 18 inches down, a cork *tampion* or muzzle-plug. If the gun had blown up, the tampion could not possibly still be in place. There was another curious point to consider. In service a tampion is always plugged into the mouth of the gun, never rammed deep into the bore. To push it 1½ feet up the barrel would require considerable pressure — pressure such as might be exerted if air was trapped in the barrel as the gun sank. But a pressure differential would only have been created if the gun had been intact when it dropped to the bottom. Did it perhaps break when it hit the sea bed? Dents and distortions around the muzzle suggested a violent impact. But if this was the case, where were the missing 8 feet or more? Had Captain Row's men recovered the breech end? Was the gun perhaps broken in the course of their operations, and was a muzzle-less *media-culebrina*

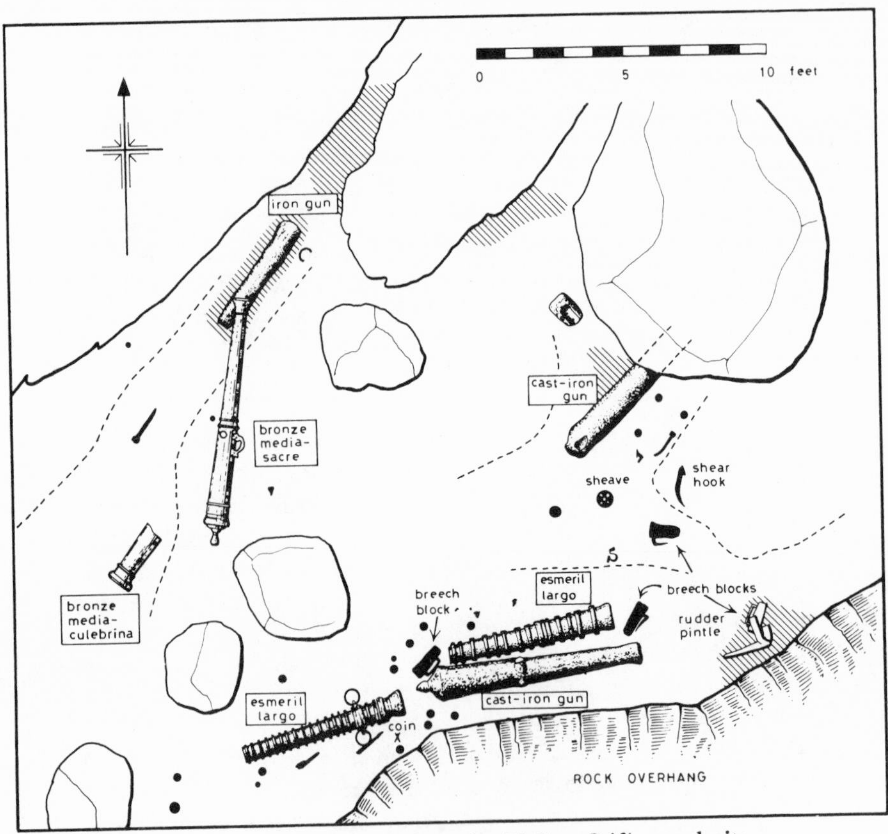

Fig. 11. Leon Gully: guns on the *El Gran Grifón* wreck site

one of their 'two brass guns of a large size'? We will probably never know.

This broken piece of ordnance is interesting in quite another respect. At the break only 2 feet from the muzzle, the bore is very noticeably off centre. The degree of error at the breech, which would have been proportionally greater, must have been enormous; simple calculation suggests that the thinnest side of the breech wall would have been about 2½ inches, the thickest about 5½ inches (the two sides should, of course, be equal). Apart from causing a serious loss of accuracy, boring off the true to this extent would have weakened the piece so much that, were it not for the evidence of the tampion, we might have been justified in suspecting that the gun had burst during firing. At any event, this particular gun must have been in some considerable danger of exploding every time it was discharged, and most certainly it can never have undergone any stringent proof-testing. If this find is typical, we can readily see why Spanish guns burst so often. It has long been known that Spanish and Portuguese gun-founding technologies were poor, and one early 17th century English expert specifically mentions 'forreigne foundings' that are 'bored awry' and 'crooked in the chase'. 'Honeycombing', or gas voids in the metal, is another casting fault which the same authority mentions and which this example displays.[1]

Badly cast guns of this sort probably made up all too large a proportion of the armament carried aboard Armada ships, and to be almost as afraid of their own weapons as of the enemy's must have deeply affected the morale of the Spanish gunners, and consequently their efficiency in action. Conversely the English, who in the main had sound guns, were able to sail into battle 'without fear about their ordnance', as a contemporary writer expressed it. Bad workmen may, in such an instance, very properly blame their tools.

Two of the iron guns found in Leon Gully yield further evidence of the poor quality of guns carried aboard at least some of the Armada's ships. They are wrought iron breech-loaders, both about 6 feet long with bores of 3 and 3½ inches. Later excavations in a neighbouring gully produced a breech-block of the right type for these guns, but too small to fit either of them, indicating the presence on board of a rather smaller piece in the same category. Such guns were built up of longitudinal strips of iron hammer-welded together on a mandrel to form the barrel, with reinforcing hoops shrunk on afterwards. As a type they predate the development of effective iron-founding techniques which took place during the 16th century. By 1588 they were certainly obsolescent as shipboard armament, for their weak construction made them dangerous to operate and ineffectual in use. That an Armada flagship — albeit not a front-line one — had to carry several such pieces in order to mount a respectable armament

[1] Apart from weakening the casting, honeycombing in the bore left jagged holes which sometimes trapped burning fragments after firing, causing serious accidents when the next powder charge was inserted.

illustrates the degree to which the Armada planners were forced, in some sectors at least, to rely on out-of-date equipment. These particular guns are probably examples of the *esmeriles largos* — big breech-loaders — of the Armada lists.

A related group of smaller guns is represented by the discovery, in Leon Gully, of four wrought iron breech blocks fitted with handles belonging to small swivel-mounted breechloaders. These breech blocks are of two types, indicating at least two individual weapons, one of about 2 inch bore and the other — apparently a longer and slimmer gun — of about $1\frac{1}{2}$ inch. The type is very common and lasted, with surprisingly little modification, from the late 14th into the 17th, and even 18th, centuries. In essence this kind of gun consists of a short barrel, either of wrought iron or cast bronze, the breech end of which incorporates a stirrup-like arrangement into which, with the aid of a wedge, a separate breech block is jammed. Normally the gun was fixed to a swivelling pintle in the bulwark, and was traversed and elevated by means of a long tiller. Its relatively quick rate of fire and ease of aiming made it an ideal weapon for anti-boarder purposes; hence its astonishingly long survival as a type. It was often mounted on the castle bulkheads fore and aft, so that enfilading fire could be directed downwards to sweep boarders from the waist. Its disadvantages were lack of power and accuracy, due to the impossibility of obtaining an effective seal at the breech, and its tendency, particularly with wrought iron types, to scale on firing and injure the gunner. In the Armada inventories guns of this type are named *esmeriles* (sometimes *versos*), while the removable breech blocks are referred to separately as *mascolos* (an Italian word) or *recameras.* The Armada galleass *Girona* has yielded a fine bronze *esmeril* and several *mascolos*, while a well preserved specimen of a complete swivel gun recovered from *La Trinidad Valencera* is described in detail on another page.

As well as the wrought iron pieces, we were able to identify five cast iron guns on the *Gran Grifón* site. The largest of these is the badly eroded piece with the 3 inch ball lodged in its exposed barrel, the location of which at the landward end of the site suggests that it may have been one of the bow chase pieces. This gun is 9 feet 6 inches long and must have weighed originally upwards of 1 500 pounds, the specifications of a small *sacre.* Next, and at the other end of the site (presumably the stern), are two rather stubby 4-inchers, each 6 feet 6 inches long and weighing in their original state about 1 200 pounds. They are probably best described as *quartos de cañons* (quarter cannons), such as are listed in Santa Cruz's 1586 'proposals' as weighing 12 quintals (c. 1 200 pounds) apiece. The final two cast iron pieces are small deck guns of about 2 inch calibre, only 4 feet in length. It is difficult to ascertain what this type was called, but if we turn once more to Santa Cruz's 'proposals' we find a large group of apparently small iron guns listed simply as 'piezas de hierro collado' (pieces of cast iron), and I suspect that it will have included just such nondescript pieces as these.

How far, on this evidence, can we now come towards assessing the nature of *El Gran Grifón*'s complete armament? We have identified two bronze guns (one *media culebrina;* one *media sacre*), five cast iron guns (one *sacre*; two *cuartos de cañon*; two '*piezas*'), two wrought iron guns (*esmeriles largos*), and breech blocks to identify a further *esmeril largo* and two swivel-mounted *esmeriles.* This total of twelve represents almost a third of the number of guns listed aboard the ship at the Lisbon muster of May 1588; or, to put it another way, it gives us a random sample of just over 30% on which to base a total assessment. Random samples, however, can be misleading. Were there perhaps other gun-types aboard the ship — especially larger ones — of which we have found no examples?

Fortunately we had evidence from a related group of finds to help us resolve this difficulty. The guns needed ammunition, and in the course of our excavations we recovered almost 100 pieces of iron roundshot. We were therefore able to determine whether the size groups represented in this ammunition sample — again a 'random' sample — would suitably serve the group of twelve guns. If not, where were the discrepancies? In particular, were there any types of shot for which there are no guns?

Seventy-two iron balls were in a condition to allow of accurate diameter measurement; they displayed clean spherical surfaces with mould lines and, in one instance, a foundry mark (the same ᑭ as identified on several pieces of *Santa Maria* roundshot). Another 20 balls, though too corroded to measure accurately, confirm the general size ratios shown by the 72. Though an absolute standardisation of sizes, as to be expected, is lacking, the roundshot falls into four distinct 'parcels' which agree perfectly with the four groups of gun types we have identified. There are no unaccountable outsiders.

Table of Measurable Iron Roundshot Recovered in 1970

Shot diameter inches	Number in sample	Appropriate to
4.1-3.8	16	*Media culebrina* *Cuarto de cañon*
3.5-2.75	35	*Sacre* *Media sacre* *Esmeril largo*
2.6-2.0	17	*Esmeril* (note: barrel bore generally exceeded chamber bore in these pieces)
2.0-1.3	4 (+ 2 lead)	'*Pieza*'

In addition to the iron roundshot we found two $1\frac{1}{2}$ inch lead balls and five socketed lead hemispheres. These latter range in diameter from 2.25 to 3 inches, and they represent a type of bar shot joined in pairs with a rod of wrought iron, fragments of which remain in some of the sockets. This can be identified with the *trundle shot* described by John Smith in his *Sea Grammar* of 1627 as '. . . a bolt of iron sixteen or eighteen inches in length, at both ends sharp pointed, and about an handful from each end a round broad bowle of lead according to the bore of the peece cast upon it.' The calibres of the *Grifón* examples suggest that they were intended for the *esmeriles* and *esmeriles largos.* This kind of shot, together with bar shot, linked shot, and chain shot, was normally used to bring down an enemy's tackle and rigging at close range.

The twelve guns do seem, therefore, to be a fair random sample of the ship's armament as a whole. It follows that we can attempt a tentative estimate of the complete armament, always remembering that while the conclusions we reach are not likely to be accurate as far as detail is concerned they are almost certainly correctly indicative of character, which is much more important. The estimate is obtained simply by multiplying the sample of guns by three, which gives us thirty-six out of the required thirty-eight, and conveniently making up the discrepancy by adding the 'two brass guns of a large size' known to have been raised during the 18th century, the exact nature of which I have quite arbitrarily guessed.

El Gran Grifón *Estimated Armament 1588*

Type of gun	Number identified on site (August 1970)	Estimated total	Lewis's estimate (700-ton hulk)
Media culebrina	1 + 1 (1728?)	4	3
Sacre	1 + 1 (1728?)	4	3
Media sacre	1	3	3
Cuarto de cañon	2	6	—
'Pieza'	2	6	—
Esmeril largo	3	9	—
Esmeril	2	6	—
		38	

Thus we have obtained what we set out to find — first-hand knowledge of the kind of armament *El Gran Grifón* carried as flagship of a second-line Armada squadron. As a result we must disagree with Professor Lewis's contention that this particular ship, because she was a flagship, was probably armed according to front-line specifications (*Armada Guns,* p. 156). She was not.[1] On the other hand, if we take his estimated figures for a hulk of this size (ibid., p. 162), we find that our figures are in quite remarkable agreement with his. Though Professor Lewis's estimate covers only the larger calibre pieces (4-pounders and upwards) they show how accurate is his conclusion, which was based on very tenuous and difficult evidence.

What is to be learned from this new knowledge of *El Gran Grifón*'s armament? First, it adds positive support to Professor

[1] But with almost uncanny intuition Professor Lewis, whose overall concern was to arrive at a *minimum* estimate of the Armada's complete gun-strength, has subtracted 3 from his original total of 18 first-rate auxiliary warships to allow for possible errors of judgement—as this one has turned out to be (*Armada Guns*, p. 156).

Lewis's general estimate of the armament provided for the hulks, and perhaps for some of the smaller ships in the front-line squadrons as well. Second, it emphasises how broad was the gap between this kind of armament and the offensive ship-smashing policy which dictated the kind of guns carried aboard major fighting ships such as the *Santa Maria de la Rosa* and *Trinidad Valencera* or *San Salvador.* The most emphatic point to be made about the *Grifón*'s armament is that it was wholly defensive. Whether or not our estimated figures for her gun types come anywhere near the truth in detail, *all* the evidence we have recovered points to this general conclusion. *Medias culebrinas* and *sacres* are long-range guns and, at any range, are not real ship-killers; thus the ship's main battery seems intended to be off-holding rather than destructive. For the same weight of main gun she could have carried *pedreros*; seven- or eight-inch stone-throwers which could have given her a much more formidable close-range firepower. But we found no hint of such pieces on the site; indeed, we found no stone shot of any calibre. As certainly as negative evidence can make it, therefore, she carried no *pedreros,* and instead relied on a hotch-potch of light-shotted and partly obsolescent guns which could, at best, do little more than keep her out of trouble.

These discoveries further emphasise the deliberate and carefully thought out policies by which the great fleet was armed. Whenever we come across evidence concerning front-line Armada ships we cannot fail to be impressed by the weight and quality of their armament; when, as with *El Gran Grifón,* we glimpse guns aboard a second-line ship we are equally struck by their essentially defensive concept and obsolescent appearance.

Such logical common sense, in apportioning the available guns to suit the operational roles of the various groups of ships, had not been in evidence from the Armada's inception. On the contrary, only three months before the fleet sailed, the whole state of its preparation and in particular the arming of the ships had been in hopeless confusion. Professor Mattingly, who carefully studied the voluminous official correspondence of this period, has graphically described the disorder which prevailed throughout the Armada at the time of Santa Cruz's death in February 1588. Whatever other qualities he may have had, the ageing Captain-General had been no staff-officer.

> At Lisbon, [writes Mattingly], '. . . there was a kind of frozen chaos. In the mad week or so preceding the marquis's death, guns and supplies had been tumbled helter-skelter on the ships, and crews herded aboard with orders to stand by for instant departure and on no account to go ashore. There were soldiers and mariners on most of the ships without money or arms or proper clothing. There were crews, the commands of unlucky or incompetent masters, who had no food. Some ships were laden far too deeply for safety : some floated practically empty. In the wild scramble towards the end every captain had apparently grabbed whatever he could get his hands on, particularly in the way of additional ordnance. Some ships had more guns than they had room for; others had almost none. One galleon had several new bronze pieces stowed between decks amidst a hopeless clutter of kegs and barrels; one Biscayan scarcely bigger than a pinnace had a huge demi-cannon filling most of her waist. Some had guns but no cannon balls; some had roundshot but no guns to fire them.'

This was the shambles which the Duke of Medina Sidonia inherited after professing, in all humility, his lack of suitability for the command. He could scarcely have misjudged himself more. Though ably supported by his experienced squadron commanders it was he, and he alone, who provided the leadership and impetus which, by the time the fleet sailed in May, had brought some kind of order out of the chaos. Very little written evidence of this great upheaval, however, has found its way into the archives. The Duke was probably far too busy with practical realities to bog himself down in paper work. But one fact of great significance is on record. The front-line squadron of Guipuzcoa (of which the *Santa Maria de la Rosa* was a prominent member), which we know to have been grossly under-gunned as far back as 1586, received, in March 1588, between seventy and eighty guns which had been requisitioned from the 'foreign hulks' in Lisbon harbour : that is, almost certainly, from the twenty-three Baltic ships of Gomez de Medina's stores squadron. The hulks, as non-combatants, did not need the extra guns, while the fighting ships of Guipuzcoa clearly did.

We spent three months on Fair Isle during that idyllic summer of 1970, and on only three days did the weather prevent us from diving in Stroms Hellier. We would set out in the Gemini from North Haven each morning after a good breakfast at the hostel and steam the three miles to the wreck site, making our way through the awesome cave passage which runs under the jutting outcrop of Sheep Rock (this was both a short cut and, if the sea was rough, a way of avoiding the nasty tide-race at the rock's tip). Puffins, shags and guillemots would skim the water at our bow, and occasionally the bewhiskered face of a curious seal would bob up on the surface to stare at us with round, intelligent eyes. A family of grey seals lived in the caves at the end of Stroms Hellier and sometimes, while we were at work on the sea-bed there, a streamlined grey shape would streak purposefully past on its way to fishing grounds far out to sea. Sometimes the seals would sing deep in their cave, and the towering walls of Stroms Hellier would reverberate with eerie music.

We normally remained on the site until about three in the afternoon, by which time each of us would have completed his one-and-a-half-hour stint in the water. Then we would climb to the cliff top, leaving the boat moored in the geo beneath, and eat our pack lunches. Often we had small discoveries to show each other, and enter up in the finds register. Most frequently they were musket or arquebus bullets — eventually we had over 4 000 of these — or scraps of sheet lead from the ship's sheathing and scuppering, which could be picked up all over the site. All were carefully catalogued, and the find spots noted. Occasionally the discoveries would be more exciting; as with the *Santa Maria,* the small finds from *El Gran Grifón* were not numerous, but they were varied. We found a leaden seal, bearing the crown and arms of Philip II. No doubt it had once been wired to a bonded bale or cask in Lisbon docks, to prevent pilfering as stores for the great enterprise were stockpiled. We found pieces of soldiers' equipment, too; part of the barrel of an arquebus, a tunic button, a belt fitting, and wedges of lead evidently hacked from the larger ingots for issue to individual men for casting shot. A well preserved bronze sheave, or pulley wheel, turned up. A small bronze cube with a hole drilled through its centre puzzled us until we consulted our copy of Mainwaring's *Seaman's Dictionary* (compiled about 1623) and read 'COAKS are little square things of brass with a hole in them, put into some of the greatest wooden shivers (sheaves) to keep them from splitting and galling by the pin of the block wherein they turn'. We had found exactly what Mainwaring described. The wooden sheave had rotted away completely, leaving only the brass 'coak' or bearing bush. Many have been found by Robert Sténuit on the *Girona* site, and one has since turned up on the *Trinidad Valencera.*

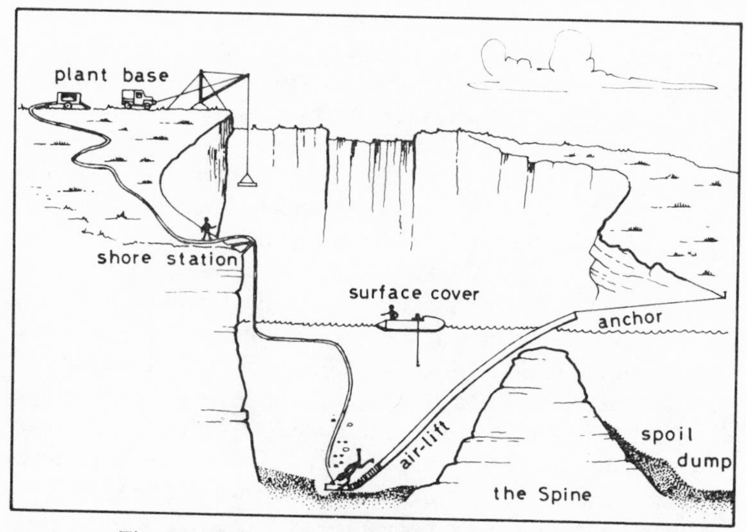

Fig. 12. Techniques of working *El Gran Grifón* site

As we airlifted in Leon Gully to expose the guns there we came upon a solitary silver coin; a 4-*real* piece of Philip II, minted at Toledo. Nestled close to it — close enough to have given the electrolytic protection which explains the coin's fine condition — we found part of a finely tempered steel blade which may perhaps have been manufactured in that same famous city, the ancient and proud capital of Castile which was renowned throughout Europe for the magnificence of its steel. Beneath a large rock we discovered an elaborately decorated hinged pewter handle, which we have since identified as belonging to one of the so-called 'Hanseatic' flagons, a broad bottomed type often associated with shipboard use (these flagons were popular at sea, no doubt because they would not topple easily with the movement of the ship). Fragments of other pewter vessels have also turned up.

In the course of the excavations in Leon Gully we recovered numerous fragments of a very large bronze cooking pot with angular lug handles. It is difficult to put across in cold print the thrill of bringing back these otherwise meaningless scraps of bronze, to read in the Armada lists of 1586 that each warship required for its galley a large 'calderon de cobre', or communal cooking pot, and to realise that the scraps in one's hand must have come from exactly such a utensil. The realisation somehow brought us very close to the men who once lived in the cramped and heaving confines of the great stores flagship.

On 17th July H.M. Fleet Tender *Brodick* arrived with the sixteen-strong team from the Naval Air Command Sub-Aqua Club (N A C S A C) led by Commander Alan Baldwin. Unluckily, they had been storm-bound for nearly a week at Wick, which cut down their working stay on Fair Isle to a fortnight. None the less, they were a strong, keen outfit, many of whom had already gained archaeological experience on other N A C S A C projects. We found them to be kindred spirits, and on the first evening, after they had set up camp and we had briefed them on what we had done, they entertained us with the hospitality for which the Royal Navy is legendary. At the same time, plans for their participation in the project were worked out.

The following day everyone in the N A C S A C team made a familiarisation dive on the wreck, and Chris Oldfield instructed those who had not yet had experience with an air lift on its use. Meantime, Alan Baldwin organised a systematic sweep of the whole wreck area and its surrounds, to back up and confirm our own preliminary searches. Over the following three days the Navy men, now divided into four separate work teams, used flotation bags and chains to lift a number of heavy boulders from Leon Gully to facilitate further excavation there. We had already removed a considerable quantity of smaller rocks, in half-ton netloads, using Chris Oldfield's winch-hoist on the Gemini.

Since N A C S A C were completely independent in an operational sense (they had three aqualung compressors and four outboard-powered inflatable craft), it was decided that during the remaining ten days of their stay they should utilise their manpower to provide continuous shifts throughout the day to operate the air lift from dawn to dusk and so complete the excavation of Leon Gully. This gave them the concentrated excavation work they wanted, while it gave us a welcome break to complete preliminary treatment of the finds and to carry out much needed maintenance of equipment. N A C S A C's excavation of the gully was competent and thorough, and not even the smallest objects seem to have escaped their eyes. During their work they spotted, and recovered, several tiny copper rivets and a minute scrap of gold. Their larger finds included two breech blocks, assorted shot, more fragments from the bronze caldron, a pewter mug handle, a small bronze mounting, and some pieces of animal bone. The positions of these finds were plotted by the team surveyor, Mike Ballentyne, and incorporated into our own master plan.

Though the total tally of finds was small, the N A C S A C divers did make two discoveries of considerable significance. One was a curved steel blade, 15 inches long, its inner edge still viciously sharp. This is probably a shear hook, a cutting blade which was attached to a ship's yard-arm in order to tear down an enemy's rigging during grappling. Significantly, the Spaniards still used such weapons in 1588 (grappling and boarding, it will be remembered, was their primary aim), while the English regarded them as obsolete, pointing out — probably rightly — that they were as likely to cause distress to their owner by catching foul as they were to inflict damage on an adversary. Shear hooks were also mounted on long poles which could be wielded by hand, and in this form were often used for cutting away the opponent's anti-boarder netting (netting was usually heavily tarred as a precaution against this, tarred rope being especially difficult to cut).

The second important find made by N A C S A C in Leon Gully was a wrought iron rudder pintle, one of the six or more hinged bindings on which the rudder was hung. The find confirms that this end of the wreck is the stern, and in consequence the fore part of the ship (where the lead ingots and the abraded iron gun were found) lies hard against the overhanging cliff, in accordance with the traditional story of the wrecking. The ship must have broken her back on the jagged pinnacle of Castile, and then the disjointed hull will have sunk into Grifon Gully with the tall castlework of the stern collapsing sideways and spilling its contents into Leon Gully. The pattern of finds in Leon Gully confirms this, as most of them are concentrated at the base of the cliff in a way that suggests that the material slid down across a sloping deck. The paired *esmeriles largos* and *cuartos de canon* in this gully may well be the paired upper and lower stern chase pieces carried in the stern.

These discoveries strongly suggest that the remains of the lower stern and midships sections lie in Grifon Gully, and this gully will therefore contain the bulk of the wreckage. After N A C S A C left we made a start to excavating the narrow head of Grifon Gully, and this is where we recovered most of the lead and iron shot. We found that the whole gully bottom is crammed with concreted remains, mostly of badly decomposed iron objects. We did not continue beyond initial explorations, however, for complete excavation of this gully will pose complex and expensive problems of recording and conservation, and the task is therefore better left until we are properly equipped to tackle it.

After the first week in August we did little further excavation, though we had a fortnight's diving ahead of us before the season could be considered complete. Syd Wignall arrived to make a film record of the work, which was subsequently shown, in conjunction with the *Santa Maria* material, as a full-length feature on B B C 2's archaeological programme 'Chronicle'. We had planned to make the heavy recoveries at this stage, so that they could be fitted into the film sequences. Chris Oldfield constructed a crane on the overhanging cliff top and, using his Land-Rover winch, we lifted the lead ingots directly ashore. The guns were too heavy to lift by this method, and so they were raised by the Gemini hoist — an ingenious invention of Oldfield's, which allows a load of half a ton or more to be slung directly beneath the boat and so carried to the pier side to be lifted out of the water by crane. We only raised three pieces of artillery — the bronze *media culebrina* muzzle, the bronze *media sacre,* and the smaller of the two wrought iron *esmeriles largos.* The other iron guns we have left on the sea bed until suitable conservation facilities are available. Though Stroms Hellier was calm on the day we carried out the lifts, we had some anxious moments bringing the guns round to the North Haven, one at a time, for unpleasantly choppy squalls were blowing off the exposed headlands. All was well in the end, however, and it was a moment of considerable triumph when we hoisted the guns ashore.

The final few days were spent in measuring, weighing, drawing and photographing all the finds to complete the excavation record. Everything was to go into the County Museum at Lerwick where the curator, Tom Henderson, had made arrangements for conserving the material. With great dedication Mr. Henderson has persevered with this painstaking and very time-consuming work, and the results of his efforts have proved outstandingly successful. The *Grifón* finds now have a permanent home in the County Museum.

While we were completing detailed cataloguing of our finds in the museum we made a final discovery. As we counted out the great pile of lead musket and arquebus bullets which had accumulated during the season we found about a dozen which showed a very characteristic splaying and flattening on one side — the unmistakable mark of high-velocity impact. This feature is quite different from the ordinary flattening caused by the pressure of moving rocks which a large number of the other bullets displayed and, as ballistic authorities confirm, could only have been caused if the ball had been fired at close range against a solid object. Beyond serious doubt these must be English bullets shot into *El Gran Grifón* during the Channel battles. No doubt they had lodged deep in the timbers of the hull, eventually to drop to the sea floor as the wrecked ship disintegrated in Stroms Hellier. Contemporary accounts of the fighting tell how the *Grifón* was engaged at 'half musket shot' (about 50 yards) off the Isle of Wight at dawn on 3rd August 1588, probably with Sir Francis Drake's swift and powerfully-gunned *Revenge*. These spent bullets are surely unique souvenirs of this fierce and one-sided action.

For the time being at any rate, work on the *Santa Maria* and *El Gran Grifón* was finished. Three years of exploration on these two wrecks had amply vindicated Sydney Wignall's dream of studying the Armada through archaeological research. But, once begun, a study of this kind can never be completed. There remained more to learn, and more questions to be answered. Paradoxically, some of these questions had emerged *because* of our work.

Some of the answers were destined to be found, though we did not know it at the time, far to the south-west of Fair Isle, off the northern coast of County Donegal.

THE WRECK IN O'DOHERTY'S COUNTRY

THERE was nothing unusual about the dive planned for 20th February 1971 by members of the City of Derry Sub-Aqua Club in the broad sandy bay of Kinnagoe, on the Inishowen Peninsula of North Donegal. Thirteen hardy divers turned up on that cold and blustery Saturday afternoon to carry out routine training under the instruction of their diving officer, Charles Perkinson. In the back of each diver's mind was the knowledge that somewhere within the 2-mile wide bay lay the remains of one of the Spanish Armada's largest ships, *La Trinidad Valencera,* but none of them really expected to find the wreck, for they had been diving in the area for two years, and several other parties had unsuccessfully searched there as well. In any case, it was generally thought that the wreck lay somewhere towards the eastern end of the bay, and not in the west, where they were now going to dive. As Charles Perkinson briefed the divers, however, he sent them off with an exhortation which had become almost traditional: 'Keep your eyes peeled for the *Valencera*!'

One of the pairs, Archie Jack and Paddy Stewart, entered the water beside one of the low spurs of rock which runs across the beach into the sea near the western end of the bay. Below the water the spur continues as a low kelp-covered reef rising a few feet above the rippled sandy bottom, some thirty feet down. The two divers started to swim along the edge of this reef, using it as a navigational guide. Some 300 yards from the shore they were on the point of turning back, when they noticed an isolated rock some yards away from the main reef rising out of the sand. Vaguely interested, for they still had plenty of air in their cylinders, they swam over to investigate. As they drew close they

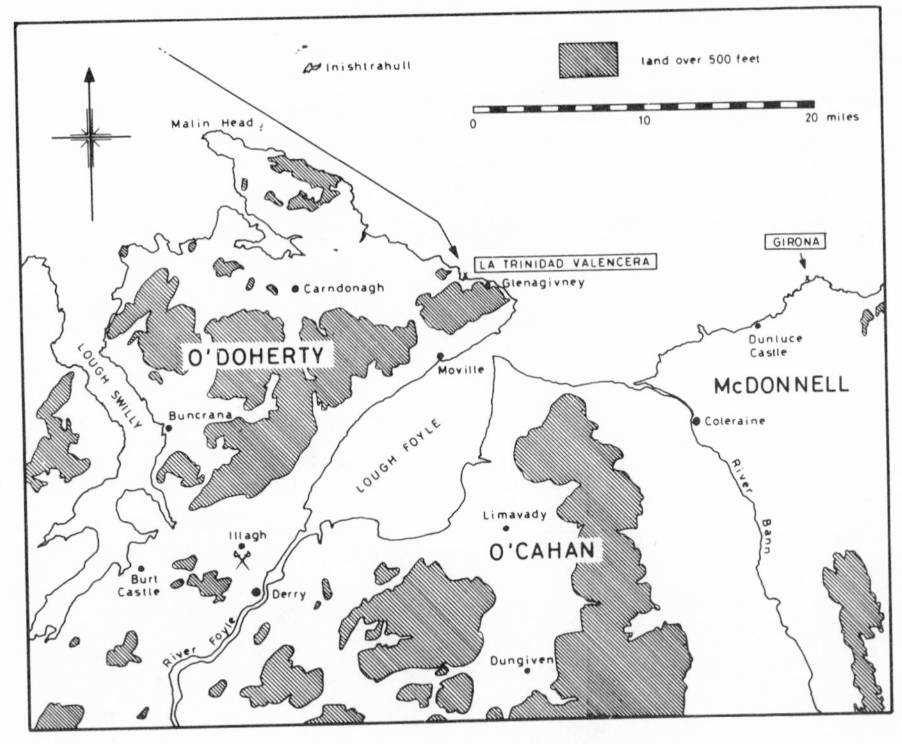

Fig. 13. O'Doherty's country

saw something resting on top of the rock — something long, regular in shape, and pastel green in colour. It was a ten-foot long bronze gun.

One diver stayed close to the find, while his companion hurriedly surfaced to shout for assistance. A marker buoy was hurried to the spot and made fast to the gun. Charles Perkinson then instructed the other divers to carry out a search of the immediate area for further clues, but first he had to calm them down. In the pandemonium of excitement which had quite naturally gripped the divers control was essential, since the light was fading, they were a fair distance from the shore, and some of the divers were relatively inexperienced. It says a lot for the discipline of the Club that the search which followed was controlled and effective, and that, in spite of the obvious temptation to carry on, it was called off before light conditions became too bad.

When the thirteen gathered on the beach for a de-briefing they began to piece together all they had seen. It was difficult at first to correlate everything exactly, but other guns had certainly been spotted. One had been seen not far from the first, its crisply decorated breech protruding from the sand next to a big iron anchor ring. Not far away was a large spoked wooden gun-carriage wheel. On the other side of the reef, in a shallow gully, a very large bronze gun had been found. Though it had been lying upside down, one of the divers had discerned the Spanish arms on its breech, beneath which he saw the name PHILIPPVS REX and the date 1556. Beyond any doubt this was the wreck of *La Trinidad Valencera,* and its discovery could scarcely have been more opportune. In the archaeology of Armada wrecks — on the *Girona,* the *Santa Maria de la Rosa,* and *El Gran Grifón* — one thing had so far been lacking, and that was first hand evidence of the heavy battery guns carried by a major fighting ship. The PHILIPPVS REX gun had a bore of 7¼ inches, which identified it as a 50-pounder ship-smashing full cannon, the largest type of gun carried by either side. If this important wreck could be examined properly, our picture of the Armada ships would be almost complete.

La Trinidad Valencera had sailed with the Armada in Martin de Bertendona's Levant squadron. She was, according to Spanish musters, the fourth largest vessel in the fleet. At 1 100 tons she was exceeded in size only by her own flagship, *La Regazona* (1 249 tons), by the flagship of the Guipuzcoan squadron *Santa Ana* (1 200 tons), and by the Andalusian flagship *Neustra Señora del Rosario* (1 150 tons). She carried a listed armament of 42 guns, of unspecified type and size, and a total complement of 360 men, of whom 281 were soldiers.

The senior officer on board was Don Alonso de Luzon, *Maestre de Campo* (colonel) of the 2 900-strong Regiment of Naples, three of whose twenty-six companies sailed with the ship. The companies were that of Don Alonso himself (each *Maestre de Campo,* in addition to commanding a *tercio,* had his own company of soldiers), and those of Captains Hieronimo de Aybar and

Don Garcia Manrique de Lara. Among other attached personnel four young *aventureros* are listed in the musters: they were Don Francisco de Rivadneira (with eight retainers), Don Rodrigo de Lasso (five retainers), Don Sebastian Zapata (three retainers) and Don Diego Fernandez de Mesa (one retainer).

La Trinidad Valencera, like many other front-line Armada ships, was not a warship in the true sense of the word, but a large merchantman specially converted for warlike use. She had originally been a privately owned ship of the Venetian Republic, built as a bulk-carrying merchant vessel. In Venetian sources she is always known as *La Balanzara,* while the Spaniards sometimes refer to her as *La Venetiana Valencera.* This ship had, at some time during 1587, entered a Sicilian port, probably to take on a cargo of grain. Sicily was an important grain producer during the 16th century, and the Venetians held long-standing contracts for its transport. But Sicily also belonged to the King of Spain, and while the ship was docked there she was commandeered by Spanish officials to convey part of the Sicilian Regiment to Spain, where it was required for the forthcoming Armada. In a letter written to the Duke of Medina Sidonia on 3rd June 1587 the King speaks of the ship as 'a Venetian vessel with thirty-two pieces (of artillery) which has been brought to Gibraltar'. When she reached Lisbon, some time before 7th January 1588, the Marquis of Santa Cruz ordered that the *Valencera* should be impounded to take part in the campaign herself. Her captain (and possibly owner), variously named as Oratio, Horatio Donai, Horatio Donayo and Horatio Donago, was ordered to grave (clean, caulk and tar) his ship but, naturally reluctant to make his vessel even more useful to the Spaniards, he at first refused to do so. In some way, however, he was prevailed upon to change his mind, for in a progress report sent to the King on 19th March it is stated that '*La Venetiana Valencera* is fully equipped and ready for sailing'. During this time the ship appears to have received an increment of ten guns over her own original armament of thirty-two pieces, for when she sailed in May she carried a total of forty-two. The nature of this extra armament, and the reason for carrying it, will become clear when we examine the guns found on the wreck.

La Trinidad Valencera (as we shall call her from now on) was not the only Venetian vessel pressed to take part in the Armada.

1 Breughel engraving (c. 1560) showing a Mediterranean-built merchant ship similar to those used as temporary warships in the Armada. *Santa Maria de la Rosa* was one such: excavations have shown that her mainmast, like the mast of the ship in the engraving; was positioned well forward in the Mediterranean fashion

2 (a) The team kits up at Dunquin jetty

2 (b) Setting out for the search area. Great Blasket island is on the right; Dunmore Head and the Sugarloaf Rock are on the left

3 (a) The broken anchor lost by Marcos de Aramburu in 1588 is brought ashore at Dingle

3 (b) The main anchor of the *Santa Maria de la Rosa*, hooked foul on the northern edge of Stromboli Reef

4 (a) The metal detector demonstrated to the team by Jeremy Green. (*Left to right:* Jeremy Green, 'Mick' Roberts, 'Smudge' Smith, Karl Bialowas, Chris Oldfield, Alf Slingsby, Jack Sumner and Colin Martin)

4 (b) Ballast stones, showing (*top centre*) the concreted iron ball with the knife cut made by Mike Edmonds when he identified the wreck

5 (a) Martin, Wignall and Grattan with some of the first recoveries made from the *Santa Maria de la Rosa*

5 (b) Main hull timbers after excavation (scale in feet)

5 (c) Positioning a survey grid on the wreck site. Timbers from the wreck can be seen in the left foreground

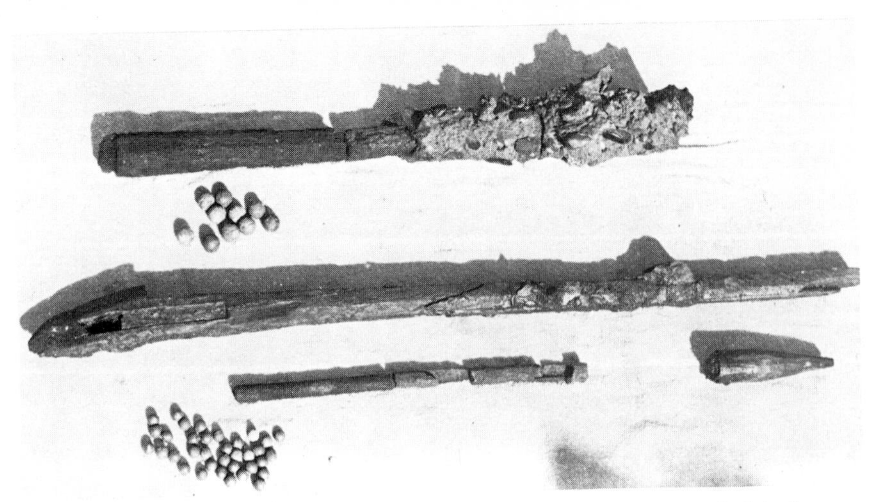

6 (a) Steel musket barrel (*top*) with concretion partly removed; ¾-inch bullets suitable for the weapon shown below. (*Below musket*): wooden arquebus stock with shot and fragments of barrel. The object at the bottom right is the butt end of a pike or similar weapon

6 (b) Types of shot from the *Santa Maria* wreck site, identifying the guns she carried

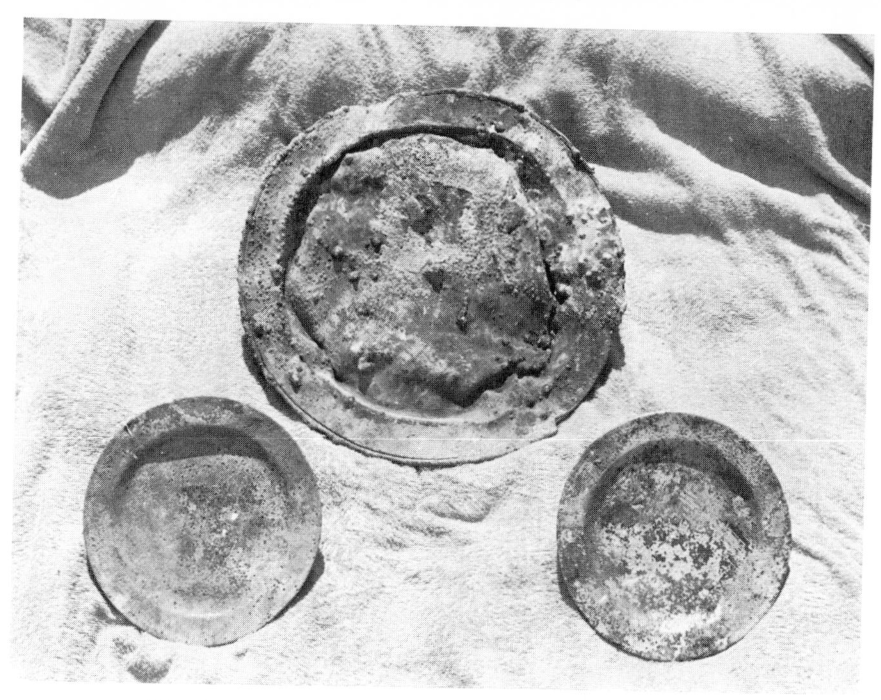

7 (a) Pewter plates; the lower pair are the Matute plates

7 (b) The Matute inscription

8 (a) Pewter medallion of the Virgin with the string still knotted in its loop

8 (b) Waiting to dive – Mike Stewart (by the engine) and Chris Oldfield. This is how those who have dived there remember Blasket Sound – wet, cold and hostile

9 A Baltic hulk similar to *El Gran Grifón*: engraving after Breughel (c. 1560)

10 *El Gran Grifón* wreck site at Stroms Hellier

11 The bronze *media sacre* is hoisted ashore

(*a*) *reverse*

12 Silver 4-*real* coin of Philip II (Toledo mint) from *El Gran Grifón*

(*b*) *obverse*

13 A Mediterranean carrack, or large merchant ship, similar to *La Trinidad Valencera* from an engraving by Breughel (c. 1560). Note the swivel guns at the stern and on the forecastle pointing downwards, and the large gun evidently mounted on a field carriage in the waist

14 Navigators' dividers found on the wreck site

15 (a) A large turned wooden bowl, exposed just prior to lifting

15 (b) An unbroken olive jar, revealed during excavations

16 A child's leather boot: the author carefully removes from concretion one of the most poignant finds made from the Armada wrecks

The Venetians, though nominally supporters of Philip's cause, relied wholly on trade for the existence of their maritime republic, and in consequence liked to maintain friendly relations with everybody. England, as it happened, was an old and valued customer, and her recent conflict with Spain had not prevented Anglo/Venetian trade from continuing. 'The Spaniards are ill pleased to see Venetian ships trading with England,' the Venetian ambassador at Madrid had written in 1587, and no doubt the charge of trading with the enemy helped ease Spanish consciences — if they were ever troubled — when Venetian and other Mediterranean ships were seized for the Armada in 1587 and 1588. Philip was especially anxious to secure large merchant ships which could carry the heavy battery artillery which was needed to bring his auxiliary fleet up to what he considered to be front-line warship standards, and the biggest merchantmen were usually to be found in the Mediterranean. In February 1588 the masters of the Venetian ships *Regazona* and *Lavia,* which had inadvisedly docked at Lisbon, 'were informed that the King required those vessels . . . the commissioners reported that these ships were the finest, the best armed and manned of all that lay in Lisbon, and on no account should his Majesty let them go'. Vigorous diplomatic protest by Venice was of no avail, and though Philip's commissioners offered their profound apologies and regrets to the ambassador, they stressed that 'because of the great need for big ships of the build of those two Venetians which are lying at Lisbon, he (the King) cannot release them . . . the Venetian ships are so powerful that they can give battle to ten or twelve Englishmen'. The *Regazona* and the *Lavia* sailed respectively as flagship and vice-flagship to the Levant squadron, and of that whole squadron of ten great ships (including *La Trinidad Valencera*) only the *Regazona* and one other returned to Spain. The *Lavia* was wrecked on the Irish coast, perhaps at Streedagh Strand, Co. Sligo.

In the storm which forced some of the Armada to shelter in Corunna, and others to ride out the tempest at sea, many of the clumsy Levanters and equally unweatherly supply hulks were driven towards the Scilly Isles. Among them were *La Trinidad Valencera* and *El Gran Grifón,* flagship of the hulks. By 11th July (the day after the *Santa Maria de la Rosa* had been remasted at Corunna) the *Valencera* had reached Vivero, and was present at the muster held at Corunna on 13th July, when she is listed with a complement of 415 men — an increase of 53 over the Lisbon figure.

The *Valencera* was undoubtedly the strongest and best armed ship in the Levantine squadron, and she was hotly engaged in most of the running fights which took place between the Eddystone and Gravelines. She was involved in the desultory long-range exchanges with Lord Howard and others at the start of the battle, and she became more closely engaged during the actions off Portland Bill and the Isle of Wight. Early in the fighting the *Valencera* and Don Alonso de Leiva's *Rata Encoronada*, also of the Levant squadron, were detached as separate striking units with two galleasses attached to each, though whether these units were employed as such in action, or with what effect, is not known. In the final rearguard action off Gravelines the *Valencera* was one of the dozen or so ships which fought in Medina Sidonia's close support and so saved the retreating Armada from destruction.

How *La Trinidad Valencera,* in company with *El Gran Grifón* and two other hulks, became separated from the main body of the fleet during the north-about voyage is recounted on an earlier page. Somewhere off the north-west coast of Ireland, it will be recalled, the *Valencera* and the *Grifón* took on survivors from the *Barca de Amburg* just before she went down, and shortly afterwards the remaining ships lost contact with one another. The *Valencera* was still off the north Irish coast when, on the night of 12th September, she was caught in a storm which caused a severe leak forward. Continuous shifts at the pumps failed to keep the water from rising and she was forced to run, almost foundering, for the coast. She passed between Malin Head and Inishtrahull Island, with her crew ignorant of their position, for they mistook that island for the Blaskets, 250 miles away at the southern end of the country. The Blasket landfall was one relatively well known to the Spaniards (see pp. 32–3) and so perhaps the *Valencera*'s crew were vainly searching for Smerwick harbour when they found shelter at the western end of Kinnagoe Bay, not far from the entrance to Lough Foyle. It seems from the evidence now obtained from her wreck that the ship was drawing as much as twenty-five feet of water, which implies that she had upwards of seven feet of water in her hold and must therefore have been close to sinking, when she grounded on a reef, perhaps during an attempt to beach closer inshore. She seems to have settled quickly with her stern on the sand and her bow on the reef, though the water was far too shallow to cover her completely. There she sat for about two days, relatively intact, until on 16th September she broke her keel and fell apart.

As soon as the *Valencera* grounded Don Alonso de Luzon escaped in the ship's boat, which was damaged, and with 'five more of the best of his company landed first, only with their rapiers in their hands', as he was later to state under interrogation to his captors. He also explained how, with their own broken boat and a boat they hired from O'Doherty clansmen, some of the survivors were brought ashore with their weapons and valuables. Others escaped by swimming, though it appears that forty or so were drowned when the ship broke apart. The Spaniards almost certainly landed on a small shingle beach, now called Port Kinnagoe, which lies some 200 yards from the wreck site, where they would have found an easy landing and fresh water.

> When they first landed [said Don Alonso] . . . they found four or five savage people — as he termeth them — who bade them welcome and well used them, until some twenty more wild men came unto them, after which they took away a bag of money containing 1 000 reals of plate (i.e. silver coins) and a cloak of blue rash, richly laid with gold lace. They were about two days in landing all their men, and being landed, had very ill entertainment, finding no other relief of victual in the country than of certain garrans (small hill ponies), which they bought off poor men for their money, which garrans they killed and did eat, and some small quantities of butter that the common people brought also to sell. Who they were that brought those things unto them he knoweth not, only that it was in O'Doherty's country;[1] and said that before he and the rest of the gentlemen of the company yielded themselves, none were slain by the savage people.

[1] O'Doherty country covered the whole of Inishowen. In 1541 the clan chief, Séan Mor O'Doherty, submitted with other Ulster chiefs to Henry VIII, and was granted a knighthood. His son and successor, Sir John Og O'Doherty, submitted to Queen Elizabeth but later revolted. In 1588 his loyalties were divided; though nominally pro-English, he was in fact anxious to help and support the Spanish cause. An O'Doherty stronghold stood at Glenagivney, about a mile from where the *Valencera* was wrecked.

The terrible events which took place after the landing are described in great detail by two of the survivors, both private soldiers in the Neapolitan *tercio,* Juan de Nova and Francisco de Borja. These men at length reached France where they were examined by the Spanish authorities about their adventures, and the main part of their statement follows:

> They learnt that (the countryside in which they landed) was held by the Queen of England's troops, and that at a castle called Duhort (Doherty?)[1] there dwelt an Irish bishop named Cornelius. They therefore took their way hither, and after having been three days on the road they arrived within a day's journey of the place. Colonel Alonso de Luzon thereupon sent a messenger forward to the bishop, saying that, as he was a Catholic, they begged him to help and advise them. He replied that they might come to the castle, and make an appearance of taking it by force, firing their arquebuses, etc., and it would then be surrendered to them. This was for the purpose of preventing the Queen's officers from saying that he had surrendered it voluntarily.
>
> The Colonel and the whole of them set forward, and when they arrived within sight of the castle those within discharged a piece of artillery towards the part where the Queen's garrison was. The Colonel, therefore, fearing treason, refused to enter the castle, but directed his steps by a marsh towards another dismantled castle near. They then discovered that the Queen's forces were approaching them, to the number of 200 horse, and as many footmen, arquebusiers, and bowmen.[2] The

[1] Almost certainly Sir John Og O'Doherty's stronghold at Illagh, about 3 miles N.W. of Derry. A few fragments of tumbled walling at the site of the castle can still be seen.

[2] This force, actually only 150 strong and badly equipped, had come from Burt Castle, about five miles away on the shores of Lough Swilly. The commanders were an 'affected' Irishman called Major John Kelly, and two English captains, Richard and Henry Hovenden. Most of the soldiers under their command were not English troops, but lightly armed Irish irregulars. Militarily, they seem to have been a much weaker force than Don Alonso's Spaniards, and Kelly displayed considerable cunning (albeit coupled with treachery and gross inhumanity)in bringing about Don Alonso's surrender and his men's destruction. Kelly's threat of the imminent arrival of 3000 of the Queen's troops was a hollow one: the English could not have mustered that many from the whole of Ireland. The precarious position in which the English undoubtedly found themselves in the face of well armed bodies of men such as Don Alonso's force provides a motive, if not a moral justification, for what followed.

Spanish force therefore halted, and the enemy did likewise; drums being beaten on both sides for a parley. The enemy asked them what they wanted in the Queen's dominions, to which they replied that they were Spanish soldiers who had been cast upon the island by the wreck of their ship, and they begged that they might be allowed, upon due payment, to obtain a ship to take them back to Spain. They were told that this could not be, and that they must surrender as prisoners of war. They replied that if this was the only alternative, they would rather die fighting, as befitted Spaniards. The English answered that if they did not surrender at once 3 000 of the Queen's troops would come shortly and cut all their throats. They still persisted, however, in their refusal to surrender, and they remained halted all that night. The next night the enemy sounded the attack at two or three points, and a skirmish commenced, which continued the whole night.

The next morning, whilst they were endeavouring to better their position, they heard the enemy's drums again sound for a parley. The Colonel and Captains Beltran del Salto and Hieronimo de Aybar went down to the level of the bog to hear what they had to say. The major of the enemy told them that they had better lay down their arms and he would conduct them to the Queen's governor in Dublin, 30 miles off,[1] who would send them to the Queen. The major then made them many offers and promises, if they would surrender, and in view of this, and that his men were dying with hunger, and that the enemy had cut off all his supplies, the Colonel replied that he would lay down his arms on fair terms of war, if they would keep their promise, and allow each man to retain the best suit of clothes he had. They gave their word that this should be done, and the Spaniards laid down their arms. As soon as the enemy had possession of them, and conveyed them to the other side of the bog towards Dublin, they fell upon the Spaniards in a body and despoiled them of everything they possessed, leaving them quite naked, and killing those who offered the least resistance. The Colonel complained of this to the major of the enemy's force, the reply being that it had been done by the soldiery without his orders, but he gave his

[1] Dublin was really more than 120 miles away; this obvious lie suggests that Kelly never intended to take his prisoners there, and had planned the massacre from the beginning. Even his promise to bring the captives unharmed to the presence of the Lord Deputy was a cynical one; Fitzwilliam had sworn to hang every Spaniard who fell into his hands.

word that the men should all be dressed on their arrival at a castle where he intended to pass the night, two miles from the place where they then were. When they had traversed half this distance the major said that as the road was so bad they would bivouac in the open for that night. They did so, the enemy forming square, inside of which they placed the Colonel, Don Rodrigo Lasso, Don Sebastian Zapata, gentlemen volunteers; Don Diego de Luzon, and Don Antonio Manrique, attaches; Don Beltran del Salto, Hieronimo de Aybar, Juan de Guzman, and Don Garcia Manrique, Captains; and the Chaplain-General and Judge of the regiment, the Vicar of the shoeless Carelites of Lisbon and two other friars, the other soldiers being left a stone's throw away, naked, in which manner they passed the night.

The next morning, at daybreak, the enemy came to separate some other officers who were amongst the soldiers, and put them inside the square with the rest. The remaining soldiers were then made to go into an open field, and a line of the enemy's arquebusiers approached them on one side and a body of his cavalry on the other, killing over 300 of them with lance and bullet; 150 Spaniards managed to escape across a bog, most of them wounded, and sought refuge in the castle of Duhort, where Bishop Cornelius received them and conveyed 100 or so, who were unwounded, to the Island of Hibernia (Islay?). Those who were wounded remained in the castle, under the care of the people there, who were Catholics, but many of them died every day. They were sent, under a guide, to the house of a savage gentleman named O'Cahan,[1] where they remained for three days, both he and his people displaying great sympathy with them in their sufferings, feeding them and waiting upon them hand and foot. On the fourth day they went with another guide to a brother of his, also named O'Cahan, twelve miles from here.[2] He welcomed us with the same kindness as his brother had done. The day after our arrival mass was said for us, but this was an exception in our honour, as they usually have mass only once a week. On the third day after their arrival he sent them with another guide and letters to another gentleman named Sorleyboy,[3] begging him to provide them with a boat, as they were Catholics as

[1] Near Dungiven.

[2] Outside Limavady.

[3] Sorley Boy McDonnell, joint lord of the 'Route' between Ireland and his kinsmen in the Scottish Isles.

he was; this gentleman possessing vessels, as he lives on an arm of the sea.[1] He received them with much kindness, and kept them twenty days, mass being said for them. There was at the time no boats there, but he sent for some three miles off. Two boats were sent and eighty soldiers embarked in them, to be taken to an island off Scotland, which is only ten miles off,[2] the rest remaining in the castle until the boats should return.

In the meanwhile the Governor in Dublin had learned that this gentleman had sheltered the Spaniards, and sent to tell him, in the Queen's name, not to ship any more Spaniards on pain of death and confiscation of all his property, and to surrender to the English those he still had with him. He replied that he would rather lose his life and goods, and those of his wife and children, than barter Christian blood. He had, he said, dedicated his sword to the defence of the Catholic faith, and those who held it, and in spite of the Governor, the Queen, and all England, he would aid and embark the rest of the Spaniards who came to him; and he came back to them (the Spaniards) with tears in his eyes, and told them the Governor's demand and his reply thereto. So when the boats came back he shipped the rest.

When they arrived on the Scotch island on the other side, they learned from a savage who spoke Latin that, on the same day that the English had massacred the soldiers, they had conveyed the Colonel and the rest of his officers on foot, all naked as they were, to Dublin, fourteen miles off, where they were put in prison, except those who died on the road of hunger, thirst, and exhaustion. He said that the man who ordered all the soldiers to be murdered was an Irish earl named O'Neil.[3]

They (the deponents and their companions) then proceeded on their way, being guided by men sent from one gentleman to another, until they arrived in Edinburgh, when the King

[1] Sorley Boy's stronghold was at Dunluce Castle, on the Antrim cliffs near the Giant's Causeway, not far from where the galleass *Girona* was later wrecked.

[2] Probably Islay, which is actually just over 20 miles from Dunluce.

[3] Hugh O'Neill, Earl of Tyrone. O'Neill, greatest and most powerful of the Ulster lords, commanded the English forces there in 1588; Henry Hovenden was his secretary and trusted adviser. How far O'Neill was really implicated in the Illagh massacre, if at all, is not known; later, however, he was himself to seek Spanish aid in the great rebellion which he led against English occupation towards the end of Elizabeth's reign.

was.[1] By his orders they were kept lodged in the town for 30 days, being fed and clothed the while. He then sent them to France, dividing them amongst four Scottish ships which, as the weather was against them, had to coast along the English shore, and twice had to cast anchor in English ports. On one occasion the Governor of the place, learning that there were Spaniards on board the ships, sought to take them out, but the shipmasters said that the soldiers had been delivered to their care by the King of Scotland to carry to France, and had ordered them, on pain of death, not to abandon them.[2] They therefore refused to surrender them, but would defend them with their own lives. They sent a boat to acquaint the King of Scotland of the occurrence, and he informed the Queen of England that, as the Spaniards had appealed to him, he had provided ships to take them across, and he begged that they should not be molested in her ports. She therefore gave orders that they were not to be interfered with. Twenty days had passed in the meanwhile, the weather still having detained them in port, but at last they set sail and all arrived in France.[3]

A number of other survivors found refuge among the Irish clans. In 1596 eight Spanish soldiers wrecked with the Armada, including two from *La Trinidad Valencera,* were still in Ulster living under the protection of Tyrone and petitioning the King of Spain — somewhat optimistically — for back pay. Contrary to popular belief the local Irish in the main behaved well towards the Armada survivors; though as fugitives from the sea the Spaniards were, by long tradition, considered fair game for robbery,

[1] King James VI of Scotland. William Asheby, an English agent in Edinburgh, reported on 23rd October that '50 Spaniards, poor and miserable, (are) passing through this country, who were wrecked in a ship in the north of Ireland called *La Ballanzara* of 1200 tons . . . the 20th of October there came to Edinburgh 20 Spaniards and 16 Italians; the rest are sick.'

[2] An original copy of the safe-conduct issued to the Spaniards at Edinburgh is preserved in the Scottish Record Office. The document is signed by the town's provost, John Arnot, and is in fact an early form of passport.

[3] Their arrival at Havre de Grâce on 26th December is reported by the Armada's Pilot-General, Marolin de Juan. 'There arrived here some Scottish ships with 32 Spanish soldiers from our Armada lost on the coast of Ireland. They belonged to the Venetian ship *Valencera,* which carried Don Alonso de Luzon, Colonel of the Regiment of Naples, and many private gentlemen, who, they say, remain prisoners on the island, most of the soldiers having been killed.'

they were otherwise generally treated with compassion and humanity, and sometimes even helped on their way, by the indigenous Gaelic population. The English authorities and soldiers, and the 'affected' Irish in their pay, were the ones responsible for most of the slaughter. Of the latter, perhaps the most horrific example is that set by one Melaghlin M'Cabb, who is said to have slain eighty shipwrecked Spaniards with his gallowglas axe.

Don Alonso de Luzon and his companions had been spared the Illagh massacre not for any humanitarian reason but because of the large ransoms which might be exacted for their safe return. Starving and destitute, stripped of all their possessions, in some cases even of their clothing and footwear, they were marched overland more than 100 miles to the grim castle of Drogheda, on the coast north of Dublin, where they were incarcerated. They were interrogated under the direction of Sir Henry Wallop, with the Welshman David Gwynn (who we met on an earlier page in connection with the questioning of the *Santa Maria*'s survivor) acting as interpreter. The depositions of Don Alonso de Luzon and Don Baltasar Lopez de Arbor, Sergeant-Major of the Neapolitan *tercio,* have survived, together with a full list of the other Armada prisoners held at Drogheda. Some were evidently members of the *Valencera*'s original crew; the captain, Horatio Donai; Michael of Venice, master-gunner; Domingo de Jorge, ship's clerk; Theodorini the Greek, a sailor; and Augustino, the ship's surgeon-barber. With them was Jacques Flamenco, a Fleming, who had been master of the hulk *Barca de Amburg.* As well as the proud names of the captured officers and *aventureros* — the high-born Dons, Captains, Ensigns, Sergeant-Majors and Provosts — we also glimpse some of what would have been called the 'lesser' sort, men such as Juan de Guzman, a private soldier; Juan Moreno St. Angelo, an Italian drummer; and Francisco de Soto, Don Alonso de Luzon's batman. Yet others are listed as having died on the nightmare march to Drogheda; these included Don Diego de Luzon, Don Alonso's younger brother, and Hernando de Canavera who 'died crossing a river'. The most touching and pathetic entry of all simply runs: 'Died before they surrendered — Don Pedro de Salto, aged from 14 to 15 years.'

Don Alonso de Luzon and Don Rodrigo de Lasso were eventually taken to London, where three years later they were still awaiting repatriation. Of the remaining captives none appear to have survived the blind and terrible vengeance of Lord Deputy Fitzwilliam, who continued to order the execution of Spanish prisoners long after the 'fury and heat of justice was past', as one English official, lamenting the waste of so much valuable ransom material, put it. Fitzwilliam's savage attitude towards the shipwrecked survivors is grimly summed up in his own words, written to Lord Burghley on 7th November 1588 : 'Since it hath pleased God by His hand upon the rocks to drown the greater and better sort of them I will, with His favour, be His soldier for the despatching of those ragges which yet remain.'

The Venetians, not unnaturally, sought compensation from Spain for the ships which had been taken illegally from them and then lost. On 7th January 1589 the Venetian ambassador at Madrid wrote to the Doge and Senate of Venice : 'I will do all I can for the Venetian ships, and if those interested in the *Lavia* and the *Valencera* are sure that the ships have been lost, and will send me a power of attorney, appointing me their agent, I will not only endeavour to recover the sums due but will try to secure for the owners some gratification, such as a contract for grain in Sicily or something of that kind.'

But the ambassador strove for compensation in vain, for the King of All the Spains and the Indies had been driven to the verge of bankruptcy by his great 'Enterprise of England'.

MASTER REMIGY'S GUNS

THE problem which faced the members of the City of Derry Sub-Aqua Club after their discovery of *La Trinidad Valencera*'s remains was a formidable one. They had made, they realised, an outstanding historical discovery, but they were unsure of how best to deal with it. The salvage of ancient shipwrecks requires money and special resources, and the Club possessed little of either. All they could draw on was enthusiasm and common-sense. An urgent meeting to discuss the situation was called by the Club's chairman, Jim Whelan, and from the first it was unanimously agreed that whatever happened the site should be treated with archaeological respect. The Club then took practical steps to get the project under way, and appointed Steuart Mossman as organiser and co-ordinator of its practical working, while Father Mick Keaveney, one of the original finders, was asked to look after the financial affairs. A bank loan was arranged to cover initial expenditure. Stan Donaghy, the Club's Publicity Officer, then got in touch with the Press and Television with a view to securing support from these quarters.

As soon as administrative arrangements were made a pontoon raft was moored over the wreck and preliminary operations began. Diving Officer Charles Perkinson, assisted by John Davidson, took charge of the programme, supported by a shore party organised by Gerry Heatley. The rocky tongue which the ship had struck, and the flat sandy sea bed surrounding it, were minutely searched, and a number of loose objects were found. All were marked, and their positions were then plotted by Eamonn Molloy who — being a surveyor by profession — had taken on the job of surveying the site. Early finds included several different sizes of iron and stone round-shot, a crushed copper kettle, a pewter jug, fragments of pottery, a bronze steelyard weight with a lead core, and two sheet copper steelyard powder ladles — one for a 50-pounder whole cannon, and the other for a gun of *sacre*

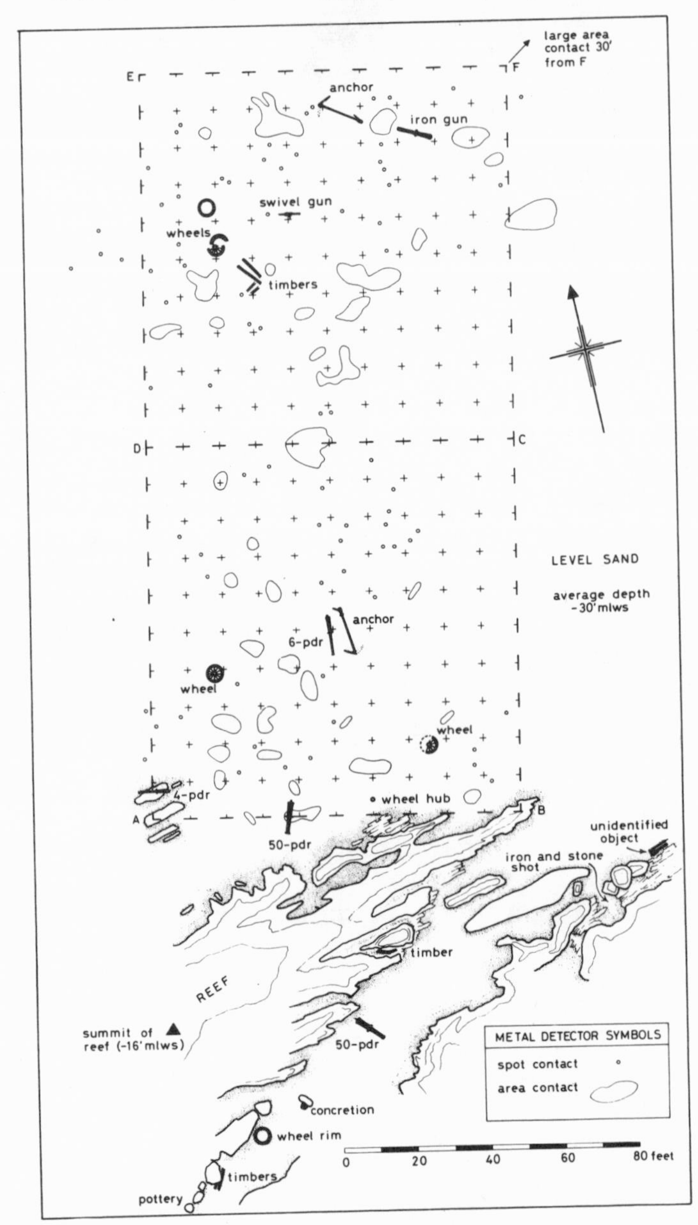

Fig. 14. Wreck site plan of *La Trinidad Valencera*, Kinnagoe Bay, Co. Donegal. Commanded by Don Alonso de Luzon, lost 14th September, 1588, and rediscovered 20th February, 1971

size. The most interesting item was discovered when a piece of concretion was broken open to reveal, in a splendid state of preservation, a pair of brass navigator's dividers. These finds were taken to the conservation laboratory at the Ulster Museum in Belfast, where they were cleaned and treated by the laboratory director, Stephen Rees Jones, who had worked on the finds made by Robert Sténuit from the Armada galleass *Girona*.

My own involvement in the *Trinidad Valencera* came through a stroke of good fortune. At the end of March 1971 — not long after the *Valencera*'s discovery — Sydney Wignall and I had been at Bristol University, presenting papers on our Armada researches to an international symposium on marine archaeology. Paul Johnstone and Ray Sutcliffe, of the BBC programme 'Chronicle', who had presented Wignall's Armada film, were also there, and at the end of the conference they received word from the City of Derry Sub-Aqua Club that some of the *Valencera* guns were to be raised the next day — which happened to be Good Friday. Johnstone and Sutcliffe were most anxious to obtain underwater film of the lifting operation, but no suitable film crew could be found at such short notice, and in any case only two seats could be obtained on the London-Belfast flight. Wignall, who had a great deal of filming experience, was first asked to go out and do the job, but had to decline for business reasons. He suggested that I might take it on. Though I knew almost nothing about filming, the chance was too good to miss. The following morning Ray Sutcliffe and I boarded the Belfast aircraft with a hired underwater movie camera stowed among our luggage, and in the course of the flight Sutcliffe taught me how to operate the camera and briefed me on filming techniques. A car was waiting at the airport to speed us over the border to Kinnagoe Bay. Most of the club members had already gathered at the wreck site, where a hired trawler belonging to skipper Len Forbes of Portrush was already moored. Forbes had improvised a side lifting tackle with a crane jib and hand winch lashed athwartships, and two guns — a 7¼ inch whole-cannon and a small culverin type — had been raised and brought ashore. We had arrived just in time, since only one gun remained to be lifted, although someone claimed to have seen part of another large gun sticking out of the sand which had since become covered up. On board the trawler, I struggled into borrowed

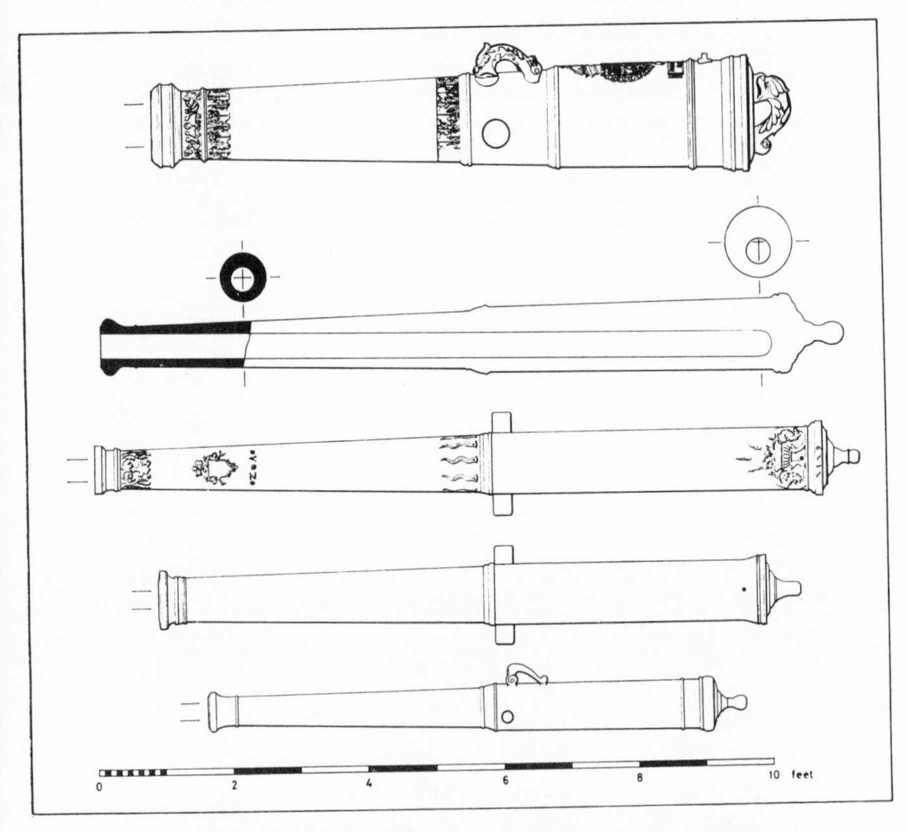

Fig. 15. Bronze ordnance from Armada wrecks. (*From top to bottom*): 50-pounder curtow (weight 5429 lb) from *La Trinidad Valencera*: one of a pair bearing the full arms of Philip II (including the arms of England – Philip II had married Mary Tudor in 1554). The gun was cast by Remigy de Halut, *Fondeur Royale* at Malines Royal Gunfoundry, near Antwerp

9-pounder demi-culverin muzzle from *El Gran Grifón* with a conjectural reconstruction of the remainder (estimated weight 3000 lb). Note off centre bore – evidence of poor gunfounding technique

6-pounder Venetian gun (weight 2632 lb) from *La Trinidad Valencera.* The founder, Z. A., is Zuanne Alberghetti of Venice

4-pounder (estimated weight 2000 lb), probably Venetian, from *La Trinidad Valencera*

3-pounder demi-saker (estimated weight 1000 lb) from *El Gran Grifón*

diving equipment and followed Eamonn Molloy, the club member who was conducting the survey of the wreck site, over the side. The bulky film camera was handed to me, and I swam down in the wake of Molloy's bubbles to the sea floor and swam down with him on a conducted tour of what had so far been found.

I spent more than 6 hours in the water that day, shooting reel after reel of film, and in spite of an ill-fitting wet suit I never noticed the cold until, in the evening, I almost collapsed from heat-loss and exhaustion. I filmed everything I could find on the wreck site — the emblazoned breech of a bronze gun sticking out of the sand, two huge iron anchors, and several massive 5-foot diameter wooden guncarriage wheels. Then two club divers, Andy Robinson and Danny O'Donnell, began to dig the sand away from the bronze gun — a long culverin type — in order to pass lifting strops underneath it. I filmed them close-up while they worked, then moved slowly away to get a long shot. As I rose upwards and backwards my kicking fins raised clouds of sand from the sea floor, and among the swirling vortices I glimpsed something bright and yellow. Filming forgotten for the moment, I dropped back on to the sand, laid the camera down, and swam to investigate. The object I had spotted turned out to be a tiny bronze knob, only just peeping through the rippled sandy desert of the sea floor. A few strokes of my open palm fanned more sand away, and more of the object emerged. Soon it was recognisable as the sprightly tail of a bronze dolphin, the breeching loop of a very large gun, as bright and untarnished as if it was new. By now Eamonn Molloy had joined me, and in a few minutes we had dug out most of the breech, to find that the gun — which was lying upside down in the sand — was exactly similar to the 7¼-inch whole-cannon which the club members had raised the day before. This was the gun which had earlier been spotted, only to be lost again in the shifting sand.

Molloy surfaced and called for his measuring tapes, and together we triangulated the gun's position in relation to the other finds. After a brief discussion we then decided to raise this new gun before lifting the culverin, since it was obviously a more dramatic and important find, and the ideal filming conditions which at present prevailed might not continue. I will never forget the moments which followed. First Robinson and O'Donnell put a strop through the breech dolphin in order to pull the gun out of the sand and turn it right way up for lifting. As the winch on the trawler took up the strain the huge weapon began to lift tail first from the muddy silt, an unbelievably impressive sight which I followed through with the whirring film camera. Finally, when the ornate muzzle broke free, a great cloud of black smoke belched forth, almost as if a ghostly gunner had set it off. The 'smoke' turned out to be the charcoal remnants of its original powder charge.

The gun was lowered back to the sea bed and tipped right way up so that strops could be passed round it for the final lift. As it lay there I began to examine the escutcheons and markings, which were so clear and crisp as to give one an uncanny impression of having been transported back in time. There, in all its pomp and heraldry, was the full escutcheon of Philip II in the very first year of his reign, 1556: a shield surrounded with the chain of firestones and rays of the Order of the Golden Fleece (of which Philip was Grand Master) with a royal crown above it and a box below it carrying the words PHILIPPVS REX. The shield included not only the armorial devices of Philip's own titles and wide dominions, but also the lions and fleurs-de-lys of England, for in 1556 Philip was the consort of Mary Tudor, Queen of England, and so as titular King of England he quartered that country's arms on his shield.

A neatly cut inscription on the base ring of the gun read thus:

IOANES . MĀRICVS . A . LARA . FIERI . CVRAVIT
OPVS . REMIGY . DE . HALVT
ANNO 1556

Which may be translated

Juan Manrique de Lara saw to my coming into being
The work of Remigy de Halut
1556

Naturally, we searched the archives to identify these men and, with the help of Robert Sténuit, and Marcel Kocken of the Malines Museum, we found them. Juan Manrique de Lara, who ordered the gun to be cast (*fieri curavit*) is well known as a soldier and statesman of considerable standing. His family held the dukedom of Nájera, the ancient seat of the Kings of Navarre, and took their title from the small town of Lara in Old Castile famed for the Seven Infantes who were martyred by the Moors in 970, and whose tombs may still be seen in the little church of San Millan de Suso at Nájera. Under the Emperor Charles V he had been Keeper of the Keys of the Royal Household, and as Imperial Ambassador at Rome he had undertaken the tricky negotiations involved in securing Papal dispensation for the marriage of Philip to Mary Tudor in 1554 (for Mary, though a devout and pious Catholic, had once committed the mortal sin — under cruel duress—of recognising her father Henry VIII as supreme head of the Church). Between 1551 and his death in 1574 Juan Manrique de Lara was Captain-General of Artillery for the Kingdoms of Aragon and Castile, and he saw much action both in Italy and Germany. In 1556, when these royal guns were cast at Malines, he was serving as Captain-General of Artillery in the army of Flanders.

Two Manriques de Lara took part in the Armada: one, Don Rodrigo (probably Juan Manrique's grandson) sailed as an *aventurero* with thirteen retainers aboard Don Alonso de Leiva's *Rata Encoronada,* and presumably perished in the wreck of the *Girona*; the other, Don Garcia Manrique de Lara (perhaps a younger brother), was an infantry captain in Don Alonso de Luzon's regiment on board the *Trinidad Valencera* herself. Don Garcia was captured along with de Luzon and the other survivors of the *Valencera* wreck, and was eventually executed at Drogheda.

Remigy de Halut, who cast this gun, was Master of the Royal Gunfoundry at Malines, a town near Antwerp in the Low Countries. Malines had been renowned as a bronze-founding centre for many years: even before the advent of cast metal artillery in the second half of the 15th century fine bells had been produced there. The most famous of the Malines master-founders was Hans Poppenruyter, who began making high quality bronze ordnance in the 1480s and who, in the course of the first two decades of the 16th century, cast more than 144 guns for Henry VIII of England. In these years Henry amassed, in the words of the Venetian Ambassador to England, 'cannon enough to conquer Hell'. Work for England was suspended at the Malines foundry in 1526 because Henry, always short of money, proved a bad payer. In the meantime, however, Poppenruyter had secured an even more important customer. In 1520 Charles V, who in that year became ruler both of Spain and of the Holy Roman Empire, had bestowed upon Malines the profitable honour of making it his Royal Gunfoundry, with Poppenruyter assuming the title of Founder Royal. Under the patronage of Charles V, and not a little helped by the wars prevailing throughout Europe, the Malines foundry flourished.

In 1526 Poppenruyter married Hedwige van den Nieuwenhuysen, who was evidently a lady of spirit and character for she took on much of the administration of the foundry. Poppenruyter died in 1534, leaving no legitimate heir, and for two years the redoubtable Hedwige continued to run the foundry on her own. But no woman, however strong-willed and competent, could undertake the heavy, dangerous, and highly skilled work of a master-founder, and so she began to look around for a suitable mate — a man whom she might contract first of all to be her co-director in the foundry and, only secondarily, her husband. The man she found was Remigy de Halut.

Remigy (or Remy) de Halut, Viscount of Burges Saint-Winoc, had been born at Braine-le-Château (not far from the village of Waterloo), and in his youth he had served in the artillery regiment of Philip de Montmorency. No doubt, as was common at that time, his training as a gunner included an apprenticeship in the gunfounder's art, possibly under Poppenruyter himself; at any event he must have had the qualifications Hedwige was looking for. They were married at Malines on 7th July 1536, and shortly afterwards Charles V confirmed Remigy's appointment as Founder Royal in succession to Hans Poppenruyter.

Remigy de Halut proved to be as skilled a gunfounder as his predecessor, and the production of fine guns of all types and calibres continued. In 1550 Charles V decided to establish a centre for his entire field artillery service in the Low Countries at Malines, and by the following year a great arsenal and munitions depot had grown up around the foundry. Garrison troops and workshops personnel were stationed there under the command of a Grand Master of Artillery, who between 1550 and 1564 was Philippe de Stavele, Knight of Glajon. Remigy de Halut continued as Founder Royal, and under him two important reforms in gunfounding technique were introduced. The first, which was only partially successful, was an attempt to standardise gun-types by laying down strict formulae by which calibre, barrel length, total weight of metal, and thickness of barrel walls were to be calculated. The second reform was the introduction of proof-firing. Each gun cast at the foundry, before being passed fit for service, was fired three times in succession with a charge of fine-grained powder equal to the weight of its shot — about twice the normal powder load.

Hedwige van den Nieuwenhuysen died in 1562, Remigy de Halut in 1568, and by the latter date the foundry had fallen into decline. The Treaty of Câteau Cambrésis, which was concluded between Philip II and Henry II of France in April 1559, brought to a close the rivalry between the Hapsburg dynasty and the French crown which had caused interminable warfare in Europe for more than forty years, while at the same time religious dissension in the Low Countries began to flare into bitter armed conflict. Malines was sacked in 1566, 1572, and 1580, and although the foundry continued spasmodically into the 17th and 18th centuries its golden age was over by 1560.

The foundry itself, which stood near the old Brussels Gate just inside the city walls, had originally been a residence of the Count d'Egmont, and was converted into a gun-foundry in Poppenruyter's time. The original building survived into the 19th century as an orphans' home, and was finally demolished in 1837. Several prints of it exist, and the modern street name of Egmont still commemorates the site.

The two royal guns cast by Remigy de Halut for Philip II in 1556 and recovered from the wreck of *La Trinidad Valencera* more than 400 years later are fitting monuments to this great foundry at the height of its fame, when Malines was the centre of the gunfounding art in Europe. The superb workmanship of the guns is evident not only in the basic techniques of their manufacture, but also in the skill and artistry with which they have been embellished. It is difficult not to feel an overpowering sense of history in the presence of these sinister, but none the less strangely beautiful, monsters of destruction. From the twined acanthus borders on their muzzles to their twin lifting dolphins, their escutcheons, inscriptions, and breech dolphin, they are magnificently evocative of the long-dead world in which they had been created. In 1556, as Remigy and his apprentices had carved out the intricate wooden patterns from which they would make the mould for the royal escutcheon with its encircling necklace of the Golden Fleece they would have known that, in January of that very same year, the new king had held a Chapter of the Order of the Golden Fleece at nearby Brussels. There, a number of new Knights of the Order — including Philippe de Stavele, Grand Master of Artillery at Malines — had been invested. In that year, too, Philip II twice passed through Malines on journeys between Brussels and Antwerp, and while there is no record of his actually having visited the foundry to see the guns, it would be strange if he did not take the opportunity to do so as he passed by the Brussels Gate. These guns, after all, had been cast in his own Royal Gunfoundry, and they may even have been the very first to bear his arms as King of Spain.

The weights of the two Remigy guns are stamped just above the escutcheons: 5 316 and 5 260 pounds respectively. The former actually weighs 5 429 modern pounds of 453.6 grammes, giving a unit for the Spanish weighing of 463 grammes. Allowing a margin of error for both weighings this unit is almost certainly the Castilian pound of 460 grammes (see Lewis, *Armada Guns*, pp. 208–16).

In the deposition taken after his capture Don Alonso de Luzon speaks of 'four cannons of brass' as distinct from the ship's other artillery of brass and iron, and the Remigy guns must be two of them. These guns were clearly not carried by the ship in her original role as a Venetian merchantman, and must therefore be part of the increment added at Lisbon to bring her gun-strength from its original thirty-two to the forty-two pieces listed in the final muster. There were, undoubtedly, two other guns of similar size aboard the *Valencera,* and the remaining six pieces of the increment are likely to have been heavy guns as well, probably including stone-throwing perriers ($6\frac{1}{2}$-inch stone shot has been found on the site) and perhaps heavy culverins. In this increment we can see the actual process whereby the Spaniards attempted to convert some of the larger ships in their auxiliary squadrons to heavily armed warship standards.

When we study the Remigy guns more closely further significant points emerge. In the first place these guns, for their class, are very short and lightly metalled. Twelve English whole-cannons inventorised at the Tower of London in 1595 weighed on average 8 500 pounds apiece, and this is the figure Professor Lewis adopted as a 'typical' whole-cannon in his categorisation of Armada gun-types, assessing it as 'a $7\frac{1}{4}$-inch muzzle loader of some 18 calibres in length, firing a 50-pound iron round-shot over a (relatively) medium range'. But, apart from calibre and weight of shot, the Remigy pieces come nowhere near this specification. They are only two-thirds of the weight, and three-quarters of the length. They are therefore not, by all the accepted criteria, whole-cannons at all, but specially lightened, cut-down versions of this class of gun. This provides us with a clue to where they originally came from.

In the early years of the 16th century Hans Poppenruyter, Remigy's predecessor at Malines, cast a matched set of siege guns for Henry VIII of England called the 'Twelve Apostles', which were described as 'large curtows weighing 56 hundredweights (i.e. 5 600 pounds — the 16th century hundredweight, or quintal, was 100 and not 112 pounds) apiece'. Another source states that Poppenruyter's curtows were 50-pounders and weighed 5 500 pounds. In English sources these same guns are referred to as 'curtails' — no doubt because they were in fact heavy siege guns 'curtailed' or cut-down for field use. At Malines, it will be remembered, the King of Spain maintained not only a royal gunfoundry but also, from 1550 until the Treaty of Câteau-Cambrésis in 1559, the headquarters of his land artillery service. During this time there was manufactured at Malines — probably mainly by Remigy de Halut — a heavy mobile siege train similar to, but much larger than, the one made earlier in the century by Poppenruyter for Henry VIII. Immediately after Câteau-Cambrésis most of the guns stockpiled at Malines, including the siege train, were shipped to garrisons in Spain and Italy.

We know quite a lot about this siege train and its strategic disposition in 1586 for the Marquis of Santa Cruz, in the plan he drew up for the invasion of England in that year, wanted to take it with him. It consisted, according to the Marquis, of fifty-four what he called *cañones reforzados*, twelve of which had been stationed at Messina and Palermo in Sicily, seventeen at Naples, and twenty-five at Cartagena, Malaga, and Lisbon. These *cañones reforzados* weighed on average, he tells us, 55 quintals (5 500 pounds) apiece, and they fired a shot in excess of 40 pounds. Taking into account variations in the 16th century pound unit, the average weight of these guns would have been, in modern terms, somewhere between 5 300 and 5 700 pounds—a bracket which encloses the true weights of the Remigy guns. That these two guns were actually part of Santa Cruz's fifty-four *canones reforzados* therefore seems almost beyond question.

There is further evidence to suggest that the guns of this siege train were of a highly standardised type and that they were used as ship-ordnance in the 1588 Armada. Among the guns found by the English aboard the captured Guipuzcoan *San Salvador* are two which are described as 'cannons' and registered as weighing, 'by the Spanish mark', 5 222 pounds and 5 329 pounds respectively. The Remigy guns, as already noted, weigh — also 'by the Spanish mark' — 5 316 and 5 260 pounds. Thus the four Armada 50-pounders of which we have certain evidence are within a hundredweight — or less than 2% of the total weight — of one another. Nor is it only in the matter of gun weights that an impression of standardisation manifests itself. The bore of the Remigy guns — 7¼ inches — is closely paralleled too. Shot suitable for such guns has been recovered both from the *Santa Maria* site and the Tobermory wreck, where, in addition, a 17th century salvor reported finding a gun 'which would carry a 48-pound ball' and another 'eleven feet length, and seven and one fourth part of measure in the bore . . .'

In early February 1588, when the old Marquis of Santa Cruz was still in command of the fleet as it lay in a state of confused half-preparation at Lisbon, the Venetian ambassador at Madrid wrote to his government that '. . . on board (the Armada), besides its own artillery, they have embarked twelve heavy siege guns and forty-eight smaller ones, with a double supply on gun carriages and wheels for the field batteries, and 600 mules . . .' The twelve 'heavy siege guns' were probably big culverins drawn from the sixteen mentioned as being available for the Armada in the 1586 list and described as 'culverins to dismantle the traverses' (i.e. of a fortress). These were very large guns — bigger than the Remigy curtows — each weighing 60 quintals and throwing a 25-pound shot. No doubt, then, the forty-eight 'smaller ones' were none other than the *cañones reforzados* from the same source. But under Santa Cruz there is no hint of evidence to suggest that any of these guns were being carried other than as cargo. After Medina Sidonia took over the fleet on the Marquis's death, however, a different picture emerges. The twelve 'heavy siege guns' appear again, as cargo, as do twenty-one lighter campaign pieces (evidently 5-pounder *sacres*). In the cargo section, however, there is no trace of the forty-eight presumed *cañones reforzados* of the earlier lists. Why? Because, I believe, they had been distributed among some of the larger auxiliary vessels in a desperate attempt to create more capital ships. Unfortunately Medina Sidonia's Lisbon muster does not break down the total gun-strength of the fleet into numbers for each type but it does say, quite specifically, that the guns 'for the ships' include 'many *cannons*, culverins, demi-culverins and perriers'.

On the *Trinidad Valencera* site we have come upon the remains of six massive spoked wooden guncarriage wheels, reinforced with iron, of the type normally associated with field use. Guncarriage wheels are listed in Santa Cruz's 1586 proposals as *ruedas herradas* (iron-bound wheels) for cannons, demi-cannons, culverins and demi-culverins, along with wooden axletrees and tallow for greasing the bearings. Two such wheels were found in close proximity to one of the Remigy guns — so close, in fact, as to suggest that these were the wheels upon which it had been mounted; that is to say that the gun had been mounted on a large two-wheeled carriage and not on the more usual shipboard truck carriage (the type with four small 'trucks' or wheels). Further evidence to suggest that these wheels were actually in use as guncarriages aboard the *Trinidad Valencera* and were not, for example, lying dismantled in the hold for land campaigning, comes from the fact that we found no examples of the much smaller limber wheels which were used to support the trail when the gun was on the move. Both types of wheel would surely have been in evidence if these had been dismantled guncarriages in transit.

Research into the matter shows that at this period the Spaniards were in the habit of using field carriages aboard ship. Early in the 17th century Sir Henry Mainwaring wrote that 'the fashion of those carriages we use at sea (i.e. truck carriages) are much better than those of the land (i.e. two-wheeled field carriages with trail); yet the Venetians and Spaniards and divers others use the other in their shipping. I think it rather that they want good timber to make them after the fashion of ship carriages than that they approve more of the field carriages, for only elm doth make them, whereof they have none'.

Sir William Monson, who in his youth had taken part in the

Armada fight, penned a very similar observation: 'They (the Spaniards) carry their great ordnance upon field carriages, which makes them the more dangerous and unserviceable, for their piece so lying cannot be traversed from side to side but must be shot off directly forward as they lie.'

Whether all large guns carried on shipboard by the Spanish auxiliary vessels were mounted on such carriages is not yet clear, but an interesting hint is to be gleaned from the gun-inventory of the captured *San Salvador,* in which it is stated that the guns found aboard the ship are listed

> 'with their *old* carriages'

and again, stored in the hold

> 'item, three *old* carriages like the other'.

What exactly did the English compiler mean by 'old' carriages? Did he mean that they were worn, and perhaps unserviceable? It seems hardly credible that a ship so well-gunned and important as the *San Salvador* would have had all her ordnance mounted on broken-down carriages. If, however, 'old' is used here in the sense of 'obsolete' the meaning is much clearer. Field carriages on shipboard, to an Englishman of 1588, would certainly have appeared out-of-date.

Several contemporary illustrations show Spanish and Italian merchantmen with guns mounted in this way. A particularly relevant example is to be found among the murals in the great Hall of Battles of Philip II's monastery-palace, the Escorial. One of the murals depicts the Spanish naval victory over the French off the Azores in 1582. In it the Portuguese galleon *San Martín* (flagship of the Armada six years later) is seen towing the French flagship clear of the battle. In the background are other galleons, and a number of auxiliary armed merchantmen (the types are readily distinguishable, long galleon as against beamy roundship). The *San Martín* and her sister galleons appear to be armed in a conventional way, with continuous rows of gun-ports along their sides suggesting a well organised and powerful armament. The merchantmen, however, display a very hotch-potch and sparse arrangement of gun ports in their hulls and a motley collection of small pieces hanging out of their tall temporarily-built castleworks. But the larger of them carry, quite unmistakably, big guns mounted on field carriages in their waists. The overall height of the pieces, because of the wheels, must have precluded their being mounted on a lower deck. I am certain that a similar practice was adopted by the Armada in 1588 by using guns of the land artillery service in order to convert a selected number of the auxiliary fleet — including *La Trinidad Valencera* — into what were intended to be front-line capital ships.

How would guns like the Remigy curtows, mounted on field carriages in a ship's waist, actually fare under battle conditions? The problems caused by recoil, particularly with heavily shotted guns, were considerable. In 1811 Sir William Congreve wrote: 'Numbers of men are constantly maimed, one way or another, by the recoiling of heavy ordnance used on board ships of war. Most of the damage is done by the random recoil of the carriage which, moving with the gun along no certain path, is much affected by the motion of the vessel and the inequalities of the deck. It is difficult to know, within a few feet, to where the carriage will come.' With short-barrelled large-bore guns the problem was especially acute. There is a passage particularly appropriate to our own case in *Boteler's Dialogues,* written in 1634, in which a sea-captain is asked what he thinks of 'those kind of great guns called *curtals*?' The captain replies that, 'in respect of their unruly reverse, they are both troublesome and dangerous; and in regard of their shortness, of little or no execution beyond the common mortar piece'.

Very little is actually known of shipboard gun-drills during the 16th century; for instance, it is not certain whether the guns were run out for action and then boused taut and belayed against recoil in this position, subsequent loading either being performed by lowering a man overboard to load the piece from outside the hull or by freeing the tackles and hauling the gun back by hand, or whether, as was to become universal practice by the mid 17th century, the recoil, under the restraint of a breeching rope, was allowed to carry the gun inboard for loading, with tackles used to run it out again. It seems unlikely, however, that guns like the Remigy ones could have been allowed to recoil inboard.

The technical difficulties of working such guns must have been formidable. The overall length of the mounted piece, because of the trail, would have been as much as double the length of the gun itself—up to twenty feet. The forward edge of the carriage would come to within about two feet of the muzzle and so, allowing for the thickness of the ship's frame timbers and skin, the gun when fully run out would barely protrude beyond the outside edge of the bulwark. Such a gun, if mounted on a deck of forty-foot beam, would occupy half of the deck space when run out and considerably more when brought inboard. The *Trinidad Valencera*'s maximum beam was probably of the order of forty feet, but the waist deck, because of the inward sloping of the hull above the waterline ('tumble-home'), would have been considerably less, and the problems of working big guns there would have been correspondingly greater.

The mechanics of a field carriage demand that the gun be mounted above the axle, and a thick bed is required above that on which to seat the piece. Because of this the line of recoil is high. The recoil axis of one of the Remigy guns, mounted on a field carriage with 5-foot wheels, would run at least 4 feet 6 inches above deck level. In land use, when the gun was usually allowed a free recoil, this would be of little consequence. But at sea, where the gun must be kept under a measure of control in a strictly limited space, very considerable problems would arise. For one thing, the big wheels would seriously interfere with the breeching and tackles. For another, the breechings, if seized below the recoil axis, would cause the gun to jump violently upwards as well as backwards, particularly if it was being fired at high elevation. The recoil problem would be such that the gun could only be kept under control by being lashed firm to the ship's side; this however would have imposed a severe strain on the hull structure particularly if the vessel was, like the *Santa Maria de la Rosa* or *Trinidad Valencera,* of weak Mediterranean build. The recoil of a gun like one of these curtows would have been especially violent, for though it threw a missile of considerable mass it did not itself possess sufficient weight to absorb, by its own inertia, much of the equal and opposite reaction.

Finally, who actually worked these guns in action, and what experience did they possess? Trained gunners were at a premium in Spain, for their special skills were ones which the average Spaniard, if he ever thought about it, could scarcely comprehend. When battle was imminent such men did not panic; on the contrary they strove to remain icy calm in action, as they coolly fiddled with plumb-bobs and quadrants, calculating such imponderable things as trajectory, range, and other ballistic secrets. Few Spaniards or Portuguese showed an aptitude for the gunner's art, and most of the ninety-five gunnery experts who sailed in the Armada with their Captain-General of Artillery, Alonso Cespides, were Germans or Italians. On average, then, there were only two trained gunners available for each of the fighting ships. This appears to have been a standard practice; the flagship *San Martín*, when engaged six years earlier under Santa Cruz at the Battle of Terciera, had among her crew two captains 'being seafaring men and having great sea experience' whose duty it was to 'attend the artillery'. Under their overall supervision each gun was allocated a gun-captain and six assistants drawn from the soldiers. We may presume that a similar arrangement was used by the Armada ships.

There is nothing to show that the members of these gun-crews had any previous artillery experience to speak of, or had been trained in shipboard gun-drills at all — even if, as is unlikely, any standard form of gun-drill existed. Untrained and inexperienced seven-man crews attempting to work guns like the field-mounted Remigy pieces in action at sea would inevitably come to grief. Even in the early 19th century, when the Royal Navy's gun-drills had reached—after nearly three centuries of constant development and practice—a state of near perfection, a 32-pounder (which weighed the same as one of the Remigy guns, but which would not have had nearly so violent a recoil and was mounted on a much more suitable carriage) required fourteen highly trained seamen to work it. It is not unreasonable to suppose, therefore, that the great Spanish 50-pounder guns of 1588, for all their apparent power and magnificence, proved virtually useless in action because it was simply impossible for their crews to operate them effectively under battle conditions at sea.

Something of the difficulties encountered by Iberian sea-gunners of this period may be gauged from the following observations of the Dutch traveller Van Linschoten, who experienced a minor action with some small English privateers aboard the 1 600-ton Portuguese carrack *Santa Cruz* in 1589. 'When we shot off a piece,' he writes, 'we had at least an hour's work to lade it in again, whereby we had so great a noise and cry in the ship as if we had all been cast away.'

A similar picture of chaos, though more widespread and far more terrible, may perhaps be discerned in the battering which, in 1588, the Armada suffered off Gravelines, when in the final stages of the battle the English — who, having sea-trained gunners, doubtless worked their guns competently enough — closed the range. Howard and Drake, it would appear, had at last realised that the wide bronze mouths which gaped from the waists of the biggest Spanish auxiliary ships were, in reality, all but harmless.

The two smaller bronze guns recovered from Kinnagoe Bay during the 1971 Easter week-end were also of considerable interest. The larger was 11 feet 4 inches in length overall, with a bore of 3¾ inches and a weight of 2 632 modern pounds (its breech mark of 2 529 pounds shows that it was weighed in Venetian pounds of 472 grammes). It is a 6-pounder *sacre,* decorated around the breech with a design of swans, sea creatures and flowering plants supporting a flame-emitting vase. The flame motif is continued on the chase of the barrel, and the muzzle is encircled with entwined foliation. This flamboyant artistry breathes the spirit of the Italian renaissance, an impression confirmed by the initials of the gun's maker — Z. A. — which are cast on the chase beneath a foliated shield. The initials are those of Zuanne Alberghetti, a gunfounder who worked during the mid-16th century at the great arsenal in Venice. The gun must have been part of the *Trinidad Valencera*'s original armament, which she had carried as a Venetian trading ship to protect her from Turks or Barbary pirates in the days before she was caught up in the events which were to lead to her wrecking on the north coast of Ireland.

A similar origin may be presumed for the smaller gun, although its surface is too pitted and abraded for any inscription or decoration to have survived, apart from a small fragment of a spread wing near the muzzle. This piece is 9 feet 7 inches long, has a bore of 3 inches (making it, approximately, a 4-pounder), and weighs some 2 000 pounds.

Much later in the season we brought up yet another gun — a small and very heavily concreted one which looked like a breech-loading swivel piece though the encrustations were too thick for us to be sure at first. We took it to Stephen Rees Jones's conservation laboratory at the Ulster Museum where, for ten days, he worked with painstaking care to remove the concreted outer shell without damaging what was inside. The result, when he had finished, was breathtaking. Inside the protective concretion the entire gun had been perfectly preserved. It was rather an unusual piece, for its barrel was cast in bronze but the breech chamber and removable block, as well as various other fittings, were of wrought iron. The pre-cast barrel (on which is stamped its weight, 125 pounds) would have been brought from the foundry to the blacksmith's shop, where an iron stirrup was forged over the two bronze lugs at the breech end of the barrel. The smith then made up the remaining parts of the gun—a long tiller extending from the rear by which the gunner aimed and held it, and a swivelling pintle fastened round the trunnions by which the piece could be set into a reinforced slot in the side of the ship and so traversed and elevated in any direction. He also made a removable breech-block or *mascolo,* very similar to the ones we had found on the *Gran Grifón* site (he probably made two of these, so that the gun could be fired more rapidly), and finally he fashioned the triangular wedge which was used to secure the breech-block in the stirrup, fastening it to the gun, so that it would not be lost, with five links of twisted iron chain. Similar guns are known to have been made in Venice from where, presumably, this one comes too.

Incredibly, the gun remains fully loaded and ready for action, just as its gun-captain left it in 1588. There is a 3¼-inch stone roundshot in the barrel (4-pounder), a fine-grained powder charge in the breech-block, and a small twist of hemp in the touch-hole to keep the powder dry. On top of the breech-block are nine small punch marks, and nine corresponding marks are to be seen on the side of the gun. These are identifying marks to avoid the wrong breech-block being put in the chamber. In Spanish fleet instructions dated 1597, ships' chief gunners are ordered to 'have a care of your powder and cartridges to be kept below in ballast, and a careful man to have charge of them and to have numbers set down upon every cartridge according to the piece . . .'

The wedge which locks the breech-block in place has a folded leather pad behind it to ensure a tighter fit and to absorb some of the recoil. The marks of the mallet with which the gunner knocked the wedge home, and knocked it out again after firing, can clearly be seen; he evidently used the mallet with his left hand, probably looped on his wrist with a thong, leaving his right hand free for aiming and loading. The butterfly-shaped iron wedge, with its aiming slot (a sort of primitive back-sight), would have helped to shield the gunner's eyes from the flying fragments which such guns tended to throw back on firing. The long tiller would have allowed the gunner the further precaution, if he held it at arm's length, of keeping his face some 5 feet from the breech as he took aim.

The gunner must have had at least one assistant, who probably stood on the right hand side of the gun, to apply a burning linstock to the touch-hole at the word of command. With a third man sponging out and reloading the spare breech-block the gun crew would have been able to maintain a fairly high rate of fire — two or perhaps even three shots per minute.

Apart from raising the five guns, the 1971 season on *La Trinidad Valencera* was mainly spent in a careful survey of the site. It seemed likely that a great deal of material — including parts of the ship herself — lay buried in the sand. A metal detector survey would be the best way of determining the extent of what was there. We made contact again with Jeremy Green of the Oxford Laboratory for Archaeology, who had carried out the *Santa Maria* survey in 1969, to find that he was on the point of leaving to take up a post of marine archaeologist with the Western Australian Museum. But he was able to spare us a week, and in the course of that week he and I completed a metal detector survey of the site.

Unlike the *Santa Maria,* the wreck of the *Valencera* lay in such shallow water that we could spend an unlimited time on it. In five days, working for four hours underwater each day, we gridded out two 100-foot square blocks of the flat sandy sea-bed and subjected it to a minute survey both of visible and buried features. Each swath of the survey, 10 feet wide by 100 feet long, was marked out with measuring tapes, and we completed the examination of each of these corridors as an individual operation. Green went in front, walking over the sea bed as he swept every square inch with the detector's circular coil, making targets with coloured stones. I followed behind, recording all the contacts on a gridded plotting board. Though the rate of progress varied considerably with the intensity of contacts the average over the complete survey of 20 000 square feet was thirty minutes per swath of 1 000 square feet, giving a total time of ten hours for the whole two-man operation.

The results, when we had plotted them on a master-survey, told us a great deal about the wreck. As we had suspected, much of it lies buried in the sand. Many of the large contacts obviously represent more guns, and we could see that the two main concentrations of wreckage lie apart from one another, suggesting that the ship had broken in two. For the rest of the season I stayed in Donegal with a charming Irish family whose house overlooks the wreck site, working with the Club members at weekends to explore and survey the entire site and its environs. The site was clearly enormously rich in material and much of it, through being well buried in the muddy sand, was incredibly well preserved.

Responsible excavation of this wreck, and especially the conservation of finds, will be a major task. Happily its finders, the City of Derry Sub-Aqua Club, intend to conduct the project properly and see it through to the end. The 1971 season was an exploratory one, and since then the Club, in conjunction with the St. Andrews Institute of Maritime Archaeology, B B C 2's 'Chronicle' programme (which has put up a major grant), and other interested parties, has carried out two further seasons on the site. A conservation laboratory has been established at Magee University College in Londonderry, and excavations are beginning to yield an extraordinary variety of finds. We have a growing collection of pottery and pewter ware, together with some wonderfully preserved lathe-turned wooden bowls, plates and dishes. Smaller finds include wooden buttons, tool handles, and even a bay leaf. Ship's fittings are represented by two wooden pulley blocks—one with a rope still rove through it—and a massive anchor cable, 5 inches in diameter. A barrel-load of Baltic tar, still pliable and sticky, retains its strong, characteristic smell. Most of the finds, however, are of military equipment and stores, reminders that the Armada was as much an army as a fleet. These include steel helmets of the so-called 'Spanish' morion type; leather boots and shoes; rope-soled sandals (issued to muleteers); musket and arquebus stocks, some with owners' initials carved on them; wheels, axles and yokes from wagons and hand cars; palisade stakes, hand spikes, earth baskets and scaling poles for the field pioneers; a blacksmith's bellows; and a keg full of gunpowder.

Such finds are bringing us ever closer to Philip II's *Armada Felicissima* of 1588, and to the people who took part in it. To us the events, and especially the people, now seem very real.

Postscript

THE BLUFF THAT FAILED

WHY did the Armada fail? Until recently most historians have been content to throw the blame on the Duke of Medina Sidonia, basing their judgement of his incompetence on his reaction to the order appointing him captain-general of the fleet in succession to the Marquis of Santa Cruz: 'I have not the health for the sea,' he wrote to the King's Secretary, Juan de Idiáquez, 'for I know by the small experience I have had afloat that I soon become sea-sick, and have many humours . . . the force is so great, and the undertaking so important, that it would not be right for a person like myself, possessing no experience of seafaring or war, to take charge of it. I have no doubt that his Majesty will do me the favour which I humbly beg, and will not entrust me to a task of which, certainly, I shall not give a good account; for I do not understand it, know nothing about it, have no health for the sea, and have no money to spend upon it.'

Was Medina Sidonia really the ignorant, faint-hearted creature his own words suggest? Or were there deeper, more obscure motives behind his self-professed unsuitability for the command? Whatever he may have thought himself, the King clearly regarded him as the right man for the job, and refused to listen to his objections. And no one, we may be sure, better knew the qualifications required of the Armada's commander than its instigator, Philip of Spain.

The first important consideration was Medina Sidonia's rank; he was the premier nobleman in Spain. Santa Cruz's death in February 1588 had robbed the Enterprise of a unifying commander; a man with sufficient prestige (and Santa Cruz's prestige was enormous) to hold the respect and obedience of his subordinates. In an age when social position was all-important, he was a difficult man to replace. If one of the abler squadron commanders — Recalde, perhaps, or Oquendo — was to be appointed over the heads of his brother officers, who were all prickly dons of approximately equal social status, sensitive veins of pride would be deeply touched. The Duke of Medina Sidonia so outranked them all that none could feel — nor did they feel — any resentment at serving under him.

But an even more vital consideration made Medina Sidonia perhaps the King's only logical choice for the command. In February 1588 the whole Armada project was on the verge of collapse: after two years of mismanagement it had become bogged down in a hopeless morass of administrative chaos, due in some measure at least to Santa Cruz's failings as a staff officer. In the glorious traditions of Spain's old navy Santa Cruz had few peers; standing on the fighting-platform of a galley as he manoeuvred the Christian reserve into position to smash the Turkish line during the climax of Lepanto, or braced sword in hand on the quarter deck of a galleon as he directed the annihilation of a French fleet off the Azores, he had been a very big man indeed. But in the great port of Lisbon, amidst the pressures and jealousies and pettifogging administrative difficulties of gathering an Armada together and looking after its men and equipment, Santa Cruz was out of his element. When he died — worn out, some said, with frustration and overwork — he left behind a shambles of unseaworthy ships and rotting supplies and, more critically, for it is infectious and less easily cured, of dispirited and disillusioned men.

What the Armada urgently needed, if it was not to continue eating greedily and uselessly into the King's purse, and seriously undermining Spain's prestige in Europe by its continued postponement (it had originally been scheduled to sail in early 1587), was not another fighting admiral but a top administrator. Medina Sidonia's administrative talents were among the best available in Spain. He virtually ruled the rich southern province of Andalusia, where he was much liked and respected for his efficiency, humanity, and fair dealing. Nor, in fact, was he entirely lacking in military and naval experience, particularly on the all-important administrative side. In 1580 he led the army which received the submission of the Portuguese Algarve, and in the following year he was given the task of organising a military expedition to North Africa. He commanded the relief force sent to Cadiz at the time of Drake's raid in 1587, and his prompt arrival probably saved the city from being captured and sacked: the King himself commended him for it. From the early 1580s until the end of his life (he died in 1615) he was much involved in the complex administrative business of fitting out and arming the ships of the transatlantic *flotas*, and in the even more demanding task of procuring supplies and recruiting crews for them. Finally, he had taken part in planning the Armada project from the very beginning. On grounds both of rank and experience, then, the Duke of Medina Sidonia was eminently qualified to command the Enterprise of England.

In the three months which elapsed between his reluctant acceptance of the command and the fleet's sailing at the end of May Medina Sidonia achieved what others more experienced than he had considered to be impossible. Under the leadership of this modest, likeable, conscientious and tenaciously hard-working aristocrat the hulls of the ships were breamed and caulked; the ballast was rummaged and the bilges cleaned out; tall fighting castles were added to the larger of the merchant vessels; new anchors, tackle, masts, rigging and sails were acquired and the old repaired. The guns were distributed among the ships according to a deliberate policy which made maximum sensible use of what was available, and right up to the last moment strenuous efforts were made to obtain new pieces, particularly large ones. Shot and powder quotas went up to the unprecedented average of fifty rounds per gun (more for some of the front-line ships), and supplies of small-arms ammunition were similarly increased. Provisions and water were stowed in the holds according to a carefully planned turnover system whereby the oldest stocks were consumed first to avoid their going bad (the fact that they did go bad was due to factors entirely beyond the Duke's control). Most important of all, the fleet's once abysmal morale was replaced by a pious fervour to sail.

And yet, after the fleet had put into Corunna at the end of June, Medina Sidonia again wrote to the King, urging him in the strongest terms to call the whole thing off. The Duke was certainly no coward, and so we can only suppose that his persistent efforts to have the Armada abandoned arose from higher motives than those of timidity or fear. He was, in fact, desperately concerned that the Armada would, despite its apparent strength and the obvious quality of most of its men, fail or be defeated, and so bring disaster and dishonour to Spain. Medina Sidonia knew, as we who have dived among the timbers of his ships also know, that many of his front-line vessels were weak and totally unsuited to naval warfare — particularly warfare involving artillery. He also must have known that the big field guns mounted in the waists of the more important auxiliary ships might look impressive, but were not likely to be of much use in action. He was probably worried about much else besides: about the obsolescence and unserviceability of a large proportion of the Armada's ships and guns; about sub-standard roundshot which had resulted from a rushed programme of iron founding by contractors whose technical abilities were notoriously bad at the best of times; about the certainty that his fleet would not be able to out-sail the English ships and so achieve the close-quarter combat in which Spanish advantages would prevail; and, most of all, about the impossibility of effecting the rendezvous with Parma without a suitable deep-water port and in the face of certain opposition by the Dutch Sea Beggars and the English fleet. Medina Sidonia had clearly grasped what modern historians, with all their advantages of hindsight, have also grasped: namely, that the plan was one which had little chance of success. But it was also the King's plan, Philip II's great crusade, his self-imposed destiny. No one, not even the first Duke in the land, could tell an absolute monarch that he was a fool. Medina Sidonia therefore resorted to every subterfuge he could think of in attempting to persuade Philip to abandon the Enterprise, including his own quite unjustified self-denigration — in effect the deliberate sacrifice of his honour, which to a Spanish nobleman was more precious than life. The Duke knew that the best service he could possibly render his King was to prevent the Armada sailing at all, and this he tried to do by refusing to take on the gargantuan administrative task of putting it into operational shape. He was, almost certainly, the one man in Spain who could actually get the Enterprise under way; equally, and he knew it, he was probably the only man who fully realised that it was unlikely to succeed. History has proved him right: no one can deny that it would have been better for Spain if the Armada had not sailed at all.

But the King insisted, and of course the King had the last word. Having irrevocably taken on the task, Medina Sidonia carried out his instructions with exemplary skill and fortitude. Despite a 5-day running battle in the English Channel he brought his Armada, in good order, to the appointed rendezvous — in itself a superb feat of leadership and seamanship. That the Duke relied heavily on the support of his more experienced subordinates to carry it out only emphasises his genius for command. After the fireship débâcle at Calais and the collapse of the invasion plan the Duke's great flagship *San Martín* was always to be seen where the fighting was hottest, and where she was most needed; now that he had only his own honour to consider the Duke was quite heedless of personal safety, on occasion even climbing into the galleon's tall fighting tops to observe the progress of the battle. Accusations of cowardice made by the Duke's many detractors are totally unsupported by primary evidence — all of which is quite to the contrary — and can be dismissed without comment. That so many ships finally got back to Spain was due, in no small part, to the discipline and good sailing instructions which originated from the flagship. Medina Sidonia may have been blamed by many for the disaster, but he was not reproached by the one man who was in a position to know the whole truth. Philip II, that lonely and enigmatic monarch, knew well enough where the real blame lay, and he carried it on his conscience for the rest of his life.

The truth seems to be that Philip did not intend, and did not really expect, his great fleet to have to do battle at all. Medina Sidonia was never told this, although in his cabin he carried sealed orders which he was to hand to the Duke of Parma when the rendezvous was effected or, in the event of the rendezvous not taking place, to return unopened to the King. These secret instructions, which are now preserved at Simancas, clearly indicate Philip's real expectations of the Armada :

> If the result be not so prosperous that our arms shall be able to settle the matter, nor, on the other hand, so contrary that the enemy shall be relieved of anxiety on our account, and affairs so counter-balanced that peace may not be altogether undesirable, you will endeavour to avail yourself as much as possible *of the prestige of the Armada* (my italics), bearing in mind there are three principal points upon which you must fix your attention :
>
> First, that in England the free use and exercise of our holy Catholic faith shall be permitted to all Catholics, native and foreign, and that the exiles may return.

> Second, that all places in my Netherlands which the English hold shall be returned to me.
>
> Third, that the English shall recompense me for the injury they have done to me, my dominions, and my subjects; which will amount to an exceedingly great sum. (This third point may be dropped; you may use it as a lever to obtain the other two.)

A modern historian, Dr. I. A. A. Thompson, whose paper 'The Appointment of the Duke of Medina Sidonia to the Command of the Spanish Armada' (*Historical Journal,* Vol. 12, 1969) should surely silence hostile criticism of Medina Sidonia for all time, stresses that

> Philip's overriding objective was not to conquer England but to stop English interference in his affairs. . . . For years every rumoured concentration of Spanish shipping had caused panic in England, now it was necessary for Philip to prove that he was able to put an Armada to sea, that the threat was a real one. For a man reputedly as afraid of war as a child was of fire, the ideal success would be diplomatic. But was not the threat of war diplomacy also? — as the Venetian ambassador put it, 'vigorous preparations for war are the surest way to secure favourable terms for peace'. With the Armada in the Channel, it was not impossible that the English Catholics would rise; that would be enough, Elizabeth would have to negotiate seriously. The *first* task of the Armada was to parade, to sail up the Channel and beat its chest before England's gates. What mattered most was that it should look imposing, hence the inflation of its size by including as many ships as possible, however unserviceable, and exaggerating the number of troops by issuing false muster rolls, all duly printed and publicised by an official propaganda machine.

In other words the Armada was to be a gigantic bluff, an overwhelming threat to England which *looked* utterly invincible even if in fact it was not. That, Philip thought, would suffice. Had his quite limited and very reasonable demands been met the fleet would, no doubt, simply have turned in its tracks and sailed majestically home, honour, political expediency, and religious duty satisfied without the uncertainty (and expense) of putting it to the test of battle. Of course, an expedition on this scale could not be entirely bluff; the effect of invincibility would only be possible if all the elements of a formidable fighting capacity were actually there or at least appeared to be, and, more important, the participants — up to and including the commander — wholeheartedly believed that they were sailing on a holy crusade to punish the heresy and wickedness of England.

Visually, the reality of the Armada under sail must have been enormously impressive. Medina Sidonia, as we have seen, probably saw through the bluff, though he was much too loyal to tell anyone. So too, no doubt, did some of his senior subordinates — Recalde certainly did. But, to the majority, the Armada really was *La Felicissima* — the Most Fortunate. Some even called it, though this was never an official title, *La Invencible.*

Even the English were, at first, overawed by its appearance. 'We durst not venture to put in among them,' wrote Lord Admiral Howard after viewing the Armada in its battle-formation off the Lizard, 'their fleet being so strong.' He added that he 'never supposed that they could ever have found, gathered and joined so great a force of puissant ships together, and so well appointed them with cannon, culverin, and other great pieces of brass ordnance . . .' Henry White, a volunteer aboard the English ship *Mary Rose,* put the matter even more bluntly: 'The majesty of the enemy's fleet, the good order they held, and the private consideration of our wants did cause, in my opinion, our first onset to be more coldly done than became the value of our nation and the credit of the English navy.'

Only in the closing stages of the campaign, after the rendezvous with Parma had failed and the fireship attack had driven the Armada into retreat, did the English use their advantages in gunnery and sailing to full effect. They had discovered, at last, that despite its formidable appearance and iron discipline the Most Fortunate Armada had serious and indeed fundamental weaknesses.

The key elements of the final battle are well summed up by the contemporary Dutch writer, Emanuel van Meteren, as published in Hakluyt's *Voyages*:

> . . . the English ships having used their prerogative of nimble steerage, whereby they could turn and wield themselves with the wind which way they listed, came often times very near upon the Spaniards, and charged them so sore, that now and then they were but a pike's length asunder: and so continually

> giving them one broadside after another, they discharged all their shot both great and small upon them, spending one whole day from morning to night in that violent kind of conflict, until such time as powder and bullets failed them. In regard of which they thought it convenient not to pursue the Spaniards any longer, because they had many great vantages of the English, namely for the extraordinary bigness of their ships, and also that they were so nearly conjoined, and kept together in so good array, that they could by no means be fought withall one to one.

Ship to ship the English could out-sail the Armada and take much more punishment than it could, gun to gun they could outshoot it, and so the final result was as inevitable as it was tragic. Man to man they were not put to the test; circumstances, and England's sensible tactics, dictated that they should never come to grips. I am of course prejudiced, but I believe that for discipline, seamanship, and sheer persevering courage the Spaniards were the better side. Never, in spite of all its disadvantages, did the English find the Armada a soft target; not even in the final battle off Gravelines were they able to defeat it in a military sense. The Enterprise may have failed, but Spanish valour remained constant to the end.

The English could well rejoice in their deliverance; a deliverance in which, it must be said, their navy had played a considerable part. Philip's bluff, if bluff it was, had failed disastrously. Militarily the Armada was, from the first, unworkable, though Philip cannot in his blackest nightmares have foreseen a catastrophe on the scale that occurred. The equinoctial gales of 1588 — the Winds of God, as the Protestants would have it — brought about the Spaniards' final crushing downfall off the wild Atlantic coasts of Scotland and Ireland, and in so doing gave us the wrecks from which, four centuries later, we have tried to answer some of the outstanding historical questions about the Armada, and vindicate the honour of whose who took part in it.

Honour is the one thing they did not deserve to lose.

Appendix 1

THE *GREY DOVE* AFFAIR

by

SYDNEY WIGNALL

THE expedition's 1969 season on the wreck of the *Santa Maria de la Rosa* opened with a detailed survey of the wreck site and its immediate environs using a metal detector. Trial excavations of the metal detector 'Targets' suggested that sufficient artefacts would be forthcoming to justify a colour documentary television film of the operations. Owing to the ever present plankton cover, which at times stretched from the surface to a depth of 30 feet or more, lighting conditions on the sea bed were far from satisfactory. Colour filming was out of the question unless we resorted to underwater floodlighting. I therefore decided to return to England to collect the necessary equipment from my colleague in St. Helens.

Arriving home late on 19th May I slept the sleep of the just, to be awakened at 8 a.m. the following morning by a telephone call from Joe Casey. Had I seen the *Liverpool Daily Post*? Indeed I had not. Casey read out the contents. It came as an unpleasant shock.

'Million pound mystery surrounds destination of ex German "E" boat. The actual destination of the *Grey Dove* is being kept secret by its consortium of business owners . . . but it is understood to be the area off the South West coast of Eire where other teams are searching for treasure. The *Grey Dove* will carry ten professional divers and high pressure sand blasting equipment to search for the *Santa Maria de la Rosa,* a galleon of the Spanish Armada. The galleon is thought to have on board 50 000 gold ducats worth about £1 000 000 when she foundered off the Irish coast. Yesterday the consortium refused to say anything about the destination or the aims of the expedition.'

I immediately got in touch with the Editors of the *Liverpool Daily Post* and was given the telephone number of their man on the spot. He informed me that he hit on the story by pure chance when visiting Birkenhead docks to investigate a labour dispute. One of the dissatisfied port employees had asked him, 'Why bother with us? There's a better story over there on the other side of the dock; that big black boat is going to search for Spanish treasure.'

The journalist was unable to ascertain who the owners were, but did glean some knowledge about the 'consortium of businessmen'. The trail of clues led him to a floating drinking and dining club in Canning Dock, Liverpool. The reporter walked aboard the floating club, asked for the owner, and in his own words was 'seen off very sharply'.

Realising that the organisers of the *Grey Dove* expedition were likely immediately to cross the river Mersey to instruct their crew members to keep their mouths shut, he returned to the *Grey Dove* at once, and boldly walking aboard, found his way to the engine room.

Squatting down alongside a crew member who was busily engaged in mechanical maintenance, he said 'I've just joined the expedition, what's the news?'

What the journalist learnt provided the basis for his newspaper column and confirmed my worst fears. We were about to be invaded by a treasure hunting expedition led and organised by very determined people. I immediately instructed a private detective to keep a close watch on the *Grey Dove.*

Politicians regardless of their affiliations are notably tardy in introducing legislation which is not vote catching. The Irish people, as inheritors of English law, are also cursed by the weaknesses inherent in the 1894 Merchant Shipping Act. The onus for protecting an ancient shipwreck falls on its excavator. The museums, and institutions which were fulsome in their praise of my efforts to defend the wreck of the *Santa Maria de la Rosa,* were remarkably reluctant to pay a penny piece towards so just a cause.

The Committee for Nautical Archaeology of London offered moral support and suggested that they would bring to bear any guns that might be of assistance. Mr. George Naish of the National Maritime Museum suggested that he would be willing to travel to Ireland in the capacity of a professional expert witness to testify on my behalf. Strange as it may seem, I had to decline this welcome offer of support for very strange reasons. The title of salvor in possession could only be proved by those participating in the 'occupation of the wreck site'. I was very much on my own.

The title of 'Salvor in Possession' has a somewhat unusual origin.

It appeared to be associated with a simply commercial salvage operation. It was far from that. It was in fact concerned with a treasure hunt for an alleged fortune in gold ingots, which were supposedly smuggled out of Germany in 1916, in the Dutch steamship *Tubantia.*

After the First World War, rumours persisted about a German plot to smuggle the Kaiser's wealth out of Europe in a merchant ship. The gold was allegedly hidden in Dutch cheeses. As the story of hidden treasure always excites the most gullible, it was not surprising that in 1922 a salvage consortium fitted out a diving vessel and set forth into the North Sea to locate the wreck of the *Tubantia* and enrich themselves with the Kaiser's gold.

In due course the wreck of the *Tubantia* was located and salvage work began. There was no sign of the Dutch cheeses or German gold. The wreck of the *Tubantia* became another commonplace salvage operation for non-ferrous metal. The salvors had attempted to purchase the title of the *Tubantia* but no owner was to be found.

During the second season's salvage operations another salvage company appeared on the scene, anchored close to the wreck site and proceeded to interfere with the operations of the original salvor.

Salvor Number One took newcomer Salvor Number Two to the British High Court. The law was now faced with a quandary. Neither the plaintiff nor the defendant had any legal title to the wreck.

The judge decided in favour of the plaintiff. He found that as they had located the *Tubantia* and had expended a considerable sum of money and had been in consistent occupation of the wreck, during which time salvage operations had continued, they were, as he put it, 'Salvors in Possession'.

Salvor Number Two, defeated and humbled, did not appeal the decision. Salvor Number One, exultant in victory, promptly went bankrupt. The *Tubantia* had not from their point of view been a financial success.

The 'Tubantia Case History' then became law in England. It was not law in the Republic of Ireland, but the Irish courts often recognised English 'Case History' when the laws on their statute book did not suffice.

The Tubantia case was all I had. It offered a glimmer of hope. The salvage licence from the Spanish Government would not be valid in law until the Irish government determined on the validity of the Spanish claim of title to the wreck of the *Santa Maria de la Rosa.* Such a claim was lodged during the course of my court action, by the Spanish Embassy, with the Irish Ministry of Transport and

Power. But these things take years, and I could not wait years for the *Grey Dove* was about to set sail from Liverpool to Kinsale.

Dr. Peter Davies of Liverpool University, who acted in the honorary capacity of Northern representative for the Committee for Nautical Archaeology, had a look at the *Grey Dove* as she took on board her diving and salvage equipment and battened down ready for the voyage across the Irish Sea. What he saw led him to pose a question to the Board of Trade. The *Grey Dove* was carrying a large compressor and several 40 gallon oil drums on deck. Could this be construed as cargo? If so, the Merchant Shipping Act was being violated because a cargo-carrying vessel must have a Plimsoll mark on her side marking the level to which her authorised amount of cargo submerged her. The *Grey Dove* did not have a Plimsoll Line. The Board of Trade prevented the *Grey Dove* from leaving until the complaint was investigated. That delay gave me a vital 24 hours in which to act.

The Board of Trade decided in their wisdom that the *Grey Dove* was not a cargo vessel and therefore did not require a Plimsoll Line. She duly sailed 24 hours late for Ireland. I was already there interviewing my lawyer John P. King. Mr. King cancelled all office appointments and we spent the day in consultation with Mr. Donal Barrington (Leading Counsel) and Mr. Fred Morris (Junior Counsel).

'Salvor in Possession' was something new both to my counsel and my lawyers. Fred Morris commented that I was the first client he had ever had who gave him all the information required for a brief, including case history.

During these consultations I received a telephone call from Colin Martin in Dingle. Two brothers, members of my 1968 expedition, had turned up in Dingle, ostensibly on vacation.

At the beginning of the 1969 season I had been faced with the unpleasant task of informing a considerable number of divers that there would not be a place for them on the 1969 expedition. The reasons for this are obvious. Once the wreck had been located, the main objective would be to carry out a detailed survey followed by a responsible excavation. Numbers would have to be cut down to the barest minimum. I needed specialists in survey, drawing, engineering, etc. The term 'Expert Diver' suggests that those who merit that description are of prime importance to a marine archaeological expedition. In fact he has proved nothing more than that he can be relied upon not to get himself or anyone else in trouble during his aquatic perambulations.

The two brothers had no qualifications other than those of divers of limited experience. If I had invited them to join me in 1969, I would have added to the expedition expenses without any compensatory gain in work effectiveness. They were not the only ones to feel angry at not being invited to join our second season.

Events in Blasket Sound in 1969 confirmed in my own mind that I had made a wise choice in selecting the team for that season. We occasionally had our disagreements, and at times tempers flared. On one occasion, an expedition member ill advisedly attempted to strike one of his colleagues. I had to talk very sternly to that young man, and threaten to 'put him on his bicycle'. Such incidents cleared the air, and we were none the worse for them.

The brothers were a different kettle of fish. On announcing my selection of personnel for 1969, I had been warned that I had not heard the last of them. It would be relevant to the story if I were to acquaint the reader with details of the two brothers' participation in my 1968 expedition.

The 1968 expedition personnel of over forty divers was recruited through an article in the journal of the British Sub-Aqua Club, *Triton.*

By the end of February 1968 all vacancies had been filled and I had a full complement of between eight and fourteen divers scheduled for every weekly roster from April to September. At this point I was refusing further volunteers at a rate of two to three per day.

Only three weeks prior to our starting date I received some unwelcome news. A man who had promised to make available a 35 foot vessel, complete with crew, decided that business commitments precluded him from participating in the expedition. There was no time to negotiate the charter of another vessel, so I decided to proceed with our initial search phase of the expedition relying entirely on high-speed inflatable boats (a wise choice as it turned out).

I then received a telephone call from a man whose name was unknown to me. He claimed to have a grievance. He and his brother and two other divers were to have been the crew of the charter vessel which did not turn up. They had planned for some time for their presumed participation in the expedition and had even gone so far as to relinquish their employment. After two days of pleading by telephone, in which they offered the use of a 16 foot inflatable boat and outboard motor, the two brothers won the day. They accepted my proposal that they might not even be allowed to enter the water and they would be in fact reserves. I duly posted to them the indemnity forms which I required every expedition member to sign. The said forms absolved me from any responsibility for accidental injury or death. They also clearly set out the terms under which a volunteer might join the expedition. I had absolute authority, held all copyright, and would determine what amount, if any, reward would be paid to any individual, subject of course to the expedition being allocated a salvage reward by the wreck's owners, the Spanish Government.

I already had nearly eighty indemnity forms in my file. They included all the accepted members of the expedition. For reasons which Colin Martin has explained elsewhere, only forty-two of these participated in the expedition.

In a covering letter to the brothers I stated that failure to sign the indemnity forms would preclude them from participating in the expedition. With only two weeks to go before setting off for Ireland I was enmeshed in the usual morass of organisational detail. I forgot about the brothers and as a consequence failed to notice that they did not return the signed indemnity forms. Events in the High Court of Admiralty in Dublin over a year later left me in no doubt that this was a deliberate act of policy on their part. It was to be one of their several very flimsy weapons in court.

To return to events in Dublin in May 1969. After consultations with my legal representatives I was invited to a meeting the following day by his Excellency Don Juan José Pradera, the Spanish Ambassador to Ireland. His Excellency asked to be kept fully informed as to the proceedings in the High Court and added that the matter was being followed with the utmost interest by the Minister of Marine in Madrid.

23rd May saw the typing of my affidavit, pleading for an injunction to restrain the *Grey Dove* expedition from interfering with the wreck of the *Santa Maria de la Rosa.* It had to be word perfect and it consequently took many hours to formulate. The affidavit had to be accompanied by exhibits which would be seen to prove that my expedition was not only in possession of an ancient shipwreck but that shipwreck had been established as that of the *Santa Maria de la Rosa* beyond any shadow of doubt.

Arrangements were made for a hearing in the High Court of Admiralty before Judge O'Keefe, President of the High Court of Ireland, at 5 p.m. We could not make the deadline, and several postponements were arranged. At 6.15 p.m. the affidavit was completed. I now had to swear to the truthfulness of same, on oath, before a Commissioner of Oaths. Similar oaths would have to be sworn as to the authenticity of the exhibits, one of which was a piece of 'Matute' plate.

We got in touch with a Commissioner for Oaths just as he was locking up his office and was making his way home. He was apprehended by John King's chief clerk and myself on a Dublin sidewalk just as he was unfurling his umbrella. It was raining hard and we tried to avoid ruining the affidavit. There was no time to type another copy. Passers by were puzzled and mystified to see the goings on. An entire bus queue stopped boarding their bus to witness the proceedings. I stood without hat or coat, rain running down my face, hand on bible, and holding the piece of 'Matute' plate in my left hand, swearing an oath.

'I think he's making his last will and testament,' a woman was heard to say. 'And that thing in his hand must be all his worldly goods,' someone else enjoined. They were not far from wrong.

As a result of last minute telephone calls, Judge O'Keefe agreed to hold court in his home in Dublin. We met at that address late in the evening and my senior counsel Donal Barrington put forward my case. In my complete ignorance of court procedure, I was not aware that I could not address the Judge, nor for that matter would he address me. The matter was being sworn on affidavits, and it was Judge O'Keefe's concern to ascertain if I had a case which merited the issue of a restricting order.

When the Judge was in doubt on any point he questioned Donal Barrington and Fred Morris. They in turn consulted John King, senior, who then consulted me. At times there appeared to be confusion both in terms and in interpretation, due to the fact that marine archaeology and marine salvage were subjects completely outside the province of everyone present other than myself. At last Judge O'Keefe made an order to his clerk; 'That the defendants be restrained from interfering with Mr. Wignall's programme of work on the wreck of the *Santa Maria de la Rosa.*' Donal Barrington immediately caught my worried eye. 'With respect M'lud, that would give the defendants the right to salvage the wreck, right alongside my client, just so long as they do not interfere with his work.'

Judge O'Keefe saw the point and corrected the order. It read as follows : 'Restraining the defendants or their servants or their agents from interfering with the said wreck or its contents or artefacts. This injunction will remain in effect until Thursday 5th June 1969 when an application should be made for its continuance.'

The hurdles had not all been cleared. The court order had no validity until it was registered in the High Court of Admiralty. We had obtained our court order at 8 p.m. on the Friday evening. The courts were now closed until Monday morning. In the meantime the *Grey Dove*'s departure from Liverpool was close at hand.

Judge O'Keefe realising our dilemma consented to 'allow the plaintiff to notify any of the defendants by telephone, telegram or letter'.

We returned to John King's office and the letters were duly typed and posted, the telegrams despatched by telephone. By the following morning the *Grey Dove* people would be in possession of telegrams which carried the full weight of the law.

At Mr. King's home Mr. and Mrs. King, their son John, my two barristers, Donal Barrington and Fred Morris, and myself consumed in celebration no less than twelve bottles of champagne. The writer and one unnamed member of the legal profession were advised by Mrs. King to avail ourselves of Dublin's excellent taxi service. We were in no fit state to drive. I tumbled into my hotel bed at 3 a.m. I had not had any sleep or any food for the past forty-eight hours.

The following morning I travelled to Dingle by car. I showed the Superintendent of the Garda (Police) my Court Letters which I proposed to serve on the two brothers personally. Superintendent O'Colmain provided a police escort, and I duly presented the letters confirming my restraining order.

On 25th May the *Grey Dove* and crew arrived at Holyhead harbour en route for Ireland. She was suffering from a mechanical fault in her propeller shaft. From that moment we called her the *Lame Duck.* The press besieged the *Lame Duck* clamouring for comments on my court order. A member of the *Grey Dove* expedition made the following statement to the *Daily Telegraph,* 'We are carrying on our salvage operations.' This was duly printed in the press on 26th May. I was amazed at the effrontery of these people and their abysmal ignorance of the law. They were prepared to defy an order of the Irish High Court of Admiralty, the consequences of which would assuredly result in their committal to prison for contempt of court. I eagerly awaited their arrival in the waters of the Irish Republic.

Three days later, on 28th May, the *Liverpool Daily Post* ran a story based on a telegram that the owners of the dining club in Liverpool had sent to the President of the Irish Republic, Mr. de Valera. The substance of the telegram was as follows :

> In September 1588 a Spanish ship of war believed to be the *Santa Maria de la Rosa* sank in Blasket Sound. Further up the coast a Spanish force attacked and seized Ballycroy castle. We believe therefore that any treasure or salvage that may be found must be handed over to the honourable Commissioners of Irish Wrecks and no part to the Spanish Government who were undoubtedly the aggressors and would be occupiers. If we obtain the permission of the Irish court to dive on this wreck, which may be the *Santa Maria de la Rosa,* any finds would be handed over to the Irish Receiver. We would furthermore please ourselves to conduct the operations with extreme care and respect for items of archaeological value. Title can

> then be decided on the floor of an honest Irish court. We respectfully draw your attention to the above facts which are intended to illustrate our good intentions and utmost respect for the law and authority of the Republic.

The newspaper article stated that the backers of the *Grey Dove* expedition were prepared to spend up to £37 500 over a 5 year period.

The point at issue for me and for any other person professing more than a passing interest in marine archaeology was that this cable confirmed that the *Grey Dove* expedition was a pure salvage operation. There is far more to marine archaeology than just lifting artefacts piecemeal from the sea bed.

I decided that I had to expose the *Grey Dove* consortium to the scrutiny of all responsible bodies interested in marine archaeology. In order to do this I issued a list of all the scientific and historical bodies who were supporting our expedition. The press lapped it up and saw to it that it fell into the hands of the *Grey Dove* consortium. I hoped that they would react to it. They did. In the *Daily Telegraph* of 30th May, we learned that the *Grey Dove* had docked the day before in Kinsale harbour near Cork. A member of the expedition confirmed in an interview that he and his colleagues were going to fight the case.

The following day the *Grey Dove* expedition reacted to my disseminated list of scientific and historical supporters with a counterblast which shook me as much as it shook the Committee for Nautical Archaeology. The headline in the *Liverpool Daily Post* of 31st May read as follows, 'Gold Hunters call in experts'. 'Swedish marine archaeologist Per Lundstroem has been called in by Liverpool treasure hunters to help in the reclamation of the Spanish Armada ship sunk off the coast of Ireland.'

The Mr. Lundstroem referred to was in fact Dr. and not Mr. Per Lundstroem, Director of the Maritime Museum of Sweden and the man in whose care the *Wasa* project had been placed.

It was highly unlikely that Dr. Lundstroem, a man of the highest reputation, would get involved with the owners of a floating drinking club.

I telephoned Miss Joan du Plat Taylor, secretary of the Committee for Nautical Archaeology in London. She cabled Dr. Lundstroem asking for an explanation. I decided to have a hand in the matter and despatched the following telegram to Dr. Lundstroem at the National Museum in Stockholm.

> My expedition working on wreck of *Santa Maria de la Rosa* Blasket Sound Ireland for past year with support and approval

of Irish and English historical and academic authorities. Invitation to you by Liverpool consortium to lead expedition comes from private treasure seekers who have been repudiated by all competent bodies. I obtained injunction in High Court of Admiralty Dublin last week restraining Liverpool consortium from interfering with wreck. They approached you with intention of using your name in an effort to set aside my injunction in the Irish High Court next Thursday 5th June. Please cable your dissociation from Liverpool consortium. Urgent. Wignall. c/o Committee for Nautical Archaeology. London. May 31st.

The next morning John King telephoned to inform me that he had received a letter from the Irish Minister of Transport and Power, Mr. Erskine Childers.[1]

Dear Mr. Wignall

Thank you very much for the record of marine research which you carried out in the Blasket Sound. I have read it with great interest. You have made a valuable addition to the military history of the period. The authorities seem convinced that you have located the wreck of the *Santa Maria de la Rosa.*

It is particularly praiseworthy that the underwater explorations have been carried out in a scientific manner and that such great care has been exercised in ensuring that the salvaged objects were not damaged in the course of salvage and were preserved so well. I hope that your plans for developing the techniques of underwater research are as successful as you deserve for your initiative and industry.

Yours sincerely
Erskine Childers

We were beginning to build up a file on the statements of the *Grey Dove* expedition leaders which could do them real harm in court. Their press statement that they intended treating the wreck with the respect that it deserved, and that all items of archaeological interest would be treated with care was exposed for the sham that it was when a member of the expedition was interviewed on Radio Merseyside on 29th May. Joe Casey was listening to the radio at the time and taped the interview. This is what was said.

'All this talk of archaeology is poppycock. People don't spend this sort of money on archaeology and as far as I am concerned

[1] Mr. Childers, late President of the Irish republic, died in 1974.

this is a straightforward business venture and we will recover all items of value as quickly as possible.'

The heavens now started to open up. Colin Martin rang me from Dingle. A team of amateur divers had arrived from England and were sitting on the cliff tops looking down on the wreck site. I asked Martin to suspend operations and take the buoy off the wreck. Joe Casey, in England, was approached by a professional salvage company who asked if Wignall was open to a deal. If he would give a 50 per cent share of any treasure to said company they would bring in a 'Bucket Dredger' to tear the wreck of the *Santa Maria* apart for the coin. If Wignall did not do a deal, then they would *wait until he had lost his court case,* and then pitch into the free for all on the wreck site and Wignall would get nothing. 'After all,' they said, 'nobody could have rights to a 400 year old wreck . . . it's only Flotsam and Jetsam.'

A London news agency telephoned to ask for my comments on the 'Continental expedition'. 'What continental expedition?' I asked. 'The one from Belgium and Holland who have stated that they are going to Ireland to salvage the treasure from the *Santa Maria de la Rosa.'* I laughed this one off. It must be a joke. It was no joke. They turned up in Dingle a couple of weeks after I had won my court case. I showed them the court order and they drifted away to enjoy the pastoral beauty of the Irish countryside.

In the meantime Dr. Lundstroem had replied to my cable. His answer lay in the office of the Committee for Nautical Archaeology for a week, due to the absence of Miss du Plat Taylor. When it did arrive in Dublin, the hearing of 5th June had taken place and the *Grey Dove* consortium, represented in court by the two brothers, had made their pleadings.

What I heard in court, sworn on oath by the defendants, amounted to the weakest brief I had ever heard. Spanish title to the wreck was no longer brought into question. It was not even mentioned. The brothers did not dispute my claim to be 'Salvor in Possession'. In fact they agreed with my plea. What they did claim was that they were also 'Salvors in Possession' with me, on the basis that a form of partnership existed between us, and that they were my co-adventurers. The brothers were no ordinary pair of divers; they now claimed to be professionals. They claimed that all the other members of my expedition were amateurs and were therefore subject to my 'Form of Indemnity', but that this did not apply to them. They defied me to produce their signed indemnity forms. It was not until that moment that I realised that the brothers had not returned the signed forms in March of the previous year.

Judge O'Keefe adjourned the hearing for me to put in my

counter affidavit. Immediately after the hearing, I received a copy of Dr. Per Lundstroem's cable. He had never heard of the *Grey Dove* expedition and would not have any dealings with them. I itched to get back into court and for Donal Barrington to lay that evidence before Judge O'Keefe. The two brothers, in their opening affidavit, had sworn on oath that they were arranging for Dr. Lundstroem to take charge of the archaeological side of their expedition. The court had been misled.

The brothers had stated in court that my salvage vessel, *Jimbell,* a 50 foot Motor Fishing Vessel, was undergoing refit in Dublin Docks and that there was little likelihood of me being able to start salvage in the near future. What on earth did they think we had been doing since 2nd April? *Jimbell* in fact was on her way round the coast of Ireland, a three day trip to Dingle. What a tale her skipper had to tell when she reached her destination.

It is pertinent at this point to point out that *Jimbell* had been undergoing a long refit. The day before she sailed from Dublin, she underwent trials in Dublin Bay. All was in order and she sailed the next day.

On the way to Dingle it became apparent that her automatic bilge pumps, newly installed, were not working. The radio telephone which had just been overhauled by Marconi refused to function. There was a wobble in the propeller shaft. The engine was jumping out of its mounting and sea water was pouring in through the stern gland. A close examination showed that *Jimbell* had been sabotaged the night before she left Dublin. The propeller stern gland had been loosened and the engine and gear box holding down bolts had been loosened.

The matter was reported to the Dublin police and the Dock authorities. The culprits were never apprehended.

In due course my counter affidavit was read in court. I produced all the expedition records. Affidavits were shown by all my expedition members to the effect that the form of indemnity in 1968 applied to all members of the expedition, and that the brothers, far from being professional divers, and my co-adventurers, were amateur divers.

Then the brothers slipped up, their counsel read out all his copies of my correspondence with the two brothers, and lo and behold! amongst them was my original letter of early 1968 mentioning the enclosed indemnity forms, and stating clearly that failure to sign them would preclude them from the expedition.

Judge O'Keefe then asked why the other defendants who were named alongside the brothers were not in court. If the brothers thought that they had a right to work on the wreck as my 'co-adventurers', how could that include defendants who had not been members of my expedition in 1968? None of these questions were answered. Judge O'Keefe then asked a question which raised laughter in the court: 'If Mr. Wignall as leader of the expedition does not have the right to exclude 1968 expedition members from his expedition in 1969, where do we draw the line? As the 1968 expedition had forty-three members does this mean that Mr. Wignall must allow all of them to return in 1969, to the point where we have divers with their feet in each other's mouths on the sea bed?' Again the defendant's counsel had no answer to that question.

During this brief two day sojourn in Colwyn Bay I received another surprise. Casey rang from St. Helens and suggested that a telephone chat with a Liverpool supplier of boating equipment might be of interest. His story blew away the false impression of the *Grey Dove* expedition having unlimited finances, as had been suggested in their press interviews. The man concerned had sold an outboard motor and an inflatable boat to the brothers for the Irish expedition. In his own words: 'I knew that they had been members of your expedition in 1968 and thought that the boat and engine were for you. I realised that they were not for you when the boat and engine were collected by two men who paid me with a rubber cheque which has bounced three times.'

Back into court we went. My evidence about the cheque was read out by Donal Barrington. It was greeted by glum silence on the part of the defending counsel. Then we put in our death blow: Dr. Per Lundstroem's disavowal of the *Grey Dove* expedition.

The counsel for the defendants admitted that our claim was correct and said that it was all due to a misunderstanding, and that his clients were at this moment attempting to obtain the services of another eminent marine archaeologist.

On the day of the final hearing I had further information. The *Grey Dove* expedition no longer had a salvage boat and they did not know it.

Again I was in the debt of my vigilant friend Joe Casey. Picking up a yachting magazine and reading through the list of vessels for sale or charter, he saw one, the description of which closely resembled the *Grey Dove.* The yacht was in the hands of a Liverpool ship broker. I rang him, giving my name but he did not recognise who I was. He said that he had the *Grey Dove* on his books and confirmed that she was available for immediate charter or was for sale subject to an acceptable offer.

Our case was so strong, my barristers did not use this evidence. Donal Barrington asked me if I wished to request a further adjournment, or would I let my case rest on the evidence so far produced, which both he and I thought was overwhelming. I was sick and tired of the whole business. The impartiality of the Irish High Court was apparent to all concerned. We waived the right to produce further evidence.

It was all over very quickly. Judge O'Keefe did not sum up and deliver a judgement. He gave his judgement and then summed up.

'I am going to continue Mr. Wignall's injunction. Anyone reading the affidavits could only infer an intention by the defendants to oust from the property Mr. Wignall and those working with him. I think that if I did anything else there would be open warfare in the Blasket Sound, and it would be instigated by the defendants as a whole.'

I now had the full protection of the law. If the *Grey Dove* crowd wanted to set my injunction aside they would have to file a case in court. They had in fact about three weeks to do this. Even then, the court would probably set a date for the hearing at least six months ahead. I had won the whole of the 1969 season. The *Grey Dove* case was so flimsy I doubted if their financial backers would risk any more funds. On 31st July, the *Grey Dove*'s counsel came into court and announced that his clients would not be continuing the case on the grounds that they did not have the funds to do so.

I was awarded costs and expenses which I knew to be in excess of £1 000. The full extent of the costs would take time for the lawyers to assess. In the meantime, my chances of obtaining them were slight. No sooner had the verdict been announced than the entire complement of the *Grey Dove* expedition shook the dust of Ireland off their feet and placed themselves outside the jurisdiction of the court. The *Grey Dove* raised her anchor and was gone on the first favourable tide.

What had we gained? The answer is, a new and more powerful weapon for the defence of shipwrecks of historical importance. Unlike the *Tubantia* salvors who had to wait until their wreck was interfered with before they could act, I had prevented the wreck of the *Santa Maria de la Rosa* being despoiled by prompt action. The case of the *Santa Maria de la Rosa* is now part of legal history. But effective as it might be, it can only be a stopgap until the United Kingdom and the Republic of Ireland pass the legislation so necessary to protect the shipwrecks of antiquity lying around their shores.

Appendix 2

ARMADA SHOT: A POSSIBLE REASON FOR FAILURE

by

SYDNEY WIGNALL

IN the month of August 1588, one of the most unusual scenes ever witnessed in the history of naval warfare was enacted off the coast of Flanders. Two great fleets, comprising 290 ships, sailed up into the North Sea, hurried along by a freshening wind, neither fleet able to inflict a mortal blow on the other. The reason for this inability of one side or the other to obtain a decision was due to the silent batteries of cannons and culverins. Both the English and the Spaniards were out of shot.

The Battle of the Narrow Seas was drawing to a close and neither side could claim to have won an outright victory.

The losses in ships were so small that we are bound to ponder over the apparent ineffectiveness of broadside gunnery at the time. The Spaniards had lost only one ship sunk, the *Maria Juan.* Two other great galleons, the *San Felipe* and the *San Mateo,* badly damaged by gunfire, had turned towards the Flemish coast and run aground to avoid capture. The other three Spanish losses, the *Neustra Señora del Rosario,* the *San Salvador* and the *San Lorenzo,* can be attributed to accident.

What of the English losses? There were none, nor for that matter was any serious hull damage recorded on any of Queen Elizabeth's royal galleons. A great naval victory? One of the momentous conflicts in maritime history? A sober unbiased analysis of the sea fight in the Channel might suggest that it was a sea battle, the tactical importance of which has been exaggerated.

How did it come about that Philip II's mighty 130 ship Armada could not sink or seriously damage any of Elizabeth's galleons?

The earlier skirmishes off the English coast were fought at beyond point blank range and no serious damage was done on either side.[1]

Off Gravelines, both sides were presented with the opportunity to force the battle to a conclusion. The fight raged for five hours, and now at last the range was down to point blank; no more than 100 yards or so. This is confirmed in the testimony of Sir William Wynter[2] on the English side, and Purser Calderon[3] speaking from the Spanish point of view.

As the battle drew to a close, the *Maria Juan* sank with heavy loss of life. The *San Mateo* and the *San Felipe* ran themselves aground on the Flemish shoals and were captured by the Dutch Admiral Justinus of Nassau.

The Spaniards had expended most of their stock of 123 790 rounds of ammunition. It was by their estimation enough for a five day fight. The English, according to Drake, in a letter to the council dated March 1588,[4] would be entering the battle with powder and shot for only 1½ days fighting.

The Spaniards had an advantage over the English in the weight of metal thrown; their heaviest battering pieces consisting of 50 pounder whole cannon, a size of ordnance with which the English were not armed. The Queen's fleet relied on the lighter-shotted 9 and 18 pounder culverins plus a few demi cannon.[5]

The Spaniards held a further advantage. Their gun powder consisted entirely of 'fine corned'[6] or pistol quality powder; whereas the major proportion of the English powder was of the inferior 'Serpentine' quality, which had a much lower maximum pressure when ignited, with a consequent reduction in muzzle velocity.

A change of wind direction brought the Gravelines encounter to a close. The Armada was blown into the North Sea, followed at a respectable distance by the English. In the words of Lord Howard of Effingham, 'We put on a brag countenance.'[7]

Spanish losses in men are unknown, but with decks crowded with

[1] State Papers. Dom.Eliz. ccxiii. July. 1588. Cecil to Walsyngham. 'There were few men hurt with any shot nor any vessel sunk, they shoot very far off.'

[2] Ibid. Wynter to Walsingham. 'When I was furthest off in discharging any of the pieces I was not out of shot of their arquebus, and most times within speech of one another.'

[3] State Papers Spanish. Edited by M. Hume (1899). Vol. IV. pp. 444/5.

[4] State Papers Dom.Eliz. cclx. 40. March 1588.

[5] M. Lewis. *Armada Guns* (London, 1961) p. 186.

[6] C. F. Duro. *La Armada Invencible* (Madrid 1885) Vol. II. No. 110. p. 83.

[7] J. Bruce. *Report on the internal defence of the Kingdom* (London, 1798). App. LX. p. cclxxxiv.

infantry, the death toll must have been considerable. The total English casualties in men was under 100.[1]

Could it be that the Spanish 50 pound and 32 pound shot, when fired at point blank range, was ineffective against the sides of well built oak ships? Proof that this was not so was evidenced in a series of tests carried out at Woolwich Arsenal in 1651 by Professor John Greaves.[2] At that time there had not been any improvement in the quality of smooth bore guns or the propellant. Iron shot ranging from 32 pound demi cannon down to 9 pound demi culverin was fired at point blank range at butts of oak and elm. Three butts were set up, each being 19 inches in thickness. The distance between butts one and two was 42 feet, and between butts two and three, 24 feet. Nearly all the shots fired burst through butts one and two and struck butt three. In every instance the powder charge was considerably less than that used by both the English and the Spaniards in 1588. The 1651 Woolwich tests confirmed the devastating effect of iron shot when fired at point blank range.

Further confirmation of the remarkable degree of shot penetration is shown by the fact that during the Napoleonic wars, vessels of the Royal Navy when 'Doubling' (attacking a French ship on both sides) were instructed to reduce the powder charge in their guns by 50 per cent. It had been learned by experience that a 32 pound ball, propelled by a full charge of powder, could smash through both sides of an enemy vessel and still possess sufficient velocity seriously to damage an English ship on the far side.

The first samples of shot raised from the wreck of the *Santa Maria de la Rosa* were despatched to Peter Start of the Department of Chemistry, University College, Dublin. Analysis suggested that the shot was rich in sulphur, but further tests proved this to have been caused by 380 years immersion in the sea.

If the poor quality of the Spanish shot could not be proved by analysis, could it be proved by a study of the historical records? As I investigated, so the evidence began to pile up, suggesting that the Spanish cast iron of the 16th century was markedly inferior to that manufactured in England.

The quality of the shot used by both sides has never before been investigated in detail. Historians had therefore unknowingly created

[1] State Papers. Dom.Eliz. ccxiv. Fenner to Walsyngham. 'God hath mightily protected her Majesty's forces with the least losses that have ever been heard of, being within the compass of so many great volleys of shot both great and small. I verily believe there is not three score lost in Her Majesty's forces.'

[2] C. Ffoulkes. *The Gun Founders of England* (London, 1969) p. 97.

a constant: the 'Ballistical Constant' which assumes that all iron shot is of identical quality.

All samples of Armada shot proved to have been quenched, i.e. they had been rapidly chilled from the hot state immediately after casting. This was illustrated by masses of concentric annular rings, giving the appearance of a shot within a shot within a shot, etc. This would make the ball brittle.

Why had the Spaniards quenched their shot? There could be two reasons. One indicated an inadequate knowledge of the craft of iron founding; the other, an emergency programme of shot moulding which had forced the Spaniards to adopt a dangerous procedure.

An examination of the Spanish records for the year 1588 provided confirmation that Spain had undertaken a rapid expansion in shot casting. In March of that year, the Duke of Medina Sidonia, commander in chief of the Armada, complained in a letter to Philip II that the shot allowance of 30 rounds per gun was inadequate.[1] He raised the total complement of shot from 70 000 to 123 790 rounds in only two months. This would amount to a total production of 350 to 400 tons of cast iron shot. A remarkable achievement when viewed against the knowledge that Spain's yearly output of cast iron was far less than the 1 000 tons per annum cast by the English.[2]

To produce such a large quantity of shot in a short space of time might have influenced the Spaniards to quench their shot, in order to speed up production. But there is other information available to us which suggests that Spain in point of fact had no viable industry for the casting of iron in the 16th century, and that her knowledge of ore smelting, iron casting and metallurgy was slight. Perhaps the Spaniards in their ignorance had always quenched their newly cast red hot iron?

In the early 16th century, bronze guns were much in favour and cast iron ordnance was looked upon with a jaundiced eye. The cast iron pieces often blew up under proof test, and the gun which stood a proof test was usually of such enormous weight that it was unsuitable for shipboard use.

Spain's advent into the field of colonial and European expansion found her with practically no capacity for smelting and casting good quality iron — a state of affairs that was to last well into the 17th century. Attempts to establish foundries for gun making were a dismal failure. The volume of production was lower than in Eng-

[1] Duro. op. cit. Vol II. No. 110. p. 83.

[2] H. R. Schubert. *History of the British Iron and Steel Industry* (London, 1957) p. 250.

land and the quality of the products was poor. The arsenal town of Medina del Campo was one of Spain's great commercial centres and boasted the largest iron foundry in the country. By the middle of the 16th century it fell into decline. The other large foundry at Malaga produced cast iron of such poor quality that its production fell to almost nothing by 1590.[1]

Philip II had within the boundaries of his various Kingdoms some of the finest bronze founders in Europe. His subjects in Flanders and in Italy produced cast bronze guns which were equal in quality to those cast in the Tower of London. None of these master gun founders lived in the Iberian peninsula, and as a consequence, whenever Philip required fine bronze ordnance he was forced to order his guns from Italy, the Low Countries, or from England. On occasion he tempted foreign gun founders to set up in Spain.[2]

The gun founders of the Low Countries, being predominantly Protestant, avoided service in Spain owing to their fear of the Inquisition. As a result, a first class indigenous Spanish iron founding industry did not emerge until well into the 17th century.

This state of affairs can be attributed to several causes, one of which was the lack of a commercially minded middle class. The great wealth flowing in from the Indies was to blame for this. The fleets of Nova Hispania and Tierra Firme, sailing to Seville from Havana brought Philip his royal tax of 20 per cent of all gold, silver and precious stones mined in the Indies. This enormous wealth was all bespoke in advance to maintain Spain's armies. Such was the wealth accruing annually to Spain, the necessity to set up home industry did not arise. If Philip wanted bronze or iron guns, or shot, he imported them from abroad. Spain as a consequence was constantly bedevilled by a balance of payments problem, and in the words of the Venetian ambassador, 'This gold that comes from the Indies does on Spain as rain does on a roof; it pours on her and flows away.'

Opposite economic factors brought about the rapid development of bronze and iron founding in England. Henry VIII rapidly dissipated the fortune left to him by his father. This is confirmed by the continental gun founder Poppenruyter, who cast bronze guns for Henry and was unable to obtain payment for them.[3]

War with the French forced the almost bankrupt Henry to turn

[1] A. Carrasco. *Memorial de Artilleria de Bronce* (Madrid, 1887) p. 185.

[2] J. Vernaux. *Chronique Archaeologique de Plays de Liege* (Liege, 1937) pp. 6–13.

[3] C. Ffoulkes op cit. p. 109.

to home industry. The French gun maker Peter Baude was sent to the Weald of Sussex, the seat of the English iron founding industry. There he instructed the master iron founder Ralph Hogge in the art of casting ordnance. Hogge cast England's first cast iron gun in 1543.[1]

Years of iron founding in a small way had long since taught the Sussex craftsmen like Hogge the negative influence of quenching hot cast iron. The English also had an accident of nature acting as their ally in the smelting and casting of good quality iron. This accident of nature was not appreciated by the English nor was it known to England's Spanish and Continental rivals. It consisted of masses of tiny fossilised sea shells in the ore. These were known as 'Greys'. Their presence provided the 'flux' that was necessary to extract the maximum quantity of slag from the smelting ore.[2] Thus the term 'grey iron' for good quality cast iron came into use and is still a common expression in the iron industry.

Grey iron was described thus: 'always a fine, genuine, good sort of metal; possessed of every good quality that can be desired'.[3]

Iron ore smelted without a flux was rich in slag and produced a very brittle cast iron which was known in the trade as 'cold shot'.[4] There is every indication that Spain's entire cast iron production in the 16th century came under this heading.

A further improvement was obtained by 'fining' or 'refining' the molten iron as it was smelted, or re-heating and fining after smelting. This included the removal of all impurities and dross at the liquid stage. It was learned in England as early as 1496 that it was essential for iron intended for the casting of shot to be refined 'before' it was despatched to the shot moulder. Otherwise, the unrefined iron, containing many impurities, might produce a poor quality brittle shot.[5]

In 1574, the Spaniards in their desperation to obtain good quality iron guns and shot tried to purchase thirty-eight guns from England for the Netherlands. Elizabeth reacted immediately and placed a ban on the export of guns. The governor of the Netherlands then turned to the gun founders of Liege. One of the most prominent of these, Wathier Godefrin, undertook in 1575 to cast 300 guns and 46 000 rounds of shot in six months. The guns were delivered on time and they all burst when subjected to proof test. Godefrin was thrown

[1] H. R. Schubert op cit. pp. 171–2.
[2] H. R. Schubert op cit. p. 229.
[3] H. Horne. *Essays concerning Iron and Steel* (London, 1773) pp. 60–62.
[4] H. R. Schubert op cit. pp. 233–4.
[5] Ibid. p. 273.

into prison.[1] We can presume that his shot was as deficient in quality as his guns.

In the same year, an attempt was made to influence Flemish gun founders to set up industry in Spain. They refused, and Spain reacted by offering throughout Europe the panic price of £20 per ton for cast iron guns . . . double the current figure in England.

In 1587 disloyal English merchants smuggled 140 bronze culverins to Naples, thereby allowing Philip to dismount many larger pieces from the Naples fortifications to fortify his ships.[2]

In 1603, fifteen years after the Armada failure, a number of Flemish gun founders set up industry in Spain at the expense of the state. The quality of their products was so poor, the scheme was abandoned with heavy financial loss.[3]

In or about the year 1622, Spain for the first time produced good quality cast iron guns and shot.[4] Six years later, the English gun founder John Browne was able to cast an iron gun which was lighter than a bronze gun, and which withstood double the proof charge of powder.[5]

England had led the field in the production of good quality cast iron for nearly eighty years. The proof is still available, for there are in existence today culverins and whole cannon cast in iron in the 16th century.[6] The Spaniards were unable to cast iron guns of equal size until well into the 17th century.

Was the poor quality of Spanish cast iron evidenced in fields other than guns and shot? The answer to this is 'Yes'. There is ample evidence that Spanish iron anchors of the period were of poor quality. The Netherlanders, as subjects of Spain, sailed in their thousands in Spanish ships. It was they who originated the nautical expression 'As meagre as a Spanish anchor'. Positive identification of several Armada anchors in recent years provided physical evidence of the poor quality of the Spanish anchors of the period. During our 'swim line' searches of Blasket Sound[7] we located a half anchor,[8] which we could positively identify as that left on the

[1] J. Lejeune. *La formation du Capitalisme moderne diens la Principaute de Liege au XIV siecle* (Liege & Paris, 1939) p. 185.

[2] M. Lewis op cit. p. 137.

[3] A. Carrasco op cit. p. 187.

[4] A. Carrasco. *Memorial de Artilleria de Hierro* (Madrid, 1889) p. 67.

[5] State Papers Dom.James. 1625/6. Vol. 25. No. 79.

[6] H. R. Schubert op cit. p. 251.

[7] S. Wignall. *Santa Maria de las Rosa.* 1968 interim report (Dublin), pp. 28–49.

[8] C. F. Duro op cit. Vol. II. pp. 315–26 (Spanish text). S. Wignall op cit. pp. 114–22 for English translation.

sea bed by Marcos de Aramburu, who witnessed from the galleon *San Juan* the sinking of the *Santa Maria de la Rosa.*

A direct line from Aramburu's half anchor to the wreck site of the *Santa Maria de la Rosa* is intersected by the latter ship's main anchor and the submerged rock pinnacle on which she struck. The *Santa Maria*'s anchor had an arm and fluke broken off. This poor quality anchor had presumably sealed her doom at 2 p.m. on 21st September 1588.

It has been suggested elsewhere that the Dutch saying 'As meagre as a Spanish anchor' was related to the thin or light construction of the anchors.[1] The construction of the Aramburu and *Santa Maria* anchors belies this. The *Santa Maria* anchor even had its ring intact. The ring, being the weakest part of the anchor, should be the first thing to break — that or the tip of a fluke. A well-constructed anchor would not break at the crown as did that of the *Santa Maria.* Aramburu's anchor illustrated even more clearly the technical deficiency of the Spanish iron industry. It had snapped in two at the strongest part; the middle of the shank.

The Spaniards may have cast better quality guns in bronze than in iron. But the quality of their bronze ordnance fell far below that of the English and Flemish gun founders. We found evidence of this both on dry land and underwater.

In April 1969 we carried out a metal detector survey at Dun an Oir,[2] the site of a Spanish-Papal landing in 1580, and we located and excavated the burst breech of a Spanish bronze gun. The casting was flawed to a dangerous degree. In 1970 we located the *Gran Grifón*, flagship of the Armada squadron of hulks, off Fair Isle.[3] One of the finds consisted of the muzzle of a bronze demi culverin of 4.20 inch bore. The bore was well out of true. This gun had been badly positioned on its core when cast,[4] indicating a lack of professional skill on the part of the gun founder.

There now remained one other source of historical information which might prove or disprove the poor quality of Spanish iron shot — the English state records. How much damage had Elizabeth's royal galleons suffered in the final point blank engagement off Gravelines?

The matter was summed up very clearly by Sir John Hawkins, Treasurer to the Navy, a few days after the battle had ended, in a

[1] W. J. Van Nouhuys 'The Anchor' *Mariners Mirror.* 1951. Vol. 37. p. 44.

[2] J. N. Green and C. Martin *Metal detector survey at Dun an Oir.* 'Estratto da Prospezioni Archaeologique'. (1970).

[3] C. Martin *Gran Grifón.* Interim report (1971).

[4] C. Ffoulkes op cit. p. 17.

letter to the Queen's secretary, Walsingham. 'Our ships, God be thanked, have received little hurt.'

Proof of the lack of damage to the Queen's ships is contained in the report of the survey of the Navy completed on 28th September 1588. The survey was carried out by the most able marine architects of their day, Pett and Baker.[1] The only mention of damage to a royal galleon was the reference to a new mast for the *Revenge*, which was 'spoiled by great shot'. The survey was minutely detailed, new rigging, new sails, replacing rotten knees and ribs. Boats were replaced after being cast adrift (it was common practice to tow a pinnace behind). Pennants and flags to be renewed. No mention of even minor hull damage.

The total estimate for repairs over and above the ordinary annual account of ship's maintenance and refit was only £1 300. The major part of this was for victualling shipwrights and for careening and caulking.[2] It must be remembered that in other years, the Queen's entire fleet would not be at sea. 1588 saw all of the royal galleons in action. For this reason the annual ordinary account would be inadequate, hence the further expenditure of £1 300. A very small sum, indicating, as Hawkins put it, 'little hurt'.

Why had the Spanish shot failed to inflict serious damage on the English galleons? The majority of historians have evaded this question. One fallacious hypothesis was put forward by the 16th century writer Camden, who suggested that the Spanish ships were built so high out of the water that their shot flew over the tops of the English galleons without hurting them. Camden was a landlubber and not an eye witness to the battle. Furthermore, his theory is not confirmed by Hawkins, Howard, Drake, Frobisher, Wynter or the Fenners. They were in the thick of battle and would have mentioned inaccurate shooting if they had witnessed it. Camden's theory was repeated by the late Professor J. A. Froude.[3] Sad to say, it is still taught in many English schools, not as an unqualified assumption, but as a matter of historical fact.

The greatest authority on Spanish and English ordnance, the late Professor Michael Lewis, suggested that the English with their superior seamanship were able to keep the range open, so that they remained out of the range of the Spanish whole cannon, but close enough for their own lighter shotted culverins to inflict punishment.[4] In a later work, Professor Lewis destroyed his own hypothesis by

[1] J. K. Laughton. *Defeat of the Spanish Armada* (Navy Records Society, London, 1894). Vol. II, pp. 250–4.

[2] J. Bruce. op cit. App. XL.I p. cxcvi.

[3] J. A. Froude. *English Seamen in the 16th Century* (London, 1901), p. 266.

[4] M. Lewis. *The Spanish Armada* (London, 1960) pp. 166–7.

proving that the Spaniards in point of fact carried more of the 18-pounder long range culverins than the English.[1] The latter hypothesis, however, still ignored the final 100-yard range point blank battle off Gravelines, when the Spanish whole cannon should have severely damaged the English ships.

The English, not having any of the 50-pounder whole cannon, their largest ordnance being the 32-pounder demi cannon, should have undoubtedly received the worst of it — but they did not.

If we examine all the recorded broadside gunnery engagements between English and Spanish ships in the 16th century, we are presented with massive testimony to the ineffectiveness of the Spanish gunnery.

The first gunnery battle took place at the Mexican port of San Juan de Ulua (now Vera Cruz) in 1568.[2] John Hawkins in the *Jesus* of Lubeck, anchored between Spanish galleons, perceived that an attack was about to take place and, warping his ship off shore, opened fire with his main armament. Although greatly outnumbered and armed only with culverins and stone firing perriers,[3] he put at least 60 shot in to the Spanish Admiral's galleon, setting her on fire. A couple of Hawkins' broadsides into the Spanish Vice Admiral were enough to make her blow up. In the face of Spanish fire ships, and attempts at boarding, Hawkins retreated to a smaller vessel and escaped. The *Jesus* fell into Spanish hands.

In 1583 a decisive battle was fought at the Port of San Vicente on the coast of Brazil between the English galleon *Leicester* of 400 tons and three Spanish Biscayans of 300, 400 and 500 tons. Captain Edward Fenton, in command of the *Leicester,* described how the Spanish *Santa Maria de Begona* bore down on him, guns blazing, in an attempt to board. The *Leicester* opened fire with her main battery armament, and in due course the *Begona* sank. The *Leicester* suffered no serious damage. The battle is well documented in Fenton's narrative of his voyage[4] and also in the journal of the Spanish admiral and hydrographer Don Pedro Sarmiento de Gamboa, who arrived at San Vicente a few days after the battle and raised several of the bronze guns of the sunken *Santa Maria de Begona.*[5]

[1] M. Lewis. *Armada Guns.* Table opposite p. 162.

[2] J. S. Corbett. *Drake and the Tudor Navy* (London, 1898) p. 114.

[3] M. Lewis. 'Guns of the Jesus of Lubeck', *Mariners Mirror.* July 1936. Vol. xxii. pp. 324–6.

[4] Hakluyt Society. *The Troublesome voyage of Captain Edward Fenton* (Cambridge, 1959). Second Series. No. CXIII. pp. 269–70.

[5] Hakluyt Society. *Narrative of the voyage of Pedro Sarmiento de Gamboa* (London, 1895). Vol. XCI. p. 269.

APPENDIX 2

In 1589 the Spanish plate fleet, arriving in the Azores from Havana, was beset by numerous English Reprisal Pirates. One such encounter was witnessed by the Dutch diarist Jan Hyghen Van Linschoten, who watched the battle from the quayside at Angra on the island of Terceira.[1] An English raider armed with only three guns attacked a Spanish galleon armed with twelve guns. The Spanish ship sank with heavy loss of life.

In 1591 Sir Richard Grenville in the galleon *Revenge,* off the Azores island of Flores, took on the combined might of the entire Spanish Indian Guard. At least half a dozen Spanish galleons, some of which displaced 1 500 tons, fought the *Revenge* for 16 hours, until, all her shot expended, the *Revenge* surrendered.

The sea fight off Flores had been fought at all times at point blank range and for some of the time the *Revenge* and some of the Spanish ships were locked side to side. The *Revenge* was armed with only 39 guns, the largest of which were 32-pounder demi cannon. Some of the 1 500 ton Spanish ships carried 90 guns, many of which were the 50-pounder heavy battering pieces. An English survivor informed Sir Walter Raleigh that the *Revenge* had been hit by at least 800 Spanish shot.[2] When the *Revenge* surrendered to Don Martin de Bertandona, she was completely dismasted, most of her crew dead or wounded, and the last round of shot had been fired. She was not in sinking condition. A few days later, under jury rig, with a Spanish prize crew aboard, she met her end in a typhoon and was wrecked against the cliffs of the island of Terceira.[3]

What damage did the *Revenge* do to the Spaniards? She sank, by the Spanish admission, one galleon of 1 000 tons and another of 1 200 tons. English survivors claimed that after the battle ended, a third galleon foundered, and that a fourth, being badly holed, had to be beached to save her from sinking. Several other ships were mauled including those of Bertandona and Aramburu.

A most revealing engagement was fought between Sir Richard Hawkins in the *Dainty* (a sister ship of the *Revenge*) against two Spanish fregatas, off the coast of Peru in 1593.[4] In that action the *Dainty* was armed with 32-pounder demi cannon, and the Spaniards

[1] Hakluyt Society. *The voyage of Linschoten to the Indies* (London, 1885) Vol. II. No. LXXI. p. 293.

[2] Hakluyt Society. *Principal navigations. A true report of the fight about the isles of the Azores between the Revenge and the Armada of the King of Spain. Sir W. Raleigh* (London, 1927) p. 7.

[3] Hakluyt Society, Linschoten. op. cit. Vol II. LXXI. p. 313.

[4] Hakluyt Society. *The Observations of Sir Richard Hawkins* (London, 1847) p. 214.

with culverins and demi culverins. A complete reversal of the artillery situation in the Channel battle of 1588.

The action, which lasted for three days and two nights, was fought most of the time at point blank range, and in Hawkins' own words, 'In which time, the enemy never left us, day nor night, beating continually upon us with his great and small shot'.[1]

Hawkins suffered grave handicaps from the very beginning of the fight. His master gunner was incompetent and allowed the two Spanish frigates to pass close alongside the *Dainty* while a complete broadside of English guns lay unloaded. On another occasion this same master gunner was seen to place the shot down the barrel and the charge of powder after it. Hawkins' crew, by his own admission being intoxicated, refused to put on their body armour, thereby suffering many needless casualties.[2]

The general level of incompetence, from which Sir Richard Hawkins cannot be excluded, lost the *Dainty* to the Spaniards. She surrendered when there were insufficient unwounded men to load the guns and trim the sails. In over thirty years of face to face gunnery battles between English and Spanish ships, not one of Elizabeth's galleons was sunk in action. The loss of the *Dainty* emphasises the fact that a badly crewed and commanded English galleon could not be sunk by Spanish broadside gunnery, even though the range was down to point blank and the odds two to one.

Sad to say, Richard Hawkins, lacking the vision of his illustrious father, blamed the loss of the *Dainty* on the English 'Race Built' galleon design. Her decks being flush, he said, could be swept by enemy fire. He advocated the return to high charged galleons with lofty castlework. Unfortunately for England, his advice was accepted and the admirable, fast, seaworthy and virtually unsinkable *Revenge* class were no longer constructed. The lead in the design of fighting ships passed first to the Dutch and later to the French, never to be regained by England.

A reader may wonder why I have not referred to Drake's attacks on Cadiz in 1587 and Coruna in 1589. The reason for this is that they were not true broadside gunnery actions, ship against ship. In the former, Drake punished the poorly armed galleys which sought to attack him. In the latter action, Spanish ships at anchor were not fully manned and were unable to fight back.

It is probable that the true quality of the Spanish iron shot will never be known. Samples of shot from the *Santa Maria de la Rosa,* the *Gran Grifón* and the *Girona* present us with badly deteriorated spheres of crystalline iron oxide, which we know to have been

[1] Ibid. p. 212.
[2] Ibid. p. 217.

quenched, but which tell us nothing about the ore smelting and iron casting methods of 16th century Spain. We know that the Spaniards possessed a good quality haematite ore. That they produced poor quality iron guns, anchors and shot is an established historical fact. A mass of circumstantial, historical and physical evidence would suggest that it was in the fluxing and smelting of the ore, the refining after smelting and in the casting and quenching techniques that the Spaniards were years behind the English.

What would happen to a poor quality iron shot when fired from smooth bore gun? There are two factors to be taken into consideration, and they are respectively the relative acceleration of the shot due to the action of the propellant forces in the gun barrel, i.e. 'black powder' which has a very high initial maximum pressure, and the decelerating forces created by the two-foot thick oak sides of the ship against which the iron shot strikes.

The black powder with high maximum pressure will strike the ball a very hard blow, much harder than modern cordite which has a low maximum pressure. This is alleviated to some extent by the fact that the propellant forces are uniformly applied over half the surface of the iron shot. Nevertheless, if the shot is of poor and brittle quality, its structural integrity might be weakened. On striking the target the decelerating forces are concentrated initially over a very small area of the shot. From this we might surmise that a badly smelted and cast iron spherical shot might be weakened by the massive blow imparted by the high pressure fine-corned black powder, and that its complete disintegration would probably take place when the first terminal contact with the target is made.

What magic formula did the English use to cast a good 'grey iron' which was the envy of their continental competitors? There was no magic formula. All of the practices of the 16th century iron founders of the Weald of Sussex are known to us. They weathered their ore for several months, allowing the elements to wash out impurities. The ore was then crushed and washed. The smelting was, unknown to the English iron founders, fluxed to a high degree by the presence of the fossilised grey shells in the ore. This produced an iron free from slag. After smelting the iron was refined several times by reheating, the surface dross and other impurities being removed at this stage.

Prior to casting, the gun and shot moulds were dried and warmed. Casting was carried out at as even a temperature as possible. Cooling of the cast objects took place gradually, quenching being avoided.

The English could not keep their practices secret forever. In 1619 a Dutchman, Jan Andries Moerbeck, applied to the States General for a patent to cast guns in the Netherlands from ore which he wished to import from England. The fact that Moerbeck had applied for a 25-year exclusive patent proved that he was on to something quite new and revolutionary in the gun founder's art. His ore undoubtedly came from the Weald of Sussex. He was granted a 12-year patent.[1]

Iron founders of the Low Countries were now able to examine an ore which was quite different from their flux free, but otherwise good quality, haematite ore. The 'greys' could be replaced by other fluxing elements of similar calcerous origin. Limestone became the substitute. Allied to the English methods of iron founding, the new technique for fluxing spread across the continent to Germany, and in 1630 a Spanish gun foundry at Lierganes, near Santander, operated by Germans, was producing first-class quality iron guns and shot.[2] For the "Invincible Armada' they arrived 42 years too late.

In September 1970 Dr. W. H. F. Tickle of the British Steel Corporation supervised a detailed analysis of 7-inch bore 'whole cannon' and 5¼-inch bore 'whole culverin' shot from the wreck of the *Santa Maria de la Rosa*. The final paragraph of Dr. Tickle's report is most revealing.

'Both samples of Spanish shot show high graphitic structure. It might be argued that after three centuries immersion in sea water re-hydration of ferric oxide had taken place and, due to imperfect reduction in the original manufacturing process, Fe_20_3 has been a major constituent in an iron matrix. The Fe_20_3 had re-hydrated with the passage of time through centuries of sea immersion to furnish the structure examined. The drillings lose up to 10% weight when retained at 105°C for a few hours, which would correspond to $Fe_20_3H_20$. This is more or less in line with the X-ray diffraction results, for $Fe_20_3 \times H_20$ was established as the core material. This is most improbable even if it is thermodynamically possible. What is more likely is that crushed haematite ore was thrown into the molten iron, making a mush which was finally formed by mould into a cannon ball. This would aid the rate of production but produce an inferior product.'

The full implication of Dr. W. H. F. Tickle's hypothesis becomes plain when we examine the system used for casting shot. The act of smelting iron is known as a 'campaign'. Once the blast furnace is up to temperature, the iron founders try to keep the 'campaign' in operation as long as possible. Once the 'campaign' was opened

[1] G. Doorman. *Patents for inventions in the Netherlands* (The Hague, 1942) p. 118.

[2] A. Carrasco. op cit. *Artilleria de Hierro*. p. 67.

and molten iron was run off, there was a drop in temperature, which if continued for too long a period, reached a point when smelting became impossible and the founders were forced to end the campaign, strip out the smelted iron and unsmelted ore, and start a new campaign, which might take several days to reach critical working temperature. Consequently, iron founders delighted in founding guns, which necessitated only one opening of the campaign for a short period of time. Casting shot was unpopular because it required repeated opening of the furnace, which often resulted in the loss of a campaign.

The Spanish iron founders were painfully aware in the 16th century that their cast iron guns were of poor quality. They did not know the reason why. If their cast iron was poor, surely a little subterfuge to increase production and lessen the risk of loss of a campaign would pass unnoticed? A poor quality gun paraded its imperfections when discharged. A poor quality shot, once fired from its piece, was no longer available for inspection. The shot cast from such dishonest methods would be fractionally lighter in weight than a pure cast iron shot. It would be brittle, and this brittleness would be increased if the shot was quenched. It is possible that the failure of the Spanish Armada was due to poor technology and not to any shortcomings in the quality of the Spaniards' seamanship, gunnery, or fighting spirit.

Appendix 3

ORDER OF BATTLE OF THE SPANISH ARMADA

with brief notes on the subsequent fate of the ships

by

COLIN MARTIN

THE following lists are based on the muster of 9th May 1588 as published at Lisbon in the same year. In addition to the well known listings of tonnages, numbers of guns, soldiers, and mariners, there have been included the columns, ignored by historians from Captain Duro onwards, which show the quantities of roundshot, gunpowder, lead, and match issued to each ship. These are revealing figures, for they indicate the relative strength of each ship's armament. In the few cases where something of the actual gun-types aboard an individual vessel is known the gunpowder figure allocated to that ship (allowing for what was needed by the soldiers for their small-arms — the powder, being fine grained, could be used for either purpose) appears to be about right for each gun to fire off its full quota of roundshot (60 rounds per gun for the ships of the Castile squadron and the galleys; 50 rounds per gun for the rest). Using the known armaments as a yardstick we can therefore gauge the approximate fire-power of the other ships from their shot and gunpowder quotas alone. Without going into the tedious calculations involved in this statistical approach, I believe that the figure of 65 quintals represents a fairly rigid dividing line between 'front-line' battery armaments and less powerful, essentially defensive, 'second-line' ones. The front-line ships as defined by this formula are marked in the table with asterisks. These ships, as a group, display a number of special characteristics. They comprise twenty-three vessels which, though representing only 18% of the fleet's total number, account for 37% of its total tonnage. These twenty-three fighting ships carried 43% of the Armada's gunpowder ration, and aboard them sailed no less than 78% of the fleet's *aventureros* — hot-blooded young noblemen who would naturally have chosen the ships most likely to be in the thickest of the fighting. It is indeed these same ships which crop up, again and again, in contemporary accounts of the battles. This front-line group, moreover, sustained by far the highest ship-casualty rate in the fleet — some 57% losses during the campaign and its aftermath compared with the Armada's overall loss of about 30%.

It is also of interest to note which ships are *not* on this list. We should single out for special comment the Castile squadron — the vaunted galleons of the Indian Guard — whose members, on average, carried the same powder ration as the lowly and lightly-armed *El Gran Grifón* (though, since Castile's ships carried fewer guns, the average size of each piece would have been correspondingly greater than the *Grifón*'s). Another surprise is the Levantine flagship *La Regazona* — the biggest ship in the fleet — with only 35 quintals of powder (which suggests that her 30 guns included nothing larger than a demi-culverin), compared with the 125 quintals issued to her cannon-carrying sister Venetian *La Trinidad Valencera*.

The columns showing the fleet's losses and survivals have been compiled mainly from two documents in the Simancas archives, published by Duro (*Documentos Números* 180 and 181), which were evidently drawn up during October 1588 and list the ships which had safely returned to Spanish ports (180) and those presumed to have been lost (181). These two documents, which were probably compiled at slightly different dates, are not wholly reliable and do not always agree; some ships are on both lists, while others appear on neither. Where this is so, the discrepancy is noted in the table. In the 'remarks' column information about the fates or survivals of the various ships (from a variety of sources, mostly contemporary) is summarised, together with the names of important individuals associated with them.

It should be noted that the appearance of a ship in the 'missing' column does not necessarily mean that it was lost. The 'missing' list was compiled after most of the survivors had returned, but a few had yet to reach port. It is almost certain, in addition, that at least some of the hulks listed as missing had made straight for their home ports in the Baltic, while a great many of the *pataches* and *zabras* probably sought shelter on other coasts. Because of this doubt, which can never now be resolved, it is impossible to reach an accurate estimate of the Armada's total losses; though great, they were probably not as high as has sometimes been supposed: 30%

— or about 40 ships — is a likely approximation. Many of the ships which did return, however, were unfit for further service, and human casualties on all of them were extremely high — often in excess of 50%. Of the 30 000 or so men who set out on the crusade in May 1588 barely one in three lived to see the following spring.

SQUADRON OF PORTUGAL, Commanded by The Duke of Medina Sidonia

Ship	Tons	Soldiers	Mariners	Guns	Round-shot	Powder (quintals)	Lead (quintals)	Match (quintals)	'Safe' List	'Missing' List	Remarks
**San Martín* capitana general	1000	300	177	48	2400	140	23	18	At Santander		Medina Sidonia. Prince Ascoli (but see pp. 48–53). Francisco de Bobadilla (*Maestre de Campo General*). Arrived in port with main body of fleet 21st September
**San Juan* almiranta general	1050	321	179	50	2500	136	23	18	At Galicia (Corunna)		Recalde, with survivors from *San Juan* of Fernando Horra (see p. 54). Arrived 7th October. This ship was captured in Drake's raid of April 1589.
**San Márcos*	790	292	117	33	1650	85	18	15		X	Marquis de Peñafiel. Lost in Ireland?
**San Felipe*	800	415	117	40	2000	85	18	15		X	*Maestre de Campo* Don Francisco de Toledo (*Tercio* of Flanders). Grounded on Flemish banks and captured by Dutch.
**San Luis*	830	376	116	38	1900	69	18	15	At Santander		*Maestre de Campo* Don Agustin Mexia.
**San Mateo*	750	277	120	34	1700	82	18	15		X	*Maestre de Campo* Don Diego Pimentel (*Tercio* of Sicily). Grounded on Flemish banks and captured by Dutch.
Santiago	520	300	93	24	1200	46	18	15	At Santander		

**Florencia* (*San Francesco*)	961	400	86	52	2600	75	18	15	At Santander	A brand-new galleon built for the spice trade by the Grand Duke of Tuscany. Impounded at Lisbon for Armada in 1587. Beyond repair on return. Often mistakenly believed to be the Bermory ship.
San Cristobal	352	300	78	20	1000	22	12	9	At Santander	
San Bernardo	352	250	81	21	1050	30	12	9	At Galicia	The 'Nao of Miguel de Aranivar'? (see p. 53).
Zabra Augusta	166	55	57	13	650	9	4	3	At Santander	
Zabra Julia	166	44	72	14	700	10	4	3	At Santander	

SQUADRON OF BISCAY, Commanded by Don Juan Martinez de Recalde

**Santa Ana* capitana	768	323	114	30	1500	71	22	10		*Maestre de Campo* Nicolas de Isla (Indian Guard *Tercio*). Recalde's flagship, though Recalde himself was aboard the *almiranta general* throughout the campaign. Separated from the fleet in the Bay of Biscay: sheltered in the Bay of La Hogue, and took no part in the fighting.

* Front-line ship

Ship	Tons	Soldiers	Mariners	Guns	Round-shot	Powder (quintals)	Lead (quintals)	Match (quintals)	'Safe' List	'Missing' List	Remarks
**El Gran Grin* almiranta	1160	256	73	28	1400	72	22	18		X	Don Pedro de Mendoza. Lost off Clare Island, Co. Mayo. Survivors executed.
Santiago	666	214	102	25	1250	47	13	8	At Guipuzcoa		
La Concepcion de Zubelzu	468	90	70	16	800	45	15	8	At Guipuzcoa	X	On both lists—in fact returned safely.
La Concepcion de Juanes Del Cano	418	164	61	18	900	30	11	6	At Guipuzcoa	X	Ditto.
La Magdalena	530	193	67	18	900	38	11	6	At Guipuzcoa		
San Juan	350	114	80	21	1050	36	7	4	At Santander		Entered in the 'Safe' List, mistakenly, as belonging to Diego Flores' squadron (Castile).
La Maria Juan	665	172	100	24	1200	61	14	8		X	Sank off Gravelines 10th August.
La Manuela	520	125	54	12	600	30	10	9	At Santander		
Santa María de Monte-Mayor	707	206	45	18	900	38	15	12	At Santander		
Patax La Maria de Aguirre	70	20	23	6	300	2				X	
Patax La Isabela	71	20	24	10	500	3					
Patax de Miguel Suso	96	20	26	6	300	2				X	
Patax San Estéban	78	20	26	6	300	2					

SQUADRON OF CASTILE, Commanded by Don Diego Flores de Valdés

(The first ten ships in this list were galleons of the Indian Guard)

**San Cristobal* capitana	700	205	120	36	2160	88	28	25	At Santander		Flagship of Diego Flores though he, as Chief-of-Staff, spent the campaign aboard the *San Martín*.
San Juan Bautista almirante	750	207	136	24	1440	53	27	23	At Santander		Marcos de Aramburu. Arrived Santander 14th October.
San Pedro	530	141	131	24	1440	48	19	25	At Santander		Probably the ship commanded by Francisco de Cuellar, who was later relieved of this command and transferred under arrest to another vessel (perhaps *La Lavia*, of Levant) which was subsequently wrecked on Streedagh Strand, Co. Sligo.
San Juan	530	163	113	24	1440	49	19	20		X	This ship, which is confused in the 'Safe' List with the *San Juan* of Biscay, was commanded by Don Diego Enriquez, son of the Viceroy of Peru. It was wrecked on Streedagh Strand.
Santiago El Mayor	530	210	132	24	1440	47	19	19	At Santander		
San Felipe y Santiago	530	151	116	24	1440	47	18	19	At Santander		
La Asuncion	530	199	114	24	1440	49	19	19	At Santander		

Ship	Tons	Soldiers	Mariners	Guns	Round-shot	Powder (quintals)	Lead (quintals)	Match (quintals)	'Safe' List	'Missing' List	Remarks
Nuestra Señora del Barrio	530	155	108	24	1440	49	19	22	At Santander		
San Medel y Celedon	530	160	101	24	1440	48	20	19	At Santander		
Santa Ana	250	91	80	24	1440	27	11	12	At Santander		
Nuestra Señora de Begoña	750	174	123	24	1440	52	22	25	At Galicia		Indian Guard Merchantman.
La Trinidad	872	180	122	24	1440	48	20	27		X	Indian Guard Merchantman. In company with Aramburu till 15th September (see p. 25). Subsequent fate unknown.
La Santa Catalina	882	190	159	24	1440	49	23	24	At Santander		Indian Guard Merchantman.
San Juan Bautista	652	192	93	24	1440	47	20	24		X	Indian Guard Merchantman. 'Nao of Fernando Horra'. Captains Gregorio Melandez and Diego de Bazan. Scuttled off the Blaskets after Recalde had taken off her guns.
Patax Nuestra Señora del Socorro	75	20	25	24	1440	3	3	3		X	
Patax San Antonio de Padua	75	20	46	12	720	3	3	3		X	

SQUADRON OF ANDALUSIA, Commanded by Don Pedro de Valdés

**Nuestra Señora Del Rosario* capitana	1150	304	118	46	2300	114	21	10		X	Don Pedro de Valdés. Captured by Drake in Channel. Brought to Dartmouth.
San Francisco almiranta	915	222	56	21	1050	43	15	12	At Santander		
San Juan	810	245	89	31	1550	50	16	13	At Santander		
San Juan de Gargarin	569	165	56	16	800	21	9	8	At Santander		
**La Concepcion*	862	185	71	20	1000	83	15	12	At Santander		
Urca Duquesa Santa Ana	900	280	77	23	1150	30	19	15		X	Wrecked in Loughros Mor Bay, Co. Donegal. Second shipwreck of Don Alonso de Leiva.
Santa Catalina	730	231	77	23	1150	41	15	12	At Santander		
La Trinidad	650	192	74	13	650	20	15	12	At Santander		
Santa María del Juncal	730	228	80	20	1000	31	17	14	At Santander		
San Bartolomé	976	240	72	27	1350	32	15	12	At Galicia		
Patax el Espíritu Santo	70	33	10	10						X	

SQUADRON OF GUIPUZCOA, Commanded by Don Miguel de Oquendo

Ship	Tons	Soldiers	Mariners	Guns	Round-shot	Powder (quintals)	Lead (quintals)	Match (quintals)	'Safe' List	'Missing' List	Remarks
**Santa Ana* capitana	1200	303	82	47	2350	106	25	18		X	Miguel de Oquendo. This ship reached San Sebastian, but after anchoring her magazine took fire and she was burned with 100 men on board. Oquendo, who was already on shore, died shortly afterwards.
**Santa María de La Rosa*. almiranta	945	225	64	26	1300	80	20	16		X	Foundered in Blasket Sound, Co. Kerry, 21st September 1588. Wreck located 4th July 1968.
**San Salvador*	958	321	75	25	1250	130	20	16		X	Magazine exploded during the fighting on 31st July. 200 killed. Ship subsequently abandoned to the English, who brought her to Weymouth. Later sank.
San Estéban	936	196	68	26	1300	43	18	14		X	Perhaps the 'Ship of San Sebastian' lost at Dunbeg, Co. Clare. Survivors of the Dunbeg wreck were executed by the Sheriff of Clare.
Santa María	548	173	63	20	1000	43	11	9	At Guipuzcoa		
Santa Bárbara	525	154	45	12	600	22	10	8	At Guipuzcoa		
San Buenaventura	379	168	53	21	1050	20	10	8	At Guipuzcoa		
La María San Juan	291	110	30	12	600	14	8	6	At Lisbon		

Santa Cruz	680	138	36	18	900	30	8	6	At Santander		
Urca Doncella	500	156	32	16	800	28	9	8		X	Sank at Santander
Patax La Asuncion	60	20	16	9	450					X	
Patax San Bernabé	69	20	23	9	450						
Pinaza Nuestra Señora de Guadalupe			15	1	50					X	
Pinaza Magdalena			14	1	50					X	

SQUADRON OF LEVANT, Commanded by Don Martin de Bertendona

La Regazona capitana	1249	344	80	30	1500	35	22	18	At Galicia		Martin de Bertendona. A Venetian merchant ship impounded by Philip II.
La Lavia almiranta	728	203	71	25	1250	39	15	12		X	Another Venetian merchantmàn. This ship was probably wrecked on Streedagh Strand, Co. Donegal, with Judge Advocate-General Martin de Aranda and Francisco de Cuellar aboard.
*La Rata Encoronada	820	335	84	35	1750	80	19	15		X	Don Alonso de Leiva's ship. A Genoese vessel. Stranded and burned in Blacksod Bay, Co. Mayo.

Ship	Tons	Soldiers	Mariners	Guns	Round-shot	Powder (quintals)	Lead (quintals)	Match (quintals)	'Safe' List	'Missing' List	Remarks
**San Juan de Sicilia*	800	279	63	26	1300	69	19	18		X	Commanded by Diego Tellez Enriquez, son of the commandant of the Order of Alcantara. Almost certainly the ship blown up in Tobermory Bay, Argyll.
**La Trinidad Valencera*	1100	281	79	42	2100	125	19	16		X	Don Alonso de Luzon.* A Venetian merchantman. Wrecked in Kinnagoe Bay, Co. Donegal. Remains discovered 20th February 1971.
La Anunciada	703	196	79	24	1200	46	15	11		X	A Ragusan ship. Scuttled in the Mouth of the Shannon.
San Nicolas Prodaneli	834	274	81	26	1300	40	17	13		X	Captain Marino Prodaneli.
**Juliana*	860	325	70	32	1600	67	12	12		X	Probably lost somewhere off Co. Donegal. Survivors from this wreck, with others from *La Lavia* and *La Trinidad Valencera* were still in Ulster in 1596.
Santa María de Vision	666	236	71	18	900	32	12	10		X	
La Trinidad de Scala	900	307	79	22	1100	41	23	18	At Santander		

* (*Tercio* of Naples)

SQUADRON OF HULKS (URCAS), Commanded by Don Juan Gomez de Medina

El Gran Grifón capitana	650	243	43	38	1900	48	19	15		X	From Rostock. Juan Gomez de. Medina. Wrecked on Fair Isle. Remains found 9th June 1970.
San Salvador almiranta	650	218	43	24	1200	40	11	9	At Santander		Pedro Coco Calderon.
Perro Marino	200	70	24	7	350	7	3	2	At Santander	X	Evidently reached Santander.
Falcon Blanco Mayor	500	161	36	16	800	24	8	6		X	Although listed as 'Missing', this ship was not lost during the Armada campaign, for she was captured by the English in the Channel on her way back to Hamburg in January 1589.
Castillo Negro	750	279	34	27	1350	23	8	6		X	Lost at sea off N.W. Ireland.
Barca de Amburg	600	239	25	23	1150	31	8	6		X	Foundered at sea after her people had been transferred to *La Trinidad Valencera* and *El Gran Grifón*.
Casa de Paz Grande	600	198	27	26	1300	26	8	6			Sailed from Lisbon but was not present at the Corunna muster. Probably did not take part in the campaign.
San Pedro Mayor	581	113	28	29	1450	21	5	4		X	Hospital ship. Wrecked on Bolt Tail, Devon, after completing 'north-about' voyage. Crew survived.
El Sanson	500	200	31	18	900	24	9	6	At Galicia		

Ship	Tons	Soldiers	Mariners	Guns	Round-shot	Powder (quintals)	Lead (quintals)	Match (quintals)	'Safe' List	'Missing' List	Remarks
San Pedro Menor	500	157	23	18	900	34	8	6		X	
Barca de Anzique	450	200	25	26	1300	29	7	6			
Falcon Blanco Mediano	300	76	27	16	800	19	4	4		X	Don Luis de Cordoba. Lost in Connemara, perhaps at Dalvillaun, near Inish Boffin. Most of the survivors (though not Don Luis) executed in Galway.
Santos Andres	400	150	28	14	700	20	6	6	At Santander		A Scottish Ship?
Casa de Paz Chica	350	162	24	15	750	12	5	3	At Santander		
Ciervo Volante	400	200	22	18	900	19	6	5		X	
Paloma Blanca	250	56	20	12	600	11	3	3	At Galicia		
La Ventura	160	58	14	4	200	8	3	3	At Santander	X	Evidently reached Santander.
Santa Bārbara	370	70	22	10	500	12	6	5		X	
Santiago	600	56	30	19	950	24	3	3		X	Lost off Ireland.
David	450	50	24	7	350	8	3	3		X	Listed as missing, but since she was not present at the Corunna muster it seems that she did not take part in the campaign.
El Gato	400	40	22	9	450	8	3	3	At Santander		
Esayas	260	30	16	4	200	5	3	3	At Santander		
San Gabriel	280	35	20	4	200	5	3	3			

SQUADRON OF PATACHES AND ZABRAS,
Commanded by Don Antonio Hurtado de Mendoza

Nuestra Señora del Pilar de Zaragoza, capitana	300	109	51	11	550	18	11	5		X	
La Caridad, inglesa	180	70	36	12	600	20	3	3		X	An English ship.
San Andres, ecoces	150	40	29	12	600	14	3	3			A Scottish ship.
El Crucifijo	150	40	29	8	400	5	3	2		X	
Nuestra Señora del Puerto	55	30	33	8	400						
La Concepcion de Carasa	70	30	42	5	250	2				X	
Nuestra Señora de Begoña	64	20	26			1				X	
La Concepcion Capetillo	60	20	31	10	500	2					
San Jerónimo	55	20	37	4	200	1				X	
Nuestra Señora de Gracia	57	20	34	5	250	1			At Santander		
La Concepcion de Francisco de Latero	75	20	29	6	300	2				X	
Nuestra Señora de Guadalupe	70	24	42						At Santander		
San Francisco	70	20	37							X	
Espíritu Santo	75	20	27						At Santander		
Trinidad, Zabra			23	2	100						

Ship	Sold-iers	Mari-ners	Row-ers	Guns	Round-shot	Powder (quin-tals)	Lead (quin-tals)	Match (quin-tals)	'Safe' List	'Missing' List	Remarks
Nuestra Señora de Castro			26	2	100					X	
Santo Andres			15	2	100						
La Concepcion de Valmaseda			27	2	100					X	
La Concepcion de Somanila			31							X	
Santa Catalina			23							X	
San Juan de Carasa			23							X	
Asuncion			23	2	100					X	

Note: On some Spanish lists two other 70-ton Zabras.

GALLEASSES OF NAPLES, Commanded by Don Hugo de Moncada

Ship	Sold-iers	Mari-ners	Row-ers	Guns	Round-shot	Powder (quin-tals)	Lead (quin-tals)	Match (quin-tals)	'Safe' List	'Missing' List	Remarks
**San Lorenzo* capitana	262	124	300	50	2500	132	16	22		X	Don Hugo de Moncada. Ran aground off Calais after the fireship attack. Don Hugo killed. The French eventually took possession of the wreck, and her guns were returned to Spain.
**Patrona* (*Zuñiga*)	178	112	300	50	2500	118	16	22		X	Not in fact lost. Arrived in great distress at Le Havre after the north-about voyage, where she remained, unserviceable, for almost a year.

**Girona*	169	120	300	50	2500	130	15	22		X	Captain Fabricio Spinola, Knight of Malta. Don Alonso de Leiva's third and final wreck. Lost on Lacada Point, Co. Antrim, where her remains were located by M. Robert Sténuit on 27th June 1967.
**Napolitana*	264	112	300	50	2500	118	14	22	At Santander		

GALLEYS OF PORTUGAL, Commanded by Don Diego Medrano

Capitana	106	106	303	5	300	15	5	5			Not present in the fighting.
Princesa	90	90	200	5	300	15	5	5			Not present in the fighting.
Diana	94	94	192	5	300	15	5	5		X	Wrecked at Bayonne. David Gwynn, who was a galley slave on this ship, escaped to England.
Bazana	72	72	193	5	300	15	5	5			Not present in the fighting.

SELECT BIBLIOGRAPHY

Though references have been avoided in the text, the historical facts as narrated are well supported by documentary source evidence. Most of the material has been published and is fairly easily accessible. This bibliography includes the most important of the published works consulted, and is intended to provide a working guide for the reader who wishes to probe more deeply into the background of the subject.

Anderson, R. C. *Italian naval architecture about 1445,* Mariner's Mirror, 11 (1925).

Anderson, R. C. and Salisbury, W. (eds.) *A treatise on shipbuilding and a treatise on rigging written about 1620-1625* (London, 1958).

Biringuccio, Vannoccio. *The Pirotechnica* (1540) translated from the Italian with notes by Smith and Gnudi, (1959).

Boteler, N. *Dialogues* (1634) ed. with notes by W. F. Perrin (London 1929).

Carr-Laughton, L. G. *Gunnery, frigates, and line of battle,* Mariner's Mirror, 14 (1928).

Carr-Laughton, L. G. *Early Tudor guns,* Mariner's Mirror, 46 (1960).

Carrasco, A. *Apuntes para la historia de la fundicion de la artilleria de bronce,* in Memorial de Artilleria, ser. 3, vols. XV and XVI (Madrid, 1887).

Cipolla, C. M. *Guns and sails in the early phase of European expansion, 1400-1700* (London, 1965).

Corbett, J. *Drake and the Tudor Navy,* 2 vols. (London, 1898).

Danaher, K. *Armada losses on the Irish coast,* The Irish Sword, 2 (1956).

van Doorslaer, G. *L'ancienne industrie de cuivre, II: L'industrie de la fonderie de canons* (Malines, 1910).

Grattan, J. *'How to find': the divers swim-line search,* British Sub-Aqua Club Paper 2 (London, 1972).

Green, J. N. and Martin, C. J. M. *Metal detector survey on the wreck of the Santa Maria de la Rosa,* Prospezioni Archeologiche 5 (Rome, 1970).

Ibid. Metal detector survey at Dun an Oir.

Green, W. Spotswood. *The wrecks of the Spanish Armada on the coast of Ireland,* Geographical Journal, 27 (1906).

Green, W. Spotswood. *Armada ships on the Kerry coast,* Proceedings of the Royal Irish Academy, 27 (1909).

Hakluyt, R. *Voyages and Documents,* (1598-1600), selected with an introduction and a glossary by Janet Hampden (London 1968).

Hardie, R. P. *The Tobermory Argosy* (Edinburgh, 1912).

Hardy, E. *Survivors of the Armada* (London, 1966).

Henrard, P. *Documents pour servier a l'histoire de l'artillerie en Belgique: Les fondeurs d'artillerie,* Annales de l'Academie d'Archeologie de Belgique, 45 (1889).

Hume, M. *Some survivors of the Armada in Ireland,* Transactions of the Royal Historical Society, New Series, 11 (1899).

Ireland, J. de Courcy review of E. Hardy (op. cit.) in Irish Historical Studies, 15 (1966).

Jones, F. M. *The plan of the Golden Fort at Smerwick, 1580,* The Irish Sword, 2 (1954).

Lane, F. C. *Venetian shipbuilding and shipbuilders of the Renaissance* (Baltimore, 1934).

Lane, F. C. *Venice and history — the collected papers of Frederick* C. Lane (Baltimore, 1966).

Lewis, M. A. *The Guns of the Jesus of Lubeck,* Mariner's Mirror, 22 (1936).

Lewis, M. A. *The Spanish Armada* (London, 1960).

Lewis, M. A. *Armada guns* (London, 1961).

Mainwaring, Sir H. C. *Seaman's Dictionary* (1623), ed. with notes by G. E. Mainwaring and W. G. Perrin (London, 1920).

Martin, C. J. M. *El Gran Grifón — an Armada wreck on Fair Isle,* International Journal of Nautical Archaeology, 1 (1972).

Martin, C. J. M. *The Spanish Armada Expedition, 1968-70,* in D. J. Blackman (ed.), Marine Archaeology, Colston Papers 23 (London, 1973).

Mattingly, G. *The defeat of the Spanish Armada* (London, 1959).

Melvill, J. *The autobiography and diary of Mr. James Melvill* (1589), ed. by R. Pitcairn (Edinburgh, 1842).

Monson, Sir W. *Naval tracts,* ed. by M. Oppenheim (London, 1902).

Nani Mocenigo, M. *La sala d'armi nel Museo dell'Arsenale di Venezia* (Rome, 1908).

Nani Mocenigo, M. *L'arsenale di Venezia* (Venice, 1927).

O'Rahilly, A. *The massacre at Smerwick (1580)*, (Cork, 1938).

Padstow, P. *Guns at sea* (London, 1973).

Palacio, Diego Garcia de (MS) : see Artinano, G. de 1920 *La architectura naval Española* (Madrid, 1920).

Parry, J. H. *The age of reconnaissance* (London, 1963).

Reid, E. S. (ed.) *Statistical Account of Shetland,* 1791-1799 (Lerwick, 1925).

Robertson, F. L. *The evolution of naval armament* (London, 1921).

Sibbald, R. (ed.) *A description of the Isles of Orkney from the mss. of Robert Menteith, Laird of Egilsha and Gairsa, dated 24th September 1633* (Edinburgh, 1845).

Sténuit, R. *Treasures of the Armada* (Newton Abbot, 1972).

Tenison, E. *Elizabethan England,* Vol. VII (London, 1940).

Thompson, I. A. A. *'The appointment of the Duke of Medina Sidonia to the command of the Spanish Armada,* Historical Journal, 12 (1969).

Waters, D. W. *The Elizabethan navy and the Armada campaign,* Mariner's Mirror, 35 (1949).

Vigon, J. *Historia de la artilleria Española,* 3 vols. (Madrid, 1947).

Wignall, S. 'Underwater search systems', in *Surveying in Archaeology Underwater* (Colt Monograph V, London, 1969).

Wignall, S. *The Armada shot controversy,* in D. J. Blackman (ed.), Marine Archaeology, Colston Papers 23 (London, 1973).

PUBLISHED CONTEMPORARY DOCUMENTS AND STATE PAPERS

Anon. *Certaine Advertisements out of Ireland* (London, 1588).

Anon. Printed copy of *La Felicissima Armada* (the Lisbon muster), annotated in the hand of Lord Burghley and others, Lisbon. British Museum Catalogue 192 f 17 (1) (1588).

La Armada Invencible (vols. I and II) : State papers and letters relating to the Spanish Armada, mostly in Simancas, compiled by C. F. Duro (Madrid, 1884 and 1885).

SELECT BIBLIOGRAPHY

La Armada Invencible: Documentos procedentes del Arcive General de Simancas, compiled by G. H. Oria (Valladolid, 1929).

State papers relating to the defeat of the Spanish Armada, 1588 (vols. I and II), compiled by Sir John Laughton (London, 1894).

Calendar of (Spanish) letters and state papers relating to English affairs, Vol. IV (Elizabeth) 1587-1603, ed. M. Hume (London, 1899).

Calendar of state papers (Ireland) Elizabeth, August 1588-September 1592 (London, 1885).

Calendar of state papers (Venetian), VIII, 1581-91 (London, 1894).

Calendar of the Carew manuscripts, 1589-1600 (London, 1869).

Acts of the Privy Council (New Series), XVII and XVIII, 1898 and 1899 (Norwich).

Tabeller over skibsfart og varetransport gennem Øresund 1497–1600, ed. N. E. Bang and K. Korst (Copenhagen, 1906-33)

INDEX

INDEX

INDEX